FALKIRK DISTRICT LIBRARIES
30124 01442039 4

MOB 1

KU-099-111

In the Shadow of the Nile

BY THE SAME AUTHOR

Caprice
My Sister Clare
Tomorrow's Rainbow
Glamara
Fragile Heritage
The Crimson Falcon
The Talisman of Set
Summer of the Flamingoes
The Chosen Ones
The Last Reunion

IN THE SHADOW OF THE NILE

Sara Hylton

C

CENTURY

LONDON SYDNEY AUCKLAND JOHANNESBURG

First published in Great Britain in 1993 by Century
Random House UK
20 Vauxhall Bridge Road, London SW1V 2SA

Century Hutchinson South Africa (Pty) Ltd
PO Box 337, Bergvlei 2012, South Africa

Random House Australia Pty Ltd
20 Alfred Street, Milsons Point, Sydney, NSW 2061
Australia

Random House New Zealand Ltd
18 Poland Road, Glenfield, Auckland 10
New Zealand
0 7126 5626 X
Typeset by Pure Tech Corporation, Pondicherry, India
Printed and bound in Great Britain by
Clays Ltd. St Ives PLC

To my brother Cyril

Ah, Moon of my Delight who know'st no wane,
The Moon of Heav'n is rising once again;
How oft hereafter rising shall she look
Through this same Garden after me – in vain!

And when Thyself with shining Foot shall pass
Among the Guests Star-scattered on the Grass,
And in thy joyous Errand reach the Spot
Where I made one – turn down an empty Glass!

from *The Rubáiyát of*
Omar Khayyám

1

In all the years John Halliday had been a passenger on some liner returning to the East he never grew tired of the ballyhoo of a departing ship. He stood on the deck, looking down on the familiar scene. There was nobody to see him off, nobody to shed tears or wave fluttering handkerchiefs, but he smiled as his eyes fell on a short, plump man struggling along the crowded quayside while behind him a porter pushed his mountain of luggage.

He'd known Tubby Rowlands a long time. While he, himself, had been gainfully employed at the British Embassy in Peking, Tubby had been drifting aimlessly from one doubtful occupation to another, fortified by money left to him by a favourite aunt and subsidised by a family who were relieved that he was far enough away not to cause them embarrassment. Halliday wondered idly where Tubby was going and what he intended to do when he reached his destination.

Halliday had spent over a year in a London hospital recovering from a war wound which had responded too slowly, so that his job in Peking went to another. He'd been advised to take things easy for at least a year and in that time the war ended and England had more or less returned to normal.

He'd spent his extended leave from the Foreign Office in Scotland revelling in the mists and lonely lochs, walking tentatively until his limbs grew stronger. Ready to resume his work, for three long years he kicked his heels in London. Then, at last, had come the interview that informed him he was to go to Egypt until there was an opening for him in the Far

East. He wasn't enthusiastic about Cairo, but he was glad to become a useful human being once more. He was thirty-eight years old and had left the army with the rank of Major after collecting a DSO and a mention in dispatches. In two months' time it would be 1923 and his need to get back into life's mainstream was urgent.

He looked down at his fellow travellers who thronged the quayside and mounted the gangways, and he knew from experience at which stage most of them would leave the liner. Only a handful would depart at Gibraltar and the next port of call was Alexandria. Here would disembark the dowagers and the débutantes, peers of the realm and go-getting young blades in search of the sunshine of Egypt until it was time to return to London for the start of the Season. In Egypt by day they would slavishly follow the tourist guides in their search for culture, but at night they would dance the time away in hotel ballrooms. There would be flirtations in the shadow of the pyramids, romances in the silences of the temples . . . and the Sphinx would continue to wear that strange, elusive smile. Last year, next year – in a thousand years it would all be the same. Those people would be uninterested in his role in the Middle East. He was not one of them.

After Alexandria, the ship would sail onwards across the Arabian Sea and an entirely different group would leave her at Bombay. Bronzed, long-term officers serving in the Indian Army, most of them accompanied by wives who would greet one another warmly, and soon be making arrangements to meet at the sports clubs to watch their men playing polo, or for women's talk over tiffin while they would smile knowingly at the sight of fresh-faced young subalterns with their pretty pink-and-white wives.

Tearful parents fluttered their handkerchiefs on the quayside and pale-faced children battled with their tears as they were left behind to finish their education in England. Among this motley crowd he could distinguish groups of civil servants, urbane and unruffled, upholders of the white man's burden from England to the far-flung corners of the globe.

After Bombay the liner would be half-empty. There would be room for the remaining passengers to spread themselves in the comfort of the lounges and play serious bridge. They could smile, in superior isolation, at the remembered scandals and promises of new ones.

'God, how I hate all this!' came a petulant voice beside him and, looking down, he saw that Tubby Rowlands stood at his side, his eyes gazing cynically down on the crowded quayside.

'The sooner we get under way and we can all settle down, the better I'll like it,' Tubby went on plaintively.

John smiled. 'Enjoy your leave?'

'It was all right. I lost a packet on the Derby and my grandmother took me to the cleaner's every night playing gin rummy. She's gaga most of the time, but she can recognise the spots on a pack of playing cards, all right. Last I heard you were still on the sick-list. Fully recovered now?'

'More or less.'

'And heading for Cairo. God, I wish I was. I'd know people and at least there'd be some sort of life I could relate to.'

'Where are you going to, Tubby?'

'Bombay. My brother Algy has a pal who works on a tea plantation. He's offered me some sort of a job – but I ask you, what do I know about planting tea? You'll be all right; tea dances at Shepheards, tennis at the Sporting Club at Gazira, weekends on some houseboat on the Nile . . . How did you manage to fall into something like this?'

John smiled. 'I didn't. I wanted to go back to the Far East. I've never been one for the fleshpots.'

'Wish I was having your opportunities – I'd certainly know how to make better use of them! Never thought of getting married?'

'Not for many years.'

Tubby said, ruefully, 'Funny, isn't it, how one wastes opportunities? I wouldn't admit it to the family, but being the black sheep doesn't exactly fill me with euphoria. Having to admit that you've been one hell of a fool doesn't come easy.'

'You mean that you regret missing out on all England has to offer, that you'd have been happier toeing the line your family laid down for you?'

'In a way. That lot'll be coming back for the Season, the balls and Ascot, weekends in country houses and Goodwood. Don't tell me you haven't missed it, too!'

'I haven't. My father was a loner after my mother died, never happier than living in some remote place miles from anywhere. He called the social scene superficial and empty and, in many respects, I agree with him.'

'Lucky you! If I was as rich as you are I'd be having one hell of a time.'

John merely smiled. The band was playing a selection of tunes from some of the London shows and Tubby remarked grimly, 'Oh, Lord, we have the streamers to come yet, and "Auld Lang Syne". I'll be comfortably sheltered in one of the lounges when we reach that stage!' Suddenly he whistled softly under his breath. 'Well, well, what have we here?'

John followed his gaze to where a tall, fashionably dressed woman was pacing along the quayside. Instinctively, the crowd parted to allow her and her two companions to pass. Dressed for travelling, the three women wore dark, tailored clothing and the veils on their hats completely covered their faces, a fact that had not prevented Tubby from recognising them.

John was not particularly interested but Tubby warmed to his subject.

'I wonder if the beautiful Laura will set Egypt alight as she's set London alight these last few months? There's an awful lot of money riding on that girl, Halliday, in the marriage stakes, I mean.'

'Who are they?'

'The lady is the Honourable Mrs Levison-Gore, the girls her daughters Laura and Margaret.'

'Levison-Gore? Wasn't he in the Forty-ninth Lancers, killed in that rumpus in Amritsar?'

'That's the husband. I've heard a lot about her from my mother. Apparently, she burst into London society when she was seventeen – rich American mother, English father of no particular note. It didn't take them long to ingratiate themselves with the right people and it soon became apparent that the Earl of Mallonden was the quarry she had in mind. His mother had other ideas and the old girl rules the family with a rod of iron; has a thing about foreign blood in the family. The Earl married his cousin Muriel, but the lady in question captured his younger brother, Hugh.

'But what the mother didn't manage to accomplish, the daughter most certainly will. She's tipped as being the debutante of the year; she's undeniably beautiful, a great rider to hounds *and* intelligent. I wish you could see her without that damned veil. I can't imagine why women have to cover their faces when the wind's hardly blowing!'

'There'll be plenty of opportunities to see the lady during the voyage,' John said evenly.

'Just don't develop any leanings towards her. They would be futile.'

'And the other daughter?'

'Margaret. Pretty, nice girl, not as devastating as her sister and a year younger. Well, I must say this voyage promises to be a lot more interesting than I'd thought it would be.'

Halliday was not listening. His eyes were on a tall, slender young man walking along the quay followed by several attendants carrying his luggage. He was immaculately attired in pale grey and his stature was considerably enhanced by the bright red tarbush he wore on his dark, sculptured hair. His long graceful strides brought him quickly to the gangway where the three ladies were standing and he paused, waiting for them to mount it before him.

As they stepped on to the deck one of them dropped her purse and, bending down, he recovered it and handed it to her. She looked up into what she considered the most handsome, remote face she had ever seen, and he stared down through a delicate veil into eyes the colour of violets and a coral mouth curved into a smile.

The two men looking down on the tableau were unaware that in that brief moment passions were forged that would illuminate the future and change lives as yet unborn. The three ladies moved off along the deck and the young man turned in the other direction to go to his stateroom.

'Do you know him?' Tubby asked curiously.

'Prince Ahmed Hassan Farag. His mother, Princess Ayesha, comes from a very wealthy Cairene family and his father is a distant relative of the Khedive. They own a vast estate in the Fayoum, the largest oasis in Egypt, and own palaces in Alexander, Cairo and Luxor. They are big farmers in the Fayoum, specialising in breeding Arab horses, and are Copts as opposed to being Moslem.'

'I can see you've done your homework, John. So what has Prince Ahmed Hassan been up to in England then?' Tubby enquired.

'I was instructed to make myself *au fait* with influential Egyptian families. As for the Prince, he's been educated in England – Winchester and Oxford – and attached to the Egyptian Embassy in London. Now he's going home to a way of life neither of those respected establishments will have prepared him for.'

'Why's he going back?'

'He's engaged to be married – some girl chosen by his family.'

'Ah well, here come the streamers!' Tubby exclaimed. 'See you after dinner, old boy. I don't suppose we'll be on the same table. Interesting to see who'll be on the captain's table. It certainly won't be me and I have the feeling you're not really interested!'

Halliday merely smiled as Tubby disappeared through the crowd that thronged the deck. Streamers were flying on to the crowds below and they were reciprocating in kind. The last floral offerings were being carried aboard, while lingering visitors were being hurried down the gangplanks. The ship's siren was vying with the strains of 'Auld Lang Syne' and, as the last chords died plaintively away, the great liner slid from the quayside and, nosed by her attendant tugs, was soon sailing majestically down Southampton Water like an ageing empress surrounded by her courtiers.

Tear-stained faces gazed wistfully at the disappearing shoreline, minds still obsessed by parents and children left behind, but now, from the lounges, came laughter and the cheerful sounds of crockery.

John Halliday remained at the ship's rail watching the autumn sunlight shining on the smudge that was England but his mind was on other days when, as a small boy, he had made this same departure time and again to spend holidays with the father he adored. That boy had loved the streamers and the band, the kindly wave of a departing housemaster and, like today, he had been the last to leave the ship's rail . . .

2

Lavinia Levison-Gore stood in the middle of her daughters' cabin, surveying it with a small frown on her handsome features.

'It's not too bad, I suppose,' she grudgingly admitted. 'We did book the passage rather late and I'm not even sure now if it was a good idea.'

'To come to Egypt, do you mean, Mother?' her daughter Margaret said in some surprise.

'I mean to sail from Southampton! When your father and I came before the war we went overland and sailed from Marseilles. I enjoyed the journey through France and the sea-voyage was a short one. However, we're here, so we might as well make the best of it, though my cabin will probably be smaller than this one!

'I hope, by this time, Elsie has unpacked. I'll send her in to you if she has – but remember, girls: nobody makes a thing about dressing for dinner on the first night out. A simple afternoon gown is all that is required – there will be plenty of time for the other stuff later. There's nothing to see through the portholes, Laura, so I suggest you remove your hat and do something with your hair.'

Laura turned and started to struggle with her veil while her mother looked on in some exasperation. 'I'll have a word with the purser later on to see if we can move into larger cabins,' she said irritably.

'Don't fuss, Mother,' Laura said. 'There's nothing wrong with this cabin and we were told the ship was full.'

'It'll be half-empty after Cairo and I'll have a word with the purser about our table, too. With our connections we should be on the captain's table. I'm going to insist on it. Do try to remember, Laura, that this is the start of your big year and I'm quite determined that you are to have the best of everything, my dear.'

'Yes, Mother.'

Lavinia turned at the door to say, 'You look very nice in that cream lace blouse, Margaret. Wear it tonight; and I would think about wearing the jade silk with those jade beads Granny Mallonden gave you at Christmas, Laura. As I said, nobody dresses up too much the first night out, but one naturally sets the seal on good taste for what comes after!'

She swept out of the cabin without another word and the two sisters sank on to their beds, convulsed with laughter.

The sisters were very different.

Laura was the taller of the two, her beauty more vibrant. Her shining hair had often been referred to as strawberry blonde and it was true that it had a pinkish glow to it. Her eyes were a deep velvety violet and her full curving lips were coral against the creamy tint of her skin. But though she was considered the most beautiful girl to have arrived on the social scene that Season, Laura Levison-Gore was not vain about her beauty; she simply accepted it with gratitude.

Margaret, on the other hand, was the traditional English rose with soft fair hair and blue eyes. She was pretty, but not instantly beautiful, her face softer, less animated than her confident, glowing sister.

'What do you bet she'll get her own way about sitting at the captain's table?' Laura said shrewdly. 'Mother tries too hard. She'll die of mortification if Poppy lands Edward and Poppy has got most of the Mallonden clan behind her.'

'She's not nearly as pretty as you,' Margaret said loyally.

For a long moment Laura surveyed her face in the mirror, then, with a graceful shrug of her shoulders, she said, 'We have to remember that Poppy came out last year and she was earmarked for Edward then. If he hadn't been in Japan at the time, no doubt this year they'd have married. Mother is delighted that I'm going to have a chance.'

'I hate it when she talks like that, and you sound just like her. Does it matter that you might not want to marry Edward?'

'He's not bad looking and he's awfully rich! Besides, he'll be a marquis and that counts the most with Mother and the Mallondens.'

'Does it count with you?'

'I'm not sure. Haven't you always had the feeling that we come a very poor second after Poppy? Granny Mallonden's never forgiven Mother for snaffling Father and Poppy is, after all, her eldest son's daughter. She's *Lady* Poppy and that's supposed to make her a fitting consort for any old marquis.'

'I still don't think it's a good enough reason to marry him, Laura, simply to beat Poppy and Grandmother.'

Laura got up from her bed and went to sit beside Margaret. She put both her arms round her sister and hugged her gently. 'You're the nicest thing, Meg! But don't get too complacent – it'll be your turn next year.'

'It will serve them all right if I marry a country curate and retire to the country to grow dahlias.'

'You'd be happy doing that, wouldn't you, Meg?'

'Of course . . . if I was in love with my husband. Love seems to be the last thing everybody else is thinking about,' Meg said sadly.

'That's something that comes later. Do you know, I've never exchanged a word with Edward Burlington! He could be the most dreadful bore.'

'I can't understand why we had to pack everything in a terrible hurry. One minute we were going to spend a few weeks with Aunt Josie in Sussex and the next we were rushing about like mad getting ready for Egypt. Will Poppy and her parents be in Egypt already?'

'I shouldn't think so, they're probably still spinning after the speed Mother's moved at.'

'Oh, do you think that's why she's rushed us so, simply to arrive before Poppy so that Edward sees you first?'

'Edward's known Poppy since they were children. Mother says we did meet just once when I was about five. He certainly won't remember me.'

'I suppose we'd better unpack,' Margaret said. 'I'm simply dying for a cup of tea. Do you suppose Mother would mind if we went in search of one?'

'Why don't we ask her?' Laura said cheerfully.

They found their mother sitting in her cabin watching her maid unpacking. She looked pale and was sipping slowly from a glass of water.

'One of my headaches is coming on. All this rush has been too much for me,' she said in a low, plaintive voice.

'Have you taken anything for your headache, Mother?' Laura asked gently.

'The usual tablets. Laura, you should be unpacking. I doubt if Elsie will have time to help you.'

'We thought we'd go and find tea but if you don't feel like coming with us, Mother, can I arrange to have something sent to you?'

'I couldn't possibly face all those crowds in the tea lounges. People simply flock there as soon as the ship leaves port and they'll be stuffing themselves with crumpets and scones. It would make me feel quite ill simply to watch them.'

'But you don't mind if we go?' Laura persisted.

'I would like it better if you waited for dinner and made your entrance then.'

'Mother, I don't want to make an entrance, I just want a cup of tea!'

'Very well, then, but don't chat to just anyone. That's the mistake most people make as soon as they get on board – they chat to the people nearest them and find they are saddled with them for the rest of the voyage.'

'One has to be polite, Mother.'

'One can be polite without committing oneself to days of looking out for one another, of being together! By the way, we *are* sitting at the captain's table . . . Not the cream lace, Elsie. It's far too elaborate for the first night out, the coffee satin is better.'

Dutifully, the maid returned the cream lace to the wardrobe, bringing out the beige gown instead while Mrs Levison-Gore leaned back in her chair, closing her eyes wearily.

By the time the two girls arrived in the tea lounge, many of the other travellers had left to seek out their cabins and the place was relatively deserted apart from several elderly gentlemen who were happily exchanging reminiscences in a far corner of the room, and two nannies hurrying their charges over the last cream bun.

They sat near the door, aware that the conversation across the room had momentarily ceased and that several pairs of eyes were regarding them appreciatively. Tea and a selection of cakes arrived immediately and, after Meg had selected an éclair Laura said sharply, 'You'll end up a positive dumpling if you go on at that rate. You wouldn't be having it if Mother was here!'

'Well, she isn't, is she?'

'No. Have you noticed anything?'

Meg looked around her with interest. 'Only the men in the far corner; they're all staring at us.'

'And they're all terribly old. It isn't that. Haven't you noticed we're starting to roll a bit? I wouldn't eat that cake if I were you!'

Replacing the cake on her plate, Meg sat back in silence and then, meeting Laura's mischievous gaze, she said, 'Oh golly, yes, I can feel it, but we can't be all that far out.'

'I know, but the wind started to blow while we were still on the quayside. Meg, do you know what this means?'

'That it's going to be rough and we'll probably be sick!'

'Of course we shan't be sick! I'm a very good traveller. But Mother isn't. She'll never come in for dinner if the ship continues to roll and that means you and I will be on our own.'

'Oh dear! It will be terrible sitting at the captain's table without Mother. What on earth shall we talk about?'

'Don't be a ninny, Meg. We're old enough and sufficiently educated to hold an intelligent conversation. Why don't we go along to the purser's office and find out who we'll be sitting with?'

The purser's office was empty apart from a short, stout man busily viewing the dining-room plan, so they stood aside until he had finished. When he turned to leave, his face lit up with a beaming smile and the two girls smiled back politely.

'I say,' said Tubby Rowlands affably, 'I hadn't thought to meet you again so soon.'

Laura frowned in an effort to remember where they were supposed to have met before, while Meg stood back uncertainly.

'You don't remember me,' Tubby said ruefully. 'Oh well, I'm used to people not remembering me. We met at my brother Algy's house at the end of

September. You were fresh out of that school near Interlaken and I remember thinking that London had better watch out.'

Laura smiled, not at all displeased by his remark.

'I remember you now! You were arguing with some other man about horses.'

'That was me. You might say it's the only subject I'm knowledgeable about and even then they quite often let me down. I suppose you're wintering in Egypt?'

'We're there until the end of March. And you?'

'No such luck. I'm heading for India and the hill country, tea-planting . . .'

'Really? I hadn't realised you were a tea-planter.'

'I'm not. It's an entirely new venture. I see you're sitting at the captain's table.'

'Do you know who we are sitting with? Will you be one of us?'

' 'Fraid not. We'll have a look, shall we? Here we are,' Tubby said cheerfully. 'You've got Sir George and Lady Galbraith – he's the shipping magnate; a Mr and Mrs Hiram Oppenheimer from Pittsburgh; Lady Moira Hesketh bound for Bombay and Prince Hassan Ahmed Farag leaving at Alex; and the captain, of course.'

'We don't know any of them, do we, Meg?'

'You soon will. People make rapid friendships on board ship.'

'That's what Mother says.'

Tubby grinned. 'I suppose she's warned you not to get stuck with the first people you meet.'

'Something like that.'

'It's not bad advice. I remember my first voyage out East; I got stuck with the friendliest crowd the first day and they turned out to be a gambling school who took me for a ride. I'm a lot more careful these days.'

'I'm sure you are,' Laura said. 'I'm so glad to meet

you again. No doubt we'll be seeing more of you during the voyage.'

The two girls left him with friendly smiles and a little later, when he met John Halliday in the lounge, he recounted the meeting with some degree of gratification.

Back in their cabin the two sisters giggled over their meeting with Tubby. Their mother had been anxious to know whether they had spoken with any of their fellow passengers and, on being told of their brief chat with Tubby, she frowned ominously.

'I do hope he's not going to latch on to us,' she said testily. 'He's the black sheep of the family, you know. Women and gambling. Cost them a fortune with one scrape after another, although his grandmother has a soft spot for him even if his mother has not.'

'I liked him,' Laura said. 'I'll bet he's a lot more fun than Algy. He's not nearly so stuffy.'

'Laura, I have not brought you on this holiday to cultivate people like Tubby Rowlands! Be gracious to the man, by all means, but don't encourage him. Did you find out who we are sitting with?'

Dutifully, Laura recounted their names and Lavinia frowned. 'I don't know any of them, but I suppose they are people of note. I suppose the Egyptian Prince could be the young man boarding the ship when we were.'

'He was awfully handsome,' Laura said brightly.

'Indian princes, Egyptian princes!' her mother said contemptuously. 'Never forget that they are *foreign* and that your grandmother disapproves of foreigners whether they are royalty or not. Once again, girls, be gracious and distant – you are cultured English ladies, not to be dazzled by foreign titles.'

Laura and Margaret faced her dutifully and then,

as the ship rolled, Mrs Levison-Gore groaned miserably. 'I doubt very much if I shall go in for dinner. I've never been a good sailor so we will dine in our cabins.'

'There's no reason why *we* shouldn't go, Mother,' Laura exclaimed. 'Tomorrow you'll be feeling much better and surely you want to know what the others are like?'

'Oh, very well,' their mother said wearily. 'Go, by all means, but remember, you must wear nothing flamboyant and don't get too friendly.'

Dutifully, they wore the gowns their mother had recommended, giggling helplessly as they staggered into them while the ship rolled. Meg said, 'If this goes on, the dining room will be empty.'

As she struggled to fasten Laura's dress, their mother's maid put her head round the door. The girls took in her pale green countenance, hastily telling her to go to her cabin and they would see that there was somebody to administer to her sickness.

Elsie was glad to go and, a few minutes later, looking in on their mother, they found her lying on her bunk moaning miserably. A nurse stood beside her and seeing the two girls she grinned cheerfully. 'She'll be all right in the mornin', girls, it takes most of 'em like this if they're not good sailors. Are you two going to be all right?'

'Of course,' Laura said stoutly. 'We're on our way to dinner. I don't suppose we can do anything for Mother now you're here.'

'Not a thing. You go and enjoy yourselves.'

'Elsie, Mother's maid, isn't feeling very well either,' Margaret said.

'I'll get somebody to see to her. Now then, my dear, try to get some sleep. Tomorrow's goin' to be a beautiful day and you'll be feeling much better,' she said stoutly, but her patient continued to moan and Laura and Meg made their grateful escapes.

'Tomorrow we'll get the inquisition – tonight we're going to enjoy ourselves,' Laura said.

'I don't see how. We'll be sitting with a lot of older people. And there won't be any dancing if the weather gets worse,' Margaret added mournfully.

Indeed, the wind had now risen in a steady crescendo and rain pattered on the glass surrounding the passageway to the dining room. Inside the dining room, however, it was quiet and a small orchestra played a selection of musical-comedy numbers although there were a good many empty places.

The head waiter greeted them with a smile and escorted them across the room to the captain's table. He performed the introductions to the people already sitting in their places but there were only three of them, the American couple and Lady Hesketh.

Lady Hesketh smiled pleasantly and Mrs Oppenheimer immediately said, 'Are you two girls on your own, then? I understood the purser to say your mother was with you.'

'She is,' Margaret said. 'She isn't feeling very well so she's decided not to come down for dinner.'

'Poor dear! Hiram and I are *never* ill. We get some very good tablets from our doctor long before we embark. I'll let your mother have some, though they work better if one takes a course of them well in advance.'

'Thank you. I'm sure Mother will be most grateful.'

'I see from the place-names that your mother is the Honourable Mrs Levison-Gore. What does that mean, exactly? I must say, the structure of the English aristocracy has me defeated!'

'Father was the second son of an earl so Mother isn't entitled to be called Lady Levison-Gore.'

'Poor you! Still, I don't suppose you're at all bothered. With your looks you'll have all Cairo at your feet. Are there some nice young men waiting for you?'

The girls simply smiled and, from across the table, Laura's eyes met Lady Hesketh's gentle smile.

'The captain doesn't appear to be joining us,' Mrs Oppenheimer remarked and her husband said, 'He's better occupied on the bridge than making conversation down here. Are you leaving the ship at Alex, Lady Hesketh?'

'No. I'm sailing on to Bombay.'

'Is that so? Prefer it to Egypt, do you?'

'I'm joining my husband in India.'

'Army, I suppose.'

'No, the diplomatic service.'

'We're doing the round trip – right out to Singapore, then we're heading back on her return journey. My good lady wanted to stop off in Egypt until after Christmas but I decided otherwise. We've done Paris, Rome and London and a sea-voyage is what we need now.'

By this time Laura was wishing desperately that her mother hadn't been quite so insistent about sitting at the captain's table. She couldn't face a week of listening to Mr Oppenheimer holding forth.

At that moment the head waiter reappeared, bringing with him the young Egyptian she had first encountered earlier that afternoon. He was wearing an immaculate dinner jacket and he bowed gravely to the rest of them before taking his seat next to Lady Hesketh. Meeting his straight gaze, Laura could feel the warm blood colouring her face and she looked down quickly, giving her full attention to the food on her plate. Conversation had momentarily died until Mr Oppenheimer decided it was time that introductions should be performed, ending by saying, 'Well, it looks as though we're going to be the only people eating dinner. The rest of them seem to have succumbed to the gale. I hope to God the captain's not one of them.'

He and his wife laughed heartily at his witticism

and, across the table, Prince Ahmed's lips twitched and Laura surprised a glint of amusement in his dark eyes.

Moira Hesketh was thinking that there were many compensations for growing old. One could view the passing show with a detachment which the young had still to experience. She was amused by the brashness of the Oppenheimers, entranced by the beauty of the two girls, and she hadn't missed the covert glances which Laura directed towards the young man sitting next to her.

Prince Ahmed Farag, whom she knew a little about, was a splendid example of young Egyptian manhood. It gave her immense pleasure to watch his eyes which flashed like black agate, his dazzling teeth, the exquisite contour of his pillar-like throat, and yet with all his Eastern glow of colour she felt the strange immobility of his countenance, which was characteristic of his Egyptian blood.

Over dinner he spoke very little. Silence suited his strong features and dignified bearing and she marvelled at the thick lashes which fringed his eyes. Lady Hesketh knew, instinctively, that he was well aware that he had captured the attention of the delectable Miss Laura Levison-Gore and sat back in her chair, totally entranced. This was only the first night out, yet already, the voyage held promise of certain entertaining distractions which she hoped would prove to be entirely light-hearted.

Moira Hesketh searched her memory for all she had heard regarding the girl's mother. If she remembered correctly their father had met his death in India and their mother was unpopular, regarded as a social climber and something of a snob. But the girls were pretty, particularly the older one. It was a pity she'd decided to give Egypt a miss; a few weeks' delay might not have mattered and Johnny had advised her to spend a few weeks in Luxor, but now she was voyaging on and she would not see the launching of the Misses Levison-Gore.

Gathering her wits, she turned to her companion to ask, 'Are you spending some time in Cairo or have you other plans?'

'I have no great love for Cairo. I find it noisy and dirty. The sooner I can return to my home in the Fayoum the better I shall like it.'

'You live alone?'

'I spend some time with my parents in Cairo and in the Fayoum, but I have a house in Luxor of which I am particularly fond.'

'Ah Luxor! I lost my heart to Luxor many years ago. I was a young bride returning with my husband to India and we spent our honeymoon in Luxor. It was a time of enchantment which I have never forgotten.'

Ahmed smiled, his white, even teeth flashing behind his firmly chiselled lips, pleased by her praise of the white town nestling on the banks of the Nile, and Lady Hesketh permitted herself a nostalgic journey into the past with its memories of that charming Italian hotel with its white pillared loggia from which the guests looked out every evening on the glory of the desert sunset . . .

After a long silence, Lady Hesketh said quietly, 'I believe I met your father once, a long time ago, at the opera house in Cairo. Tell me, you have spent most of your life in the West, I believe. How easily will you be able to change from one sort of society to another?'

He shrugged. 'Perhaps not easily at all. I think the storm is getting worse and we do have the Bay of Biscay to cross.'

He had changed the subject so adroitly that she was hardly aware of it. She took the hint, however, and asked no further questions about his future in the land of his birth. Instead, she addressed the two sisters, asking, 'What are your plans for the next few months? Are you remaining in Cairo or spending some time in Luxor?'

'Mother has it all in hand. We're expecting my cousin and her mother to join us in Cairo shortly but after that we're not really sure what we shall do,' Laura answered.

The orchestra was playing a selection of melodies from *The Merry Widow* and Mrs Oppenheimer remarked, 'I don't suppose there'll be dancing the first night out. Do you dance, Your Highness?'

'I doubt if I shall have much time for dancing when I arrive home.'

'But you'll dance on the ship, I hope. It's my bet these two young things can hardly wait to get their feet on the dance floor.'

He smiled but offered no comment and the two girls looked down at the table with blushing faces. After a few minutes Laura raised her eyes and found herself staring into two dark, inscrutable eyes, in a face whose incredible beauty left her heart racing.

Beside him, Lady Hesketh felt the first faint stirrings of alarm while, at his table near the wall, Tubby Rowlands downed his brandy and made for the bar. Passing John Halliday's table he said, 'See you in the bar, Halliday?'

'I'm afraid not,' John Halliday replied, 'I've promised to make up a bridge four.'

'Oh well, I'll take a look round and see what's cooking. Interesting situation at the captain's table, don't you think?'

'I haven't been aware of it.'

'You will be, dear boy, you will be!' After which cryptic remark, Tubby made his unsteady way across the dining room and out on to the heaving deck.

3

The ship sailed on; friendships were forged, romances blossomed. Out came the gladrags and, night after night in the ship's ballroom, Laura and Meg danced the night away while their mother watched from her seat at the edge of the ballroom to see that the girls entered into no liaison with the wrong type of man.

Lady Hesketh looked on with amusement. She had declined to sit with Mrs Levison-Gore because she had decided she didn't much care for the woman – and Mrs Levison-Gore had long since decided that the Oppenheimers were hardly her sort.

Sir George and Lady Galbraith were never in evidence. He retired immediately after dinner to talk business with anybody who was prepared to listen while his wife played bridge. And Prince Ahmed went in search of his own amusement and, much to Laura's chagrin, never appeared in the ballroom.

She took this as a personal affront. She was young and beautiful – the most beautiful girl in the ballroom, her mother told her – and not once had he suggested that they dance. She was wise enough, however, to keep her annoyance to herself. She knew if she broached the subject with her mother, Lavinia Levison-Gore would be horrified that she should even think of dancing with so obvious a foreigner.

Her mother had found her in conversation with Tubby Rowlands one morning on deck and had later voiced her acute displeasure.

'I don't want you encouraging him!' she had snapped. 'He's a fortune-hunter and a ne'er-do-well.'

'Oh mother!' Laura had protested. 'I'm not going to *elope* with him. He simply makes me laugh. He knows *everybody* and he's outrageous in the things he says.'

'I'm well aware of what he says and what he's like,' her mother said sharply. 'I've heard the most awful stories about that man.'

'What sort of stories?' her daughter demanded eagerly.

'I don't propose to repeat them!'

An unrepentant Tubby was subjected to a very cool nod of Mrs Levison-Gore's head whenever they met, but it did not deter him from trying to amuse her daughters.

'She hates my guts,' he confided to John Halliday, 'but she needn't worry. I'm not out to capture either of her offspring.'

A remark which amused Halliday considerably when he looked down at Tubby's rotund form and the enchanting beauty of the girls in question, particularly the older one.

Their mother took to her bed again as they crossed the storm-tossed Bay of Biscay and Laura decided she would use that time gainfully and set out to enchant the young Egyptian.

She's a minx, thought Lady Hesketh, watching the dimpled smiles come and go, the sparkle in her incredible violet eyes, and the young man's obvious interest.

The boiling sea calmed suddenly halfway through dinner and Laura said, happily, 'How marvellous! We shall be able to dance after all.'

Lady Hesketh had no doubt that a bevy of young officers were waiting to dance with her, but that was not what Laura wanted. She wanted this grave, remote man who smiled gently at her sallies and left the table immediately the meal was over.

Laura pouted prettily after he had afforded them his polite bow before striding off across the room.

'Really!' she said petulantly. 'Wouldn't you just think he'd unbend a little now and then? It wouldn't do him any harm to dance with me, so why won't he?'

'He's probably got some girl back home he's going back to,' Mrs Oppenheimer said philosophically. 'Don't they keep harems these days? I always understood the women in these Eastern countries were little more than chattels.'

'Oh, I wonder if there is someone,' Laura breathed. 'Can't we find out?'

'*Not* a very good idea,' Lady Hesketh said firmly. 'Prince Ahmed is obviously a very private man and we must respect that he comes from a very different culture. He would resent any prying into his private life.'

'I doubt if he'd object to *my* questions,' Mrs Oppenheimer said sharply. 'After all, he's probably realised I'm one of those brash Americans who don't kowtow to foreign royalty. I'm genuinely interested in the man – and I'm old enough to be his grandmother!'

Laura giggled. 'But of course,' she said happily, 'you could ask him all the questions I wouldn't dare to.'

For the first time Lady Galbraith entered the conversation, saying, 'His father is deeply involved with Egyptian politics and is a great landowner and his mother is rarely seen in society although I have met her. She is charming and cultured but, like most Egyptian women, she is very involved with her family. Prince Ahmed is the eldest of several children and is betrothed to an Egyptian girl of his parents' choice. It was no doubt something arranged when they were little more than children.'

Completely unchastened, Mrs Oppenheimer said, 'This voyage is probably his last opportunity to live like a Westerner, then. He shouldn't let the chance pass by.'

Lady Galbraith frowned and her husband said testily, 'Only years of involvement with the Eastern races can enable us to know how they act and how they feel. Personally, I think it would be an imposition to question him on any aspect of his private life.'

With that, both he and his wife excused themselves and left the table, while Mrs Oppenheimer said huffily, 'God, but they're stuffy! Don't you worry, honey, I know you're just *dying* to find out everything you can about that young man and I'm going to help you. Don't you agree, Lady Hesketh?'

'It's doubtful if you will penetrate his reserve, Mrs Oppenheimer, and you have no reason to do so. Neither of these girls lack partners on the dance floor – rather the reverse, I think!'

After dinner Margaret excused herself on the grounds that she wanted to see if her mother was feeling better, and later, as Laura rose to leave the table, Mrs Oppenheimer caught hold of her hand, saying, 'I know where you'll find him, my dear. He's usually in the bridge room or on deck, staring disconsolately at the elements.'

Laura blushed but managed to say haughtily, 'I'm not going looking for him, Mrs Oppenheimer. I'm accustomed to men looking for me.'

The rest of them watched her cross the room.

'How wonderful to be so young and so sure,' Lady Hesketh murmured with a small sigh, and Mrs Oppenheimer said, 'But how unfortunate when the only man she's remotely interested in remains so strangely aloof!'

'For all concerned, it would be better, perhaps, if he were to remain aloof,' Lady Hesketh answered evenly.

'Oh, I don't know. After tonight we'll be entering calmer waters and the girls' mother will back in circulation. I'm a great romantic at heart, aren't I, Hiram? Let those two young things live a little before it's too late, is what I say.'

Lady Hesketh kept her own counsel. She had grown up with English prejudices and her married life in India had conditioned her to accepting the barriers of colour and class that the British erected around themselves, the strong belief that East was East and West was West and never the twain should meet. God would have saved the world an awful lot of trouble if he'd made us all the same colour, she reflected grimly.

She was still busy with her thoughts when John Halliday paused at her table to ask if she would partner him in a game of bridge and she was grateful for his intervention.

'I hope I didn't interrupt something special,' he said as they crossed the room.

'You came at exactly the right moment – before I crossed swords with Mrs Oppenheimer!'

He smiled. 'She is a lady of strong opinions, I believe.'

'Yes, *very* strong opinions. And she has a mischievous sense of humour. I'm rather relieved that they are not leaving the ship at Alexandria.'

'I'm surprised to hear that. I would have thought you'd have been relieved to see them go.'

'I think Mrs Oppenheimer will do less damage on board than she would in Egypt.'

Lady Hesketh had known John Halliday a great many years and she regarded him as the very best kind of diplomat. She was sorely tempted to tell him of her conversation with her table companion but refrained. Yet she couldn't quite rid herself of the disquiet she was feeling . . .

Instead, she said easily, 'Do you intend to stay in one of the hotels in Cairo?'

'Actually, no. I'm sharing a flat in Heliopolis with another chap I've yet to meet. Frankly, I'm hoping my stay in Egypt won't be too long because I want to return to the Far East.'

'I'm thinking now that it would have been very nice to spend a few weeks in Egypt.'

'Why don't you?'

'Sheer laziness. Packing, unpacking, embarking, disembarking . . .'

At that moment Meg came hurrying along the deck and Lady Hesketh said, 'Did you find your mother better, my dear?'

'She was asleep so I didn't disturb her. Is Laura still in the dining room?'

'No, she left some little time ago. I've no doubt you'll find her on the dance floor.'

The girl smiled and hurried away. Lady Hesketh looked after her thoughtfully. 'I remember how it was to be eighteen with all of life waiting round the corner. But she's a sensible little thing – it's the other one that worries me.'

'Surely not! Isn't the other one destined to set London alight? Egypt too, if the people in the know are to be believed.'

She smiled doubtfully. 'I'm being fanciful. If Johnny were here he'd be the first to say so. He's always maintained that I have an unfortunate habit of seeing drama in everything.'

'Something about this voyage is worrying you?'

'Yes but I'm not going to spoil my game of bridge by worrying about it.'

'I hope you're not expecting the ship to go down or anything like that,' he said with a teasing smile. 'A disaster at sea is the last thing I want.'

'Not that kind of disaster at all,' she said firmly. 'I sincerely hope I'm wrong, but if I'm not, one day I might be tempted to tell you about it.'

He glanced down at her curiously, but she was smiling a greeting at two men who had risen from one of the bridge tables and then they were taking their places at the table and John was acknowledging

Tubby Rowlands who stood at the bar, lifting his glass in response.

'That young man drinks too much,' Lady Hesketh said firmly.

The ship sailed on into the night while those on board enjoyed their individual pursuits. The sound of music floated out of the ballroom on to the calm night air and now that the storm had abated, the night sky was ablaze with stars as Prince Ahmed stood at the ship's rail staring out across the silvered waves. Soon now, he thought, Egypt would swallow him up in her timeless cocoon, erase every last vestige of his Western life: holidays spent in English country houses, tea on English lawns and horses ridden against a biting wind across the Sussex Downs, May balls and race meetings, the companionship of friends grasping at pleasure after four long years of war.

Could he really forget all that in the new life that awaited him? Would the glorious tragedy of desert sunsets ever replace a misted landscape shadowed by rain? Would the domes and minarets of his native land erase completely the church spires of England glimpsed across the hedgerows? And would the vaguely remembered face of Fawzia erase completely the memory of the English girl he was painfully yearning for?

He had always known that Fawzia was the girl he would eventually marry although he had not seen her since they were children. Her parents had brought her to his home the day before he left Egypt for England and Winchester College. She was eight years old, a pale, delicate little girl with great dark-lashed eyes and a gentle face. She had written to him over the years; long, stilted letters in Arabic, although she had informed him that she had an English governess and they would be able to converse in English if he would like that.

They had both accepted without question that their future lay together. In England he had watched his friends falling in and out of love, seen the trauma of pain and ecstasy and felt singularly superior that such emotions would never get the better of him. Now, for the first time, he was beginning to understand something of the pain and agony of love.

She was there in the ballroom, dancing light-heartedly with a host of young men. In Cairo she would be swallowed up by another crowd of the pleasure-seeking people who descended upon Egypt to escape the rigours and monotony of an English winter.

Ever since that first night he had been aware of her eyes looking at him, the soft blushes on her beautiful face, the hurt, childlike expression when he tore his eyes away. He had known that the American woman was intrigued by the situation, just as Lady Hesketh was troubled by it. And the girl's mother was distantly polite. He had met women like Mrs Levison-Gore before; remote, superior women who had no liking for his foreign blood or his title.

Once, a long time ago, women like her had angered him, but as he grew older, amusement had taken the place of anger, until now.

Oh well, tomorrow they would be in the Mediterranean. Soon they would reach Alexandria and she would become a part of the crowd who would dance the nights away in the ballroom of Shepheards or Mena House while he would have returned to a life he had largely forgotten.

4

Back in the ballroom Laura was entertaining a group of young men by her efforts to teach one of them the latest dance-step to hit London. He was a quick learner and, when she deemed him sufficiently proficient, she started on the next in the queue. The laughter as well as the champagne flowed freely.

It was almost midnight and Mr Oppenheimer said feelingly, 'This lot'll never go to bed. Haven't you had enough dear?'

She looked across the room to the group of young people watching Laura perform with her latest partner and, with a little wave in their direction, said, 'All right, we'll go to bed. I can do the Bunny-hug as well as the next person – I just can't keep it up quite as long as some of them, that's all!'

They moved along the deck in the direction of their rooms. The sea stretched out like a heaving silvered carpet and the wind had dropped to a whisper. It was cool and quiet after the heat and pulsating noise of the ballroom and Mrs Oppenheimer looked ahead to where Prince Ahmed leaned against the ship's rail, staring across the waves.

He did not take his eyes off the view in front of him and Mrs Oppenheimer whispered quickly to her husband, 'I've forgotten my spectacles. You go ahead, dear, while I just slip back for them.'

Before he could utter a word she had sped away and was disappearing along the empty deck in the direction of the ballroom.

Mrs Oppenheimer hurried across to the table they had vacated as though in search of something, although her spectacles were safely inside her evening bag. Then, making a detour to where Laura was about to change partners yet again, she took hold of her arm, hissing, 'He's all alone out there, just staring at the waves. Take him a glass of champagne and invite him to join in!'

Laura stared at her in silence while her new partner stood by impatiently.

'Go on,' Mrs Oppenheimer insisted. 'It's now or never!'

Laura watched her hurrying out of the room, then, making up her mind suddenly, she spun round with a gay laugh, saying, 'I'm leaving you for a little while. There's somebody I have to talk to.'

Protests went up from all directions and Meg stared at her sister curiously. Ignoring them, Laura poured out two glasses of champagne and headed for the door, calling out behind her, 'I shan't be long so do get on with it. I'll expect you all to be expert when I get back!'

She decided it hadn't been a good idea to carry two glasses of champagne so, after sipping half of one of them, she put it down on a table near the door and left the room carrying the other. Along the deck she saw the brooding figure of Ahmed, staring out to sea, and she walked quietly, suddenly afraid of the expression she might read in his eyes.

She had reached his side before he turned to see her and his eyes narrowed. As she held out the glass of champagne he was desperately aware of her face, warm with blushes, below his own.

He accepted the glass of champagne with a little smile, saying, 'Why aren't you joining me?'

She laughed a little self-consciously, 'I've probably drunk too much already. It's such fun in the ballroom yet here you are, all alone with nothing but the stars for company.'

'It is cooler out here and the wind has gone. I think tomorrow will be a beautiful day.'

For a long moment there was silence until, in desperation, she cried, 'Why do I always find it so easy to talk to everyone and yet so terribly difficult to talk to you?'

He smiled. 'I fear I would only bore you. You have far more in common with those people you have just left.'

'Do you like being alone?'

'I'm accustomed to solitude. When I was a child I wanted to hear the desert's centuries of silence rolling up like a mighty ocean. It was only when I went to live in England that I came to respect an Englishman's need for his clubs and meeting-places.'

'Will you be staying in Cairo?'

'No. Where will you be staying? Shepheards?'

'No, Mena House. Then we hope to cruise on the river.'

'That is good. Cairo is a big, dirty city. It has its compensations of fairy-tale elegance with its mosques and minarets, but Egypt, the *real* Egypt, can only be found on the Nile. You will find Egypt very beautiful at this time of the year. It is the season of the inundation when pools of clear blue water cover the land and the date palms throw their reflections into a thousand tarns.'

'I am looking forward to it.'

'You have left your dancing to talk to me and I am being ungallant. Come, I will walk back to the ballroom with you. It is cool out here.'

'They are playing a waltz. Why don't you ask me to dance?'

'I find the ballroom noisy and very hot.'

She was standing looking up at him, the moonlight silvering her hair, her eyes beseeching, her mouth tenderly smiling. In answer to the unspoken plea in her eyes he reached out and took her in his arms and they started to dance, in silence, his chin resting on her hair.

She gave herself up to the joy of the muted music and the silver moonlight. They moved as one along the silent deck with no need for words and she wanted the waltz to go on for ever but, like everything else in life, it had to end. And when it did, they stood silently, wrapped in each other's arms. He was the first to move, and still their eyes were locked in a moment of intense passion, then, with a little moan, he put his arms around her and crushed her in his embrace. She lifted her arms and, as their lips clung together, neither of them had any thought beyond that moment . . .

It was the sound of footsteps hurrying along the deck which dragged them apart. Like a sleepwalker, Laura turned to see her sister near the entrance to the ballroom, looking uncertain and afraid.

Ahmed had stepped back against the ship's rail, his face a mask of reserve. It was as if a giant shutter had come down over a person she had only just glimpsed. Now that person was a remote, distant figure unconcerned with that wild fleeting moment of passion she was still shaking from.

Shyly she held out a trembling hand towards him and, taking it, he bowed over it gravely. 'It is late,' he said stiffly, 'and your sister is waiting for you. Goodnight.'

His smile was impersonal, shutting her out as if he regretted that rare moment of intimacy, and there was nothing for it but to turn away to where her sister stood.

Her tortured eyes met Meg's, and Meg said, hoarsely, 'I'm sorry, Laura. I wondered if you'd gone to Mother's cabin.'

Laura didn't answer, and Meg said hesitantly, 'Are we going back to the ballroom? Everybody was asking for you.'

'You go back, Meg, I'm going to our cabin. Suddenly I feel very tired.'

'But what shall I tell them?'

'Anything! Tell them anything!'

Laura undressed mechanically and lay unsleeping in her bunk, staring up at the play of shadows on the ceiling. She heard Meg come into the cabin but she feigned sleep. She knew that at one stage Meg came to stare down at her but she stayed very still, with her eyes tightly shut. She heard Meg move away and, after a few minutes, the creaking of her bunk as she settled into it.

She thought about Ahmed. Would he, too, be lying sleepless or would he find her easy to forget, a girl who was light-hearted and spoilt, a girl who had danced the night away with a bevy of young men and had sought his embrace as simply another scalp to add to the others?

She tossed and turned in her narrow bunk until the first pale light of day invaded the cabin, then she eased herself out and went to stand at the porthole. The sea was calm under a pale grey sky tinged with pink, colours that reminded her of the feathers of a bird, delicate and fragile. It was hot in the cabin and she had a sudden craving for the fresh, salt-laden air outside.

The long, silent deck stretched in front of her and, hugging her robe tightly about her, she went to stand at the rail. The turbulence had gone and the sea lay before her, a gentle undulating blue. The light breeze blew tendrils of hair around her face and she waited in anticipation for the rock that was Gibraltar to appear through the early-morning mist. The first stage of the voyage was almost over . . .

The atmosphere at the breakfast table was cordial and polite. Mrs Oppenheimer's eyes darted over her companions like those of a curious bird. Laura toyed with her meal and her mother talked to Lady Galbraith about some function she had attended in Delhi while the men chatted spasmodically about golf, sailing and bridge.

'I hope we can rely on you to join us for bridge tonight, Prince Ahmed,' Mr Oppenheimer said heartily. 'I did enjoy our game last night and it's evident you're not interested in dancing.'

Across the table Laura blushed uncomfortably. For a brief moment she raised wide, haunted eyes to Ahmed but his expression remained bland and impersonal.

'We have a few days in Egypt on the way back, Prince Ahmed. It would be nice if you could show us around,' Mrs Oppenheimer asked hopefully.

'I'm afraid that might not be possible,' he said easily. 'I do not intend to remain in Cairo for longer than is absolutely necessary.'

'Well, we'll be moving around, too, won't we, Hiram? There must be somewhere we can meet.'

'I can't think why we didn't spend some time in Egypt on our last voyage out. Tell me, Prince Ahmed, when is the best time to visit Egypt?' Lady Galbraith enquired.

'I think now is the best time. It is the time of the inundation, when the desert blooms, and now in November the little farms of date trees and mud houses will appear like islands rising out of a vast lagoon. In March, when you arrive in Egypt, the pyramids will be standing high and dry on the desert sand, and the Sphinx will not be gazing upon an expanse of clear water which keeps and holds the light of Egypt. It is a great pity that you did not decide to spend time in Egypt now.'

'There, Hiram, what did I tell you?' Mrs Oppenheimer said sharply. 'You *would* sail on to the East and call on the way back.'

Mr Oppenheimer scowled. 'By the time we get back to Egypt we'll be so sick of travelling that getting back to the States is all I'll be interested in. Are we likely to be reaching Alexandria at some ungodly hour, Captain?'

'At midday,' the captain answered him. 'We shall have ten hours in Alexandria – time for you to go ashore.'

'Is there much to see?'

'There's the tomb.'

'Alexander's tomb?'

'No, simply the tomb of some unknown and very wealthy citizen of Alexandria in Roman times. But you should see it, it is magnificent.'

'Weren't Cleopatra and Antony buried in Alexandria?' Lily Oppenheimer asked.

'Her tomb has never been discovered, nor Antony's, Mrs Oppenheimer. But you can visit the place where the Rosetta Stone was discovered, and there is much of Alexandria concerned with Nelson's battle of the Nile.'

'I'd have been more interested if it had been Alexander's tomb or Cleopatra's. Whatever happened to hers, or Antony's, too, for that matter? Can you tell us, Prince Ahmed?' Mr Oppenheimer asked.

'I'm afraid not. Lost in the mists of time, I feel sure.'

'Surely Alexandria must have preserved something of Antony and Cleopatra? Weren't they the star-crossed lovers of all time? I thought Egypt was steeped in history.'

'When you have inspected all the monuments of Alexandria and spent pleasurable time in doing so, you will find that in spite of your efforts of imagination you are incapable of reconstructing the city in the days of its ancient splendour,' Ahmed said quietly. 'You will call up no picture of Cleopatra with Antony or Caesar, for Alexandria is not the Eternal City where history never fades and where the past is at one with the present.'

'I take it you are also very fond of Rome, Prince Ahmed,' Lady Galbraith said.

'In Rome, history is continuous, it has no gaps, no lapses of unnumbered centuries, as in Egypt. In Rome, Mark Antony is still standing in the Forum begging the people's pity for the great Caesar; you can hear his deathless words wherever you have ears to listen. You can still walk with St Paul along the Appian Way and it takes no stretch of the imagination to hear the clatter of horses' hoofs across the square of St Peter's.'

Laura was listening with shining eyes. This grave, cultured young man was like nobody she had ever met, and the low charm of his voice filled her with a desire that was already doomed.

'I love Rome,' Lady Galbraith said earnestly. 'I adore the shops and the way the Italians have of enjoying themselves.'

'Oh yes, we were there just before the war,' Lily Oppenheimer said eagerly. 'I do hope nothing's changed.'

Lady Hesketh smiled cynically and Laura felt she could have screamed. Why didn't they let him go on enchanting them with his knowledge, allowing her to watch his sculptured lips, the white, even teeth when he smiled, his dark eyes gleaming behind those incredible long lashes?

Later, when he excused himself and left the room, she had to cling to the edge of her chair to stop herself from going after him. Across the table her eyes met Lady Hesketh's and she surprised in them a sympathy that made her look away quickly in case Moira Hesketh should see the stinging tears she could not control.

'Are we all going ashore at Gib?' Mr Oppenheimer asked somewhat gloomily.

Nobody seemed very sure.

Only a small group of people left the ship at Gibraltar, servicemen and civil servants, some of them accompanied by wives and children and others uncertain about what they should see.

Mrs Levison-Gore had declined to go ashore, insisting that her daughters spend only as much time off the ship as they deemed necessary. Most of the passengers visited the Rock and the caves, but Laura and Meg merely looked at the shops and took tea with Lady Hesketh at the Rock Hotel.

5

How easy it was for Laura to flirt and taunt her procession of partners when she had never felt so furiously angry before – but then, she had never been in love before.

Meg watched her sister uncertainly and, from their seats at the edge of the ballroom, Mrs Oppenheimer and Lady Hesketh watched also.

Lady Hesketh thought the girl was behaving outrageously; Mrs Oppenheimer considered her a minx but thought she should have gone in search of Prince Ahmed rather than stringing a host of young men along.

'It's quite obvious he isn't interested,' she commented, 'or he'd have been here. What can a girl do when he's shown her quite plainly that he prefers the bridge room to the ballroom?'

Laura's sentiments were identical to these. Consequently, when Mr Oppenheimer tore himself away from the bridge table with the information that they'd all had enough, she was quick to entice the second officer on deck where Prince Ahmed passed them dancing in each other's arms.

It didn't help. She had no means of knowing if she had hurt him or if he was merely indifferent. She indicated to her sister that it was time they went to their cabin and the first thing she did on entering was fling herself on her bunk in a deluge of tears while Meg stood looking helplessly down on her.

'It's Ahmed, isn't it? You're in love with him!'

Laura sobbed on, and Meg said doubtfully, 'Did you think he was in love with you?'

Laura sat up then, looking at her balefully. 'I think I hate him! He's cruel. Oh, I wish I could hurt him, *really* hurt him, but he's too cold, too cynical.'

'Laura, you can't really fall in love with him. Nothing could come of it. There's Edward . . . Surely you haven't forgotten that Mother expects you to marry him?'

'I can't marry Edward, not now,' Laura said savagely. Besides, he'd be better off with Poppy – she's a lot nicer than I am. *She'd* never fall for an Egyptian prince who couldn't care the toss of a button for her!'

Laura was even more doleful when Lily Oppenheimer said over breakfast the following morning, 'I forgot to tell you, girls – the Prince was up on the Rock with that nice Mr Halliday yesterday, two bachelors together, enjoying their conversaion. All they were short of was two nice English girls to brighten up their afternoon.'

Meg scowled and Laura wished Mrs Oppenheimer would shut up.

'We took a look at those apes the British are so proud of,' Mr Oppenheimer said. 'One of them ran off with a woman's glasses and it was the best excitement we had all day. Of course she hadn't a hope of getting them back, the beast was halfway up the Rock in no time.'

'Where did you spend all your time?' his wife asked Lady Hesketh.

'We went to the shops and had tea,' she answered.

'How very civilised. I wish we'd done that, my feet were killing me when I got back on board. I couldn't have danced last night if anybody'd asked me.'

'Well, girls, we'll soon be in Alexandria,' her husband said, smiling broadly. 'I suppose you'll be going up to Cairo immediately.'

'Yes,' Meg replied. 'Mother wants to get installed in our hotel before the rest of the family arrive.'

'So there's going to be quite a party. The ship's going to be very dull when you've all left us. How many are you expecting to join you?' Lily Oppenheimer went on.

'I'm really not sure – Mother made all the arrangements.'

'And you are all sailing up the Nile together?'

'I think so, but we do intend to stay near Cairo for some time before we sail.'

'You'll be spending Christmas on the Nile, then?'

'I suppose so. Heavens, I'd forgotten about Christmas, but it will be lovely, won't it?'

'You're very quiet this morning, Laura,' Lady Hesketh said. 'Aren't you looking forward to your stay in Egypt?'

'I'm not looking forward to Egypt at all, Lady Hesketh. *Anywhere* but Egypt!'

Laura had turned large soulful eyes upon her and Moira Hesketh couldn't help but be aware of the misery in them. Briskly, she said, 'I came out to Egypt when I was a little younger than you and I had a *marvellous* time. There were the dances in the hotels and garden-parties at the Sporting Club. All I wanted to do was dance and enjoy myself but Egypt got through to me, as it does to so many people. I began to look for more from my visit – and then I fell in love with an archaeologist, a very studious, painstaking young man who didn't even know I was there.'

'Then you know what it's like, Lady Hesketh?' Laura said, feelingly.

'I think so. But you know as well as I, Laura, that it is impossible. Prince Ahmed has seen this and you must, too, if you are to avoid being made miserable.'

'But why is it so impossible? Why is he so distant? What's wrong with me?'

'My dear child! Nothing is wrong with you except your culture, your entire way of life. Your family would not accept it and, in all probability, neither would his.'

'That's archaic!'

'It is also a fact of life, my dear. Good morning, Prince Ahmed! I'd begun to think you'd decided not to eat breakfast.'

Prince Ahmed smiled briefly and ordered coffee.

'I saw you up on the Rock with that nice Mr Halliday,' Mrs Oppenheimer said coyly.

Prince Ahmed merely smiled, while Mrs Levison-Gore said curiously, 'I seem to know Mr Halliday from somewhere. Isn't he leaving the ship at Alexandria?'

'Yes,' Lady Hesketh said. 'He is in the Diplomatic Corps but was wounded in the war and his job in Singapore had to be filled while he was convalescing. He'll be working in Egypt until something in the Far East crops up.'

'Perhaps that's where we met, India or Hong Kong, perhaps?'

'Perhaps.'

Mrs Levison-Gore was not prepared to let it go at that.

'Who are his family?'

'His grandfather was General Sir Arthur Halliday and his father was the second son, Malcolm. He spent most of his life in the Far East. Married a nurse out there.'

'Of course. Now I remember. Didn't the family object to the girl? Was she coloured or something?'

'No, she was Irish. She died when John was five but John and his father never patched up their differences with the family.'

Mrs Levison-Gore smiled bitterly. 'Yes, gossip never loses anything and there was very little else for the women to do except gossip. We all suffered from it at one time or another.'

'I wouldn't have thought the English would have

objected because the girl was Irish. Some of our wealthiest families are of Irish extraction,' Mrs Oppenheimer said sharply.

Nobody spoke, while Mrs Levison-Gore silently remembered that she had been rejected for being half-American.

'I think it's terrible,' Laura said, staring angrily round at them. 'It's obscene to have people chosen for you. Like a cattle market.'

Lady Hesketh was quick to see the annoyance on Mrs Levison-Gore's face, the alarm on Meg's, and Mrs Oppenheimer's bright-eyed anticipation. To cover the long, uncomfortable silence she said quickly, 'How lovely to have a day at sea in which to please ourselves.'

'And to get ready for the Gala Ball before we dock in Alexandria,' the captain ended, equally relieved that somebody had had the sense to change the subject.

All next day there was an air of anticipation on the decks and in the lounges while people gathered in groups to discuss the evening's event.

Mrs Levison-Gore said it was quite ridiculous for elderly passengers to be behaving like children.

Lady Hesketh accepted with alacrity John Halliday's invitation to partner him in the bridge room. The Galbraiths decided they would retire early and looked forward to the time when most of the bright young things left the liner.

Mr Oppenheimer declined to accompany his wife to the ball and set about looking for a bridge partner. To Laura's chagrin, he found one in Prince Ahmed.

'What are we going to wear?' Meg wailed. 'Mother said we had to keep our new evening frocks for the social life in Egypt. The things we have in the cabin are so frumpish.'

'Just wait and see,' Laura said gleefully. 'I expected something like this might happen. Millicent Radwell warned me and you know how she travels the world on one liner or another.'

'You're hiding something,' Meg said. 'Oh Laura, I want to know, I'd rather not go to the wretched ball at all if we haven't anything decent to wear.'

Her eyes followed Laura as she went over to her trunk and dived towards the bottom.

'I just hope they're not too creased from being hidden away,' she said anxiously. 'Perhaps Elsie would see to them without Mother knowing anything.'

She produced heaps of frothy tissue paper, saying, 'This one's yours, Meg, with the pink ribbon tag on it. I hope it's one you might have chosen yourself. I kept them apart when Mother was seeing to the packing, hoping she wouldn't notice.'

Meg's fingers tore at the delicate paper, revealing in seconds the sheen of pale pink crêpe-de-chine, then, her eyes wide with wonder, she pulled out a confection embroidered with silver bugle beads and with a skirt hanging in a heavy fringe reaching to her knees as she held it in front of her.

'Oh Laura, how marvellous,' she breathed. 'This was my favourite of all the gowns Mother bought for me. Which have you brought?'

Laura held up a gown in cornflower-blue chiffon and Meg clapped her hands gleefully. 'I loved that dress, I wanted you to have it the first moment I saw it. Suppose Mother finds out?'

'She won't. She's not the least bit interested in the ball and I'll swear Elsie to secrecy.'

'But suppose she wants to see what we're wearing before it all starts?'

'Then we'll put on something from that lot and then come back to change. Stop worrying, Meg – you're going to spend your life worrying about what Mother's going to think.'

'I wish you worried a bit more. You're going to

have to behave when we get to Cairo and the family arrive. Why didn't we all travel together? I can't understand why we had to rush to get on this boat and arrive in Egypt before the rest of them.'

'That's because you're sweet and innocent, darling, and don't understand how Mother's mind works like I do.'

'How does it work then?'

'She found out about this Nile cruise from Aunt Constance who owns the dahabiyah and that she was letting the Mallondens and Edward's parents have it for several months. Mother knew exactly why they were coming here; it was to allow Edward and Poppy to meet. By fair means or foul she cajoled poor Aunt Maud into allowing us to join them on the holiday. You know what happened next – we have to get to Egypt first so that Edward meets me before he sees Poppy.'

'You make Mother seem awfully devious.'

'Mother is devious when she's up against Granny Mallonden. Heaven knows what *she's* had to say about our joining them.'

Fortunately, they were spared a long interrogation on their ballgowns since Mrs Levison-Gore misplaced her purse just before dinner and the entire first-class lounge had to be turned upside down until it was discovered under a pile of magazines. After that episode she developed one of her sick headaches which necessitated her going to her cabin immediately dinner was over. While the two girls fussed over her, they inwardly rejoiced at their good fortune.

The night's merriment soon got under way and the two girls were showered with compliments from a host of young officers vying with each other to dance with them.

Lily Oppenheimer, resplendent in pale cream satin lavishly decorated with bugle beads and just a fraction too tight for her, said coyly, 'What a pity the Prince isn't here. He'd make you a member of his harem on the spot.'

Seeing the distaste on Laura's face, she added quickly, 'I was only joking, honey, of course he won't have a harem. Egyptians don't, do they?'

Suddenly disenchanted with the evening Laura escaped on to the deck and for a long time stood staring out at the sea, glassily calm and silvered by a full moon. She was still there when, a little later, a group of men strolled along the deck from the bridge room and John Halliday said with a smile, 'Surely you're not tired of the dancing already?'

She smiled, but as her eyes met Prince Ahmed's they were all aware of her delicate face suffused with sudden colour.

Mr Oppenheimer said, 'I suppose my wife's still in there, exhausting herself and everybody else.'

In the laughter that followed Laura turned away and the men walked on towards the ballroom.

Minutes later Lily Oppenheimer joined her, saying breathlessly, 'Do come back into the ballroom, love. Everybody's there including His Highness who is sitting near the back reviewing the scene with those dark, inscrutable eyes of his.'

'Is he alone?'

'He was when I left. Some bright young thing had pursuaded Mr Halliday to dance.'

Laura hurried into the ballroom, her eyes leaping across the room to the far tables, but there was no sign of Ahmed. In spite of those wishing to detain her she crossed the room and left it by the door leading to the deck. And then she saw him, leaning on the ship's rail, gazing into the distance.

She paused uncertainly, afraid of his withdrawal, his remoteness. Then, taking her courage in both hands, she stepped forward and joined him at the rail.

He turned to look down at her, his smile polite, his attitude that of a man disposed to be courteous even when he would have preferred to be left alone.

Her voice trembled pitifully and she despised herself for her weakness and a pride that seemed to have abandoned her.

'This is our last night before we reach Alexandria,' she said softly. 'Tomorrow will be so busy we might not be able to say goodbye.'

He smiled. 'Then perhaps we should say our goodbyes now. I sincerely hope you enjoy my country, Laura.'

'But surely we shall see you there?'

'I think not. I shall be at my home – I do not intend to linger in Cairo.'

'But we are sailing on the river to Luxor and Aswan.'

'Then you are very wise. That is when you will really see and get to know Egypt.'

'Oh, I do wish you weren't so stiff and starchy! It's like talking to an image from one of your old tombs. All those young men in there are *dying* to amuse me, but not you. You wish I was miles away!'

He was staring down at her, his face etched in moonlight, his expression gentle and, for the first time, robbed of its remoteness. His voice was low, and her entire being responded to its charm.

'Are you asking me to amuse you?'

'I doubt if you'd take the trouble.'

'I could tell you a story.'

'What sort of story?'

'About a little boy who played with fire.'

'Has it a moral?'

'Yes, all good stories have morals.'

'I don't think I want to hear a good story . . .'

Her voice was trembling with nervousness but, ignoring her words, he said, 'Don't you want to know what became of the bad little boy?'

'Oh, was the boy bad?' Her voice mimicked excitement. 'Why was he bad?'

'Because he had been warned not to play with fire.'

'Who had warned him?'

'A lady called Experience.'

'What did she say to him?'

'That if he played with fire it would burn him – and it would hurt.'

'Go on,' she said. 'Did the boy play with it?'

'At first there wasn't any fire,' Ahmed said. 'Only two tiny sticks; but the boy knew that if the two sticks came too close together there would be fire, but he couldn't resist the fun of making just little sparks and flashes. Tiny ones at first and then bigger and bigger until they burst into a big, bright flame, and then he couldn't stop them burning. They burnt his hands horribly, and still he couldn't help holding them; then the flame fascinated him almost more than the pain hurt . . .' he stopped.

'And then?' Laura said, breathlessly.

'And then . . . well then . . .' he said, 'there was nothing more. Nothing at all, except the awful pain and the memory of all that the lady called Experience had told him.'

'Do you think that little boy will ever play with fire again?' she said.

'I think not.'

'Do you know the little boy?'

'Yes. I am his most intimate friend.'

'Should I like him?'

'I think not,' he said. 'He is too grave for you.'

'And you will not introduce me to the little boy?'

He shook his head.

'You are afraid he would play with the matches again?'

'Yes, I am afraid.' He looked into her eyes and said again, 'Yes, I am afraid; I think you are so eager for fun that you could not resist tempting the little boy to play with the matches. And I think you are so clever that you would drop yours before they burnt your fingers . . .'

'Oh Ahmed! You think I am heartless because you saw me flirting with all those young men. But I only flirted because you were so aloof. When you kissed me I thought you cared for me and then – then you ignored me and I was so *miserable*!'

'Darling Laura, please understand that there can be nothing for you and me. Momentarily, passion and desire united us, but there are too many things that will divide us. You're so very young and inexperienced. I live in a different world from yours, a world of which you can know nothing.'

He raised his hand and brushed away the tear which rolled slowly down her face, then he took her hand and kissed it.

With a little cry she threw herself into his arms and pressed her lips against his. For a moment she felt him trembling against her, then, resolutely, he pushed her away from him. With a grave bow he left her staring after him.

In the distance she could hear 'Auld Lang Syne' being played in the ballroom and the light-hearted laughter as people began to walk out on to the decks. The night was balmy under a deep blue sky ablaze with stars and people were strolling about or gathering in groups, reluctant to go to their cabins on their last night aboard.

Laura had no wish to linger with them. Instead, she raced along the deck, not pausing until she reached the safety of her empty cabin.

When Meg joined her she was already undressed and wearing her bath robe, but she was not asleep. Meg found her staring out of the porthole and there was something about her stance that made the younger sister suddenly afraid.

Laura turned her head and for a moment it was as though she didn't see her. Then, with a little smile, she said, 'I'm sorry, Meg. You didn't mind my not waiting for you, did you?'

'Where were you? I thought you were enjoying yourself!'

'Oh Meg, I'm so very unhappy,' Laura said, holding her hands to her face, and Meg ran forward and took her in her arms.

'This was not the light-hearted Laura whom Meg adored. Suddenly she had turned into a sad, alien woman and Meg believed she knew the reason why.

'It's Ahmed, isn't it?' she blurted out. 'What has he been saying to you?'

'I love him, Meg! I think I fell in love with him that first day when he handed me my purse. I love him so much it's like a pain here in my heart.'

'You only love him because he's different,' Meg protested. You'll soon forget him.'

'You think I'm as silly and shallow as he does!'

'I don't think you're silly at all. I just think you *think* you're in love with him now but you'll forget about him when you don't see him any more. Besides, there's Edward.'

'Edward?' Laura said stupidly.

'Oh, Laura! Isn't that why we're here?'

'I can't marry Edward, Meg. I won't marry anyone I'm not in love with and if I can't marry Ahmed I won't marry anybody!'

Meg sat down on the edge of her bed, looking at her sister stupidly. It had all been spelt out to them so many times: Laura this year, Meg next year. There had been no love to complicate matters, simply the niceties of like meeting like, the fusion of two families and the happy-ever-after. Now, if Laura refused to play her part, it would all be spoilt . . .

Laura saw her sister's pretty face tinged with fear

and uncertainty. Dear, sweet Meg who saw everything in black and white, never in shades of grey. Now she looked as if her entire world was turning topsy-turvy. Sitting down beside her, Laura said gently, 'Don't worry about it now, Meg. After tomorrow we'll go up to Cairo and toe the family line and Ahmed will . . . disappear. I'm only telling you that somehow, somewhere, I've got to see him again. When I do, I'll have a better idea what the rest of my life is going to be like.'

'In the meantime you'll meet Edward; he'll fall in love with you and you'll forget all about Ahmed. Oh, Laura I do so hope that is what will happen!'

'We'll see, darling, we'll see.'

She had to pacify Meg at this stage because Meg would mope and her mother would be alerted that all was not well. Laura had no doubts in her heart that in the end love would find a way . . .

6

They had been in their hotel almost a week and were waiting for the arrival of the rest of the party. In the strangeness of their surroundings Laura had recovered much of her interest in life. She rode with Meg every morning, trying to be cheerful as they mounted their excellent Arab steeds which were brought to the hotel for them.

The Mena House hotel on the edge of the desert afforded them magnificent views of the pyramids and Sphinx and, as they rode out to ancient Memphis, Laura told herself, 'This is Ahmed's country. This is the sort of scenery he would remember in all those long years he spent in England, and now I have to love it too.'

Dutifully, they had visited the sites around Cairo, the mosques and the Citadel, and in the evenings they had danced in the hotel ballroom. They had inspected the charming river-boat which both girls immediately fell in love with, and their mother had informed them over lunch that Edward had arrived in Egypt.

'I wonder how she knows,' Meg hissed softly. 'She must have spies out somewhere.'

'I've no doubt she's right, though,' Laura said sharply. 'I wonder if he's staying here or in Cairo?'

'Mother said he was at Shepheards,' Meg confided.

They were not left long in doubt, for their mother suggested they should go into the city and take tea at Shepheards that afternoon.

Perversely, Laura said, 'Afternoon tea here is much nicer, Mother, we can look out on the pyramids. In Cairo we're simply looking out on the promenade.'

'And the most fascinating river in the world,' her mother added caustically. 'Wear that hyacinth-blue dress, Laura, it's so good with your colouring. And don't bother with a hat, take a parasol instead.'

On their way up to change, Meg said softly, 'Notice she didn't tell *me* what to wear. You're the sacrificial lamb.'

Dutifully, Laura wore the blue gown her mother had recommended, and, eyeing her critically, Meg said, 'You look very beautiful – but you're not the same Laura I knew in England.'

'What do you mean by that?'

'In England you were fun. Since we came to Cairo all you do is sit on your own, staring into space. I think I hate that Egyptian prince for changing you. And it's time you were over him now that you're going to meet Edward.'

'Oh, bother Edward! He may not even like me and I'm not at all sure that I shall like him. I'll do my best to help Poppy along.'

'How do you intend to do that with Mother breathing down your neck?'

'You can depend on it that she'll leave us together as often as convention permits. It's then I shall tell him how nice my cousin Poppy is and how much she's always adored him.'

'You don't know that!'

'I know what the family are coming out here for. Mother's hoping to get in first but I'm not being pushed on to anybody. I know what I want and I'm going to get him.'

'You won't manage it.'

'How much are you willing to bet?'

'If I had any money I'd gamble a great deal. As it is, I just think you're being ridiculous. You'll never see Ahmed again and by this time he's probably forgotten you anyway.'

Laura picked up her parasol after giving her sister a long, hard look. Brusquely, she said, 'We'd better go down. Mother will be waiting for us.'

Mrs Levison-Gore looked very elegant in cream silk and was wearing a matching hat adorned with large, pale green roses. She waited in evident impatience and, as soon as the girls joined her, she said sharply, 'What a time you've been! I've ordered a carriage to take us into Cairo and time costs money. You both look very nice but leave me to do most of the talking.'

In the privacy of his private suite at Shepheards the Marquis of Camborne faced his eldest son, Lord Burlington, in some displeasure.

Why was it, he wondered, that he and Edward had never got on? He'd never been the sort of son he could relate to. While Edward's older brother, Rory, had been serving in the Navy and his younger brother, Peter, had been dying on the Somme, Edward had been somewhere in the Far East searching for his soul.

He'd gone off to Tibet and then to Japan, living like an Eastern monk for five long years and then, out of the blue, he'd sent a cable to say he was coming home. It was then that the Marquis and Lord Mallonden had put their heads together. It was time Edward married – and who better than Lady Poppaea Mallonden? They'd been earmarked for each other years ago, and Poppy hadn't exactly managed to capture anyone else during her year as a debutante. Now Edward was coming home and Edward's parents had decided that they would winter in Egypt and Edward should break his journey and meet them in Cairo.

Mallonden agreed that it was a good idea. It wouldn't be good for Poppy to have to face another London Season and hopefully, in the romantic setting of Egypt, Poppy and Edward might discover they had a great liking for each other.

The Marquis eyed his son with a certain grim humour. Edward was tall and lanky, not bad looking but not handsome. Still, Poppy wasn't exactly a raving beauty. She was a pleasant enough girl, hearty and decidedly horsey, but she'd be good for Edward, knock that strain of effeminacy out of him.

It was Dorothy's fault that Edward was like that; she'd tricked him out in skirts until he was nearly four. No wonder the lad was puzzled. The Marquis met Edward's pale blue gaze with a stern frown.

'There's to be no more extended trips in the Far East,' he said acidly. 'There's been a lot of talk about you being out there all through the war. Something like that isn't easy to explain to people who've lost sons in battle. And what reason could I give as to why you hadn't come home immediately the war started?'

'I wasn't in touch with civilisation, Father. The war had been on two years when I found out about it, and it wasn't possible to get home.'

'And did you find your soul?' his father asked sarcastically.

'I found a great many things,' Edward said firmly.

'I remember the last letter we had from you said you'd found a rare butterfly; that's hardly the sort of information we could be expected to entertain our friends with.'

'I must remember not to mention such rarities again,' Edward retorted.

His father frowned. 'We're sailing up the Nile as far as Aswan and we're sharing a dahabiyah with the Mallonden family. That means Lord Mallonden and his wife, Poppy of course and possibly the grandmother. I'm not sure who else is joining us, but you'll have over three months to make yourself agreeable to Lady Poppy. Need I say more?'

'It's years since we've met, Father. We might have nothing in common.'

'I tell you what you'll have in common. An old and honoured name – and money. Poppy's a nice girl; she sits a horse with great style and she's good-natured. She might not be as pretty as some other girls you're likely to meet but beauty's only skin-deep. Poppy has qualities that are more enduring than beauty. They'll be sailing out to Egypt at the end of the week, and in mid-November we're travelling up the Nile. It doesn't give you long, but it would be nice to be able to announce your engagement early in the New Year.'

'You're right, Father, it doesn't give us long.'

'Long enough! I proposed to your mother on our second meeting.'

'I'm sure you did. Grandfather'd proposed to her on your behalf months before!'

'None of this would have been necessary if you'd behaved like your brothers. Last year you'd have been in London for the Season and you and Poppy would have got together in the time-honoured way. Poor girl, she knew what her grandmother and her parents wanted, but she had to go through the farce of the London Season simply because you'd chosen to stay out of the country.'

Edward didn't answer. He knew it would do no good.

There was a timid knock on the door and his mother entered, flustered and uncertain. She looked at her husband questioningly, and he said evenly, 'We've had our talk, Dorothy. Now I think we can go down to the salon and have tea. I suppose that's what you're wanting to do.'

Edward's face conveyed nothing and, with something akin to relief, she said, 'Oh yes, I would like tea! You'll come with us, Edward?'

'I'll join you in a few minutes, Mother, I have a letter to write.'

'What sort of a letter?' his father demanded. 'Not to some woman, I hope?'

'No, Father. I'm writing to a chap I met in Nepal. I promised him a letter immediately I reached civilisation.'

'Hurry it up, then. I want us to portray a united front in the face of any party we're likely to encounter downstairs.'

They had not been seated in the salon long when a woman sitting opposite inclined her head with a gracious nod and Lady Camborne nodded equally graciously in reply.

'Who is it?' her husband muttered.

'Lavinia Levison-Gore and her two daughters. I wonder if they're in the Mallonden party?'

'Can't be! The old girl can't stand her daughter-in-law and, in any case, they'd have mentioned it.'

'Perhaps we ought to ask them over.'

'I don't see why.' The Marquis was eyeing the three ladies very carefully through his monocle. She was a handsome woman, he'd always thought so. Mallonden had said she'd always worn the trousers, bossed his brother about something shocking. One girl was a pretty little thing, schoolgirl, or little more, and the other was hidden by a potted palm. All he could see of her was a dainty foot tapping in time to the orchestra and an expanse of blue silk.

At that moment Mrs Levison-Gore murmured something to her daughters and, with a smile on her face, crossed the room to greet the Cambornes effusively.

'How nice that you're here!' she enthused. 'We thought none of our party would be here until the rest of the family arrive.'

'So you're travelling up the Nile with us?' the Marquis asked shortly.

'Well yes. My friend Constance Marsdale told me she'd rented out her dahabiyah to the family and then Maud Mallonden insisted we join them. I do so love Egypt in the winter and it will be nice for the family to be together, particularly over Christmas. The boat is big enough for a much larger party.'

At that moment Edward joined them and Mrs Levison-Gore extended a slender hand, saying, 'It's many years since I saw you, Edward, you were little more than a schoolboy. What an exciting life you must have led.'

'I doubt if it's been any more exciting than it would have been if he'd stayed at home,' his father snapped testily.

'Well no, of course not. But Edward didn't know there was going to be a war when he left, did you, dear?' his mother said. 'Would you like to join us, Lavinia? Do pull some chairs up, Edward, while Mrs Levison-Gore brings her daughters over.'

Minutes later the Marquis found himself staring at the most beautiful girl he'd ever set eyes on. Edward's eyes were positively bulging and, sharply, his father said, 'Sit next to your mother and see if you can rustle up a waiter. These Egyptian waiters seem to think tomorrow will do.'

The ladies talked about the voyage out, the newest dresses in London and what they could expect from Egypt in the way of entertainment. The Marquis watched the play of sunlight on the delicate cheeks of the girl sitting next to him, the tendrils of red-gold hair against her forehead, and occasionally the flash of even, white teeth as she laughed. Edward said little. It was sufficient for him to listen to the lilt in her voice, bask in the charm of her smile, see the velvet hue of pansies in her beautiful eyes. He was enchanted by her – and his father missed none of it.

A worldly man, it didn't take him long to realise what Lavinia Levison-Gore was about. Here they were, all of two weeks before the rest of the family were due, embarked upon the same cruise, and this beautiful girl with a fortnight's start on Poppy Mallonden. Lavinia Levison-Gore was a very determined woman!

Well, let her get on with it! He was an equally determined man – and no girl without money was going to snaffle his son or tempt him in any way from his appointed path. True, Laura was decidedly beautiful, and on her father's side at least the blood was all right. She would most certainly add a great deal of lustre to the family portraits in the Long Gallery – but it wasn't enough . . . Nevertheless, he found himself accepting an invitation for them to drive out to Mena House for dinner that evening.

Lavinia Levison-Gore was not displeased with the afternoon's events. She had been quick to realise that the Marquis would not be an ally but she also saw that Edward was decidedly smitten with Laura. To that end she instructed Laura to put herself out to be charming to him.

'Think how marvellous it will be if you can go into the Season with Edward Burlington at your side! You can enjoy all the parties and the dances with your future assured and you can show the family that the paltry money they've promised to spend on you hasn't been wasted.'

'And what about Poppy?' Laura asked bluntly.

'Well, what about Poppy? She's always had more advantages than either of you; enough money, the family behind her . . . it's not our fault if she's done very little with it. She's a nice girl and it's not her fault that men don't fall over themselves about her, though she could try more, stop being such a country bumpkin.'

'Men are so stupid!' Laura exclaimed. 'If they took the trouble to get to know Poppy they'd realise there's so much more to her. She's probably a lot nicer than me, to begin with.'

'What a silly idea! Of course she isn't nicer than you. Now Laura, I want no more of this. You know how I've groomed you for the sort of future I want for you. All Grandmother's money went on that venture of your father's and when he was killed I had to soldier on on my own with precious little help from his family. You have to repay me for all that, Laura. And Edward will be a good, kind husband, I'm sure of it.'

She swept up the stairs, leaving the two girls to follow in silence. At the entrance to her room she said, 'Wear the cream satin tonight, Laura. Let Edward see you at your best.'

'What am I to wear, Mother?' Meg asked softly.

'You always look quite lovely, my darling. Just please yourself.'

In the bedroom they shared, Laura sat down on her bed and eyed her sister miserably. 'I'll wear the cream satin and I'll be nice to everybody, Meg, but I'm not going to marry Edward. Wild horses wouldn't make me!'

'He's half in love with you already. He never once took his eyes off you at Shepheards.'

'I *know*. And we've got weeks and weeks on that wretched boat when Mother'll throw us together at every opportunity.'

Laura got up and walked to the window which looked out at the splendid view of the pyramids, and Meg could not see the yearning sadness in her eyes. Somewhere out there was Ahmed. And nothing she had seen in Edward Burlington had the power to erase his memory . . .

The dancing was over and Edward had departed with his parents for Cairo. Mrs Levison-Gore sat back in her chair, well pleased with the evening's events.

Laura had treated Edward with just the right mixture

of friendliness and aloofness, a mixture which would, in all probability, leave him anxious for more of the same. She had looked enchanting, quite the most beautiful girl in the ballroom, and when the Marquis and his wife wanted to talk about Poppy Lavinia had been benevolent about the girl, as if she was anxious to hide Poppy's plumpness, her hearty manner and homely face, knowing full well that Edward's mother was totally charmed with Laura.

The Marquis had been quick to realise that he was faced with a worthy opponent; a very clever woman who would have no scruples when it came to getting what she wanted. He was equally determined that she would not win. As soon as the Mallondens arrived he would have a talk with Poppy's father, and between them they'd defeat whatever plans the woman had for marrying off her girl to Edward.

Edward, on the other hand, was in a state of euphoria. He hadn't been looking forward to what his father called the Silly Season. He wasn't at his best with girls; the very thought of marriage to one of them made him want to turn tail and run, but here was this girl with her beauty, her soft, gentle voice, her laughter, changing everything.

Edward was not a vain man. From his earliest childhood his father had made it quite plain that all a girl would ever see in him was his title and the fact that one day she would be mistress of Sedgemoor. But Laura had been charming. She'd showed an avid interest in his travels in the Far East and the people he'd met there. She'd dimpled with laughter at his attempts at humour and thanked him warmly for a lovely evening. Surely they had got off to a very good start.

Edward hated Sedgemoor. It was too big and it cost the earth to keep it together. The family were still bouncing from the last lot of death duties and other taxes. At the same time, he could see Laura there, her portrait in the Long Gallery, descending the stairs in a fabulous gown while her guests waited to greet her.

He thought about the battle to come. His parents had informed him, without subterfuge, that Poppy Mallonden was destined to be Lady Burlington and, eventually, the Marchioness of Camborne. He was already dreading what lay ahead. He'd never in his entire life crossed his father directly. When he went off to the Far East his father had been in America so they'd never faced each other on the issue although for weeks he'd been bombarded by angry letters that had pursued him across Asia.

Edward had always known that one day he would have to go home. He'd anticipated his father's anger and was relieved when his parents had asked him to meet them in Cairo; that was before he realised that his father had something more in view than a meeting to welcome him home. He hadn't been left long in doubt.

He remembered Poppy Mallonden as a jolly, plump little girl whose only interest was her horse and when he'd asked his father outright if Poppy wanted to marry him, Lord Camborne had retorted, 'The girl's got to marry somebody! She'll be a very rich woman; she's keen on hunting, she breeds fine gundogs and she's a dutiful daughter. *She'll* not be asking any ridiculous questions of her father.'

During the evening he'd just spent with Laura he'd learned that she was fresh from her finishing school in Switzerland and had yet to embark on the London Season. Egypt was a try-out – and when he asked her if she was interested in some young man she had merely smiled and changed the subject.

His mother had gently told him that they would have months sailing on the Nile, that it was the most romantic river in the world, that Egypt would provide the perfect setting for he and Poppy to fall in love;

and, if not love, then a deeply sincere friendship might prove much better.

When they reached their hotel, his father said tersely, 'I don't want you spending all your time with that girl, Edward. I can see you're attracted but steer well clear of her to please me and your mother.'

'She's promised to ride with me in the morning, Father.'

The Marquis snorted, 'I know nothing about the girl, but I doubt if she'll sit a horse as well as her cousin Poppy!'

Edward arrived at Mena House after breakfast and was pleased to find Laura waiting for him in the gardens. She looked quite enchanting in her riding attire and informed him that she had already made arrangements for two mounts to be brought to the hotel for them.

He was enraptured by the elegant way she sat her horse and her skill in controlling the beautiful prancing animal. They rode out into the desert in the direction of Memphis and Laura was glad there was little chance of conversation. The tourists were already sampling the archaeological delights of the ancient city and she scanned the groups eagerly for a sight of Ahmed. Then, disappointed, she realised that it was not amongst people like this that she could hope to find him. Ahmed was not a tourist . . .

They returned to the hotel in time for lunch and, from his seat in the car that had brought the Marquis and his wife out to the pyramids, Edward's father watched their arrival. The girl rode extremely well, he had to admit it. She had grace and expertise – and for the first time he began to think that keeping the pair apart would not be as easy as he had supposed.

He called to them as they rode towards the hotel entrance gates. From Laura's flashing smile and Edward's besotted face he realised immediately that his son had spent an ecstatic morning.

At that moment Laura's mother walked across the sand towards the car with determination in her step.

'I've been watching out for you,' she said. 'I was hoping you'd join us for lunch Edward. Indeed, I'd like you all to join us.'

'I have to get back to Cairo, I've got to see a chap from the Embassy,' the Marquis said quickly. 'And you're hardly attired for dining in the hotel restaurant, Edward.'

'I agree, Father. I'd better get back, Mrs Levison-Gore, but I would like to invite Laura to a ball at Shepheards this evening though. I'm no great shakes as a dancer as she's probably told you. I'm out of practice, I'm afraid.'

'Nonsense!' said Laura's mother, stoutly. 'Laura will soon lick you into shape, won't you, dear?'

'I'll call for you around seven,' Edward said, then he climbed into the car with his parents, watched by Laura and her mother.

On their way back to the hotel, Lavinia linked her arm in Laura's, saying, 'I don't think we've anything to worry about, dear. Edward Burlington is already in love with you – and I suspect he's a very stubborn young man. Only a man of some strength could have risked his father's anger by going out to the Far East and deciding to stay out there.'

'You've always been dead set against me going anywhere unchaperoned, Mother,' Laura said, thoughtfully. 'Why is tonight so different?'

'Edward's parents will be there to keep an eye on you. Besides, I insisted on chaperoning you because I didn't want you to get entangled with any Tom, Dick or Harry you happened to meet. Years ago I set my heart on somebody like Edward Burlington and I do believe I'm about to see my dreams come true!'

Lavinia would have been less sure if she could have heard Laura's conversation with Meg a few minutes later. Meg was standing at the window of their room when Laura dropped her riding crop on to the bed, followed by her riding hat. She did not bother to turn round but said, 'I saw you coming back to the hotel and Mother going out to meet you.'

'Yes, she invited them to lunch but they decided to go back.'

'So when will you see him again?'

'Tonight. There's a ball at Shepheards.'

'I don't want to go to a ball at Shepheards! I'll be sitting with Mother waiting for somebody to ask me to dance, and all the men will have partners. I looked round the hotel yesterday and it's expensive and stuffy and they're all *old*.'

'Well, of course they're not *all* old, but you needn't worry, you've not been invited.'

Meg spun round and stared at her sister.

'You mean she's letting you go with him alone?'

'Quite alone. It's what's known as strategy. I've heard Uncle Mark refer to her as the General and now I understand why!'

'You're just as bad as she is!' Meg stormed suddenly. 'You're not in the least in love with Edward but you're prepared to string him along. He's nice – he doesn't deserve to be treated like this.'

Laura sat down on the edge of her bed and stared at her younger sister in surprise.

'Is that how it looks to you, Meg?' she asked after a long silence.

'Yes, it does. One minute you're in love with Prince Ahmed, the next you're dancing to Mother's tune. But where does all that leave poor Edward? Wait until the family get here – they'll have something to say about all this.'

Laura started to hang her riding habit in the wardrobe,

her face thoughtful, while Meg stared at her, suddenly contrite in case she had said too much.

'I'm sorry,' she blurted out. 'It's not really your fault, I know, but I would not let her force Edward on *me*. I'd run away before I'd let that happen!'

Laura looked at her sadly. 'Meg, I feel like a leaf in the wind,' she said. 'I've got Mother manipulating things as hard as she can. I've got Edward falling in love with me and I know it's not what his parents want, or the family. I fell in love with Ahmed on that wretched boat and I'm not even sure that I shall ever see him again, or that he'd even want me.'

'I just don't think that you should lead him on, that's all.'

'I'm not leading him on. I'm just being myself. I can't help it if he's reading more into it than that.'

'You could try being a little bit aloof, couldn't you?'

Laura smiled. 'Oh Meg, you're so awfully young! If you like Edward so much, maybe you'd like me to marry him?'

'Only if you loved him. Marrying him for any other reason is horrible. Oh, I know marriages of convenience happen all the time with people like us but I just don't want it to happen with me. I say, Mother hasn't said anything to you about me, has she? It would be like her to have found some younger son or, worse still, somebody quite hopeless just as long as he's rich and titled!'

'I think one at a time is as much as she can handle, Meg.'

'Well, when the family arrive she won't get things all her own way. Grandmother Mallonden will see to that.'

'We don't know that she's coming.'

'If she finds out that Mother is here, she'll come,' Meg said confidently, and the two girls dissolved into merriment, their momentary antagonism suddenly forgotten.

7

Laura sat under the sundeck awning on the dahabiyah which was to be her home for the next three months. It was not quite dawn, but she had risen early in order to be alone because she was so seldom alone now that the family had arrived.

Today there would be no tombs or temples, there would just be the Nile, the wide, beautiful river that was Egypt. Today she would do nothing but feel the spell of Egypt; do nothing but sit under the shady awning where the cool breeze always drifted from the bows of the boat, and watch the procession of Egypt pass along the green margin of the river's banks; do nothing but watch the fierce sunlight play on the amber sands.

To be cool and watch a sunny, hot world at work . . . what unconscious arrogance in the pleasure, but there was little else to watch all day but the antics of the Sudanese crew. There was the ostrich-feather broom-boy who watched for a speck of dust to brush away, and the brass-boys who lifted up rugs and mats to find some hidden treasure in the way of knobs to polish.

Laura knew she would be content to drift with the flow of the river when even the call of the desert and the mystery of the silent sands was so suddenly stilled, to live with the material comforts of twentieth-century civilisation while she absorbed on the river-banks the panorama of primitive life which had changed but little during the hundred centuries of Egyptian stagnation.

Her eyes were expectant. She had come to realise that there were no dawns like Egyptian dawns, just as she believed she had never seen a sunset until she had seen her first one across the vast Sahara. Now the mist was clearing and a new world was emerging, coloured enchantingly in rose and orange, turquoise and gold. Shafts of sunlight illuminated spiders' webs shimmering with dew and already, along the banks, slender half-naked figures were at work hauling up their buckets full of water from the shadoufs. From the nearby village a procession of black-robed women emerged, carrying their water-pots to the river-bank, exactly as they had on every day of Egypt's long history, and children, accompanied by straggling herds of buffalo-cows, slouched with bored steps and weary gaze across the irrigated land.

Egypt's unvarying monotony was a song in her heart with its trains of heavily laden camels standing high against the horizon and endless fields of bamboo and sugar-cane, and palms, incredibly graceful, standing proudly in lagoons of cool blue water. She had ceased to see Egypt's disorder, which was masked by the most wonderful light so that the land seemed very low while the heavens seemed high and immense.

It could have been so wonderful, but everything was spoilt. Grandmother Mallonden had received them coldly, making her displeasure evident, her cold, haughty expression showing plainly that she knew full well what Laura's mother was about.

Poppy had been placed next to Edward at the dinner-table and it was Poppy he was instructed to escort when they went ashore. Laura and her sister were expected to sit in silence, speaking when spoken to. Her grandmother had been quick to tell her that her turn would come next year when Poppy was safely engaged – and if Laura gave her any trouble there would be no money forthcoming to help her mother launch her into society.

In the privacy of her cabin Laura's mother had

said, tartly, 'You will do what I say, Laura, and not what your grandmother says. If you capture Edward we shan't want her money. Why, he can't take his eyes off you. Poppy looks like a country bumpkin beside you.'

Laura liked Poppy. She was open-hearted and affectionate and she had little or no dress sense, invariably choosing colours that vied with her florid complexion. On one occasion in Cairo Laura had attempted to advise Poppy on a suitable colour for a new evening gown, but her mother had quickly shown her displeasure. 'You are playing into your grandmother's hands, Laura. Let the girl go on making those drastic mistakes – it's not your affair and very much to your advantage.'

Footsteps along the deck heralded the arrival of Edward, sleepily rubbing his eyes which lit up when he saw that Laura was alone. He sat down beside her, saying, 'I thought I might find you here when you told me yesterday how much you loved the dawns here. We never seem to get a chance to talk alone now.'

'But it's nice for us all to be together, Edward. I haven't seen all that much of Cousin Poppy and she's so nice, Edward. Your mother is very fond of her.'

'I know what they're trying to do, Laura.'

'And you mind?'

'Yes. Perhaps I'd have gone along with the idea if I hadn't met you first, but that altered everything. Will you come ashore with me when we get to Luxor? I want to show you Karnak without anybody else around.'

'It may not be possible.'

'We can make it possible.'

'I'm not sure, Edward, but I'll try.'

He took hold of her hand and held it tightly in his, then quickly released it when they heard voices and footsteps coming close.

They belonged to Poppy and her father, and Laura

did not miss the angry frown on her uncle's face, although Poppy smiled sweetly, saying, 'Gracious, how early you are! I've promised myself I'd be up to see the dawn come up ever since we arrived but I've never managed it. Was it very beautiful?'

'Very,' Laura admitted. 'Edward missed it, too. He's only just arrived.'

'I'm glad we're not leaving the boat today. It will be nice simply to laze on deck in the sunshine. Where are we tomorrow?'

'Abydos. Mohammed says it's the most beautiful temple in all Egypt.'

'Grandmother might want to see that one.'

'I doubt it,' Lord Mallonden said. 'She can't stand the heat and it's some little way from the river.'

'I can't understand why she came to Egypt if she's not going to look at the temples,' Poppy said feelingly, then turning to Laura she added, 'She made up her mind to come when she knew you were here. Probably she wanted it to be a huge family party.'

Laura didn't speak. She was under no illusion as to why her grandmother had decided to come. Instead she rose to her feet, saying, 'Well, I suppose I'd better go back to my cabin and dress for breakfast – you're all ready, Poppy.'

She smiled briefly and made her escape. Her mother was deluding herself if she thought she could beat the family and capture Edward for her daughter. It would be her turn next year; and she thought acidly about the balls and tea dances, the race meetings and garden-parties, the suitable young men she would meet and her mother ever watchful, sizing them up and discarding those she considered unacceptable.

She leaned her arms on the rails looking out across the wide river to where a solitary man was leading his camel up a steep hill of soft sand and she thought of Ahmed.

Somewhere along the six hundred miles they were to sail they must surely find him! When they reached Luxor she would make some surreptitious enquiries, He was a prince, so obviously he would be known to a great many people. She would discover where he lived, how he spent his time, if he ever visited the temples and at what hour. Well pleased with her decision, Laura went to her cabin to change for breakfast.

Meanwhile, under the awning, Poppy's father discreetly left his daughter and Edward alone and, as usual, they had little to say to each other.

Poppy was wishing she was like Laura, easy to talk to, with an enchanting smile that embraced the person she was speaking to so that you felt she was interested in anything one had to say. Edward, too, searched around for words. But what did he know about Poppy except that she liked horses and was an accomplished horsewoman? This was Egypt, damn it. There would be no race meetings, no hunting – what in heaven's name could he find to say to her?

Poppy was the first to break the awkward silence. 'I wish Laura had knocked on my door when she went out. I'd have loved to see the dawn come up.'

'Perhaps another day,' Edward said gently.

He liked Poppy. She was a warm and considerate friend and she had a generous heart but not for a moment could he ever visualise a time when he would want to make love to her.

He could imagine Laura holding court in the halls of Sedgemoor, adorning it with her beauty, chatting easily to their guests, but not Poppy who could only talk about horses and whose mind hadn't evolved beyond hunt meetings and point-to-point races.

Probably Laura found him dull. He wasn't much use with women, perhaps because he'd given them very little thought in the sort of life he'd led up to now, but he might make the effort with Laura. He wouldn't allow his father to push him into a loveless marriage; it wasn't fair to him and it certainly wouldn't be fair to Poppy.

'Are you going ashore to look at the temple?' Poppy asked him.

'Probably. I'm an awful duffer when it comes to tombs and temples. I should have read up on it but there doesn't seem to have been much time.'

'I borrowed a book out of the ship's library,' Poppy said quickly. 'There's so much to learn and Laura's lent me a whole list I ought to read.'

He stared at her in surprise. He couldn't imagine beautiful, sunny Laura delving into the musty archives of Egyptian history. He was not to know that she had made herself read up on ancient Egyptian history because in some way it brought her closer to Ahmed because it was his history.

Poppy was staring across the river, absently rubbing at a mosquito bite on her arm, and he couldn't restrain himself from asking,

'Didn't you think it a little strange that Laura had taken the trouble to study Egyptian history?'

'Well, she's so pretty and fun-loving. It just shows how wrong you can be about people. I'd have thought you might have been more interested.'

'I've never been much of a one for ancient history, what's gone has gone. I found the mysticism of the Far East far more absorbing, perhaps I was wrong.'

His father considered that Laura was a bright young thing of a too familiar pattern, intent on enjoying herself without a single thought beyond the moment, brittle and empty-headed. Now Edward had a trump card up his sleeve. At some moment in the near future he would inform his father that Laura was probably the only one on board who knew anything at all about the country they were travelling in!

Back in her cabin, Laura was confronted by her mother.

'Where have you been?' she asked sharply. 'I've looked in here several times and you haven't been here.'

'I wanted to see the dawn come up,' Laura said calmly. 'The sunsets are so beautiful, I imagined the dawns would be glorious, too.'

'Were you alone?'

'Happily, yes, until Edward came. It was light by that time.'

Her mother's expression relaxed. 'So Edward watched with you?'

'Not really. I've told you, it was light when he appeared, then Poppy and her father joined us.'

'And you left them then, I suppose, left him with Poppy. As if it isn't enough that all my married life I've suffered the slight of having married a second son, of having daughters instead of sons, and of knowing that my mother-in-law has never approved of me.'

'I'm sure you've imagined a lot of it, Mother.'

'Indeed I have not!' her mother snapped, her face sharp with resentment. 'She objected to me because I wasn't totally of British stock, even when I brought money into the family. For years I've told myself that you and Margaret would be the ones to show her we have what it takes. I've spent a small fortune on your education, denying myself the pleasure of foreign travel, expensive clothes, suffering the handouts the family have condescended to give me. Now it seems as though it might all have been for nothing if you're not going to play your part. I want you to have Edward Burlington and I want you to capture him on this trip, then I can concentrate on Margaret.'

'What about Poppy?'

'What about Poppy? She'll marry some obscure country parson and love every minute of it. You know very well that Poppy isn't into high living. She'll be happier with church fêtes and dog shows.'

'Poppy's been more accustomed to high living than I have!'

'And what has she accomplished? A good seat on a horse, no conversation, and gaucheness instead of grace in the ballroom. You'll be doing her a favour if you marry Edward Burlington, mark my words.'

'I feel as if I'm in a slave market waiting for the highest bidder!'

'What rubbish! You are merely a very beautiful girl who wants the best. I consider Edward Burlington will have done very well if he captures you. After all, there are men who are better looking, have a great deal more charm and polish; he just happens to be the most eligible bachelor on the scene, with money and a title.'

With that, her mother swept from the room, leaving Laura staring at her sister with undisguised anxiety.

It was an unusual procession that left the boat the following morning. It was only just light but the captain had advised them to leave before the temperature climbed and before other tourists invaded Abydos.

Laura stood on the deck, watching her grandmother's hesitant attempt to walk down the gangway. She leaned heavily on two sticks, disdaining any assistance from her son or Poppy, and the rest of them hung back while Lady Mallonden said in a whisper, 'She would come. I tried to dissuade her, but it was no use.'

In an undertone to Laura her mother said, 'We know why she's come, don't we? It's to make sure Poppy is with Edward and that you're well out of the way.'

Laura didn't reply, but a few minutes later she whispered to Meg, 'It's like trying to launch a battleship! How on earth is she going to walk around the temple or ride one of those donkeys waiting there?'

A line of them waited at the bottom of the gangplank together with their donkey-boys and the Dowager Lady Mallonden looked at them in some dismay.

'You surely don't expect me to ride one of those?' she cried.

'I told you that the temple was some way from the river, Mother,' Lord Mallonden said. 'I don't know what the alternative is.'

'I want a carriage,' the old lady demanded. 'There were enough of them around the last time I was in Egypt. Why isn't there one here now?'

'This isn't Luxor, Mother, the roads are unmade and unsuitable for a carriage.'

'Then help me on to one of these. You, boy,' she said, prodding the boy with the tip of her parasol, 'find me a good docile animal and see to it that I have an attendant who knows what he's doing.'

Laura and Meg grinned at each other while the rest of the family hurried down the gangway to assist. They were more than surprised when the old lady mounted the donkey without mishap and appeared more at home on its back than she had on her own two feet.

'Here,' she called to Edward, 'I'd like a young man to look after me as well as Poppy. The others can take care of themselves.'

Dutifully Edward allowed his donkey to trot to her side, then they moved off, away from the river along the straggling village road leading to Abydos. Between them Poppy and Edward took charge of the old lady's comfort and Mrs Levison-Gore burned with anger.

The temple had been allowed to fall into a sad state of disrepair but the reliefs on the walls were so beautiful they had to admit that their journey had been well worth while. Laura stared raptly at the exquisite portraits of the Pharaoh Seti the First on every wall. In his profile she could see Ahmed and her heart began to do strange things. This was how

Ahmed's face would look under the ornate Egyptian crown, that purity of line, the dark, expressive eyes, and a mouth chiselled so exquisitely she was reminded forcefully of it pressed against hers in the kiss she was unable to forget.

A commotion at the end of the corridor dragged her away and she joined the rest of the party anxiously bending over Poppy's mother who was complaining of feeling faint.

'Perhaps we should go back, Mother,' Poppy said gently. 'It's getting terribly hot and Grandmother is sitting out there saying she's seen quite enough.'

Mrs Levison-Gore was not one to waste opportunities. 'Poppy's right,' she said agreeably. 'we should get back to the boat. Those who wish to stay longer could join us later.'

Poppy's mother was making the most of her indisposition, much to her husband and the Marquis's annoyance.

'Why not sit in the shade for a while?' the Marquis advised her. 'We've only just got here and you'll feel better presently.'

Lady Mallonden answered with a low moan and Mrs Levison-Gore said sharply, 'Well, I'm going back to the boat. Are you coming with me, girls?'

Margaret hurried to her side but Laura said, 'I do want to see more of the temple, Mother. Is there anybody who wants to stay with me?'

'I'll stay,' Edward said at once and, immediately, old Lady Mallonden said, 'You must stay too, Poppy. I've spoilt it for you by coming and your father will look after your mother so you don't need to come back with us.'

Poppy dutifully joined Laura and Edward near the temple steps while the donkey-boys milled around to assist their patrons to mount. The boys were a motley crowd, long-legged and dark-eyed, all of them wearing white skullcaps made of coarse crochet, their wit ingenious, their brown limbs so perfect it was difficult not to admire their charm despite their laughing impudence.

Poppy's mother mounted her donkey, hanging on to the poor beast's neck with closed eyes and giving every appearance that at any moment she would fall off. Poppy turned to her companions, saying swiftly, 'It's no use. Father's no help in case of sickness so I've got to look after Mother. I'll see you later.'

Laura's mother watched Poppy's return to the party with delight, and Laura and Edward waited while the ill-assorted procession moved off down the track leaving two donkey-boys behind them.

The curio-dealers were busily laying out their wares on the temple steps, all of them flagrant shams – vivid green Sphinxes, freshly mummified hawks and images of the god Osiris in every possible form – but the salesmen's patter of broken English was so droll that Laura and Edward lingered.

They addressed Laura as 'My beautiful lady', and spoke of Edward as 'Your gentleman'.

'Your gent-le-man he buy you this very nice god Osiris; him very lucky, my lady; you buy, what price you like?'

'Yes, my lady, him very ancient, two weeks back him dug up in Thebes. My word is true, my lady, very cheap god.'

But the only thing Edward did buy was a fly-switch, selecting one with very long white hair and a blue-beaded handle finished with a tassel of small white cowrie shells.

At that moment a boy stepped forward and handed a small turquoise cat to Laura. She took it in her hands, looking down at it with some degree of pleasure. It was a pretty thing, sitting upright in the form of Egyptian cats, wearing round its neck a thick ornamental collar and jewelled earrings in its ears. She smiled with pleasure, saying, 'Oh Edward, this is pretty. Don't you like it?'

Edward looked but he was unimpressed. 'How much?' he asked the boy, who promptly named a quite unmentionable price.

'Far too much,' Laura said quickly and, pulling Edward's sleeve, she whispered, 'We must go. We'll never get rid of them if we don't.'

An older man pushed the boy out of the way and held out a gnarled hand filled with scarabs.

'See, my lady, all real scarabs, very old, cartouches of great kings. See this one, this cartouche of King Seti. That his name you see there.'

Laura took it and gazed down at the hieroglyphics on the pale green stone, while a young Englishman standing near by leaned forward to say, 'They're all fakes, you know. They make them look old by feeding them to turkeys. One passing and they look like that!'

Shuddering delicately, Laura handed the scarab back and, taking Edward's hand, pulled him after her. But Edward was intrigued.

She watched with amusement while he argued with the scarab-seller, then, with a proud smile on his face, he handed over the sum they had agreed on and took charge of the scarab.

'Why did you buy it?' she asked him. 'You know it's a fake.'

'Well, of course it is, but what ingenuity to use a turkey that way. I thought it would be interesting to see what my father thought about it and you must admit it's a jolly good fake. Put beside those in the Cairo museum, I doubt if I could tell which was the real one.'

They were so busy looking down at the scarab that they were startled when a man's voice said, softly, 'It is unwise to buy from street vendors. If you wish to buy real antiques there are several traders in Cairo that I could recommend.'

A sudden brilliant smile illuminated Laura's face as she gazed up into Ahmed's eyes, while Edward looked as though he had seen a ghost, for never had Ahmed appeared so curiously Egyptian. Dark curling lashes complemented eyes of dark velvety brown; his white teeth gleamed under the smile on his clearly cut lips, Eastern lips, as blood-red as the scarlet of his high tarbush which gave an added height to his splendid physique.

Quickly regaining her composure, Laura said, 'Your Highness, may I present Lord Edward Burlington, Prince Ahmed Hassan Farag.'

Ahmed inclined his head by the merest quarter of an inch and he did not hold out his hand. Edward had not yet got over the shock of seeing what he called a full-blooded 'ancient Egyptian' in faultless riding clothes suddenly drop down from the skies.

'How do you do?' he said in a stiff and meaningless English fashion. He didn't in the least care who the fellow was; he only wished one thing – that the image with the moving eyes of ebony-black glass would take itself back to wherever it had come from, whether from the temple before them, or the plinth of some statue in the Cairo museum. He was only too aware of Laura's blushing face and shining eyes. The Egyptian's expression was enigmatic, conveying nothing. Edward could not tell whether he was pleased to meet Laura or not, but the lack of warmth towards himself spoke volumes.

Prince Ahmed Farag was unimpressed by Edward's title. More than that, he was unreasonably angered that Laura should be here with a man at all.

Ahmed had observed the arrival of the English party from the back of his stallion. He had seen them entering the temple, watched the fretfulness of the old lady and the vapours of the younger one. Then he had watched them mount their donkeys and ride back to the boat, all except Laura and her escort. He had decided he would not speak to them, then, unable to stop himself, he had witnessed their dealings with the vendors and the purchasing of the fake scarab. It gave him an unmissable opportunity and now all he could see was Laura's exquisite face, her smiling coral mouth, the wistful yearning in her violet eyes.

He asked, 'Are you enjoying your journey through Egypt?'

'Very much. I love it all – the river and the huge skies, the life along its banks – there is so much to see! I hadn't realised just how much.'

'Six thousand years of history is not seen in a few days. There will be even more to see when you reach Luxor.' He turned to Edward with a small smile. 'If you are genuinely interested in Egyptian antiques, Lord Burlington, I can recommend Ali Mustapha in Luxor. His antiques are genuine and if you mention my name he will not attempt to overcharge you.'

'Thank you Prince Ahmed. I bought the scarab as a curio and I doubt if my home is large enough to absorb any more antiques, Egyptian or otherwise, but I'll bear your advice in mind.'

Ahmed bowed politely and said, 'I'll bid you good-day then. This is a very beautiful temple, the reliefs the most beautiful in all Egypt. Enjoy them.'

It was almost noon when Edward and Laura rode back to the boat. Laura was enthusiastic about the morning they had spent in the temple, Edward rather less so, being more concerned with the increasing heat and his good sense in purchasing the fly switch.

If they had looked back they might have seen Ahmed watching their departure from the back of his horse standing high on a desert dune. He watched until they came within sight of the river, then he wheeled his horse around to gallop swiftly across the sand.

8

The Marquis of Camborne was decidedly tetchy. Mallonden had made it quite plain that his son was not coming up to scratch, and he in turn had declared that the fault lay as much with Mallonden's daughter, the Lady Poppy, as with his son. It was Poppy who had elected to return to the river-boat when her mother had the vapours, leaving the course wide open for young Laura; now, on the morning after, his wife was complaining of stomach cramps and old Lady Mallonden had accused all of them of being ditherers.

Laura's mother was obviously more than satisfied with the way things were going and it cost him a great deal to be polite to the woman.

They expected to arrive in Luxor in mid-morning and Camborne's wife had already said she intended to leave the boat for a few days' pampering at the Winter Palace Hotel. This had added to his annoyance. It was true that Lady Marsdale had put her dahabiyah at their convenience, but not without a great deal of money being handed over. Egypt was expensive and now there would be the additional cost of a stay at the Winter Palace. The only redeeming feature of it was the fact that the Levison-Gores would be remaining on board while the rest of them left for the hotel.

The woman would be furious, of course, but the Mallondens would not foot her bill and it had nothing to do with him. Thoroughly disgruntled, he made his way to the breakfast room where he found Lavinia and her younger daughter. There was no sign of any of the others and he was halfway through his breakfast when Edward appeared.

Edward had passed a restless night. He was not looking forward to the conversation he intended to have with his father and one look at the Marquis's irritable expression did nothing to boost his courage.

Breakfast was a silent meal. Mrs Levison-Gore appeared serenely at ease as she greeted Lady Poppy when she arrived in the breakfast room a little later. The same could not be said for Poppy. She had been given a severe reprimand from her grandmother the evening before when the old lady had received her family and Edward's in her stateroom in order to set out her grievances.

The Marquis eyed them all with some degree of frustration. Edward was engaged in cracking his egg, a task which seemed to demand all his concentration, while Poppy seemed more intent on passing the time of day with her aunt. After meeting the Marquis's exasperated glare she said in a trembling voice, 'Did you enjoy the temple, Edward?'

He raised startled eyes before saying, 'Yes, it's a very fine temple. We'll soon be seeing Karnak, won't we?'

'Yes, I'm dying to see Karnak. I've heard it's magnificent.'

'Damn Karnak!' thought the Marquis, savagely. He could have shaken the pair of them. It was his bet that the delectable Laura didn't talk about Karnak. The girl had been well instructed by that mother of hers.

At that moment they were joined by Laura and he did not miss the look of almost boyish delight that crossed his son's face.

There was no doubt about it, the girl was beautiful. She had a grace and style which left her cousin looking undeniably plain. He knew which one he'd have fancied if be had been in Edward's shoes, but there were higher things at stake than a pretty face and pansy eyes.

'Mummy's decided she wants to spend a few days at the Winter Palace,' Poppy was confiding to her aunt. 'Will you be joining us?'

It was the first Mrs Levison-Gore had heard of it and he had to hand it to her, the smile on her face never slipped. Instead, she said quietly, 'Oh I don't think so. We love the boat and it was so good of Maud to invite us on the cruise.'

Edward was in a quandary. He recognised that his father was not in a good mood; on the other hand, this insistence that he should marry Poppy must not go on. The girl was well enough, but it was Laura he loved, Laura he intended to have.

He waited for his father to leave the breakfast table, then, with a muttered excuse, followed him to see if he went to his cabin or up on the top deck where he liked to watch the passing scenery.

To his relief, Camborne climbed the staircase to the top deck and, without hesitation, Edward followed him.

His father was not pleased to see him. The Marquis thought that Edward should have been below, making an effort to entertain Poppy, but there was no disguising the resolute look on his son's face as he took the seat opposite. At that moment neither of them had eyes for the biblical procession of long-robed men and women, together with their animals, along the river-banks, or the Theban Hills which glowed purple under the golden rays of the morning sun.

Edward had decided, after a night spent tossing and turning in his narrow bed, to take the bull by the horns. Without any preamble he said sharply, 'Father, I'm in love with Laura and I can't possibly marry Poppy. It wouldn't be fair to either of us.'

His father's face flushed with anger. It took him several minutes to control his need to bellow with rage before he said, fiercely, 'You'll not marry that girl with my blessing! Love? What has love got to do with it? The girl's fresh out of the schoolroom and it's doubtful if she has a serious thought in her head. You owe a duty to your mother and me, to Sedgemoor. The place needs a fortune spending on it so you need a wife with money, not some pretty little thing with nothing behind her.'

'She's a Mallonden. She must have money!'

'Whatever money her mother brought into the family was squandered years ago. I know from good authority that they exist on what the Mallondens dish out. Look, I know none of this can reflect on the girl – she's a nice enough girl, even if she could end up like her mother in twenty years' time.'

'I'm not asking to marry the mother! I want to marry Laura.'

'And I say no! I won't have it.'

'Father, I am over twenty-one. I don't need your permission.'

The younger man's face was resolute and his father began to realise the enormity of the problem he had to deal with. Philosophically, he decided that blustering intimidation would do no good, it was a situation that required diplomacy. His voice took on a different tone as he said, 'It's something we've got to talk over very seriously, Edward. Spending the next few days at the Winter Palace is a good idea. I didn't think so when your mother suggested it but now I think you and I can really get down to talking like two men of the world. Let us leave things as they are for the moment and see how you feel when the girl is here with her mother and you are with us at the hotel.'

'I shan't change my mind, Father.'

'Look, my boy, you've had very little experience of women. You've spent years in one god-forsaken place after the other. When did you ever meet a woman like Laura Levison-Gore where you've been hiding out? Why, before I was your age I'd been in and out of love half-a-dozen times, but I always knew where my duty lay. I always knew I must put home and family first.'

'I wish I saw my duty as clearly.'

'You will, my boy, you will.'

The Marquis picked up the book that had been lying on the seat beside him, which indicated to Edward that the interview was at an end.

The whole group gathered on deck to witness their arrival in Luxor later that morning and, whatever their private troubles, none of them could but be impressed by the columns of Karnak rising upwards against the brassy blue of the sky, or the delicate pillars of the temple of Luxor, pink and ethereal, viewed from the landing-stage.

Bags were packed and stood waiting to be taken ashore while Mrs Levison-Gore stood on the deck with an inscrutable smile on her face.

'I'm sorry you're not joining us,' her sister-in-law said unhappily, but old Lady Mallonden merely bade her a curt good-morning and anxiously shepherded the rest of them before her.

Only Edward stayed to take Laura's hand, saying gently, 'It's only for a few days . . . some bee Mother's got in her bonnet. We'll meet, of course, and we must see Karnak together.'

Laura watched their departure with a feeling of relief. She did not want to see Karnak with Edward. Her plan had been formed during a night of sleepless tossing and turning. As soon as possible she intended to find the shop of Ali Mustapha. One of the boatmen was sure to know where it was situated, and Ali Mustapha would tell her where she could find Ahmed.

If she saw the temple at all, it would be with Ahmed. Through his eyes she would see Karnak whole and entire, beautiful as it was meant to be. Only Ahmed could clothe Karnak with the imperial majesty it deserved.

Meg joined her at the rail, her face pale, and Laura was sad to see that her sister's eyes were filled with tears.

'Why are you crying, Meg? Surely you're not sorry to see the back of them?'

'I'm sorry that they've been unkind enough to leave us here. Why couldn't we go with them?'

'I thought you liked the boat. It's much more romantic than the hotel.'

'It's not romantic at all, just the three of us. We're the poor relations and that's why we haven't been invited.'

'Well, I like being a poor relation. This way we don't have to suffer Granny Mallonden watching every move we make; or watch them trying to manoeuvre Edward away from us and poor Poppy's anxious searching for something to say to him.'

'If they can't talk now, before they're married, how are they going to get along after?' Meg asked innocently.

'How indeed,' Laura murmured.

There were things on Laura's mind other than Edward and his relationship with her cousin. How would her mother expect them to spend their day? This was Luxor, glorious in history, the site of ancient Thebes whose temples had been the marvel of the ancient world and which still stood for modern generations to marvel at and admire.

Somewhere within those clefts in the purple hills was the Valley of the Kings, the Valley of the Queens, and the tombs of countless noblemen. She wanted to see them all, but in which order would her mother elect to visit them?

In her cabin, Mrs Levison-Gore was decidedly out of countenance. She had watched the others depart with a smile on her face and deep anger in her heart.

She had learned over the years to accept this sort of discrimination; hadn't she always been the foreigner? Lady Mallonden couldn't have treated her more ungraciously if she'd descended upon them from darkest Africa instead of a respectable old Bostonian family.

She would win, of course. Laura was her trump card and she had little doubt that Edward was about to play it. She stared through the window of her cabin at the pink columns of the Temple of Luxor in whose precinct rose an equally enchanting minaret. In the glory of that golden morning it was impossible to see anything out of place in the structure of a Moslem mosque within the grounds of a pagan temple.

After lunch, she decided, they would saunter through the gardens that lined the river's bank and take a look at the temple. There would be time enough for Karnak and the royal valley during the next few days and Edward would not leave them in isolation. She had no doubts at all about *that.*

It did not take Laura long to realise that she had lost her heart, lost it impulsively, completely and ungrudgingly, lost it for ever, to golden Luxor. In those first moments she had no thoughts for great imperial Thebes with her splendour and hundred gates. To Laura, Luxor, without all the trappings of Egypt's past, still shone with a royal beauty which gave her her rank as Lady of the Nile. Laura was only aware of Luxor's enchanting smile and pagan soul and, with the help of her donkey-boy who spoke commendable English, she gave herself up entirely to discovering the enchantment of the place.

After visiting the temple, her mother and Meg were glad to retire to drink afternoon tea on the deck of the dahabiyah but Laura was happy to ride along the banks of the river until, at one point, the boy pulled her sleeve, saying, 'Do you know, missy, what lies on the summit of those hills?'

'The Valley of the Kings?' she offered haltingly.

'No, missy. If you climb to the topmost peak you find yourself on the rim of the Sahara. I go there when I want to be by myself, to be close to Allah.'

'I hadn't thought of the desert like that.'

'Where you feel closest to God?'

She shook her head in a puzzled fashion and, with a little smile, he went on, 'In the desert men walk and talk alone with God, they put away vain thoughts and boastful things, they become again as little children.'

They rode back to Luxor in silence. Joseph, for that was the boy's name, was busy with his own thoughts and Laura was feeling the enormity of Egypt's past. On that vast plain there were scattered the greatest monuments in all Egypt, the greatest monuments of antiquity that the world had to offer, but she had never thought much about the Sahara, rolling into an abyss of space with its silence, nothing but golden sand and sky.

As they reached the quayside and the long lines of river-boats moored there, Joseph smiled at her, saying, 'You pleased with Joseph, missy? You ask him to ride with you again?'

'Oh yes, Joseph, I am very pleased with you. Where can I find you when I need you again?'

'Always here near the river. I come every morning to see if you need me, very pleased if you do, not unhappy if you do not.'

She laughed. 'Tonight, Joseph, I need to find the shop of Ali Mustapha. Do you know it?'

'Oh yes, missy. Very expensive. He sell only real antiques, not manufactured, you know. I can take you there. What time?'

'I'm not sure. I want to go alone.'

He nodded wisely. 'I wait until you come. It takes about fifteen minutes – it is out towards Karnak.'

Impetuously, she said, 'Do you know Prince Ahmed Farag?'

He frowned in an effort to collect his thoughts, then he shook his head with a little smile. 'Missy, Joseph is only donkey-boy, superior donkey-boy with good English, but this man is a *prince*.'

She laughed. 'Of course. I'm sorry, Joseph. I met Prince Ahmed on the boat from England. Perhaps Mr Mustapha will know him.'

'But of course. He know everyone with money to spend. If you buy from his shop it will cost you much money.'

'I'm sure it will, but I just want to look this evening. What time does he close?'

'Close?'

'Yes. What time does he shut up his shop for the night.'

'My lady, he *never* close. He sleep with one eye open if there is money to be made.'

She laughed. 'I'll see you tonight, Joseph. Wait for me here.'

She watched with impatience when her mother picked up a magazine after dinner and Meg decided to tinkle on the piano. Would they never go to bed? In desperation she said, eventually, 'I think I'll go to bed, Mother. It was hot on the streets this afternoon and I am rather tired.'

'I told you you should have come back to the boat with us. The heat of the afternoon is far too intense to have you rambling all over the place, particularly in a foreign town.'

'I'll see you in the morning, then. Don't disturb me, I'll be asleep as soon as my head hits the pillow.'

In her cabin Laura hurriedly changed into a long riding skirt and shirt-blouse, then she laid pillows along the centre of the bed and pulled the sheets around them. From the door she looked back to reassure herself that the bed looked occupied, then, noiselessly, she opened the door and closed it after her.

She reached the gangway without meeting a soul and then her heart sank when she saw one of the boatmen walking along the deck. She held up a finger to her lips and he smiled. 'Please don't give me away, Hassan,' she said softly. 'I want to see the temple by moonlight.'

He grinned at her and, in the darkness, she could see his gleaming teeth and the glint of gold in them. 'Best time to see, Mees Laura. In moonlight temples look whole again.'

She smiled and crept silently down the gangway, looking around anxiously for Joseph as she hurried along the quayside.

He appeared from nowhere, holding out to her the reins of his cream-coloured donkey before mounting another. Seeing her surprise he said, 'I borrow from my brother. Now we go to Mustapha shop and onwards, perhaps.'

'Onwards?'

'Yes, if he tell you where Prince Ahmed live.'

She stared at Joseph in some confusion. She was rapidly learning that, in this strange, exotic land, one had only to think something to have it suddenly appear. In this seemingly ordinary donkey-boy she had discovered a deeper soul, capable of anticipating her needs before they had been given expression.

The African night was balmy and there was the scent of jasmine mingled with more exotic fragrances. They rode down streets where the shops were open to the skies and on the pavements were spread all the herbs and spices of the East, illuminated by lanterns swinging gently in the cool evening breeze.

They encountered no other Europeans along the busy street and passers-by looked curiously at the blonde Englishwoman riding by with her donkey-boy at a time of day when most of her compatriots would be happily ensconced in the large Western hotels or in the river-boats moored along the quayside.

'Here is the shop of Mustapha,' Joseph announced quietly. 'See there, my lady.' He pointed to where a striped awning sheltered the dimly-lit window of a narrow shop.

He helped her to dismount and for a few minutes she gazed through the window at a collection of stone figures and broken pillars. She turned to stare at Joseph, who smiled cheerfully. 'You enter, my lady. Ali Mustapha not put his best things in the window for robbers to see. Inside you will find what you want.'

He pulled back the curtain over the door so that she could pass in front of him and she found herself in a dark little shop illuminated by only one lamp burning on the counter. She thought at first that the shop was empty until her eyes became accustomed to the gloom and then, from the back, a very old man shuffled forward to peer short-sightedly across the counter.

For a moment, Laura wished that Joseph had entered the shop with her, but the old man was busy applying a match to another lamp standing on the counter and then the shadows receded and she was able to look around with interest at the shelves filled with stone heads and glass cases containing statuettes made of alabaster and basalt.

The old man smiled, showing several ancient and rotting teeth.

'You are Mr Ali Mustapha?' Laura asked gently.

He shook his head. 'My son,' he said.

'May I speak with him?'

He nodded and disappeared into the back of the shop, leaving her alone.

She was able to see a vast mummy case reared up against the wall and she shuddered delicately at a mummified hand adorned with several rings in the show-case on which her bag lay. With a little cry she snatched it away and when she looked up she saw that another man faced her, a tall, very thin man with faintly slanting eyes and a dark beard.

'Mr Ali Mustapha?' Laura enquired.

He nodded. 'You are looking for something special, Madame, something very old?'

'I am interested in buying an Egyptian cat if the price is right,' Laura said.

He smiled. 'I have many cats. What do you think of this one?'

He reached under the counter and brought out a ceramic cat in the traditional Egyptian pose. She took it in her hand and looked at it from every angle while he watched with a half-smile on his lips.

'I have seen many cats like this one in the shops in Cairo and on the vendors' stalls. It is very well done, but hardly antique, Mr Mustapha.'

He smiled. 'I did not say it was antique. Most visitors to my shop would be happy to buy it, but you think I might have some other? Some cat that is very old?'

'Yes.'

'Why did you come here? Is it that some person recommends my shop to you?'

'Yes. Prince Ahmed Farag.'

She watched his face, but not a single muscle betrayed that he knew the man she referred to. Instead, he reached under the counter and produced another cat, this time fashioned in black basalt and quite the most beautiful she had ever seen. The smooth black stone felt cold in her hand, but there was no denying the exquisite workmanship, from the aware, slanting eyes to the rounded curves of the cat's body. It felt ready to spring into life and Laura's eyes shone with admiration.

'Can you tell me anything about it?' she asked him. 'Where it was found, who it belonged to?'

'It was found in the tomb of a noble near the ancient site of the city of Bubastis. The cat, my lady, was worshipped in Bubastis in ancient times. It is very old – and expensive.'

'How expensive?'

'Five thousand Egyptian pounds.'

Laura gasped. 'I would love to have it, Mr Mustapha, but I cannot afford anything like that.'

Reluctantly, she replaced it on the counter but continued to look at it with longing eyes.

'Did Prince Ahmed not tell you that the antiques I sell would be expensive, my lady? He is aware of it, for he has bought many things from me over the years.'

'No, he didn't tell me. I was with a friend who had just bought a scarab from a street vendor. Prince Ahmed merely said that if he wanted the genuine thing he should visit you.'

'But your friend not with you now?'

'No, I came alone.'

She watched as he replaced the cat in the case under the counter and was about to turn away when her courage returned to her. She loved the cat, she dearly wanted it – but she had not come to his shop in search of such a treasure. She had come to discover where she could find Ahmed.

'Does Prince Ahmed often frequent your shop, Mr Mustapha?'

He raised his hands in a noncommittal fashion and she turned away with the feeling that she would learn nothing here. She had reached the door when he said, softly, 'His Highness is a dedicated collector of things ancient Egyptian. You should ask him to help you when you buy or you could quite easily buy something of no value.'

'I would welcome his help, but I do not know where he lives. In the Fayoum, I think.'

'The Fayoum, Luxor, Cairo . . . Prince Ahmed is a very rich man with many homes. Now he is in Luxor so perhaps you are fortunate, Madame.'

He was smiling, a vaguely amused smile which brought the warm blood to her face and, seeing her about to turn away again, he came to lift up the curtain so that she could pass out of his shop. When she looked up to thank him, she saw that his face was not unkind.

'Prince Ahmed's house is on the bank of the Nile near Karnak. A large white house with iron gates. You cannot miss it. I know that he is there, for he came into my shop this morning.'

'Thank you, Mr Mustapha, I will remember.'

'He come, he go, tomorrow may be too late.'

Then Joseph was tugging at her arm saying, 'Come, my lady, donkeys wait.'

She allowed Joseph to lead without knowing if he had heard Ali Mustapha's instructions or not, and presently they reached the broad road beside the river with the lights shining in the dark depths of the water and, ahead, the towering, moonlit columns of Karnak.

They rode without speaking until at last they came to a pair of immense ornamental gates. A large river-boat was moored at the landing-stage and, beyond the gates, the short drive was shadowed by waving palms. The house behind the trees and oleander bushes gleamed white and, from one of the lower windows, a light streamed out into the darkness.

Laura stood at the gates with one foot poised as though she would take flight and it was Joseph's face, split in a wide grin, which restored her courage as he said softly, 'I wait here for you, missy. I wait all night if you like, then I take you back to your boat.'

'I shan't be long, Joseph,' she said diffidently. 'I

merely want Prince Ahmed's advice on an antique I wish to buy.'

Joseph was astute enough to smother the smile that threatened to illuminate his face while Laura opened one of the gates and quietly closed it behind her.

9

Prince Ahmed Farag was in a reflective mood. He stood on the terrace of his house looking at what he considered to be the most impressive view in the world, a view that superseded all others.

The towering columns of Karnak were bathed in silver moonlight. Giant pylons and obelisks raised by ancient Pharaohs in honour of their gods dwarfed the surrounding countryside, shining dramatically in the dark waters of the Nile as they had done for innumerable centuries. Once, long ago, he had tried to count Homer's hundred gates but he had found it impossible for there was a haunting sadness about Karnak's imperial ruins.

His schooldays in England had been happy ones. His fellow pupils soon forgot his title when they realised that they liked him. They invited him into their homes and they showed him their country, introducing him with great pride to their cathedrals and old churches, boasting with pride that these were very old, Norman or Saxon, and Ahmed had felt compelled to tell them that Egypt's monuments were already ancient when William the Conqueror had invaded Britain.

Oxford's dreaming spires filled him with a sense of euphoria. He was privileged to be a part of that great seat of learning, but one night, as he looked out across the city from his chambers, he resolved that when he returned to his native land he would spend more time in his father's house on the banks of the Nile with the pillars of Karnak stretching before him. The house was comparatively new, the view was as old as time, and Ahmed was now far removed from that young man who made his plans so confidently.

War had come to England. He had seen his friends, transformed by their new uniforms, go off to fight cheerfully for their country and soon the world he had known had gone for ever. When the war ended, some of his friends came back, others didn't. But in those few short years he had spent at the Egyptian Embassy in London he had come to realise that England was changing – but not as much as Egypt. In Egypt, the British were masters and he would have to live under their protectorate. Resentment grew in his proud heart.

The man sent to London to replace him had been quick to tell him that Egypt was reeling from the presence of the British on her soil. Though the British had not conquered Egypt, many of those in authority behaved as though they had. Those people who had once been Ahmed's friends would now consider themselves his superiors.

There had been bitterness in his heart on the day he left England. The boat had been crowded with British officers and civil servants going back to India, the Far East and Egypt, and his seat at the captain's table had exposed him to Mrs Levison-Gore's haughty condescension and Lady Hesketh's unguarded compassion.

Then there had been Laura. From that first moment when he looked into her incredible eyes, he had desired her. He had never been in love before. Since boyhood he had mixed happily with the sisters of his friends without a single one of them making his heart beat faster; and always, in the background, had been the shadow of Fawzia, the girl he would one day marry. Fawzia, the girl chosen by his parents as the ideal partner for their eldest son. She was beautiful, gentle, and of an amiable disposition. But Ahmed had been back in Egypt for two months and, with one excuse after another, had made it clear that he was not yet ready to meet her, a fact that did not endear him to his father and troubled his mother.

At any one time during the past eight weeks he had known where he could see Laura but he had refused to give in to his desires, punishing himself mercilessly by keeping his distance. But on the day he had met her at Abydos in the company of Lord Burlington he had been unable to stop himself speaking to them.

The Englishman had been predictably patronising, but he had seen Laura's eyes light up with joy, and although he knew the terrible hopelessness of it, he had inwardly rejoiced.

With a sigh he turned away from the glory of Karnak and went inside the house. His servant had lit the lamps and he pulled the long curtains across the windows facing on to the garden, shutting out the silver moonlight and the jewelled sky. He could hear the gentle rustling of the wind through the palms that surrounded the house, and from somewhere close by came the sound of a reed pipe.

What was the point of staying on in Luxor when it meant denying all the things he wanted to do for Egypt? he asked himself. There was work to be done in the Fayoum; he had a vast estate to administer and a host of workmen to care for, as well as the promise he had made to himself to improve the life of those living in the villages there. He had done nothing since he had been home except think about Laura and follow her surreptitiously in her passage along the Nile.

Irritably, he pulled the bell rope. His servant appeared noiselessly, bowing deferentially while he waited for his instructions.

'Pack my bag, Lutvi. I have decided to return to the Fayoum tomorrow.'

'Yes, Master.'

'And close up the house. We shall not be returning for some time.'

Lutvi bowed again and silently withdrew. He was becoming accustomed to his master's desire for change. He might almost think the Prince was lovesick for some woman, but there was no woman. His master lived a solitary, celibate life.

Never had Ahmed looked so Egyptian. He had discarded his European dress and was wearing a long, white robe which moulded his graceful figure and highlighted his profile . . .

He crossed the room to pull the drapes on those windows facing the river, and it was then that he saw a figure in white flit before his window. He went quickly to the door to investigate. As he reached it he heard a soft tap and he opened the door to reveal Laura staring up at him, tantalisingly unsure, her face pink with embarrassment. With a small bow he stood aside so that she could enter.

For several minutes they stood in silence, staring at each other, then, a little breathlessly, she said, 'I'm sorry to intrude, Ahmed, but I took your advice and went to see Ali Mustapha. He told me where you lived.'

Ahmed stood looking down at her impassively. She rushed on helplessly, in an endeavour to explain.

'He has a cat . . . it's very beautiful but terribly expensive. I didn't buy it because I wasn't sure I could trust him. I thought you might advise me.'

Ahmed's voice was deliberately cold as he answered her. 'You can trust Ali Mustapha implicitly. If you told him I had sent you he would not attempt to deceive you. Did he tell you where the cat came from?'

'From the site of ancient Bubastis, he said. Wasn't that the city where the cat was once worshipped?'

'Yes. Our ancient people were fond of their animal-headed gods, as you must have noticed during your passage through Egypt. Pasht was their name for the cat goddess. I should tell you that it was not the cat they worshipped but her prowess in keeping the granaries free from vermin. The poor people in Egypt had innumerable local gods.'

'Thank you, Ahmed. I am very ignorant about ancient Egypt – I wish I knew more.'

'There is no reason why you should. The gods and kings of ancient Egypt will play no part in your life when you return to England.'

'Even so, I should have read more about them before I came out here. But your house is beautiful, Ahmed. It is so romantic here on the banks of the Nile, and so close to Karnak.'

He permitted himself a small smile and hurriedly Laura continued, 'You must have superb views of Karnak.'

He walked across the length of the room and pulled back the drapes, revealing Karnak in all its splendour under the bright full moon.

Laura gasped with delight, joining him at the window. Before he was aware of it she was through the window and out on to the terrace, gazing enraptured at the view before her.

He went to stand beside her and, while she looked at the pillars of Karnak, he looked down at her golden hair glowing in the moonlight and the expression of awe and wonder on her face.

'How beautiful it is,' she breathed at last. 'We haven't seen Karnak yet – I think we're to go there tomorrow – it's wonderful to be seeing it like this.'

'How did you come here, Laura?' he asked curiously.

'I came with Joseph, my donkey-boy.'

'And where is he now?'

'Waiting for me outside. He will wait as long as I am here.'

She turned to face him. The embarrassment had gone and, instead, her eyes looked straight into his.

He found himself drowning in their beauty. The coldness he showed towards her covered a desire greater than any he had ever known, and she meant to shatter it. She had placed herself at a great disadvantage by coming uninvited – he might at least show some sort of pleasure in their meeting.

She was not to know that his heart burned with desire for her, that he wanted to sweep her into his arms and hold her close but something old and sane held him back. It was impossible that this daughter of England could ever be his; both his family and hers, were hidebound in prejudice and the girl's mother had barely been polite to him on the voyage. His family too were steeped in pride; any involvement with Laura would horrify them. He had to be strong for both their sakes.

Gently, she placed a hand on his arm and, triumphantly, she felt him tremble. She knew that he desired her. Why, then, didn't he take her in his arms and tell her so? Aggrieved, she said plaintively, 'I should not have come here, Ahmed. I can see that you are annoyed. I am sorry, I should go.'

She turned away and walked back through the house towards the door. For a moment her hands fumbled with the unfamiliar latch and then he was beside her, helping her to open it.

Their eyes met and, in a gentle voice, he said softly, 'It is not safe for you to come here so late, even with your donkey-boy, Laura. Suppose your family have missed you? What will you tell them?'

'Please don't be troubled on my behalf. Goodnight, Ahmed.'

'Laura, please . . . I have been ungracious. Tell me about the cat you admired in Mustapha's shop. I am sure I can obtain it for you at a very reduced price – please, will you allow me to see what I can do?'

Disposed to forgive him for his churlishness she

turned to smile. 'Oh Ahmed! Do you really think you can? It is a beautiful little cat in black basalt, all smooth and round, not stiff and starchy at all as Egyptian cats are usually depicted.'

'If I tell him about the English lady who admired it he will remember. Now, how long are you in Luxor?'

'Tomorrow we are visiting Karnak and in the evening there is a fancy-dress ball at the Winter Palace. Everybody seems anxious to go, so I expect we shall be there. The rest of the party are staying there but we are remaining on the boat. Oh, Ahmed – couldn't you come to the ball?'

'No, it isn't possible. Perhaps we could meet somewhere and I could explain about the cat.'

'I could come here. Please, Ahmed! Oh, I wish I wasn't going to that wretched ball, but I could come the next night. You will be here, won't you? Ahmed, I couldn't bear it if I didn't see you again! I've spent the last weeks hoping somewhere, anywhere, I might see you!'

Before he could collect his thoughts she was running away along the path. He saw Joseph come forward out of the shadows pulling her donkey.

Above the rustling of the palm fronds he heard the clatter of hoofs receding into the night, then he turned and rang for his servant.

'We shall not be returning to the Fayoum until two days after tomorrow, Lutvi!' he instructed him.

Lutvi merely bowed. Something had occurred to change his master's mind but whatever it was it did not concern him. In Egypt the great ones were never questioned by their menials – it was a tradition as old as the temple shimmering in the moonlight. In his own time his master would make his plans clear . . .

10

Mrs Levison-Gore decided to defer their visit to Karnak until the day after the ball.

'We really don't want to tire ourselves out tramping around the temple and then be expected to dance through the night,' she explained over breakfast. 'There's a Frenchman staying at the Winter Palace who has emptied his Paris salon in order to provide his customers with a great many costumes to choose from. I expect he'll be terribly expensive, but I suggest you choose something simple and elegant – let your beauty do the rest.'

'What do you mean by simple, Mother?' Meg asked curiously.

'Something Grecian, perhaps. I'm not even sure if they're for hire or if they're for sale. We'll go to see him directly after breakfast. Your aunt's not an early riser and I suggest we get in first!'

A room had been set aside within the Winter Palace, filled with glass cases which the Frenchman had had sent over from Paris. Within them were crinolines in silks and satins, powdered wigs and delicate fans, Roman togas, Red Indian feathered head-dresses, Pharaonic crowns and Mandarin silks and brocades.

Mrs Levison-Gore showed her preference for a dark-blue crinoline with a high powdered wig and a jewelled lorgnette. She had a slender figure and Monsieur Phillipe clucked around her like an old hen in his haste to show his approval.

Laura wandered around the cases with a frown on her face while Meg immediately chose a Dresden shepherdess costume which suited her pink-and-white English complexion.

Monsieur Phillipe gave Laura his full attention. How he longed to dress this beautiful English girl in the garb of a Grecian goddess or nymph, but she was disinterested in everything he showed her.

'Has Mademoiselle nothing specific in mind?' he asked, plaintively.

'I'd really like to go as an ancient Egyptian princess,' she said hopefully.

Before he could answer her, her mother cut in sharply, 'Really, Laura, you are too fair. Egyptian princesses were invariably dark, I'm sure.'

Monsieur Phillipe clapped his hands excitedly. 'But yes, Madame, she could wear a wig! See, I have something quite exquisite right here.'

He flung open a glass case at the end of the room and brought out a delicate white gown with a pleated skirt, equipped with a wide jewelled belt and a matching jewelled collar. Then he produced a head-dress in dark lapis lazuli, shaped like a bird, which he set aside before bringing out a straight blue-black wig which he placed on her head. The hair fell on to Laura's shoulders in shining strands, curling up at the ends. He laid the head-dress on her hair so that the wings of the bird fell against either cheek and the regal vulture's head was raised proudly over her brow.

Laura spun round and both her mother and sister stared at her in speechless amazement. The Frenchman was saying excitedly, 'Mademoiselle will make up her eyes so,' and he produced a photograph of an ancient Egyptian princess taken from one of the reliefs on a temple wall. He had little doubt that the girl's violet eyes would do justice to the kohl the salon would use.

'Is Madame pleased?' he ventured at last and, in spite of her better judgement, Mrs Levison-Gore had to admit that her daughter looked entirely enchanting. All Laura could think of was, 'Ahmed will like this

– this will surely convince him that we can be right together.'

Later in the afternoon Laura sat in a hairdressing salon having her nails delicately tinted and her eyes expertly made up. She was aware of the steady hum of conversation around her, then suddenly she was jerked wide-awake when a Frenchwoman sitting nearby said casually to another, 'Did you notice that divine Egyptian in the shop of Ali Mustapha this morning? He was looking at a terribly expensive black cat.'

The Englishwoman she spoke to smiled knowledgeably. 'His father is Prince Omdeh Farag, quite a force in government circles, I believe, and terribly rich.'

'I wonder if he bought the cat?'

'Oh yes, I saw a small fortune change hands. I wonder if it's one of his wedding presents for Fawzia Hadji? It could well be.'

Laura watched the two women leaving the salon with deep resentment in her heart, then something of the enormity of what she had done came over her. Ahmed had bought the cat and she would have to pay for it. How on earth could she, out of her not very generous allowance? And what could she say to him?

The cat had been an excuse to see him, but was she brave enough to tell him that, and see the shutters come down on that handsome face?

That night they drove in a horse-drawn carriage to the Winter Palace along an avenue lined with Egyptians who had come to view the eccentricities of foreigners. They wore cloaks over their costumes but Laura's Egyptian head-dress evoked great approval from the crowd, while her mother's tall, powdered wig gave rise to a great deal of merriment.

On the advice of their mother they made a late appearance and the ball was already in full swing. Laura was pleased to see that she was the only girl in the room wearing ancient Egyptian dress and she was quickly claimed by a red-faced young man wearing a tall Pharaonic crown, but not looking the least bit Egyptian. Ahmed would have looked so marvellous, she thought longingly, but Ahmed was probably enjoying the solitude of his villa and no doubt thinking about his forthcoming marriage.

She threw herself wholeheartedly into the spirit of the ball, flattering and being flattered, gay and light-hearted, her eyes as sparkling as the champagne she drank freely, and then suddenly Edward was at her side, his eyes devouring her. He looked faintly ridiculous in his Roman toga which impeded his dancing.

'Why are you so late?' he grumbled.

'You surely haven't been waiting for me? Where's Poppy?'

'I haven't the faintest idea.'

'But she's here with you, surely?'

'I've got to talk to you, Laura.'

By this time they had reached the doors leading out on to the terrace, and he took hold of her hand, pulling her out into the warm, scented night.

She looked at his face anxiously. There was something different about him. Edward's mouth was set in determined lines and the hands propelling her along the path leading to the gardens were bruising in their intensity.

'Edward, you're hurting me! What's so urgent that you couldn't tell me in the ballroom?'

She pulled away from him, causing him to pause in his headlong rush towards the bushes.

For what seemed an eternity they stared into each other's eyes, then he said harshly, 'I've spoken to my father, Laura. I've told him it's you I want to marry, not Poppy.'

She stared at him, speechlessly, then anger made her say sharply, 'Didn't it occur to you to find out if I wanted to marry *you* before you spoke to your father?'

'But you know very well what they wanted! They

wanted me for Poppy and I don't care for Poppy – at least, not enough to marry her. Your mother made it quite plain that she wanted me to marry you and I thought it was your wish also!'

'Oh Edward, I don't know. I like you. We get along very well together but we both know what the family want. We haven't really known each other very long and you've made very little effort to get to know Poppy.'

'You mean you don't want to marry me?'

'Edward, I don't know.' She knew very well what she wanted. She wanted Ahmed, who quite obviously didn't want her. It could be that she was turning down the substance for the shadow and the last thing she wanted to do was to hurt Edward. Edward was a good person, somebody she would like for a good friend.

Her mind was filled with confusion. Her mother would be furious if she turned Edward down – and his family would be furious if she accepted him. She needed time to think! She looked back along the path where there was laughter and light-hearted chatter, then she saw her mother standing on the steps of the terrace, her eyes peering into the darkness.

'There's Mother,' she said helplessly. 'I wonder if she knows anything?'

'She could well do if she's spoken to my parents. In any event, Father's calling a meeting of the family on board the dahabiyah in the morning. What are we going to do, Laura?'

'Can't we just enjoy the dance tonight, Edward, and think about it later? Your father may make you change your mind.'

'Only you can make me change my mind, Laura, but I shouldn't have blurted it out like this. Obviously, it's upset you.'

Her mother came forward to meet them and there was no disguising the triumphant pleasure on her face.

'You're mother's told me, Edward, but we'll say no more until after the meeting in the morning. I'm sure your father will try to make you change your mind, and the others in my family will back him up. I'm afraid you're going to have to be very strong.'

He nodded determinedly, then they were back in the ballroom and the family were watching them with varying expressions of disapproval and concern. Only Poppy seemed worried. Inwardly, she was decidedly pleased. She liked Edward Burlington well enough, and she'd been prepared to do anything her family wished, but she had never seen herself as the wife of a marquis, entertaining his friends to lavish dinner-parties, long country weekends and summer garden-parties. She was no great beauty and her portrait would add no great lustre to the collection on the walls of his family seat whereas Laura would look the part, grace any function. Laura would be the bride as well as the debutante of the year.

Now she would be able to go back to her horses and her dogs, to the activities she liked best, to friends who liked doing the things she liked. One day, perhaps, there might be some nice, ordinary man who might be prepared to marry her for herself . . .

Edward dutifully asked her to dance and, seeing his morose expression, she said gently, 'Is everything all right, Edward? Was Laura pleased?'

'She's not as easy to understand as you, Poppy. I'm rather afraid I jumped it on her. I just hope I didn't misunderstand her – I thought she wanted to marry me.'

'I'm sure she does, Edward, but her mother is a very dominant woman.'

'That's what I'm afraid of. I don't want her simply to obey her mother. I want her to marry me because she wants to.'

'I've always thought Laura to be pretty strong-minded. I'm sure she'll do as she pleases.'

Laura was not enjoying herself. She couldn't think with the music blaring and the crowds milling around her. She yearned for the slow pace of the river and the solitude of the dahabiyah. She wished she could make an excuse to leave, but when she told her mother quietly that she had developed a headache her mother had merely hissed, 'I don't want you running off on your own, Laura! Try to look as if you're enjoying yourself – and I want you here for the parade at the end. Heaven knows, you wanted that costume, and it cost a great deal of money to hire it!'

So Laura waited until the end of the dance and then she joined the parade, along with Meg and Poppy in Roman dress.

Meg hissed, 'What have we done now? Grandmother's totally ignored me all evening.'

'It's not you, Meg,' Laura replied. 'She's vexed with me. Edward has told his father he wants to marry me.'

'Golly! Mother'll be over the moon.'

'I know . . .'

Meg looked at her anxiously but by this time the parade was moving and Laura soon found herself in the centre of the ring, in the company of a Roman gladiator, a Chinese mandarin and a giggling Helen of Troy. Laura and the gladiator received the first prizes while the other two had to make do with seconds. Laura surveyed the large bottle of champagne and the equally massive box of chocolates which she promptly offered to be raffled for charity, a fact that pleased Poppy enormously since the charity took care of the welfare of Egyptian horses in a country where they were largely ill-treated.

Back on the river-boat Lavinia was disposed to talk about the meeting which was to take place in the morning, but all Laura wanted to do was retire for the night. For what seemed like hours, she lay awake listening to the creaking of the boat at her moorings, the gentle swell of the river and the distant barking of dogs.

Her mother spoke sharply about her lacklustre appearance at the breakfast table.

'Really, Laura, you might at least look as though you're looking forward to meeting Edward this morning! If he sees you like that, he could well have second thoughts.'

After breakfast Laura was despatched to her cabin to freshen up and be back in the salon to meet the family when they arrived.

The Marquis made his displeasure plain. Laura was too young – why, the girl hadn't yet had a chance to live – and Edward had been enchanted by a pretty face without a thought for anything else. Poppy was mature, a fine, upstanding girl who looked as if she could breed strong, healthy sons. He called upon Edward to think again.

The Dowager Lady Mallonden said it had been her dearest wish to see her darling Poppy married to Edward and the two families joined.

Poppy's mother and Edward's mother merely wept a little, while Mrs Levison-Gore said that the two families would still be joined and she was amazed that the fact seemed to have escaped everybody's notice.

Edward sat through the proceedings with an adamant face. Laura said nothing. Occasionally Edward squeezed her hand to show her she had his full support.

The meeting ended just before lunch with the Marquis and the Mallondens being forced to admit defeat and, seeing that there was nothing more to be said, Lord Mallonden ordered champagne and Laura and Edward stood together while toasts were drunk.

'Laura should have a ring,' Edward exclaimed. 'Do you have one she could borrow, Mother?'

'Of course, dear. I have a diamond and emerald ring she may borrow until she's chosen her own.'

'Sorry, darling,' Edward said gently. 'You won't mind wearing Mother's ring for a while?'

'I'd prefer to wait for my own, Edward. What's in a ring?'

'Oh well, just as you wish, dear.'

The Marquis said briskly, 'Well, if we're all going to Karnak we'd better have lunch and arrange to meet at the hotel. I take it we'll all be going to view the temple?'

So they departed. Laura received Edward's farewell kiss dutifully and Poppy pressed her hand, saying, 'You'll make a beautiful bride, Laura. I'll gladly be one of your bridesmaids if you care to ask me!'

Laura merely smiled. Her thoughts had not got as far as her wedding, they were still entangled with the engagement, coupled with her mother's quite evident delight at the outcome of her designs. She felt trapped, wishing she could escape along the river-bank to where Ahmed lingered in his white villa within sight of Karnak's towering pillars.

11

Laura stood with Edward in the centre of the Great Hall at Karnak and marvelled to herself that when she had seen it from Ahmed's terrace the temple had appeared whole and perfect in the silver moonlight. Now she could only look at its ruined splendour and feel her heart aching with sadness for the glory that had gone for ever.

Pillars and obelisks and pylons stretched upwards against the vivid blue of the sky, giant statues of gods and Pharaohs vied with the stature of the surrounding pillars and, across the expanse of the Hall, the dust of centuries had settled between the cracks in the floor.

Its magnificence overpowered her. Their guide talked to them of the splendour of Egypt's past, but Laura could only absorb the beauty and the sunshine, the sadness and the memory of the pink of the distant hills, the golden air and the majesty of the ruins. She knew that she would never forget the rapture of her first impressions of Karnak, but, in her memory, they would be forever a part of the strangest day in her life – and the bitter knowledge that she was bound in honour to a man she did not love . . .

At Edward's wish they had left the rest of the party and wandered alone from one pillared hall to the next. They had stood by the edge of the sacred lake and imagined the festivals mirrored in its depths. Yet Edward had only wanted to talk about themselves while Laura ached to see Ahmed. Why had Edward needed to fall in love with her in Egypt, when Egypt and Ahmed were so intrinsically bound together? She would never love Edward in Egypt, and the longer she stayed here, the more remote would be the idea of loving him in England.

By the time they left the temple the sun was already setting in the western sky, and in Egypt it is either night or day, there is no twilight. From the temple gateway they saw the land of the Nile stretching like a ribband of yellow light, and the pink cliffs of Thebes turned purple and a tragic crimson under the light of the dying sun.

As they sauntered back to their carriage Laura was aware that Edward was holding her arm closely and those people they met smiled at his proprietary air. She was introduced as his fiancée and there was a great deal of whispering, for most of their English acquaintances thought that it would be the Lady Poppy who would fill that role.

Laura's mother was making the most of it, much to the Dowager's chagrin, and by the time they reached the hotel Laura was wishing she was miles away. Her face was pale as they lingered over their afternoon tea and Edward said anxiously, 'I hope you'll be able to attend the concert this evening, darling. Karnak was pretty exhausting, I know.'

'I didn't sleep very well last night,' she admitted.

'Well, of course not. I expect you were far too excited – everything has happened so quickly.'

Laura had never felt less like attending a concert, but it was being sponsored by the hotel for their British guests, and Signor Carlo Pascalli, Italy's most noteworthy tenor who happened to be visiting Luxor at the time, had agreed to sing.

When they returned to the boat a little later her mother exclaimed on Laura's pallor. 'I do hope you're not sickening for something, Laura!'

'Perhaps if I rest for a while, Mother,' she ventured.

'Then rest in the lounge. I've spread your gown

across your bed. I'll get you a sedative and wake you round about seven. That should give you ample time to get ready.'

Laura didn't sleep. Her mind was far too active, plagued as it was with an engagement she didn't want, to a man she didn't love, when all she could think about was Ahmed.

Later, Laura was glad of the open window and the gentle breeze that diminished the sultry heat of the concert room. Occasionally her mother looked across to reassure herself that she was bearing up, and Edward was overly solicitous. Signor Pascalli performed magnificently in a series of Neapolitan love-songs which at any other time she would have adored, but tonight the haunting melodies left her feeling miserable.

The concert was over and people were milling around, offering their congratulations. Her mother basked in the acclaim, but Laura whispered to Edward, 'I really would like to go back to the boat, Edward. I'm sorry to be such a wet blanket but I am very tired.'

It was a great relief to get out into the warm, perfumed night for their short walk to the quayside.

Edward took her in his arms at the top of the gangplank and she said, quickly, 'Please tell Mother I'm perfectly all right but I don't want to be disturbed.'

She lay staring up into the darkness and had no idea what time it was when she heard her mother and Meg returning to the boat. Footsteps paused outside her cabin and then went on. After a while there was silence throughout the boat.

Incredibly, her lethargy seemed to leave her. Getting up, she went to the porthole to pull back the curtains. It was quiet ashore. Only one figure sat hunched up against the harbour wall and, nearby, a donkey stood placidly surveying the scenery.

She went to her wardrobe to put away the dress

she had worn for the concert and it was then that her eyes fell upon the ancient Egyptian costume she had worn at the fancy-dress ball. She took it out and held it against her. Then, from the shelf above, she took out the head-dress and the shining wig.

She was unable to resist putting them on, and as she stared at the beautiful, alien, face that gazed back at her from the mirror, an idea came to her, an idea so incredible that she sank trembling on to the edge of her bed. The idea, however, refused to go away. She would go to Ahmed, he would be stunned by her costume, they could talk about the cat, she could tell him about her engagement, watch the expression on his face to see if he cared. Without further thought she snatched a cloak from the wardrobe and let herself quietly out of her cabin.

As she crept stealthily along the deck towards the gangway, the figure sitting beside the harbour wall rose effortlessly to its feet and, as she drew closer, she recognised Joseph whose smile lit up his face.

'Why, Joseph,' she whispered. 'What are you doing here at this hour?'

'You need me, my lady. It is too far to walk and there will be no carriages at this time.'

'But Joseph, how did you know?'

'I knew that one night you would go to him. I stay here as long as it takes.'

'There is only one donkey.'

'You ride, Joseph will walk. I have been long asleep, it is good that I walk.'

She allowed him to assist her into the saddle, and then they were trotting in the direction of Karnak and her excitement was so great that she had no thoughts for the enormity of her action . . .

Prince Ahmed Farag was not asleep. He had tossed and turned for hours, his thoughts a confused jumble after seeing Laura that afternoon with the red-faced

Englishman, his arm around her slender waist, his expression adoring as he had looked down at her. Ahmed, standing near one of the pillars in the Great Hall of Karnak, had turned away in angry disgust.

Tomorrow, he thought savagely, he would return the basalt cat to Ali Mustapha's shop. Tomorrow, he would think about returning to the Fayoum; tomorrow, he would think about Fawzia.

His reverie was shattered by the sound of someone tapping lightly on his door. At first he thought it was the wind from the river, whistling through the dovecotes in the gardens. Then, when it recurred, his heart leapt at the thought that it might be Laura.

He opened the door and she was in his room, discarding her cloak and dancing on sandalled feet across the floor. She paused before him, smiling, demanding his adulation.

His eyes kindled darkly. 'You surely haven't gone to the trouble of wearing our ancient dress merely to brighten up my dull old house, but if you have I must tell you that no queen in all her adornment could be more beautiful, no goddess more exquisite.'

'Oh Ahmed,' she breathed nervously, 'I had to show you this gown! I had to show you that I can look just as Egyptian as you can.'

Once more she spun round on her golden sandals and the pleated gown swirled about her ankles. She knew well the enchanting picture she presented and she meant to break down his reserve which had erected invisible barriers from the first day she had met him.

He smiled down at her, a singularly sweet smile. To cover the beating of his heart his voice, when he spoke to her, held an unusually gentle quality.

'Your jewels illuminate the night, Laura. They dazzle my poor eyes.'

'But they're only imitation, Ahmed. Had they been real, they would have been priceless.'

'And this is what it has come to, the dress of a queen worn to dance until dawn in a modern ballroom? You wore it for the fancy-dress ball at the Winter Palace, did you not?'

'I wore it because I loved it, because it was part of being here, part of the wonders we have seen, part of meeting you . . .'

'I'm flattered.'

'Now you are cold again! Just when I thought we might be happy together.'

'Laura – Laura, I am afraid for you. You should not be here at this hour. I have heard that you are engaged to Lord Burlington. He and your family would be horrified if they could see you now. I told you on the ship that there could never be anything between us and I meant it, Laura.'

'You mean you could never love me?'

'I mean that you are going to marry someone else – as I am. Englishmen talk glibly of their honour. We, too, have our sense of honour. Men in my country were keeping their word while your country was only just emerging from the primeval forests.

Laura, I meant it when I said there could never be what I would like there to be between us. You must go back to your family and the life you have known and allow me to do the same.'

For a long moment she stared up into his face, a face etched in bronze, stern and unyielding even though his eyes were pleading and not unkind. Now she was wishing with all her heart that she had not come. Now she hated the beautiful gown and the fake jewels which had, only a short while ago, given her such joy. They made her feel like a slave-girl adorned to give pleasure to her master, instead of a queen waiting for her royal lover. The time for laughter had gone, the moment was spoilt.

She wanted to cry, to run back along the river road

to the boat. How could she ever have thought for one moment that he loved her? Why had she been so stupid as to read into every smile, every gesture, every small polite kindness the first faint stirrings of love? Ahmed did *not* love her. She was nothing more than a pleasant diversion. Then, even as the treacherous thoughts entered her mind, she saw the unfairness of them and she blushed with shame when she remembered how she had flirted with him on the boat, invaded his life without any invitation on his part.

Ahmed watched her helplessly, aware of the expressions chasing each across her face. Despair and pride, anger and anguish.

Ahmed was not a vain man but he understood the reason for her despair and the sadness in his eyes sent her running blindly across the room to where she knelt next to a divan, her shoulders shaking with sobs. He stood watching her, his face bleak with dismay.

At last he went to her and tried to help her to her feet but she clung to the cushions, imploring him to leave her. Unthinking, he knelt beside her – and that was his undoing. Before he realised it, she was in his arms, and he found himself kissing her tear-stained face, his hands stroking her hair, his voice uttering words of endearment. Then her arms were round his neck, her lips soft and passionate against his own. No earthly power could have made him leave her then.

He had known no other woman in passion, she had known no other man. Together they explored all the tantalising, towering feelings which left them helpless and drained in the hour before the dawn.

Down the length of his body, Ahmed was aware of her limbs against his; the scent from her hair was in his nostrils, her gentle breathing fanned his cheek. He had not known such passion existed within him – and she had matched it, sensation for sensation, touch for touch.

He had no thoughts about where this night would lead them; he had only just recognised the bewildering beauty that would illuminate the years so that anything less than this would be a betrayal of all he felt for Laura in his heart. She had possessed him completely, all his strong young manhood, and he lay shaken by the memory of it, her sweetness and her strength, her gentleness and her desire.

In his innermost heart, Ahmed knew that nothing had changed. There could never be a future together for Laura and he.

The delicate white gown lay on the marble floor beside its jewelled belt and jewelled diadem. On its side rested one small golden sandal which she had kicked off the night before. Her slender, porcelain body lay in the shelter of his arms and when she stirred he placed his hand upon one of her soft breasts, gently caressing it.

Sleepily, she opened her eyes and met his searching gaze. The memory of the night before came flooding back to her so that she buried her face in his shoulder, her cheeks burning with blushes. Then, after moments when he stroked her hair, his voice murmuring endearments, she put both her arms around him and kissed his lips with great tenderness.

'Oh my love, my dearest love,' she murmured, and his arms crushed her against him.

Soon, now, she must leave him, run from his side before the gardeners began their work and her family discovered her absence. Over her head he looked towards a niche in the wall which housed an ancient stone statue of the goddess Isis. Even in this day and age there were poor people in Egypt who still worshipped at her feet. They called her a good lady, a lady who understood their troubles as she had done in ancient days, but all Ahmed could see was the cold stone face and the remote, expressionless eyes. What did they care, those old stone gods, about the littleness of love?

12

Ahmed stood alone on the river's bank looking out to where the rosy fingers of dawn touched the Theban Hills. In these first moments of the day the sands of the desert were coloured a delicate pink and the barren hills a fragile mauve, a scene so beautiful that he never tired of it, so peculiarly Egyptian that he never wearied of its sameness or its unvarying monotony.

He felt, at that moment, that he never wanted anything more definite to fill his days; that he would be content to spend his life on the river; that where the great river went, he would go too.

He did not hear Laura until she stood beside him, then he looked down at her face and his arms crept around her.

'How beautiful it is,' she murmured. 'Ahmed, I shall be happy to look on this scene for the rest of my life.'

His face betrayed nothing and, anxiously, she said, 'Ahmed, I love you! We shall be together always – please tell me that that is how it's going to be?'

His expression was infinitely sad. 'Darling Laura, I told you before that there can be nothing permanent between us. I love you – at this moment, more than anything in the world – but it isn't enough. You're a child to think that our love is all that matters. It isn't.'

'What else is there? I can't go back to Edward now! I can't spend the rest of my life with him when I don't love him, when I'll *never* love him. And you can't marry that girl you're engaged to when you don't love her! Doesn't it mean anything to you that we spent the night together, that I gave myself to you without reservation? Surely you can't think that this is something I did lightly, without thought.'

'I know you didn't, Laura. Beautiful, generous Laura, what can I say? I love you, I'll always love you, but don't you see, darling, that in the end nothing has changed. Your family will never accept me and my family will never accept you. There is no future for us together; besides, I am in honour bound to marry Fawzia. It was ordained years ago. Nothing has changed.'

'But it has. You've met me, we've fallen in love. Oh Ahmed, I hate you when you talk like this. Nothing can be the same for us ever again. We have to be together.'

He shook his head, his face adamant. More and more she felt she was beating her head against a stone wall and, in a voice quietly controlled, he said, 'Now you must return to the dahabiyah and in the days to come you must try to forget me.'

She stared at his implacable face in amazement. How could he ask her to forget him when the memory of the night they had spent together was too wonderful, too poignant ever to be forgotten? 'How can you say you love me in one breath and ask me to leave you in the next? Where will you go, what will you do?'

'I will go back to my home in the Fayoum while you must return to Luxor. I shall never forget you, Laura. As long as I live you'll be a part of me but a very forbidden part of me. One day you'll wonder how you could have imagined yourself in love with me; one day, when the sights and sounds of England have made you forget.'

Pride, anger, desolation, all were mingled in the face she turned up to him, and she was too angry to see the pain in his eyes. Haughtily, she drew herself away and in a voice which only trembled slightly she asked, 'When will you go?'

'Later this morning. Laura, please don't go with bitterness in your heart. Don't make it more difficult than it already is . . .'

She stared at him long and hard, then without another word she left him and his eyes followed her fleeing figure as she ran through his garden and out to where Joseph awaited her on the roadside.

Joseph looked at her tear-stained face sadly. His beautiful English lady loved the Prince Ahmed but did he not love her, too, that he sent her running from his house with her face filled with such anguish? As he padded beside her on his bare feet, Joseph heard her sobbing gently, and it was he who had the presence of mind to suggest that she left him before they reached the quayside.

She met no one on the way to her cabin but she hadn't been there long when there was a tap on her door and Meg came in, her face curious and accusing.

'Where have you been?' she asked sharply. 'I came in early but you weren't here and your bunk didn't look as if it had been slept in.'

'I slept very badly and I was up long before dawn prowling about the deck,' Laura lied. 'Did you tell Mother I wasn't in my cabin?'

'No, but if you hadn't been here now I would have had to tell her something. Where were you, Laura? I looked on the deck, I looked *everywhere*.'

Laura looked at her sister helplessly, then the sobs started afresh and Meg, realising the depth of her misery, went to sit next to her on the bed, holding her gently in her arms.

It was some time before Laura could collect herself sufficiently well to talk, and then the long, sorry story of all that had happened came out in breathless anguish.

'What will you do?' Meg asked in shocked amazement.

'I love him, Meg! I can't ever marry Edward and I can't go on with this engagement farce. Ahmed is leaving today and I can't let him go without me. We've got to make people see that we're in love, that we have to be together. Nothing else matters.'

'But he's told you that there can't ever be anything between you. You can't make him take you with him, Laura!'

'Meg, don't you see, if I marry Edward all my life will be a lie? I've got to fight for what I want. I don't want Mother in here, I don't want her to see me so upset. You know what she's like – she'll demand to know what it's all about and I'm not ready to face any of them just yet. Do go along to the salon and tell her I'm not quite ready for breakfast – tell her I'm still feeling a little seedy.'

'She'll come down here and see for herself.'

'Oh Meg! Do use a little initiative! Lay it on thick and hard, *make* her believe you. I'll join you when I've had time to think.'

Doubtfully, Meg left her, and for several minutes Laura paced her cabin with her hands tightly clenched. It was half past six in the morning. Soon the rest of the party would be arriving to start their tour to the Valley of the Kings while it was still early and before the other tourists arrived on the scene. She had very little time.

Hurriedly, she threw her suitcase on her bed and started to heap clothes into it from the wardrobe. She took only what she knew she could carry and, after locking the case, she sat on the edge of her bed with notepaper and envelopes.

The first letter she addressed to her mother, saying only that she realised she could not marry Edward, apologising for any distress and anxiety she would be causing and asking her mother to forgive her. She ended the letter with the words, 'One day I hope I shall be able to tell you more about my decision. In the meantime, dear mother, please try to think kindly of me and realise that I have never been more honest in my life. Your loving daughter, Laura.'

Her other letter was addressed to Edward and in it she asked him, too, to forgive her. She told him she could never have been the sort of wife he deserved and she wished him joy and happiness with some other woman who would prove more worthy of his affection.

She paid no heed to the boatmen she met on the deck, who stared at her with undisguised amazement. One of them carried her suitcase to the quayside and up the steps towards the promenade above.

She was relieved that there was no sign of Joseph and she hailed a horse-drawn carriage standing idly on the road. 'Please hurry,' she urged the driver after giving him instructions as to where to take her.

The horse was fresh and enjoying his morning gallop and she was relieved to see Ahmed's river-boat tied up beside its quay and by the silence surrounding it. After paying the driver she made her way to the boat, then, after reassuring herself that there was nobody around to see her board it, she walked cautiously up the gangplank and along the deck.

As she entered the salon, Laura looked round with pleasure at the beautifully equipped room, thinking how much more beautiful it was than the boat she had left.

For several minutes she stood at the door listening for sounds throughout the boat but she was met only with silence. Taking her courage in both hands she humped her suitcase along the passage, opening and closing doors on her way until she came to a white ornamental door which was vastly different to the rest. She opened this cautiously and was immediately confronted with a stateroom decorated and furnished in white and gold. Her feet sank into a beautiful oriental carpet and with wide, wonder-filled eyes she moved about the room, taking in the vast, fitted wardrobes and the array of cut glass on the dressing-table.

A huge bed was covered by an embossed rose-pink satin bedspread and her dazzled eyes fell on a large portrait hanging on a wall opposite the portholes. It was of a woman, a very beautiful woman with dark hair and dark eyes and a face which reminded her of Ahmed. She assumed the woman in the portrait must be his mother and that this was the room occupied by her whenever she elected to sail on the river. So where was Ahmed's room?

Leaving her suitcase, Laura left the stateroom and moved along the passage, eventually finding another room, not quite as large but equally impressive – a room which was being prepared for someone.

From the porthole she could see Ahmed's house through the trees and, after a few minutes, she was rewarded by seeing three men come along the path from the house carrying suitcases. She recognised one of them as Ahmed's personal servant. Then she heard their footsteps along the deck and the opening and closing of doors. In some haste she left the room and hurried back to the stateroom she had first found only just in time for she heard them moving along the passage.

As she waited in the stateroom, the enormity of what she had done horrified her. She had burnt all her bridges behind her – her ancestry, her culture, her family – to go to a man who might not want her, who was not of her race; who, although he might love her, was engaged to another woman. She did not know a single member of his family; she knew nothing of their way of life; she only knew she wanted Ahmed and would go on wanting him until the end of time . . .

Why didn't he come? He had said he wanted to leave in the morning and by this time the family would be aware of what she had done.

Impatiently she went to stand at the porthole and, after several minutes, she was relieved to see Ahmed walking through the gardens towards the boat.

She heard his voice issuing instructions to his servants, then his footsteps passing her stateroom. After a few minutes, with a racing heart, she let herself out of the room.

She stood at the door of his stateroom for a few moments with her hands pressed against her breast, as if by this effort she could stop the hammering of her heart. Then she reached down and opened the door. He was staring out of the porthole, looking back towards Karnak, and at first did not move, thinking it was his servant. After what seemed a century of silence he turned and the incredulity on his face brought the scalding tears into her eyes. Then she was running across the room to fling herself into his arms, her words of explanation lost because at that moment Ahmed was unable to comprehend anything beyond the fact that she was here in his arms . . .

It was much later when he instructed his crew to sail south for Aswan and neither of them spared a thought for the dahabiyah still at her moorings in the shadow of the Temple of Luxor. It was late in the afternoon and by now the western sky was tinged with all the colours of the sunset; gold and rose mingled with crimson, throwing up the hills of the west in purple magnificence. By this time the dahabiyah they left behind them was alight from stem to stern and below, in the crowded salon, two families were locked in anger and disbelief . . .

13

It didn't take John Halliday long to realise that his chief was decidedly irascible. They faced each other across Sir Archibald Darwin's mahogany desk and John took in at once his heightened colour, his narrowed eyes and the grim set of his mouth.

Sir Archibald had spent a disastrous twenty-four hours. It had started with his interview with Sultan Fuad who had informed him of a skirmish on the desert railway for which he blamed the British soldiers instead of the bandits who had invaded the train.

Anger had taken the place of diplomacy and the two men had parted with heated words. Then there had been the opera. Sir Archibald hated opera but his wife loved it. He saw nothing in the least entertaining in watching a twenty-two stone Italian tenor telling a twenty-stone diva that her tiny hand was frozen. He'd said as much in an undertone to his wife who had accused him of being a moron, so that the rest of the evening had hardly been harmonious. Then they had only been in the house a couple of minutes when he had been called to the telephone and his troubles had begun in earnest.

'I've been trying to get hold of you since early, this afternoon,' the voice at the other end of the telephone said belligerently. 'Where the devil do you civil servants get to?'

'Who is that?' he'd demanded.

'The Marquis of Camborne, speaking from Luxor.'

'What exactly can I do for you, Lord Camborne?'

'If I'd been able to get hold of you earlier you'd

have had a much better chance of doing something for me! Now I'm not so sure.'

Sir Archibald, seething, remained silent, then the Marquis went on: 'We're here with the Mallonden family and I have to report that Mallonden's niece has gone missing. Left a note for my son Edward and another for her mother and nobody's seen her or heard of her since.'

'When was that?'

'Yesterday morning.'

'You say she wrote to your son?'

'Yes, they'd just announced their engagement and the note was to tell him she'd changed her mind. The letter to her mother was equally terse. She's gone off into the blue, the women in the party are all having the vapours and my son's threatening to shoot himself. I want you to send somebody down here, somebody responsible. I want some action, do you hear me, Darwin?'

'I hear you, Lord Camborne. I'll look into it for you and send somebody as soon as possible.'

There was the sound of the receiver being replaced, then silence, and for the rest of the night he hadn't cared that his wife was sulking reproachfully.

'You'd better get down to Luxor by the next train,' he ordered Halliday now. 'Stay as long as it takes. Mallonden's niece, he said – do you know the Mallondens?'

'I met Mrs Levison-Gore and her two daughters on the boat coming out here. She's Lord Mallonden's sister-in-law.'

Sir Archibald raised his eyebrows. 'I knew her husband, poor chap. Between his wife and his mother it's a wonder he wasn't gaga. When he was killed in India, some of us were unkind enough to say it was a happy release from that wife of his. Terrible social climber she was. What were the daughters like?'

'Young, pretty,' Halliday replied diplomatically.

'Do you suppose it's one of these girls that's gone missing?'

'I have no idea. I don't know how many nieces Lord Mallonden has.'

'Well, I want you to get the picture. Check in at the Winter Palace and take it from there. Get off on the next available train.'

A pale young moon shone its light over the Temple of Luxor as John Halliday alighted, stiff and weary, from the train. At the Winter Palace Hotel he was immediately informed that his presence was requested on board the dahabiyah now anchored below the hotel gardens.

The command was unreasonable, in his opinion. He had had a very long journey, had eaten only a light lunch and felt the need to bathe and change his attire, but when he made to go to his room the manager said in some agitation, 'No, sir! You go immediately – both the English lords have said so.'

'I doubt if the English lords would wish to see me dishevelled after my journey. I do not intend to keep them waiting long.'

The looks cast in his direction were sorrowful as he made his way across the hotel foyer towards the stairs.

He bathed and changed hurriedly, then he went to the window of his room. He could see several pleasure-boats lined up along the quayside and, from a mosque nearby, came the muezzin's call to prayer. He could see men dropping on to their knees, their faces turned towards Mecca in answer to the sonorous words, 'Allah is good, there is no God but Allah.'

The balmy night enfolded him as he walked through the hotel's gardens towards the quayside. The scents of Egypt surrounded him, jasmine and cinnamon, incense and oleander, and then he was at the gangway leading to the white boat gleaming above him. A boatman in a long white robe came forward to meet him, his white teeth flashing in his dark face, and he was being escorted along the deck and into the salon. For a moment he blinked in the sudden light, then he found himself facing a group of people who eyed him with varying expressions.

He saw at once that Mrs Levison-Gore sat apart from the others, her face as cold as if it was etched in marble. Beside her sat her younger daughter, tearful and afraid, but there was no sign of Laura.

A stout, military-looking man detached himself from the group and, after eyeing John from top to bottom, said testily, 'So Darwin didn't think it important enough to come himself. I'm the Marquis of Camborne – who are you?'

'I'm John Halliday, Sir Archibald's senior assistant.'

'Well, you'd better come over here and meet the rest of them.'

Introductions were performed. The Dowager Lady Mallonden regarded him haughtily, Lord Mallonden and Edward shook hands with him, Lady Mallonden and the Marchioness smiled weakly and Lady Poppy extended a hearty hand. He was then led to Mrs Levison-Gore who looked at him without recognition and John said, 'We've already met, on the boat coming over.'

She stared at him and, after a few moments, said, 'Of course, I do remember you were quite friendly with Lady Hesketh. This is my daughter, Margaret.'

'I remember your daughter, Mrs Levison-Gore, and your other daughter.'

'That's fortunate, then,' the Marquis cut in. 'If you've met the girl you'll know exactly who you're looking for. You'd better read these two letters the girl left behind her, though they won't tell you much.'

John took the letters and read them through, silently

agreeing with his host that they conveyed precisely nothing.

'I'll need to know a little about the days prior to Miss Levison-Gore's disappearance,' John said. 'Were there any quarrels? Was she interested in anybody else? Was the young lady ill or unhappy?'

'There were no quarrels!' the Marquis answered irritably. 'She'd just got herself engaged to my son – pulled off the undisputed catch of the season – and she wasn't ill that I know of. How long are you intending staying in Luxor?'

'Until I've exhausted every avenue. Obviously we can't do anything tonight and I have been travelling most of the day. Perhaps we could start in the morning?'

'I came here to see the Valley of the Kings and I do not intend to be put off by this silly business. I suggest you accompany us there. That way you'll have the opportunity to discover what you need to know to be going on with.'

'Do you all intend to visit the valley?' John asked in some dismay.

'My son and I are going – you're coming too, aren't you, Mallonden? – and no doubt Lady Poppy will be with us. I'm not sure about the other ladies.'

'I shall go,' said the Dowager Lady Mallonden. 'I haven't come this far to be dissuaded now. Poppy will look after me.'

'Yes, of course, Grandmother,' Poppy breathed.

'How about you, Lavinia?' Lord Mallonden asked.

'Certainly not! I'm in no mood for sightseeing. I shan't rest until my daughter is back with us – and I can't think that Mr Halliday will be gainfully employed in wandering about those wretched tombs.'

'Oh well, please yourself,' the Marquis said sharply. 'Do you intend to keep Margaret with you?'

'Margaret will want to stay with me, won't you, dear?'

When Margaret didn't speak, her grandmother said irritably, 'I suggest that Margaret comes with us. Mr Halliday will want to talk to each one of us. I understand you don't feel like sightseeing, Lavinia, but you should allow Margaret to come.'

Mrs Levison-Gore dabbed at her eyes but for the life of him John was unable to detect any sign of moisture. She graciously agreed, however, that Margaret should accompany the rest of them the following morning.

'We shall want you aboard at six,' the Marquis advised him. 'We want to get there before other tourists arrive. A felluca will take us to the other side of the river, then there will be donkeys to take us to the valley. Can we rely on your being here?'

'Yes, of course, Lord Camborne. I'll be here promptly at six.'

In later years, whenever he thought about that morning, Halliday couldn't resist smiling, though the humour of the situation gave no hint of the trauma to follow.

As he rode behind the ageing Dowager he couldn't help admiring the way she sat her donkey, her back straight and uncompromising, her arthritis momentarily forgotten as her head looked this way and that so as not to miss anything on the road which wound its way like a white thread through the heart of the Theban Hills.

It was a silent journey. The two girls rode on either side of their grandmother while the Marquis and the Earl followed, with Edward and John bringing up the rear. Behind them trotted the donkey-boys, silent since the Marquis had ordered them to stop their chattering because he wanted to enjoy the peace.

They were impressed with the barren valley in which no living thing grew, no living thing moved; for all that, it was surely the most wonderful place in the world.

John was glad of the silence, for he had seen nothing more impressive, nothing more poetic, nothing that filled his heart with so much awe as that sun-bathed valley.

They rode into its stillness from the fallen city of Thebes, into a kingdom of unearthly light, a kingdom of unearthly desolation. And the further they wandered the higher the barren cliffs rose and the world of light became a world of brilliant sadness . . .

Halliday had not ridden many minutes before forgetting that this valley of the tombs of the kings was a valley of death; he had forgotten because there was nothing in the valley to remind him of death. Instead, he was entirely enthralled by the great stillness and intoxicated by Egypt's unsurpassed quality of light.

The white road pierced its way through the pink hills into fresh sunlight where no shadows lay and a landscape of rugged cliffs, now towering up like precipice-rocks from a wild sea-coast, now soaring into the blue, needle-pointed like the pinnacles of a Gothic cathedral.

As John looked ahead at Meg's dainty figure seated on her nimble-footed donkey with her grandmother riding stoically at her side he had to remind himself that, surrounding them and beneath them, were temple-tombs of five centuries of Egypt's warrior kings, tombs as deep as mines, stretching for hundreds of feet through the barren hills. Decorated palaces, hidden from the world; eternal palaces in the bowels of the earth waiting patiently for the next royal mummy.

In those moments while they wandered awestruck along passages decorated lavishly with reliefs which looked as freshly cut now as they had looked when they were completed, Laura was momentarily forgotten. In one tomb they were asked to descend a long, winding shaft to discover not a mummy but a beautifully modelled, full-length portrait figure in white limestone. And then, dramatically, the guardian of the tomb turned on one dim electric light and, at the far end of the pillared hall, straight ahead of them, lay the magnificent figure of a dead Pharaoh stretched on the top of an immense limestone sarcophagus.

It was so beautiful that when they returned to the upper world even the sunshine and the hills did not have the power to obliterate what they had seen . . .

For several minutes they all stared at each other in silence, then Lord Mallonden said, 'I have seen the Street of the Tombs in Athens; I have walked many times along Rome's Appian Way, but this Valley of the Tombs of the Kings is the most impressive God's acre in the world. What do you think, Halliday?'

'I agree with you, sir. The mark Athens made in the world was concentrated into less than two hundred years but there were Pharaohs buried in this valley for more than five centuries.'

Again there was silence until, brusquely, the Marquis said, 'I suggest we go along to the rest-room and see if we can order something to drink. We must none of us forget why we're together this morning.'

Nobody answered him. Instead, they mounted their donkeys and rode in single file towards the rest-room. John could only guess with what irritation the Marquis was regarding Laura's escapade. How much more enjoyable it would have been if he could have absorbed the brightness and pinkness and peace of the royal valley without the intrusion of a thoughtless girl!

Halliday could see the weariness etched on old Lady Mallonden's face; Poppy Mallonden's anxiety, and Meg's confusion whenever her eyes met his. He gained the impression that Meg was avoiding him. Whenever his eyes met hers she looked elsewhere and he made up his mind to question her when he got the chance. Even at that moment the Marquis said sharply, 'Have a chat to my son. Maybe they did quarrel – maybe it's just a childish whim to get back at him. And talk to that sister of hers – she may know something we don't.'

John's opportunity to talk to Edward came as they rode back in the afternoon but, faced with Edward's moroseness, he found it difficult to begin to discuss Laura. Instead, they discussed banalities until Edward suddenly blurted out, 'We hadn't quarrelled, you know. My father seems to think we'd had a lover's tiff, but it isn't true. Her absence has nothing to do with me – if anything, it's the attitude of the rest of them that has got her down.'

'What exactly do you mean by that?'

'Between them they were impossible! My parents and the Mallondens were furious that I wanted to marry Laura instead of Poppy and they made it very obvious.'

'How about her mother?'

'Oh, she was delighted, but she's a bossy, pushy woman. I wasn't much relishing having her for a mother-in-law, but we'd have got around that. Laura would have been happier without her mother breathing down her neck all the time.'

'Surely the attitude of your parents couldn't have made her leave? After all, you must have reassured her that you were old enough to make up your own mind, that nothing they could do or say would alter things.'

'Well, of course I did.'

'When was the last time you saw your fiancée?'

'We'd been to Karnak. We spent all afternoon wandering about the temple. I would have preferred to go in the morning but there'd been a fancy-dress ball at the hotel the night before and nobody was disposed to set off early. It was deucedly hot and she looked a bit frail. I put it down to the dance and the heat. However, that night they came to the hotel to a concert and Laura was still pretty tired – so tired that I took her back as soon as the concert was over. I never saw her after that.'

'What was her manner like? Was she pleased to see you? Did you arrange to meet next morning?'

'She was weary – I took it for granted that we would meet the following day. If she didn't want to marry me, why didn't she say so? Why go along with the idea at all, unless it was to keep her mother quiet?'

'Who would you suggest I talk to next?'

'It's no use talking to my parents or her mother – they'll disclaim all idea that they're in any way to blame. Talk to Meg. If anybody knows anything it's Meg.'

'Have you talked to her?'

'I've tried. She simply scoots away whenever I try to approach her. And I doubt if Poppy knows anything.'

'Do you think Lady Poppy might be secretly pleased at the way things have turned out?'

'No! Poppy's a nice girl. I didn't want to marry her, but I like her. She wouldn't do anything mean or underhand, and she's not the sort of girl to gloat over what's happened.'

John urged his donkey forward to where the two girls rode side by side, noting that Meg immediately joined her grandmother and Lord Mallonden while Poppy obligingly allowed her donkey to fall into step beside his.

'What did you think of the tombs?' he asked calmly.

'Oh gosh, they were *marvellous*. I don't think I'll ever forget them. Actually, I'd like to take another look, but I'm not sure when we're leaving.'

'You're sailing on to Aswan, I understand?'

'That was the general idea, now I'm not so sure. They're talking about going back to Cairo. We can't really continue with a holiday when there's all this going on about Laura.'

She had presented him with every opportunity for further discussion about her cousin. 'Were you and your cousin good friends, Lady Poppy?'

'Well, yes. She was a nice girl. I hadn't seen an awful lot of her, really. She'd been at a finishing school in Switzerland for two years, and the family have never been too friendly with Aunt Lavinia. It's largely Granny,' she added, lowering her voice. 'She's never got over one of her sons marrying a woman she calls a foreigner. I've never thought of the Americans as foreigners though, have you?'

John smiled. 'I rather think they wished to be foreigners some little way back, but I know what you mean.'

'Well, of course Aunt Lavinia is a bit abrasive and life hasn't been easy for her. Her husband was killed in India and she had two daughters to bring up and educate. She hated India – Granny said it was because she couldn't be in England to keep tabs on the rest of us. I like Laura; she's so beautiful, I'm not surprised Edward fell in love with her.'

'It didn't hurt you?'

Poppy smiled. 'That he preferred her to me, do you mean? No, I expected it. I've grown up with the idea that one day Edward and I would marry. When I came out last year I didn't go to many of the bunfights because I wasn't looking for someone, there was always Edward, you see, and it saved Father a fortune. Edward was in Japan and this holiday was for us to meet again and hopefully like each other enough to announce our engagement. But we reckoned without Aunt Lavinia. By the time we got here Edward had met Laura and fallen in love with her.'

'And she with him?'

'Her mother was delighted . . .'

'You haven't answered my question, Poppy.'

'I don't know . . . I'm not pretty and I've never been

the sort of girl men drool over, but I've always been a dutiful daughter. I'm not at all sure Laura was like that. She was possibly more wayward. Meg's more like me.'

'What do you think has happened?'

'I honestly don't know.'

'Is there some other man she could have gone off with?'

'Oh, I'm sure there isn't! After all, when would she have met one? She's always been with Edward, at least since we arrived here. She told me she'd had a lovely time on the voyage out, but the boat sailed on, didn't it, taking all those young officers with her?'

'Yes, the boat sailed on.'

John was thoughtful. He was remembering Laura dancing in the arms of those young officers, her exquisite face alight with enjoyment – and then the sudden blushes whenever Prince Ahmed took his place at their table, her eyes following him whenever he walked across thc room. Surely not! The Prince had given her no encouragement and by now he was safely ensconced in the bosom of his family, no doubt looking forward to his approaching marriage.

Seeing his pensive expression Poppy said, 'You came out on the same boat, didn't you? Daddy said you'd know if there had been anyone on the boat.'

John smiled. 'I'm afraid not. I rarely set foot in the ballroom. I spent most of my nights at the bridge table and shipboard romances die as quickly as they spring to life. Well, I think perhaps it's time I had a word with her sister.'

He trotted on, and immediately Meg allowed her donkey to trot ahead so that he had to press his own donkey to go after her. He was convinced by now that Meg knew something, and absolutely certain when he caught up with her and saw her blushing face and eyes that refused to look at him.

'I think you and I should have a little talk, don't you?' he said pleasantly.

'What about?'

'About your sister. Don't you care what might have happened to her?'

'Well, of course I care! She'll be all right, she always is.'

'In a strange country, without an escort? Oh, come on now. Can't you see that everybody is very distressed about it, particularly your mother?'

'She told Mother not to worry about her, that she knew what she was doing.'

'That isn't enough, Meg. Your sister is a young Englishwoman in a strange country. It's our duty to do something to help. When we find her there might well be a great deal of trouble – and not only for Laura.'

'She'll be all right,' Meg said stubbornly.

'You feel so sure about that?'

'Yes!'

'I think you know more than you are telling me. I think your sister advised you to keep silent about her movements – but Meg, you are doing a great deal of harm in obeying her instructions. If you don't tell me of your own free will I'm afraid I shall have to speak to your mother.'

'I don't know anything!'

Her lips were set in a determined line, her small hands were clenched tightly round the reins and next moment she had urged her donkey forward. By the time they reached the river the donkey had been given over to its owner and Meg was waiting at the quayside. Halliday looked at her sternly, but she leapt aboard the felucca.

When they assembled on the dahabiyah, he was about to follow her when the Marquis said, 'Well, Halliday, have you learned anything that might help you to trace Edward's missing fiancée?'

'Nothing concrete, I'm afraid, but I'll work on it.'

'I don't think you need question my wife or Lady Mallonden. How about the girl's mother?'

'Not at the moment.'

'Well, one thing's for sure, we shan't be sailing on to Aswan. She won't have gone on to Aswan alone. She's more likely to have gone back to Cairo with a view to getting a passage home to England. She's causing us all a great deal of trouble and I, for one, think my son is well rid of her.'

'Would he agree with you, do you think?'

'He's a fool if he doesn't! Edward's always been one for going his own way and, unfortunately, he's the eldest son. I regretted it once before, I regret it now . . . Dine with us this evening if you wish – though you've probably seen enough of us for one day!'

Halliday shook his head. 'I must ask you to excuse me. I have a few ideas I need to think about but I'll come down to the boat after breakfast tomorrow.'

The Marquis nodded and stomped along the deck to his cabin while John went to the gangway. It was then that he saw Meg talking to a donkey-boy by the quayside and his interest quickened. The boy had been there the evening before when he had first set foot on the river-boat, and again this morning. Interesting . . . When Meg saw him approaching, she left the boy quickly and hurried past him along the quayside with her head averted.

John was intrigued. Egyptian donkey-boys frequented the ancient sites, clamouring for trade; they knew instinctively the nationality of anybody who employed them and consequently altered the names of their donkeys to accommodate that person. By haunting the steps above the moored dahabiyah this boy was losing valuable trade – and the fact that Meg had been so eager to talk to him made John doubly curious.

He fully expected the boy to offer his services when

he drew near to him, but he looked away across the river and, pausing, John retraced his steps. The boy looked up at him timidly.

'Is your donkey for hire?' John asked him.

'Perhaps later,' Joseph said.

'But not now?'

Joseph didn't answer.

'Are you waiting for someone? You were here last night and again this morning.'

The boy shrugged his shoulders, and John decided to try his luck.

'I doubt if the lady will require you today – she has other things to do. If I need you this evening shall I find you here?'

The boy nodded.

'Very well. I shall be here at nine-thirty. Can I rely on you?'

'Yes, my lord.'

John smiled and walked on. He would question the boy later and discover why Meg had been so anxious to talk to him. His years in the diplomatic service had equipped him for dealing with wilier adversaries than an Egyptian donkey-boy!

He looked up at the dahabiyah above him. There was no sign of Meg and he was glad that she had not remained on deck to witness his conversation with the boy.

14

It was almost as light as day when John Halliday made his way through the hotel gardens to the promenade. He had no guarantee that the boy would be waiting, but he suspected that Joseph had something to tell him.

The moonlight turned Luxor into an enchanting place.

As he stepped on to the promenade into the shadows another shadow left the harbour wall and then the boy was there, looking up at him hopefully, dragging his donkey behind him.

'You want me, my lord?' he asked hopefully.

'Yes. What is your name?'

'Joseph. Where does my lord wish to go?'

'Where do people usually go in the evening if they wish to absorb a little culture?'

'Culture?'

John smiled at the boy's puzzled air. 'I should have asked Miss Laura to tell me some of her favourite places but I forgot. I was sure you would know.'

He saw the sudden gleam in Joseph's eyes and he knew he had not been mistaken.

'I not see Miss Laura all day. She not go with you to royal valley?'

'No. Perhaps she had already been there.'

Joseph shook his head. 'Miss Laura go with her gentleman to Karnak, to Winter Palace Hotel, but not to royal valley.'

'Oh well, you will know her favourite places. You can take me to one of them.'

Again Joseph looked puzzled before saying, 'Is the English gentleman interested in antiques, then?'

'Are you saying that Miss Laura hired you to take her to some antique shop?'

Joseph nodded.

'What did she buy?'

'Joseph wait outside until she came out.'

'And then where did you take her?'

The boy's face was wholly innocent. 'Where else but to the dahabiyah?'

John Halliday knew that he lied.

'Very well, then,' he said easily. 'Take me to the antique shop. By the time we arrive there you may have remembered where else you took Miss Laura.'

Ali Mustapha's shop was in darkness but as soon as they arrived a light appeared within and John could only surmise that the sound of their arrival had penetrated the darkness.

Joseph disappeared into the shadows and, with much bowing and smiling, John was ushered into the shop. A chair was immediately brought forward by an old man and a second man, who introduced himself as Ali Mustapha, offered him mint tea as well as a box containing Egyptian cigarettes.

'You look like a man who seeks something authentic, something not made yesterday in antique factory,' the younger man said.

'Actually, I'm looking for a similar article to the one bought by a friend of mine some time recently. All I know is that it was beautiful and expensive.'

Glances were exchanged between the two men and, after a few moments, Ali Mustapha said, 'This antique – was it alabaster, jewellery, stonework? We need to know more, sir.'

'I'm afraid there is very little more I can tell you. A young English lady made the purchase, a very beautiful English lady sailing on a dahabiyah. If you can tell me what she bought, I shall be interested in purchasing something similar.'

Again the men exchanged looks, then the elder of the men said evenly, 'We have sold nothing to a young English lady recently. Old ladies with money come to buy, and many English gentlemen. Look, sir, at what we have. You find something very rare without seeing what the lady said she bought.'

John rose to his feet. 'I'm sorry to have wasted your time,' he said calmly. 'Obviously I am in the wrong shop.'

'This best shop in Luxor, in all Egypt! All our articles are old, very old, all are genuine. What she like, this young English lady?'

'Tall, slender, fair-haired. If she came into your shop you would not easily forget her.'

Another exchange of glances before the older man said, 'I think I remember the lady.'

Halliday met the man's eyes and after a long pause Ali Mustapha said quietly, 'I remember the lady, too, but she did not make any purchase from my shop.'

Taken aback, John was forced to gather his wits before saying, 'But she assured me she bought something from you!'

'No, sir. She was interested, very interested in the figure of a basalt cat. It was very old and very expensive. The lady said she could not afford to buy it.'

'Then if you still have it I would like to see it. It could be just what I am looking for.'

'Alas, sir, it was sold to a gentleman very soon after the lady looked at it.'

'And the gentleman?'

'A good customer who buys much from us. I cannot tell you the name of our customer; it would not be ethical, you understand, sir?'

John understood all right. He would discover nothing further from the men in the shop. He would have to see what more he could find out from Joseph.

Mounted again on his donkey, Joseph looked up at him for further instructions and John said, 'How far is it to Karnak from here?'

'Not far, sir, but it is late. Tourists long gone. Karnak very big, better to go first in daylight.'

'Very well, we will go back to the town, then.'

'Did the English gentleman get what he came for?' Joseph asked.

'Nothing that I wanted. Did you ever bring Lord Burlington here, Joseph?'

Joseph looked doubtful. 'Who is Lord Burlington?'

'Miss Laura's English gentleman.'

Joseph shook his head emphatically.

John was thoughtful as they rode back to Luxor. He could be on the wrong track altogether; it could have been a perfect stranger who had bought the article that Laura wanted. Joseph was now his only hope. From his devotion on the quayside it was evident that he thought a great deal of Laura.

They rode in silence, with Joseph trotting beside the donkey. John was the first to break the silence. 'I would like to go to Karnak tomorrow, Joseph. Will you meet me at the same place I found you earlier this evening?'

Joseph was hesitant and, after a few moments, John said, 'If you are otherwise engaged I will hire someone else. But if you think Miss Laura may need you, she will not.'

'Miss Laura, she is ill?'

'Miss Laura may be in some danger. I think you can help her, Joseph.'

'I not know Miss Laura, I only see her with her gentleman!' And Joseph fled, tugging hard at his donkey and urging the poor beast to climb the steps leading to the promenade. The boy was clearly afraid to be in any way connected with Laura's disappearance.

John had never been confident that his ruse would work, yet he was convinced that the boy knew more than he was saying. On that frustrating note he decided to call it a day.

He was awakened early next morning by a telephone call from Sir Archibald who sounded more irritable than usual.

'Has everything been sorted out, Halliday? I need you back here as soon as possible. Things are going crazy around here.'

John was accustomed to his chief's ramblings so he remained silent, waiting for enlightenment.

'An idiot took a potshot at one of the Sultan's men yesterday and a guard was wounded; the wretched Nationalist Party are causing mayhem – hot-headed young students who mistakenly believe they are patriots and who have their own ideas about the proper governing of their country. They're threatening to murder a good many important personages in the hope of filling their posts themselves. Now, when can I expect you back?'

'The young lady is still missing. I've talked to her relatives and her fiancé without learning much, but I do have a lead and I'm working on it. Do I understand that you want me back in Cairo before this matter has been resolved?'

'I'll give you another day. If nothing comes to light in that time you'd better get back – there are more important issues than the disappearance of a flighty debutante. And if Camborne gives you any trouble, tell him you're a diplomat attached to the British Embassy, not a nursemaid!'

Halliday was not relishing his meeting with the Marquis and, after breakfast, he walked towards the dahabiyah despondently, so lost in thought that he did not see Joseph until the boy tugged at his sleeve, saying urgently, 'Sir, Joseph will speak. I tell you all I know.'

The boy was evidently afraid and John, in an endeavour to put him at his ease, smiled down at him. Summoning all his courage, Joseph told him about Laura's visit to Ali Mustapha's shop, followed by the visit to the white house on the banks of the Nile, then the second visit, of only two days later, when he had waited all night for her to rejoin him.

'Do you know who owns the white house?' John asked urgently.

For a moment the boy hesitated, then, seeing the stern expression on the Englishman's face, he said, 'It is owned by Prince Ahmed Farag. It is the prince Miss Laura loves, not the red-faced English gentleman.'

'Will you take me to the white house, Joseph?' Halliday said at last.

'I take you, sir, but the house is empty. Everybody has left.'

'How do you know this?'

'I went yesterday when you were visiting royal valley. I walked through gardens but the house is all shuttered. There was a gardener but I hid from him. The Prince's dahabiyah gone too, from the mooring place.'

'I see.'

'You think Miss Laura go with her prince? She be happy with him, they love each other. I saw them embrace when I wait for her.'

'I wish it was that simple, Joseph.'

'Joseph know Miss Laura not love her English gentleman. She very sad. But when I take her back to boat after she be with Prince Ahmed her eyes shine like stars. How beautiful she was that night, how happy!' The boy's eyes were as tender as his memories of Laura.

They stood on the promenade with the pillars of

the Luxor temple rising behind them and the broad river before them.

'You still wish to go to house near the river, sir?' Joseph asked hopefully.

'No, Joseph. I don't think it will be necessary. You have helped me a great deal.'

He reached into his pocket and pulled out a handful of notes which he pressed into the boy's hand. Joseph's eyes grew round at the sight of so much money, more than he could hope to earn in a year. With a little smile John advised him to buy something useful.

With shining eyes Joseph said, 'I buy fruit and vegetables for my mother and another donkey. Will Miss Laura ever come back to Luxor, sir?'

'I don't know Joseph. Perhaps one day, who knows.'

'You will go away now, sir?'

'Very soon, perhaps tomorrow.' He took the boy's hand and pressed it, then, resolutely, he walked on to the dahabiyah and another meeting with its occupants.

'Well,' Lord Camborne demanded. 'Have you any news for us?'

Halliday realised immediately that Lord Camborne was losing patience. The frustrations of the days since Laura's disappearance had taken their toll and John was prepared to be diplomatic.

'Nothing concrete – but I have several lines I need to follow up. I am considerably more hopeful than I was yesterday.'

'What's that supposed to mean?'

'I don't know where the young lady is – but I have a very good idea why she left and who she is with.'

'Then I want to know! My son has a right to know and so has the girl's mother. Good God, man, surely you must know what misery they've been going through?'

'Give me another day. I have to go back to Cairo tomorrow on a matter of some urgency but in the meantime I'll find out as much as I can and let you have the full story very soon.'

'Damn it, man, that's not good enough! You say you know why she left and who she is with – at least tell us that much. Where she is can come later.'

'By now she could be regretting her actions, Lord Camborne. I don't want to say anything at this stage to prevent you taking Miss Laura back into the family circle if it's her wish to return to it.'

'We'll be the judge of that! The girl has only herself to blame for anything we decide. Now why did she leave and where has she gone?'

'She left to go to the man she was in love with. Neither of them are in Luxor and where they are is something I have yet to discover.'

There was a little cry from Meg as she rushed towards her mother who sat with her face frozen in anger.

'You say my daughter is with some man or other?' she demanded.

'I believe so, Mrs Levison-Gore.'

'That is utter nonsense. Laura does not know anybody in Egypt, it is her first visit. Besides, she has been constantly with Edward since we arrived here. Edward, why don't you say something, you know that's true.'

Edward remained silent and Lord Mallonden said sharply, 'Who is the fella? And where the devil did she meet him?'

'She met him before she arrived in Cairo.'

'Where?' old Lady Mallonden demanded. 'She is little more than a schoolgirl. I don't believe in all this, it's nonsense.'

'Then allow me to continue with my enquiries,' John said in some exasperation. 'If things have quietened down in Cairo I hope to get back as soon as possible.'

'What's more important than this?' Lord Camborne demanded. 'I'll have a lot to say to Sir Archibald when we get to Cairo. There's no need for you to come back here, Halliday. We'll be in Cairo ourselves within the next few days.'

'There have been attempts on the lives of the Sultan and Lord Minton, so I think you will agree that Sir Archibald is right in ordering me back to Cairo.'

Nobody spoke and, with a brief smile, John left them to mull over what he had just told them. He had almost reached the gangway when the sound of running feet made him turn to see Meg racing along the deck towards him.

'Mr Halliday!' she called breathlessly. 'Please, tell me that Laura is all right!'

Looking down at her sternly he said evenly, 'You could have helped me more than you did. I suppose that was out of so-called loyalty to your sister?'

She had the grace to look momentarily ashamed, then she said in little more than a whisper, 'She begged me not to tell them anything and I promised! She fell in love with him on the boat coming here and even though he told her there could never be anything permanent between them, she was determined about it – Laura was always so headstrong – she didn't want to marry Edward.'

'It is a great pity she didn't show her determination much earlier!'

'I know . . . What will they do to Laura when she comes back?'

'My dear young lady, I'm not at all sure that she's coming back!'

'Well, no . . . not if she and Ahmed are married. She'll be a princess, won't she, and he's really very rich? Perhaps everything will be all right – Poppy will marry Edward and I'll be able to visit Laura here one day.'

John smiled. Oh, the sublime optimism of youth, he thought grimly, watching Meg walking back to the salon.

15

Two mornings later John faced his chief once more and found him no more amenable than on their last meeting. Sir Archibald had spent a very discomfiting few days. The Nationalist Party was in full cry; the Sultan waiting to be proclaimed king was a frightened man and those around him were feeling very insecure.

He'd been instructed by the Foreign Office to play it cool, but how could he do that when everybody else was dithering and, to cap it all, he had a wife who was urging him to retire immediately, she'd had enough; all she wanted was to get home to England, settle down in their comfortable manor and raise cocker spaniels.

Now here was Halliday telling him that Laura Levison-Gore had eloped with the son of one of the Sultan's top ministers, a man every bit as stiff-necked and autocratic as the Marquis of Camborne, and in no time it could all blow up into a political nightmare.

'Do you suppose they're married?' he demanded.

'That I don't know,' Halliday replied. 'They sailed south to Aswan, I gather, and by this time they're probably in the Sudan – or anywhere at all!'

'Well, it's stirred up a whole hornets' nest, I can tell you! Farag is a man of some consequence, a king-maker, and he's educated his eldest son to follow in his footsteps. I'll check them out in Aswan and I want you to contact Sawyers in Khartoum; tell him to keep his eyes and ears open. I tell you, Halliday, this is a problem I could have done without!'

Oblivious and uncaring about the problems she had created, Laura stood with Ahmed on the deck of his dahabiyah staring out at the display of splendour that was the night sky.

The silence of the mimosa-scented darkness was broken by the sound of singing and they turned to witness the Nubian boatmen dancing to music played on an instrument Laura had never seen before.

Wide grins illuminated the men's faces and Laura and Ahmed gave themselves up to the pleasure of watching and listening until suddenly a tall, graceful Nubian came and bowed before them. He was grave and silent and he carried a long swinging lantern of white paper and a staff like a shepherd's crook.

'It is time to go, Master,' he said solemnly.

They followed him along the deck and down the gangway, and it was then that Laura took off her shoes and walked barefoot along the rise that led to the temple of Abu Simbel.

Ahmed squeezed her hand gently, whispering, 'This temple is like no other in all Egypt . . .'

There had been so many temples, and Laura had learned a great deal from Ahmed on their journey from Luxor into Nubia. He had promised to show her this temple when the last tourist had gone and under the light of a full moon. When she had asked him why it was so important for them to visit it at that time he had said, gravely, 'To me, Abu Simbel far out-distances even the great pyramids themselves in its sense of imperishableness and infinitude of age.'

Minutes later, when she gazed at the colossal figures seated in stiff solemnity on either side of the portal in the rock, their rough strength and serenity of expression made her feel that God, at the very beginning of time, must have breathed upon the sun-warmed cliff and commanded those kingly figures into life.

The faces of the Pharaoh who had built it, Rameses the Second, were sublimely beautiful. Rameses had built the temple in honour of the Sun God but, drily,

Ahmed said he doubted that Rameses had had the Sun God in mind. Rather, he had ordered its construction as a monument to his own imperial and divine power.

'Why do you say that?' she whispered.

'As was usual when this great monarch built a temple, the god to whom it was dedicated was of minor importance compared to himself. When the building was completed it was Rameses, not a god, whom you were asked to worship.'

'Were all the Pharaohs egotistical?'

'No, like all kings there were good and bad. Even Rameses had many good points – he was not a bad king. There is the temple he built in honour of his queen, the beautiful Nefertari, which proves that even the formidable Rameses was not ashamed to fall in love.'

How she loved him! Seeing Egypt with Ahmed had been a very different experience from the one she had experienced when they were in the hands of local guides. Here was a man who loved his country and gloried in its long history. She only had to watch the way his hands lingered lovingly on sun-kissed stone and smooth, cold alabaster. As they returned to the dahabiyah she could see that a fire had been lit on the desert sand and their Sudanese crew sat in a circle around it.

Chairs had been brought out for them to watch the boatmen's performance and Laura's eyes shone with delight as she watched their genius for making music even out of two bottles and a key. As they warmed to their music she thought she had never seen such gleaming eyes – polished by passion as cut onyx – and teeth as white and sharp as a dog's.

Only one youth performed at a time, but the grace and sympathy of every performance was amazing. Beautiful brown-limbed youths bending and posturing, dancing with every nerve of the body brought into play, dancing with slim hands and slender neck and polished back, with eyes and senses, feet stepping two paces forwards and two backwards, not on their toes, but on the narrow soles.

In the shadow of the dahabiyah, under the light of the round full moon and with the unspoilt world of Nubia all around them, Laura knew that this was a night she would remember for the rest of her life, whatever it held in store for her.

She and Ahmed were desperately in love, living a life composed of sun-kissed days and dark balmy nights when she lay in his arms, warm and contented after love.

Young and selfish, unconcerned with what their love might do to others, Laura had no regrets. She missed her sister, but she had no yearnings for her mother. And Edward, poor Edward, he would soon find somebody else to love, she thought dismissively. Poppy was a nice girl. By this time he was probably thinking he'd had a lucky escape and had turned to Poppy for consolation.

The family would be glad to have her out of the way, leaving the path clear for Poppy. Edward's parents, too, would have few regrets after they'd recovered from the jilting of their son.

Ahmed kept his thoughts to himself. There were times when she found him pensively staring out across the river, his thoughts turned inwards. At those moments, how she longed for him to tell her what troubled him but he merely favoured her with his sweet, grave smile.

There were a great many questions she wanted to ask him. When were they returning to Cairo? When would she meet his parents? Where would they live and when would they marry? But that tantalising gravity she sensed in Ahmed made her keep silent and, oh, she wanted to be his wife.

More and more she was beginning to realise that, although love united them, it was that elusive Eastern part of Ahmed which divided them, a part of him that she might never understand. He seemed content to sail southwards towards Wadi Halfa and one day she asked where he intended to go when they reached the second cataract. For a moment he seemed uncertain, then, as if he was desperately seeking a reason to put distance between them and all they had left behind, he said, 'Why not into the Sudan, to Khartoum? We will take the desert train. Khartoum may interest you, darling, so much of English history is concerned with it.'

So they left their dahabiyah and boarded the white train with its wide verandahed roof and double blue-glass windows in what Laura could only think of as a light-hearted and holiday mood.

There was a great deal of bustle from excited porters when their luggage was safely deposited in their sleeping compartments and soon they were in a wilderness of golden sand, and its forests of palm trees with the occasional gazelle to be glimpsed on the horizon.

The train was luxurious by any standard – Eastern luxury coupled with Western needs. In the well-appointed drawing-room car, bridge tables were set up and Laura asked herself: Why are we rushing through this limitless desert, through a world so desolate that the very telegraph posts seem human and friendly?

From the observation car she found herself looking long and intently at a pair of railway lines laid straight across the desert, two glittering bands of metal meeting at the converging point and vanishing into space, and she thought: These two lines are our connecting link with far-off civilisation; they are our only link with the past, all that we have left behind, all that we hope to return to.

In the fierce midday hours, how arrogantly those

railway lines shone, how blue they looked, stretching on and on across the yellow sand, how strangely imbued with humanity. What curious things can give us nostalgia, she thought: two long steel lines vanishing into space, vanishing into a distance which means civilisation and human sympathy, and telegraph posts which speak of home and friends.

In the desert she had seen nothing for days but sky and sand, sunsets that had left them breathless and silence deep and profound, yet she could imagine a telegraph post making a strong man weep.

She was sorry they had come to Khartoum. Totally unimpressed by the large, opulent hotel she yearned for the peace of the Nile and the leisurely life on the dahabiyah. Here were newspapers, and open curiosity at the sight of a beautiful English girl in the company of a handsome Egyptian. Two people obviously in love, two people to be whispered about behind the potted palms by other Englishwomen over their teacups . . .

Laura had lost all count of time and she stared at Ahmed in some amazement when he pressed a long, slender package into her hands before they went down to breakfast on their third day in Khartoum. When she was hesitant in opening it he said, softly, 'Had you forgotten that today is Christmas Day, Laura? Happy Christmas, darling.'

'Oh Ahmed! I had forgotten. Nothing here seems like Christmas – you must know the sort of Christmasses we English are accustomed to spending.'

He smiled. 'You'll find the hotel will put on roast turkey and plum pudding, probably even a choir from the English Church, but there won't be snow and robins. Aren't you going to open your present?'

'But I haven't got you anything, Ahmed! I feel dreadful about that.'

'I have everything I shall ever want – and now I

have you to share it with me. Nothing you could ever give me could give me greater pleasure.'

With a delighted smile her fingers tore at the wrapping paper, disclosing a leather box embossed with gold. On opening it she stared with wonder at a long diamond necklace and matching earrings.

'Oh Ahmed,' she breathed. 'How absolutely perfect! Thank you so much.'

He smiled. 'This evening you can wear them to outshine every woman in the room – but then, your beauty has done that already . . .'

The hotel had indeed done their best. There were Christmas crackers on the tables and the hotel orchestra played the carols she had known from childhood. In the evening they danced to music played by a regimental band and Laura wore the gown her mother had insisted she wear for Edward, now adorned with the diamonds which made every woman in the room look on with envy.

Nothing was lost on the young man who had sauntered casually into the ballroom from the bar. For several minutes he stood smoking his cigarette, watching the dancing, then he left as unobtrusively as he had entered. Minutes later he was in his room, putting through a call to Cairo . . .

Two days later Ahmed informed Laura that they must go back to Cairo as soon as possible. He was holding the morning newspaper in his hand and there was an anxious look on his face which caused her alarm.

'Something is wrong, Ahmed? What is it? Why must we go back so soon?'

'There has been an attempt on the life of the Sultan and a member of his staff has been seriously hurt. I am worried about my father.'

Laura knew little about Egyptian politics, so she waited patiently for him to tell her more.

'There is trouble from the Nationalist Party – young hotheads who think they could govern Egypt better than the people who do so. They are utterly ruthless and do not hesitate to kill whoever stands in their way.'

'Oh Ahmed! And you too if you go back there,' she cried unhappily.

'It is my duty to go back, Laura.' He was gripping her hands, making her look into his eyes, eyes from which all trace of laughter had gone, eyes that were dark and deadly serious in a face whose stern beauty was compelling. 'Perhaps it's time we started thinking about the rest of our lives. We have to face reality, and reality may be very hurtful to both of us.'

She was gazing up at him with wide, questioning eyes, and he knew that she did not fully understand what he was trying to tell her.

'Why, Ahmed? Why should we be afraid of the future? We *love* each other. Oh Ahmed, you're not going back to be with her, you're not going to leave me?'

He looked at her beautiful, pleading face and the words he wanted to say would not come. He could not tell this lovely, anxious girl that love wasn't enough, that they would have to face prejudice, resentment, alienation – from both their people.

His family would not like this beautiful girl he had fallen in love with. In his father's eyes her beauty would count for nothing; the world was full of beautiful women. Men married for expediency, they made mistresses of beautiful women; concubines, not wives.

His mother was strong but dutiful – she would not take his part against his father. Laura would never understand a home conducted on Eastern principles. His father disdained any sign of Western decadence in the furnishing of his many palaces; when she left the sand and the sunshine behind, Laura would soon discover that medieval Egypt would take command, a command as old as the banners of Saladin which once swept through the ancient ramparts of a country whose history was almost as old as time.

Ahmed did not have the courage to tell her then and, like two leaves in the wind, they were propelled onwards towards sorrow and disaster . . .

16

It fell to Sir Archibald to inform the Marquis and his fellow travellers on their return to Cairo that his son's fiancée was somewhere south of Egypt with Prince Ahmed Farag. He knew for a fact, now, that they had sailed towards Aswan in the Prince's own dahabiyah. Indeed, the boat was still anchored there, because the Prince had hired another to take them on to the second cataract at Wadi Halfa and from there they had boarded the desert train for Khartoum.

Mrs Levison-Gore's face had crumpled, like a mummy exposed suddenly to strong sunlight. In an instant she appeared old and ill while her other daughter sobbed quietly by her side.

Old Lady Mallonden's face became pinched and furious and the other two women dissolved into tears, while the men looked on incredulously. Sir Archibald felt most sorry for Edward Burlington – it wasn't easy to accept that the girl you were engaged to had eloped with somebody else, and that somebody a foreigner, even if he was a prince.

'Well, there's nothing more to be said,' Lord Camborne said at last. 'The girl's gone – and if she came back on her bended knees you wouldn't want her, Edward. I think we'd all better get back to London and forget the entire unhappy episode. I'm sorry, Lavinia, she's your daughter, but there's no point in us hanging on here any longer.'

'I don't think it's quite that simple, Lord Camborne. The girl may need her family since the young man's family can't be guaranteed to accept her. Farag is a stiff-necked Egyptian official who will be as angry with the situation as you are. He will view his son's involvement with this English girl as a catastrophe and may insist that she be returned to her family.'

'Will he, indeed?' snapped the Marquis. 'And suppose the family are not prepared to take her back? The girl's escapade has ruined any hope of a life in England. The best thing that could happen to her is for her to marry this Egyptian and stay in his country. At some future date, no doubt, she'll be consigned to a harem of sorts.'

'The Farags do not keep a harem, to my knowledge,' Sir Archibald replied drily. 'This young man was affianced to the daughter of another of the Khedive's officials, so it's a very tricky business altogether.'

'What do you want us to do, then?' Lord Mallonden asked.

'Remain in Cairo for a few more days. By then I may have some more concrete news for you. Halliday's back in Luxor but I'll be recalling him tonight – the political situation is worsening.'

In a native café of dishonourable repute in a lonely suburb of Cairo, three young men, members of the Advanced Nationalist Party, were awaiting the arrival of their fourth companion.

Their talk was completely at variance with the clear heavens and the soft desert wind which moved the jasmine flowers against the archways. From the desert came the idle notes of a flute-player who was sitting cross-legged on the sand, sending across the desert sweet, fancy, birdlike notes from his long reed pipe; and the sharp barking of wolf-dogs, which bedouin farmers set loose at night to guard their flocks from raiding jackals, came from the far horizon.

At the entrance to the café, on a raised divan near the door, a bearded Turk, well-fed and yellow-slippered, lay smoking his 'hubble-bubble'. The long red tube of his pipe reached from the floor to his sensual lips, his eyes were half-closed in ecstatic enjoyment. Nothing could have looked more peaceful than this scene, or more typically Oriental. The interior of the building, which stretched a considerable way back, was filled with all-night gamblers and hashish-smokers, all of them oblivious to the three men whispering together with intent, hard expressions on their young faces.

A fourth man joined them. He was of Middle Eastern appearance but not Egyptian; he had a large hooked nose and was wearing a stained white suit, and his narrow eyes glittered in a face that was both cruel and dissipated.

He did most of the talking and in the initial period there seemed to be some opposition. Then suddenly a bargain was struck, a handful of money was produced which, not bothering to count, the man thrust into the pocket of his jacket. Without another word he rose from the table and strode out into the night.

The men who remained seemed well pleased with their bargain. They rose, shook hands and two of them departed while the third man went to the back of the café and joined one of the gambling tables. The two men left the café just in time to see the man in the white suit enter a dilapidated taxi which drove down the winding street into the city. They parted company at the junction in the road and when, several hours later, the café was raided by the police only the one man remaining there was arrested.

John Halliday received Sir Archibald's telephone call just as he was about to retire for the night. He was to return to Cairo the following day because the intelligence reports indicated that there were likely to be further attempts on the lives of important people, both English and Egyptian, and it was more important to be in the capital than chasing after a silly young girl.

'I don't suppose you've anything to report in that quarter?' Sir Archibald said.

'Only that they have left Khartoum to return to Wadi Halfa.'

'Is that so? Then they, too, could be returning to Cairo – in which case you can kill two birds with one stone.'

'You want me to approach them?'

'Certainly not! At least, not until their lordships have said what is to be done.'

Halliday went to bed wishing fervently that he was back in his old job in the Far East. Nothing like this had ever troubled him there.

It was barely light when Ahmed and Laura left their dahabiyah for the railway station in Aswan. Ahmed had given instructions to his crew to return the boat to its mooring in Luxor while Laura was finishing her packing.

Her thoughts about returning to civilisation were mixed. Like a spoilt child she had believed they could go on for ever in that dreamy state of being the only two people in the world, a world of desert sunsets and a silence so complete that even the distant tinkle of camel bells sounded like a noisy clamour in her ears.

It was a strange new world she would be returning to; the only thing she was sure of was Ahmed's love. As for the rest, it lay hidden in that dark medieval city of the Caliphs and the Mamelukes, with its labyrinth of narrow streets, its white arabesqued domes and soaring minarets. For the first time she experienced a pang of regret when she thought of all she had left behind her – long country weekends and tea dances, rides across the Sussex Downs with England's gentle rain against her face and the scented cosiness of coffee lounges in the London shops she adored.

Ahmed had been reticent about the life she might expect to lead as his wife. He told her that his mother seldom went into the city but preferred her life in the Fayoum where she was involved with matters concerning her family.

'At times she will accompany my father to functions, but she has no love for city life,' he'd said calmly – and there was something in his voice that had precluded her from questioning him further.

Laura was too happy in her love for him to look beyond the present; love would solve everything, she told herself. She was not to know that it was not their future together which troubled Ahmed now. In his Egyptian heart there were sterner matters ahead than the problem of his love for her.

Laura did not bother herself with the English newspapers, which were out of date by the time they arrived, and she did not understand Arabic. So she knew nothing of the news in the Egyptian press which was concerning Ahmed: the attempts on the lives of the Sultan, his Prime Minister and Lord Minton, which fortunately had been foiled.

Ahmed was now deploring the time he had selfishly spent sailing the river when his place was with his family. He had spoken to his father on the telephone to tell him of his intended return and his father had been distant, answering his questions in monosyllables. Yes, his mother was well. No, he had been in no personal danger. Yes, it was true that a certain element in the city was causing disturbances.

There had been no mention of Laura; all the same, he knew that his father was well aware of her existence. News travelled fast in a country where men of wealth and power were still exalted.

They were travelling light. Ahmed's servants walked

ahead with their luggage, pushing their way through the crowds of people sitting on the ground with their chickens and goats, their donkeys and camels laden with their possessions. Some of them were obsequious while others were surly – and if Ahmed was aware of it, Laura was not. She was enchanted by the novelty of it all, by a group of Sudanese dancers performing in the centre of an appreciative crowd . . .

They were in that part of the train reserved for travelling dignitaries and the attendant ushered them into a spacious compartment which would have done credit to a first-class hotel. Many tourists did not trouble to travel beyond Luxor, so the train was not full and, although Laura went to the window to gaze at the activity outside, Ahmed sat back with the morning paper in his hands.

Dawn was like a silent blush in the eastern sky when the train started its journey to the capital and Laura felt strangely sad. The golden days were over and Ahmed was different. If she had but known it, Ahmed was troubled. He did not like the emptiness of the compartments around them and he did not like their Nubian attendant. Normally, Nubians were all smiles and geniality, but this man averted his eyes when he spoke to them, and his black face only registered a certain veiled insolence.

When the man served them lunch with silent servility, Ahmed began to doubt his wisdom in deciding to journey by train. The attempt on Lord Minton's life had been made on the journey between Alexandria and Cairo and now he sensed something entirely sinister in the emptiness of their section of the train and in the attendant's manner.

He did not speak of his concern to Laura, who was serenely gazing out of the window as the train sped onwards to Luxor. It was early afternoon when they arrived there and Laura gazed nostalgically at the beautiful wide river and the pink pillars of the Temple of Luxor, visible above the housetops.

'It seems an eternity since we left Luxor,' she said plaintively. 'I wonder if the family are still here.'

He looked up in some surprise. 'That is the first time I have heard you mention them, Laura. It can't be the first time you've thought about them?'

'No, of course not,' she said quickly. 'But when we were in the south it was different. Now we're here, and it was here where it all really began. I wonder if they went on to Aswan or if they returned to Cairo?'

'I rather think they would return to Cairo. My darling girl, how could you expect them to continue with their holiday as if nothing had happened?'

What would his mother think of this girl from the West with her gay assumption that her beauty and her love were all that mattered? And would Laura crumble under the restraints her new life would place around her?

Tourists thronged the platform; English milords and their families travelling back to England for the start of the Season, Germans in knickerbocker trousers and pith helmets . . . Jumping to her feet, Laura said, 'I'm going to look for our attendant as soon as the train starts. He'll forget my tea now that the train is so crowded.'

'You needn't look for him, we'll ring for him,' Ahmed said reasonably.

'But darling, I've been sitting here all morning! I need to stretch my legs and I want to take another look at Karnak from the train. Why don't you come with me?'

He shook his head, amused at her enthusiasm. 'You won't be impressed with Karnak from the train, Laura. You would be well advised to remember it in the moonlight.'

They smiled at each other across the room. 'I won't

be long, Ahmed,' she whispered, loving his tenderness, and, with another smile, she was out of the door, sending him back to his more serious thoughts.

Laura went first to the small compartment at the end of the corridor where she hoped to find the attendant, but it was empty so she carried on to the one beyond. People were standing at the windows to catch their last sight of Karnak and a man moved aside politely to make room for her at the window.

'Great sight, isn't it?' he said with a smile.

'Yes, it's wonderful – but more wonderful in the moonlight.'

She did not recognise him – but then why should she? A prosy bachelor no longer in his first youth. Besides, while Laura had been dancing the night away on the ship coming out, he had been occupied with his cronies at the bridge table.

She was as beautiful as he remembered her and he looked down at her appreciatively while she stared out at the fast-disappearing columns of Karnak.

'What will you remember most about Egypt?' he asked with every intention of continuing their conversation.

She paused to think, then, with a bright smile, she said at last, 'The sunsets and those glorious pink hills.'

'Not the temples or the Valley of the Kings?'

'Well, I loved them all, particularly Abydos, but I shall be living in Cairo and hopefully I'll see them again quite soon.'

'You're not on holiday, then?'

'Not any more. And you?'

'I am in Egypt to work. I have a flat in Heliopolis.'

'Then we may meet in Cairo. Please tell me a little about Cairo. I believe the Opera House is quite magnificent and I remember the tea dances in the hotels. I think it is the shops I shall miss most.'

'I take it you mean shops like the English ones. There are some in the Western part of the city – but why hanker after the West when the native part of Cairo is so much more interesting with its bazaars and the life that flows and loiters along its pavements?'

'You talk as though you love the East better than you love the West.'

'Some tourists never discover the East; their eyes see no beauty except in the luxury of the European hotels and overpaid dragomans. There they dance and eat and talk, and bargain for feather fans and fly-switches, and change their dresses all day long. Very few of them would believe you if you were to tell them that a life teeming with interest lies within a stone's throw of their hotels.'

'How can an Englishman prefer that part of Cairo to the Westernised part?'

'I will tell you, my dear, what I have seen in every great city of the East that it's been my privilege to live in – a street of European cafés, where Orientals of all nations mix together and ridicule, or gaze with covetous eyes upon, the fair European travellers as they pass by in carriages or on foot to visit the shops where fools pay fools' prices for foolish things. I hope *you* will discover another Cairo with its rich architecture, the grace of its minarets and its elegance.'

'I'm so glad I've met you. I really do hope we meet again in Cairo,' she said with a radiant smile. 'You've made me feel much happier about my life there.'

Shyly, she offered her hand and he took it, smiling down at her.

'It is possible, of course,' he said gently. 'My name is John Halliday.'

'I must see if I can find our attendant,' she said, turning away. 'He's been most inattentive and I'm longing for afternoon tea.'

He watched her making her way along the compartment and out through the door at the end of it. He was returning to Cairo to inform his superior and the girl's family of all he had managed to learn about her whereabouts; now he had found out so much more. Quite evidently, she expected to marry her prince and live with him in Cairo. It was a situation which would no doubt raise questions in exalted circles.

He moved to return to his seat and his newspaper, but before he reached his compartment there came the sound of an explosion and then all he was aware of was the sickening lurch of the carriage, the lights going out and people screaming in terror. He was thrown with a jarring thud against the end of one of the seats and the entire carriage was sliding and moving sideways while above the sound of chaos a baby's shrill cry echoed poignantly . . .

In later years, whenever he thought about that explosion, John Halliday could not remember how he had managed to climb out of the mangled carriage into the late afternoon sunlight. He stared around him in dismay. The rear of the train was an unrecognisable wreck while the rest of it reeled drunkenly off its tracks.

A crowd of passengers and crew had managed to jump on to the ground at the side of the rails but others were still moaning pitifully from inside the train. His shoulder ached from the blow it had received, but he joined in helping to pull people from the wreckage and, although he worked mechanically, his thoughts were on the occupants of the wrecked carriages. Obviously the explosion was the result of a bomb planted on board the train and, as soon as he had reassured himself that there were sufficient helpers to aid those left in his carriage, he made his way along the tracks to the rear of the train.

A group of British soldiers who had been travelling at the front were already helping to move debris and lift out the bodies. A young officer, who appeared to be directing operations, said briefly, 'If you've come to lend a hand, sir, there are still some people in there, though I doubt if any of them have survived this.'

'I take it someone of note was travelling on the train,' John said quietly.

'Four British officers that we know of, two brigadiers and two colonels. There must have been some other reason to blow up the train.'

'Have you got them out?'

'Three of them, all dead. My men are still in there, some are trapped under the debris. It may take some time to release them.'

'I'll see what I can do to help.'

'Better leave it to the men, sir. You can help further down the train.'

'My name is Halliday, from the British Embassy. I was on my way back there . . .'

'Sorry, sir! Go right ahead, but you can understand the need for caution.'

There seemed to be nothing left of the opulent carriages except for rich drapes hanging grotesquely across crumbling walls.

A sergeant called out to him, 'Mind 'ow you go, sir! Test the ground before you steps on it – one o' the lads just fell through that 'ole there.'

Gingerly, John did as he had been told but he soon realised it was hopeless to try to distinguish one compartment from the next and his sympathy was with a young soldier who was visibly sick in spite of his sergeant's withering remarks.

By this time, a stream of ambulances and police cars were arriving from Luxor, as news of the disaster filtered through. It fell to John to escort bruised and battered passengers to the waiting transport.

Suddenly, his thoughts turned to Laura and he scanned the groups of onlookers for her. The front of the train leaned drunkenly but was otherwise unscathed, except that some of the wheels had left the tracks, but Laura had come from the back of the train and his eyes looked bleakly on all that was left of it.

If Ahmed Farag had been in that compartment there was little hope that he was still alive – and somebody had to break the news to her. His steps quickened as he hurried along the sand beside the track, stared at stupidly by people in the carriages above him. He climbed into the train where mothers were intent on stemming the tears of their children, where luggage had fallen from the racks above and he had to try to make his way through it. It was his guess that Laura would not have ventured too far along the train in case she came across people who had known her, and in this he was correct.

Laura had been on her way back when the explosion occurred. Caught between two carriages she had been flung against the door with her head striking the heavy brass door handle. Providentially, she knew nothing more and it was there that John found her, lying in a heap with blood matted in her hair . . .

17

Several hours later John Halliday waited in the corridor of the small hospital in Luxor for the latest information about Laura who had been carried, unconscious, from the scene of the devastation.

A little earlier he had stared down at the still form of Prince Ahmed Farag, lying lifeless under a white sheet along with the others who had died, all of them British. John had looked at the handsome face, from which death had eradicated every expression, and he had difficulty in remembering the strong, virile young man who had captivated the beautiful Laura. Now he faced the dreadful task of telling her that her lover was dead . . .

A nurse wearing a huge white coif on her head approached him along the corridor and he was relieved when she spoke to him in English.

'You are Mr Halliday?'

'Yes. Is Miss Levison-Gore able to see me?'

'She is awake but confused. Perhaps if she remembers you, Mr Halliday . . .'

'I'm not sure about that. We met on the boat coming out here, but she didn't remember me when we met again on the train.'

'Was she travelling alone?'

'No, the man she was travelling with was killed. If she had remained in their compartment she, too, would be dead.'

'I see. Well, please be gentle with her, Mr Halliday. It might not even be possible to tell her tonight.'

Laura lay against her pillows and there was no disguising the blue-black bruise on the side of her face, or the fact that she looked at him entirely without recognition.

When he told her his name, it was obvious from her blank expression that it had not registered, so he said, gently, 'We met on the voyage out. We also met on the train, Laura.'

Tears came into her eyes, but they were tears of frustration because she did not remember him.

He pulled up a chair so that he could sit beside her bed. 'How do you feel?' he asked, gently.

'My head hurts. I must have bumped it somewhere.'

'What is the last thing you remember?'

She frowned, and for a long time there was silence. Then, in a small voice, she said, 'I remember the moonlight shining on the temple from the terrace. I remember there was a boat, a river-boat . . .'

'With your mother and other members of your family?'

'Yes, I remember *that* boat. Granny Mallonden was there and Meg. But it wasn't that boat, it was another, more beautiful boat. There was music and the crew danced for us.'

'Us?' he prompted.

'Yes.' Suddenly her eyes opened wide, and she grasped his hand, asking urgently, 'Where is Ahmed? Why hasn't he come to me? Why are you here?'

'You remember now, Laura? You remember that you were travelling to Cairo with Prince Ahmed, that you were beginning a new life there with him?'

She nodded, searching his face anxiously. And then, seeing the pity in it, she cried, 'Oh, please tell me – where is Ahmed? He is safe, isn't he?'

He held her hand tightly but when he shook his head sadly she gave a tortured cry and turned to press her face into the pillows . . .

She was sitting in a chair when he visited her the next morning but the beauty which had shone like a beacon was missing. In its place was a face ravaged by pain. Her eyes were red and swollen from weeping, and she looked like a sad and weary rag doll.

Halliday took the chair opposite hers and asked, gently, 'How does the head feel this morning?'

'Will I be able to see Ahmed, Mr Halliday?' she asked, ignoring his question.

He shook his head. 'I'm afraid not Laura. His body has already been taken to Cairo at his family's request, and the funeral will take place today.'

Her eyes opened wide in shocked surprise. 'But that isn't possible! I have to be with him! Besides, it's too soon . . .'

'You forget we are in a hot country. Funerals invariably take place quickly.'

'But what about me? Don't they care about me?'

The compassion she saw in his face brought the scalding tears into her eyes. Gently he took her hand in his, saying, 'I am returning to Cairo this afternoon. Tomorrow I'll make it my business to speak to your mother.'

'My mother?'

'Yes, of course. It's over, Laura. Your future doesn't lie here. You must return to England with your family and pick up the pieces of your life. It won't be easy – but there is nothing else.'

'How long shall I be here?'

'We will try to get you transferred to a hospital in Cairo where your mother and sister will be able to visit you. Hopefully, within the next few days.'

'I see . . .'

Her voice was the voice of a child and her small, hurt face was expressionless. Helplessly, he left her, after pressing her hand warmly but receiving no response from her chilled fingers.

Sir Archibald stared at John Halliday uncompromisingly from the other side of his littered desk. He'd spent a very uncomfortable two days with the Sultan and his minister, Ahmed Farag's father, and had had an even more uncomfortable meeting with the Marquis of Camborne and the Mallonden family.

The Farag family were desolate at the murder of Ahmed. He had been the sort of man destined to do great things for his country – and if it hadn't been for his infatuation with the English girl he would have been safely back in the Fayoum instead of journeying from Aswan.

The Marquis was equally scathing in blaming most of the tragedy on Laura's pursuit of the young man.

'She'll not have an easy ride by any means,' Sir Archibald said to John. 'I've no doubt they'll take her back, but there'll be no Edward Burlington waiting to pick up the pieces. There'll be no London Season – and there'll be a great many debs relieved that the beautiful Laura has blotted her copybook and is no longer a rival.'

'That's a very cynical way of looking at things,' John said. 'I'll admit the girl's behaved very foolishly – but she's not the first girl to think it's all been worthwhile in the cause of love.'

'You're too old to subscribe to that nonsense,' Sir Archibald said, testily. 'I want you to go and see the family tomorrow morning – they're at Mena House. You can tell them that you saw Laura, who will be in a Cairo hospital by that time, and will no doubt be looking forward to a visit from her mother and sister.'

John had no illusions on that score. He doubted very much if Laura was at all eager to see her mother.

The first thing Halliday sensed the following morning was the family's hostility. And he noticed immediately that Lady Poppy and Edward Burlington were missing.

When he suggested that they should wait until the others joined them, Lord Mallonden said testily, 'We'll have a very long wait, Halliday! My daughter has returned to England to attend the wedding of one of her friends and Lord Burlington has also gone to England from where he intends to leave for the Far East as soon as possible.'

John made no coment, but addressed Mrs Levison-Gore.

'I saw your daughter in Luxor, Mrs Levison-Gore. She was slightly hurt on the train and was naturally terribly distressed at the death of Prince Ahmed. She is now in a British military hospital in Cairo. No doubt you will wish to see her as soon as possible.'

'I suppose she's expecting to rejoin the family as though nothing had happened?' the Marquis said coldly.

'I did not discuss her future plans with her. It was far too early,' John replied.

The Dowager Lady Mallonden spoke for the first time.

'We shouldn't start running round after the girl. She must be made to see how very angry and distressed we've been about all this. Poor Edward felt he couldn't face her – and you can be sure that news of her escapade will have reached England. She can't expect to carry on there as if nothing had happened. People have long memories.'

'I wasn't aware that anybody outside the family knew anything about this,' John answered her steadily.

'They know that Laura hasn't been with us. They know that her engagement to Edward came to an end. People have a nasty habit of putting two and two together and making five.'

'I intend to visit Miss Levison-Gore this afternoon. May I tell her that you will be seeing her in the near future?'

'That is up to my daughter-in-law,' Lady Mallonden said coldly. 'As I said, I think we should give the girl time to reflect on all that has happened.'

Lavinia Levison-Gore nodded. 'I agree with my

mother-in-law – Laura has been spoilt. By me, by her father when he was alive, by all those people who raved about her beauty. It didn't add to her character. I will see her presently, but I'm not sure just when.'

John let his eyes rest on Meg who looked down at her feet as if they were something to wonder at. He turned away to walk to the door and the Marquis said shortly, 'Thank you for what you've done, Halliday. No doubt we'll see you again within the next few days.'

John Halliday favoured them with a stiffly correct bow before walking out of the room.

When he reported on the situation to his chief a little later, Sir Archibald said irritably, 'I'm not in the least surprised, Halliday. I knew from the very outset they'd prove to be a stiff-necked, unforgiving lot. So the girl has to sit it out in that hospital in the hope that eventually somebody will remember her existence and pay her a visit?'

'It rather looks that way.'

'Well, in the meantime I suggest you go out there, take her a few flowers, make her feel the world hasn't quite forgotten her.

John smiled to himself as he left the Embassy. He had always known that underneath that brusque exterior, Sir Archibald had a very kind heart.

Armed with chocolates, flowers and fruit he presented himself at the hospital in mid-afternoon and was immediately accosted by a young doctor who called out, 'If you're going in to see Miss Levison-Gore, I'd like to have a few words with you first. I suppose you're a relative sir,' he went on as soon as John sat down in his office.

'Actually no, I'm not. I'm at the British Embassy. Halliday's the name.'

'Sorry, Mr Halliday. I didn't know the British Embassy were so lavish with their generosity.'

'They're not as a rule. I happen to know the young lady and I thought she needed cheering up.'

'Has she no family here in Egypt?'

'They'll be coming along presently, I hope.'

'But you're not sure?'

'No.'

The two men looked at each other thoughtfully and the doctor was the first to speak.

'The young lady will be able to leave the hospital quite soon. Her bruise has almost disappeared. But I wish I was as happy about her mental state.'

'Her mental state?'

'She's very depressed. She isn't eating and she spends hours staring out of the window. Mr Halliday, did you know that she was pregnant?'

Consternation showed on Halliday's face and the doctor said, 'Look, Halliday, the young lady's had a quite traumatic experience. She *needs* her family at a time like this.'

Halliday decided to play for time. 'Before I visit Laura, I think I should inform her family of these later developments. Will you see that she receives these?'

'Shall I tell her they're from you?'

'Only if she asks. I'll be back as soon as I can tell you more.'

An hour later he was reporting the latest developments to Sir Archibald.

Sir Archibald stared at him in dismay. 'Well, that'll put the cat among the pigeons. It'll be interesting to see how they cope with this latest revelation!'

'I suppose you want me to tell them?'

'Well, you know how it is, Halliday. I'm tied up with Allenby and the others. The trauma of this girl is nothing compared to the troubles I'm having with them!'

Later in the day, when the family was once more

assembled in the private room at the Mena House Hotel. John dropped his bombshell and waited for what was to come.

The Marquis and his wife sat back in silent condemnation. The Mallondens sat grim and implacable while Laura's mother was stony-faced. Only Meg betrayed any real emotion by putting her head in her hands and sobbing quietly.

The Marquis of Camborne had nothing to say. The problem the girl had created for them was over and he rather relished the trauma confronting his companions.

'Is there to be no end to the problems that girl is causing?' Lord Mallonden asked his sister-in-law vexedly.

Lavinia remained silent and, in exasperation, he went on, 'I suppose she's wanting to come back to us. It's what you're asking of us, isn't it, Halliday, to take her back to England and forget the whole episode?'

For the first time the Dowager Lady Mallonden took command and the resolution in her voice obliterated a great many of her years. She'd ruled her husband and her children with a rod of iron and for as long as they could remember she'd been the dominating force in their lives. Even though her husband had been dead a great many years and her son was now Lord Mallonden she was still the one who made the decisions, shaping and moulding them all into her conception of what they should be.

'We have no alternative but to take her back,' she said adamantly. 'Obviously, we can't leave her here – we don't want any more scandal than has already been created. Laura will return to England with us and none of us will ever discuss what has happened or the child she is expecting.

'There is a Home in a remote part of Scotland that I have contributed to for many years. Laura will go there as soon as we arrive in England and stay there until the baby is born. It will give her an opportunity to see other women in a similar situation – and hopefully she will learn from the experience.

'It will be her penance for all the trouble she has caused us. When she is well enough she will return to her mother's house and none of us will ever refer to the child which she will leave in the care of the Home. In time she will pick up the pieces of her life; she will re-enter society and, hopefully, make a suitable marriage.'

It was Meg who cried, 'Suppose she doesn't want to have the baby adopted? Suppose she wants to keep it?'

'That is out of the question! I want no child in our family who has been touched by the shadow of the pomegranate, no child who is half-Egyptian.'

John spoke for the first time since he had told them his news. 'What is the alternative if Laura doesn't agree with your proposal, Lady Mallonden?'

'There *is* no alternative, Mr Halliday.'

'Mrs Levison-Gore?' he said, appealing to Laura's mother.

'I agree with everything my mother-in-law has said. I did my best for Laura. Now I have my other daughter to think about,' she said firmly.

Years of training in the field of diplomacy kept John's face bland when his innermost thoughts were in turmoil. How could any of them do this to that lost, beautiful girl who was going to need all the help it was possible to give? There was no hint of his anger, however, when he said, 'I will see your daughter tomorrow and tell her the outcome of our meeting. I'll let you know what she decides as soon as possible.'

Old Lady Mallonden favoured him with a haughty stare. 'What *she* decides, Mr Halliday?' she said sharply. 'It is what *we* decide that matters now. I shall write to Laura with my views. I shall tell her to forget this child, that she should marry an Englishman who will keep alive his fair complexion and race, and not one who would taint it with the passion of the children of the East!'

She leaned back in her chair and suddenly the years rushed back to claim her. Her fingers plucked at the rug over her knees and, in a faint, weary voice she said plaintively, 'I'm tired. I'm far too old to have this upset, too old and too disappointed...'

They rushed to assist her with extra cushions and soda water while the Marquis and his wife looked on with grim detachment. John took the opportunity to make his departure and, as he walked back to the Embassy, the cool evening breeze seemed like a benediction to his troubled mind...

18

John found Laura sitting in the small quadrangle behind the hospital. It was a place of solitude in the midst of teeming streets filled with the cries of street vendors, a Western haven in the heart of medieval Cairo where memories of Saladin still lingered. A large lebbek tree stood in the centre of the lawn, stretching its kindly branches right up to the secluded harem windows which were incredibly beautiful with their old Meshrebiyeh latticework.

He took in her pallor and the languid way she gazed out across the lawns, her thoughts turned inwards, seeing nothing of the green stretch of grass and the majestic tree.

'How are you, Laura?' he greeted her.

She smiled because it was expected of her. Already he was hating his role in what he had come to tell her. He knew none of it was his fault yet he couldn't help feeling that in some strange, oblique way he too had betrayed her.

'I have been to see your mother and the rest of the family,' he began. 'I expect they will be wishing to visit you quite soon.'

She offered no comment.

'Laura, we have to talk about your future. What, exactly, are you expecting from your family?'

The violet eyes turned to stare at him, doubtful and questioning. Then, in a small voice, she said, 'Don't they want to take me home? Will they ever forgive me?'

'Yes, my dear, they will take you home and in time they will forgive you. But there is a price to pay before they do and it is for you to say if you are prepared to pay it.'

'A price? I'm not sure what you mean, Mr Halliday.'

Hesitantly, John told Laura everything that had been said the day before and, as he talked, he saw her expression change. Awareness took the place of apathy, to be followed by an anger that filled her eyes with hot, treacherous tears.

As he put out a hand to touch hers, she recoiled as if John, too, were her enemy. For a while he waited for the tears to dry, while his heart searched for the right words, words that she would not find trite and meaningless.

When they came, they did nothing to allay the hurt in her violet eyes. He read there reproach and misery, a vulnerable pride that made him feel ashamed of the messages he had brought from a family she had pinned her hopes on.

'I can't talk about it any more today,' she said, trembling. 'It's something I need to think about very carefully. Will you be able to come and see me again?'

'Of course. In the meantime I expect your mother and sister will come.'

'I don't want to see any of them until I've had time to think. Will you tell them that?'

'Very well, Laura.'

He took her small, cold hand in his and once more her eyes filled with tears.

Two days later he visited Laura again, but in some intangible way it was a very different girl who faced him in the tiny hospital ward that had been her home since she had arrived back in Cairo.

Gone for ever was that joyous expectancy that the world would be her oyster. Instead he faced a woman who had grown up too fast, a woman who had been made to face a future clouded with uncertainties.

'Did you see my mother again?' she asked him.

'Yes, briefly. I gave her your message.'

'Was my grandmother present?'

'No, only your sister.'

'And my mother said nothing about changing her mind? She expected me to obey my grandmother?'

'I can hold out no hope that your grandmother or your mother will change their minds, Laura.'

'Then I must tell you what I want to do. Firstly, I want to keep my baby. It is the only link I have with Ahmed and I loved him very dearly. I shall love this child, Mr Halliday, I shall make it my whole life.'

'That is a very great commitment for a girl who is alone in the world, with no family to care for her. Do you have any money of your own?'

'I have a little money my father left me. I also have jewels that Ahmed gave to me which can be sold. They are worth a great deal.'

'Possibly. But not worth enough to keep you and your child until he or she is old enough to fend for themself. Laura, be practical! You have not been trained to work and I doubt if there is any way you could earn a living. All your young life was dedicated to the prospect of marrying well. All those attributes that enabled you to attract the right sort of man will count for nothing in the world you'll find yourself in. And when your money has run out, what then?'

'I have to try! I don't care if I never see any of my family again. I only care about my child – Ahmed's child. Mr Halliday, do you think Ahmed's mother would receive me?'

His eyes widened.

'This is Ahmed's child. We were hoping to marry – he was coming here to ask his parents to give us their blessing. But even without it I *know* we would have spent the rest of our lives together. If they loved him, surely they must receive me? They must want to do something for their son's child.'

'You have experienced the bitterness of your family – don't you think it is possible that Ahmed's parents will be even more unapproachable?'

'Yes, it is possible, I know. But don't you see, Mr Halliday, I have to try! You can help me – surely she would not refuse to accept a visit from a British diplomat. If – if the Princess refuses to see me then I shall have to think again about what I must do – but I shall never give up my child. It isn't possible!'

When John Halliday reported once more to Sir Archibald he said scathingly, 'The girl's out of her mind! Of course the Princess won't receive her – they're no doubt blaming her for everything that has happened, and this is an Egyptian family we're talking about. They don't act like us and they don't think like us. But if you want to stick your neck out, that's your business, Halliday.'

John wrote to the Princess whom he learned was living in the Farags' palace in Heliopolis and he waited expectantly each day for her reply. He had almost given up hope when a letter arrived from Princess Ayesha to say that she would receive them the following day promptly at two o'clock.

'Don't expect too much,' he warned Laura gently. 'Don't raise your hopes too high. I know her husband. He is a man who has little love for the British. She may be prepared to meet you out of curiosity, a mother who is anxious to see the sort of woman her son fell in love with – to such an extent that he forgot his family, his fiancée and the things he had sworn his life to.'

'I don't care!' said Laura with something of her old spirit. 'I refuse to believe that she won't help me!'

Laura's first thought as they were ushered into the courtyard of Princess Ayesha's garden was that they had entered a haven of cool peace after the heat of the streets outside.

Momentarily she forgot her swiftly beating heart in the appreciation of her surroundings. The villa was like a French château, built round three sides of the square courtyard, painted white, with bright green shutters at the windows, and the garden beyond was gay with its fountain and fluttering doves. They were being escorted by a large, uniformed Sudanese figure who, at one time, John would have suspected of being a eunuch. He had to remind himself that this was a Coptic household.

They were led across a floor of exquisite Persian tiles and up a shallow staircase into a long room overlooking the garden.

Light filtered gently through the Meshrebiyeh windows and gems of stained glass still glowed like uncut jewels from the lacework white stucco which ran in a deep frieze high around the ceiling. They were shown into small anteroom where a fountain played and there they were bidden to wait.

Laura's spirits had sunk lower with every step she had taken in the palace and John, in an effort to put her at ease, said gently, 'This house is a perfect example of an old Mameluke palace. Most of them have long ago been debased but this has been allowed to survive and grow more beautiful with age.'

Laura smiled but offered no response. They sat in uncomfortable silence with the house still and quiet around them. Then, in the distance, they heard the opening of a door and footsteps crossing the room beyond. Without a word they both rose to their feet.

Laura would have known instinctively that Princess Ayesha was Ahmed's mother. She was tall and dark-haired except for the wings of silver at her temples, and she had a beautiful patrician face.

It was John who moved forward to greet her, taking Laura's arm and saying, 'May I be allowed to present Miss Laura Levison-Gore, Your Highness? I am John Halliday.'

With a gracious wave of her hand the Princess indicated the seats from which they had just risen and she took another opposite them, waiting in silence for them to state the reason for their visit.

'We have been admiring the palace, Your Highness. It is a beautiful example of an old Mameluke palace,' he said tentatively. 'You must be very fond of it.'

She smiled and he was well aware that she knew of his discomfiture, nor was she going to make it easy for either of them. At that moment the outer door opened again and the Sudanese came in carrying a huge silver tray on which rested gold filigree cups and saucers. Princess Ayesha said, softly, 'We will have tea, Mr Halliday. I am aware how you English enjoy your afternoon tea. Afterwards you shall tell me why it was so important for you to see me today.'

They watched while the Sudanese poured tea from a heavy gold teapot and a plate was handed round containing tiny almond cakes which Laura was sure would stick in her throat. As she took the cup from the Princess's outstretched hand their eyes met and she felt the hot blood rise into her face at the sudden confrontation with eyes which reminded her of Ahmed's.

John had to admire the Princess's dignity in the presence of this young Englishwoman who had so tragically changed the course of her life.

The Sudanese servant removed the tray and for several minutes there was silence in the beautiful room, so that only the sound of the fountain and the gentle cooing of doves could be heard. Then, addressing Halliday, the Princess said calmly, 'If you enjoy an Eastern garden, Mr Halliday, you will take pleasure in mine. I specially love the lotus flowers on the lagoon – I believe you call them waterlilies in England.'

'I would very much like to see your garden, Princess Ayesha,' he replied gallantly.

'I have an appointment at half past three but that gives you plenty time to look around and for Miss Levison-Gore to explain why she wished to meet me.'

Laura watched him leave the room with desperation tinged with relief. Explanations had to be in her words, not those of a diplomat. Meanwhile, the Princess was eyeing her calmly and, against all her silent promises not to give way to tears, she now felt them burning behind her eyes before they rolled helplessly down her cheeks.

The Princess allowed her to weep and Laura fumbled desperately in her bag for a handkerchief. 'Please forgive me, Your Highness, I didn't want to cry. Tears are not enough for the sadness I feel in my heart.'

'I was mindful not to receive you,' the Princess said evenly. 'Since my son's death I have told myself many times that I hated you, that it was your fault that my son is dead, that it was you who persuaded him to turn his back on his family and the woman he was to marry. So I decided I had to see what sort of woman could make my son do these things.'

Laura sat with bowed head, allowing the Princess's words to wash over her. 'I knew, of course, that you had been injured on the train. I did not expect you to come to see me, however. I thought you would return to England with your family and that would be the end of the matter. It was brave of you to come.'

'Your Highness, it wasn't I who killed your son! I loved him. I made him, for a time, forget everything else. Ahmed told me right from the very beginning that there could never be anything between us, however much we loved each other. I didn't believe him because

I was arrogant and spoilt. I wanted him and I went after him. I made him forget everything except that I loved him and I would have followed him to the ends of the earth.'

'What did you intend to do when you returned to Cairo?'

'We wanted your blessing. We wanted to marry and we hoped you would accept me. But if you had not, then we would have married anyway. It was something that had to be. . . . Please, Your Highness, I came to ask you to help me.'

'To help you! How?'

'To return to my family I shall have to promise to give up the baby I am carrying and never see it again. I would rather die than do what they ask.'

The expression on the Princess's face did not change; only the clenching of her hands in her lap betrayed how much Laura's words had shaken her.

'You are telling me that it is Ahmed's child you are expecting?'

'Of course! I was going to tell him before we came to see you. I wanted him to be as delighted as I was.'

'What sort of help do you want from me?'

'A home here, somewhere to have my baby and bring it up. I have a little money that my father left me and I have jewels that Ahmed gave me which I can sell. I don't want anything from you for myself, but you cannot refuse to help Ahmed's child.'

'You apparently attribute me with more Christian values than those found in your own family! Have you any idea what your life would be like here, a young unmarried woman with a child to bring up, not speaking a word of Arabic, a stranger to our culture, not one of us and unaccepted by the British people here?'

'I will not give up my baby! Rather than that I will kill myself, I swear it!'

The girl's face was adamant. Ayesha knew that without doubt she meant every word she said.

'I have to discuss this with my husband and other members of my family. I am not the only one who feels bitterness towards you.'

'How long must I wait?' Laura asked in a small voice.

'I will inform Mr Halliday of my decision within the next few days,' Princess Ayesha said. Rising to her feet she said gently, 'You will find Mr Halliday in the garden. I will instruct one of the servants to show you out.'

Laura rose to her feet and bowed her head, then she stood still until Ahmed's mother left the room. She found John sitting on the terrace gazing out across the desert to the pyramids beyond and, although he looked up at her enquiringly, there was nothing she could tell him.

On the way back to the hospital they discussed Laura's visit to Ahmed's mother and he marvelled at her conviction that the Princess would help her. What sort of catastrophe would it take to convince this beautiful, pampered girl that the bridges she had so lightheartedly burned had gone for ever? He did not think the Farag family would assist her in any way and every day that passed he expected to receive word from Princess Ayesha to confirm the fact.

Sir Archibald agreed with him.

'Of course they won't help her,' he said scathingly. I've heard the girl that Ahmed was to marry is marrying his younger brother, Prince Hadji. They're the same age and they know each other rather better than she ever knew Ahmed.'

'Why did they affiance her to Ahmed, then?' John wanted to know.

'Because he was the eldest. You know, John, I'm always surprised how well these marriages work. It's a pity Ahmed didn't go to claim his fiancée instead of going off on his own to Luxor and the arms of the delectable Laura.'

'If everybody knew what was going to happen, the world would be a calmer place,' John said easily. 'The Mallondens are talking about returning to England at the end of March. Did you know?'

'I knew. The Marquis and his lady went back last week. I'm glad to have him off my back, I can tell you.'

Three days later the Princess's letter arrived on John's desk and he hesitated for several minutes before opening it. In that envelope lay all that remained of a girl's dreams and hopes for the future . . .

The note was brief. It merely asked Mr Halliday to accompany Miss Levison-Gore for a further interview with Her Highness on the following Tuesday at four o'clock. He did not know that her mother and sister were at that very moment trying to convince Laura that Granny Mallonden's way was the best.

'I can't believe you are being so stupid!' her mother said angrily. 'You will be treated very well in that Home your grandmother has contributed to. You will come back to us and in no time at all you'll be back in the swing of things.'

'Looking for some man to marry me?' Laura cried. 'Somebody rich and titled? Somebody who doesn't know a thing about me and isn't likely to find out? Oh Mother, that isn't what I want! It's far better that I get out of your lives.'

'You're talking like a fool, Laura! How do you propose to keep yourself and a child? Don't think for one moment that the Mallonden family will come to your assistance if you decide not to do as your grandmother wishes.'

'Please, Mother, I don't want to talk about it any

more. I've made my plans one way or the other. When are you going home?'

'Next week.'

Laura was glad to see them go. Her mother proud and unbending, Meg looking back in tearful misery.

In the days after Halliday brought the Princess's note, nothing could dispel her optimism. She couldn't think that Ayesha had sent for her again merely to dash all her hopes to the ground. When John Halliday called for her at the hospital on Tuesday afternoon she was waiting for him, exquisitely gowned from elegant grey suede shoes to flower-trimmed hat.

They spoke little on their way to the Princess's house. Laura's spirits were high and John wished he could feel more enthusiastic.

Again the Princess received them in the room looking out across the gardens and as she entered she said, 'You need not leave us, Mr Halliday. You should hear what I have to tell Miss Levison-Gore.'

She indicated that they should sit near the window and took a carved chair opposite them.

'Obviously I have had to discuss this with my family and you must understand there is a certain degree of bitterness towards you, especially in my husband and my daughter-in-law, Fawzia, who was to have married Ahmed.

'We have been influenced by the knowledge that my son loved you and hoped to marry you if those terrible men had not taken his life. That you are expecting his child has also been a factor in influencing our decision. You can expect nothing from your own family and we cannot see our son's child thrown on the mercy on the world. We have, therefore, decided to offer you Ahmed's house in the oasis of the Fayoum. There are servants at the house and, if it meets with your approval, I will ask a special servant who has been in our family for many years to live with you there until your child is born, and afterwards if you still need her. She is an Irish woman, Bridget Murphy. She is loyal and you will have no trouble with her.'

Laura's eyes had opened wide at the mention of an Irish servant and the Princess smiled. 'Bridget Murphy nursed my two younger sons and made it clear she wished to remain with my family here in Egypt. She did not know Ahmed well; he was already in England at his prep school when Bridget came to us and there was no occasion for them to meet when he came home for holidays.

'But Laura, if you decide to adopt this way of life you will live as an Egyptian princess and not as a visiting European. You may find it a lonely life. My husband will not receive you, so you will not be welcome at our palace in the Fayoum.'

'Will I have enough money to pay my servants?' Laura asked in a small voice.

'My son was a wealthy man and we have decided to make you a generous allowance from his estate. My husband thinks that you will one day wish to return to England, in which case some decision will have to be made about your child . . . Ahmed's child.'

'What do you mean?'

'We require that the child be educated in our way of life. You cannot expect to receive the sort of help your own family were reluctant to give and then simply return to England, taking the child with you. If you do as your family have suggested you will lose the child as soon as it is born; if you accept our help, you lose your child only if you return to the West.'

For a long moment Laura stared at her with an ashen face, then she murmured, 'I shall never leave my child, Your Highness, and I shall be glad to accept your offer. When shall I be expected to leave for the Fayoum?'

'Whenever you wish. The palace is waiting for you as it always waited for Ahmed. Are there any questions you wish to ask me?'

'I knew Ahmed's house in Luxor – would it not be possible for me to go there?'

'Would you really wish to live in Luxor, surrounded by British visitors who come to look at the ancient sites or dance every night in the Winter Palace Hotel? Would you care to see their fashionable clothes and overhear their chatter about English life which is now denied to you? Could you stand to listen to Western music borne on the breeze from the ballrooms and know you have no part in it? I think not.'

For a long moment there was silence, then Laura said stonily, 'No, you are right. It is better that I do not live in Luxor. If I stay here in Egypt it is better for me to try to forget England and the life I knew there.'

'I think you are very wise.'

'What will my servants call me? Will they know who I am?'

'They will call you "my lady" and they will not be curious. They served my family and my son loyally and they will give the same sort of loyalty to you.'

'Are there any Europeans living nearby, Your Highness?'

'No. There are archaeologists working on the Roman remains near by but unless you ride there you need not meet them. Our villa is within walking distance; if there is anything you require you may approach me if we are in residence there.'

When Laura did not reply, the Princess bowed. 'I will bid you both goodbye, then. My servant will show you out.'

Their journey back to the hospital was a silent one because John was reluctant to intrude into her thoughts but, as he stood with her on the hospital steps, she favoured him with the enchanting warmth of her smile.

'You have been so kind, Mr Halliday! No brother could have been kinder and now we have to say goodbye.'

'You are going to the Fayoum in the morning?' he enquired.

'Yes.'

From the top of a table she picked up a cat modelled in black basalt and silently handed it to him. He took it, admiring its exquisite curves, the expression on its perfectly chiselled face, and Laura smiled. 'It all seems so long ago since the night I went to talk to Ahmed about that cat. He bought it for me. It was terribly expensive but I will never part with it; in some strange way it brought us together.'

Handing the cat back to her John said gently.

'Laura, it isn't going to be easy. There will be times when you will be very lonely, when you will long for the life you have left behind. I'm not convinced that you are doing the right thing.'

'I know I am. I loved Ahmed and I shall have his child. From that first moment I wanted Ahmed and I pursued him, regardless of the warning he gave me. Now there is a price I have to pay and I intend to pay it in full.'

She held out her hand which he took in his for a few minutes, then, very gently, he said, 'If there are any problems, Laura, you know where I am.'

Later that afternoon he reported to Sir Archibald who handed him a letter across the table.

John looked at him curiously and Sir Archibald said, somewhat sourly, 'Whatever the future of that young woman, Halliday, you'll be well out of it. That is your transfer to Singapore.'

John opened the envelope and scanned its contents. 'I hadn't expected it quite so soon,' he said evenly.

'Nor had I. I'd have liked you to stay on here, Halliday, until my retirement at any rate. I'd hoped they'd give you my job.'

'You're very kind, sir. I was expecting to stay here for two years at least. This has come as a surprise to me.'

'Oh well, we should be accustomed to sudden arrivals and departures. Are you quite happy with things here? I mean, the Laura Levison-Gore affair?'

'No, I'm not entirely happy but she seems happy enough. She has a childlike faith in the ultimate fairness of life.'

'Which is surprising with a family like the Mallondens. She's burnt her boats, you know.'

'Yes, I know. But, what is more important, Laura knows it also . . .'

19

From the terrace of her house overlooking the oasis of the Fayoum Laura looked out upon a view that was totally enchanting but her thoughts were turned inwards, a fact that was reflected in the wistful curve of her mouth and the expression in her eyes.

The gardens reached down to the edge of the great lake, Qarun, with its swaying bulrushes and waterfowl, framed by the hot hills beyond. She loved the Fayoum. In the three years she had lived here she had delighted in exploring the awesome ruins of Crocodilonpolis where the ancients had kept pampered crocodiles adorned with priceless gems, feeding them on costly dainties until the wretched animals died from liver trouble.

She knew every straight street in the ruins of a perfect Roman city which the sand of the desert had preserved at the foot of the hills, and she had explored on horseback the pyramids of the twelfth dynasty and the ruins of the Labyrinth. Those early months had passed quickly, so different from anything she had known before that she forgot how to be lonely, that she and Bridget were the only Western women in that part of Egypt. The Fayoum was remote; there were no ballrooms here to dance the night away and only dedicated archaeologists ever came to poke among the ancient ruins.

Now, more than ever, the tourists flocked to Luxor to see the tomb of the boy king Tutankhamun, then back to Cairo to see the marvellous things that had been brought out of it in the museum there.

Laura's eyes lit up as they fell upon Bridget, walking slowly along the path that led from the lakeside, pushing her daughter in the tiny trolley one of her servants had brought up from the village.

She had seen nothing of Ahmed's parents during the years she had lived here. Most of the time they were in Cairo or Alexandria and she guessed that they would have been more forgiving if her child had been a son instead of a daughter.

Bridget had proved to be a big, raw-boned country woman with a ruddy countenance and an Irish accent she was keen to preserve, even though she hadn't set foot in the Old Country for over twenty-five years. Her sense of humour was infectious and she was loud in her condemnation of the two families who had sent Laura into exile. It had been Bridget who had stood beside her bed to encourage her with every breath through twenty hours of pain during the birth of her child; Bridget's voice she had heard in her delirium; Bridget who had placed her baby in her arms and Bridget who had refused to leave her to become nursemaid to Fawzia's baby who was born twelve months later.

'Dade but ye needs mi more than she does,' she'd said staunchly. 'And her with all the money and the family behind her. Sure and I'd never forgive miself if I left ye to look after a girl who'll have 'em all dancin' attention!'

'Perhaps you should go,' Laura had said dismally. 'I took Ahmed away from her. Don't you think I've hurt her enough?'

'Sure and it's her pride you hurt, not her heart. If they will go on affiancin' young people when they're little more than children, what do you expect when they send them out into the world and they meet other men and women? Now she's married his brother and I don't suppose she gives Ahmed a second thought.'

Fawzia gave birth to a son and Bridget said, caustically, 'How they'll all be dotin' on him – but just you wait until they see ye, mi little beauty.'

They made no attempt to see Laura's daughter, Rosetta. And, although she wrote to tell her mother that she had given birth to a beautiful girl, she received no acknowledgement of her letter. 'They've got no heart!' Bridget said angrily. 'How can they ignore something as beautiful as this little thing?'

Rosetta *was* beautiful. She had Ahmed's blue-black hair and Laura's eyes. She was a contented and happy child and Laura's servants adored her.

There were days when Laura couldn't believe that three years had passed since the morning she left Cairo; three years of monotony, for apart from the precious time she spent with her daughter she had nothing to do.

The eastern women filled their days with trivialities. They walked down to the lake carrying their water pitchers on their heads, chattering and giggling in carefree groups. She watched them sitting on the bankings, gossiping, combing their long black hair and paddling in the shallows before filling their pitchers and walking home again.

They were curious about the fair-haired Englishwoman who lived at the big house, and sometimes the children peered through the lattice work in the white stucco walls until Bridget or the servants chased them away, screaming with laughter.

There were no English newspapers, no visitors and, although she had more than enough money, there was nothing to buy except the food they ate. Laura had taken to wearing Eastern garb, kaftans she could buy in the village stores while her Western clothes hung in her wardrobe, growing more and more old-fashioned with each passing day.

Once Bridget found her holding one of her ballgowns in front of her while she looked in the long mirror in her bedroom and said drily, 'Why don't ye go up to Cairo then? Ye could look at the King Tut treasures and buy yourself some dacent clothes.'

'Oh Bridget! When would I wear them? Who would appreciate them? Besides, if I went up to Cairo, they'd think I couldn't stay away.'

'Dade and what does it matter what they think? They're hardly ever here – and when they are they don't take the trouble to call.'

As she hurried along the path to meet Bridget and her daughter, Laura's thoughts were a confused jumble of ideas sparked off by the English newspaper which Lutvi had found in the village that morning, lying on a seat where a party of men were angling. His one thought had been that his mistress would like to read it and none of the men had seen him take it.

Laura had devoured that newspaper from cover to cover – and it had been the announcement on the page given up to betrothals, marriages and deaths which had disturbed her peace. It was the brief announcement of the betrothal of Miss Margaret Jean Levison-Gore, daughter of the Honourable Mrs Lavinia Levison-Gore and the late Colonel Arthur Levison-Gore to Edward, Lord Burlington, elder son of the Marquis and Marchioness of Camborne.

For a long time she sat staring at the newspaper, her thoughts chaotic. How her mother would be revelling in this latest development – and how the Marquis would be gnashing his teeth with impotent rage!

Meg and Edward! Never for one moment did she think that Meg was in love with Edward. And what had Edward said about Meg? He had thought she was a jolly little kid. Surely he couldn't be marrying Meg because he saw something of Laura in her?

Bridget took one look at her face before saying, 'Dade and you're lookin' mighty upset, love. Is it visitors we're 'avin?'

'No, Bridie, nothing like that.' She produced the newspaper. While Bridget read the announcement, Laura pushed the trolley over the uneven path and Rosetta pointed with glee to the tall, stately ibis wading in the shallows.

'Dade and it's not worryin ye, is it, love? Surely you'll not be thinkin' if ye'd gone home it might a bin you gettin' married to Lord Burlington?'

'No, Bridie, nothing like that! It's simply that reading that paper has brought back to me all the years I lived in the West – school, and Granny Mallonden's for Christmas, the shops and the restaurants, the theatres and the tea dances. Oh, I know it's silly and trite and that you never even think about Ireland, but I can't help it.'

'You're wrong, love, in thinkin' I never long for the Old Country – I do. I thinks about mi old father bringin' in the cows for milkin' and mi sisters squabblin' about the lads in the village. They moight 'ave married by now, but I'll never know. Every morning when I look out across the lake to the desert and the mountains I think about Ireland and the mist lyin' low across the emerald fields. Ye didn't really think that all this Eastern splendour could make up for them old whitewashed cottages and the old talk in the village street?'

'Why did you never go back, then?'

'I had a big row with mi father and mi pride wouldn't let mi go back with mi tail between mi legs. I was too proud to be tellin' him I'd missed him and the rest of them. Instead I sent a stream o' letters home tellin' them all about the riches and the palaces, the Princess and her jewels, the pyramids in the mornin' mists. Mi brother Gerard wrote to tell mi about mi Granny's death but although I wrote back to them over the years I never 'ad another letter from any of them.'

'I'm sorry, Bridie.'

'Nay, love, you shouldn't be feelin' sorry for me. I've had some happy times back in Ireland, times I can look back on with a lot o' pleasure. I doubt if there was much happiness for you with that stiff-necked family and that ambitious mother o' yours.'

'I'm sorry I read this newspaper – it's made me restless, made me think about the past when I was congratulating myself that I seldom thought about it.'

'Does it say when your sister'll be gettin' married?'

'No, but it will probably be early in November before people start to leave London in search of the sun. I don't suppose Meg and Edward will wish to come to Egypt.'

'Well, even if they do you're hardly likely to be bumpin' into them around here! They'll be with the rest o' the fleshpots, honeymoon or no honeymoon.'

As they reached the bottom of the steps leading on to the terrace, Laura took her daughter's hand and they mounted the steps together while Bridget called up, 'I'll bring you a cup o' tea, love. Tea's civilised enough for anybody.'

In the weeks that followed Laura wished wholeheartedly that she had never read the English newspaper. She was restless and it was not enough to walk by the lake or laze in the gardens. Bridget's conversation was amusing but she longed for books and music, for the sort of talk she had enjoyed with other women from her own world and the laughter they had shared.

Bridget sensed her restlessness and Rosetta sensed it also. She became fretful, preferring the company of Bridget, who was loving and fun, to that of her mother, whose mind was on other things.

One afternoon Bridget found Laura scolding Rosetta angrily for some slight naughtiness that another day she would have overlooked and, after she had taken the tearful child away to settle her in her room in the company of her dolls, she returned to Laura and in a chiding voice said, 'Yer unhappy, love, and yer takin' it out on the child. It's not like ye.'

'I don't know what's the matter with me, Bridget. In all the time I've been here I've never felt so restless.'

'It's that English newspaper, love. It gave ye a taste of all ye've bin missin' these last few years. Sure and they be silly, trifling things, but ye've got to go back and face 'em love.'

Laura stared at her in amazement. 'I can't go back, Bridget! Where in England could I go to?'

'I'm not talkin' about England, love. Dade and what would you be doin' goin' back there? I'm talkin' about goin' to Cairo for a few days. Take a look in the museum at the things they found in that tomb. Buy some pretty things in the shops, dine in the hotels. See what the English are doin'. Listen to the way they're talkin' and go to the opera.'

'Where shall we stay, Bridget? Not Shepheards – I'd know too many people – and not Mena House, I stayed there with Meg and mother.'

'There are other, smaller hotels you could stay at – and I shan't be comin' with ye, love. I'll stay right here and look after Rosetta.'

'But I want you to come with me, Bridget! You know Cairo, you could tell me what I should see.'

'I don't know the posh hotels and the Western shops, love. Nay, you won't be interested in the parts of Cairo I got to know. Like I said, I'll stay here and look after Rosetta. She wouldn't be interested in the things you'll be wantin' to see in Cairo either.'

For days Laura was torn between her desire to go to Cairo and the fact that she would be leaving her daughter behind. She had no doubt that Bridget would look after Rosetta because she adored the child, but how much more wonderful it would have been if they were visiting Cairo with her . . .

Bridget supervised her packing, pulling evening gowns and wraps out of the wardrobes, and Laura was quick to say, 'I shan't be needing any of them, Bridie. I can't possibly go to a dance in any of the hotels unescorted. All I shall need are some decent afternoon dresses and a hat or two, preferably with veils.'

'And why will you be wanting veils, then?' Bridget enquired.

'Look at my tanned skin. Once it was like porcelain, now it's baked by the sun. Besides, I don't want anybody to recognise me.'

Bridget and Rosetta accompanied Laura to the tiny railway station where she boarded the train for Cairo, a train far less opulent than any she had hitherto travelled in. She had to share a compartment with four other people who stared at her curiously, no doubt wondering why an Englishwoman was travelling alone from the Fayoum to Cairo. But in Cairo itself she caused little speculation. Swallowed up amidst its late-afternoon bustle, memories flooded back to her as she looked at the skyline of decorated domes and graceful minarets.

Several donkey-boys approached her, offering their patient beasts for her to ride, but she knew where she was heading. On the banks of the Nile were several modest hotels and she fell into step with the crowds hurrying along the wide pavements.

She felt suddenly elated by the pace of the city; the crowded roads where lavish and shabby motor cars moved slowly behind small, pattering donkeys, and camels piled high with sugarcane swayed gracefully, oblivious of the honking of innumerable horns from impatient drivers. In their midst could be seen men from the desert, riding exquisitely turned-out Arab horses, their faces proud, their bearing arrogant, completely at variance with the men riding donkeys with their feet only inches from the road under the hoofs of their mounts.

This was the city she had exchanged for staid, grey London and, as she crossed the bridge over the Nile with Shepheards Hotel facing her invitingly across the promenade, she felt few regrets. The hotel she had in mind was situated on the other side of the bridge, small and unpretentious, where those Europeans who could not afford to stay at Shepheards or the other expensive hotels found some degree of comfort.

If the clerk at the desk was surprised at a request for accommodation from an Englishwoman with little luggage, he did not show it. The room she was shown into was small and scrupulously clean and the small window overlooked a narrow passageway and an oblique view of the river and its palm-fronted promenade.

Laura's first mistake was to dress for dinner. She realised it the moment she arrived in the dining room where people were sitting at tables attired in informal clothing. They looked up with interest at the elegant Englishwoman wearing a full-length gown. She was escorted to a table at which another Englishwoman sat alone and she smiled at her companion as she took her seat. The woman looked to be in her early fifties. Her hair was liberally sprinkled with grey and it framed a pleasant face with bright, intelligent eyes.

She smiled at Laura and said, softly, 'My name is Mary Edisford. Have you just arrived?'

'Yes. It was foolish of me to think I should dress for dinner.'

'You look very elegant, my dear. Is this your first visit to Egypt?'

'No. I live here.'

Laura smiled at Mary Edisford's surprise. She had made up her face carefully and, in the somewhat dim lighting, her deep tan was obviously unnoticed.

'I don't live in Cairo, I live in the Fayoum.'

'I see. So you are visiting, just like me.'

'Yes. Is this your first visit?'

'Oh yes. I've been so looking forward to it. I live with my sister in a small village in North Devonshire. We have a draper's shop and we always take separate holidays. My sister likes beach holidays, I like cultural ones, so we do agree to differ on that score. This year it's my turn. Next year I shall stay at home to look after the shop and Edna will journey forth in search of the sun. You will be able to tell me what I should see.'

'I take it you are on a tour?'

'Yes, but they only show you the usual things, don't they? I suspect somebody who lives here would know much more.'

Laura enjoyed telling her the things she had learned from Ahmed, and her companion listened with profound interest, saying at last, 'You know so much about Egypt, yet are you never homesick?'

'Sometimes. That's one of the reasons I'm here. To hear English spoken, to listen to music and look at the shops. I'm also hoping to see Tutankhamun's things in the museum.'

'Oh yes, you must. They're absolutely marvellous and, my dear, there is so much gold, it seemed unreal. How fabulously rich the ancient Egyptians must have been! How long will you be in Cairo?'

'I'm not very sure.'

'It would be so nice if you could show me some of the things I should see. In a couple of days we're due to sail up the Nile as far as Luxor but I don't want to miss anything in Cairo.'

Laura smiled but did not promise anything. What did she know about Cairo? Practically nothing, since during the time she'd stayed there with her mother and sister all they'd ever done was attend garden-parties in the hotel gardens and dance every night in their ballrooms. It was true she'd paid a dutiful call at the museum and driven out to the pyramids, but all she knew of Cairo was what Ahmed had told her.

Thinking that perhaps her companion would find her ungracious she said hesitantly, 'Please forgive me, but I really know very little about the city. I came to know more of Egypt after I left Cairo, and I'm hoping to discover more of it during the next few days.'

She knew that her companion was curious about her. An Englishwoman living in the Fayoum? She'd seen Mary's eyes looking at her hands on which she wore several rings, but not a wedding ring, and, after a few minutes, her companion said, 'I expect you want to shop and meet friends.'

'I do want to look at the shops in the Western quarter of the city, but I don't have any friends in Cairo, at least none that I have arranged to meet.'

'Would you mind if I came to the museum with you in the morning? I'd dearly love to see the Tutankhamun treasures again and they didn't give us very much time the other afternoon.'

So the following morning they went together to the museum and Laura smiled at the dedicated manner in which Mary approached their visit. She was attired in a businesslike khaki cotton costume which would have been suitable for a trek through darkest Africa, and she had on her head an ancient pith helmet which she explained had been loaned to her by the vicar at home. Laura's choice of a cotton dress and light summer shoes seemed quite inappropriate and Mary said, doubtfully, 'I do hope you're not going to get sunstroke, my dear. The sun is very powerful in the afternoon.'

'I have a long scarf I can wear on my head,' Laura said, without explaining that the scarf was intended to cover her face lest she should meet anyone she knew, as were the large sunglasses she was wearing.

For hours they wandered through the halls of the museum, completely entranced by the priceless things found in the tomb of Tutankhamun. Laura's eyes filled with tears when she thought of how Ahmed would have loved to be standing here with her now to look at this display of ancient wealth and power . . .

It was mid-afternoon when they emerged into the blazing sunshine and Mary said, with a little laugh, 'Heavens, I'd no idea it was so late! We've missed lunch and dinner isn't until seven. I wonder if we could get a cup of tea somewhere? This side of the river is very expensive, but perhaps if we crossed the bridge . . .'

'Shepheards is quite close – you'll enjoy afternoon tea there,' Laura answered her, relieved that she need not enter the hotel alone.

'Shepheards is terribly expensive, Laura. I'm not even sure that we're dressed for it,' Mary said hesitantly.

'But of course we are! It's a cosmopolitan hotel and we shan't cause any curiosity, I can assure you.'

It was a little early for afternoon tea, so the lounge was only half full by the time they entered. Laura chose a table near the wall where they could look out across the beautifully appointed room on one hand and through the long windows overlooking the river on the other.

More than ever Mary looked like an inquisitive little bird with her head going this way and that so as not to miss anything, her bright eyes shining with enthusiasm.

There would be so much to tell Edna when she got home. Not just about Egypt and the Nile, but about this fabulous afternoon in surroundings she had only hitherto read about.

Edna wouldn't be all that interested in Egypt. She would tut-tut in all the right places, putting in an occasional 'Well, I never', but she would want to know more about Laura with her dark blonde beauty and her haunting violet eyes. Laura was the epitome of every heroine Edna had ever read about in those women's magazines and the frothy romances she borrowed from the public library. Laura was mysterious, sitting in the discreetly-lit tearoom wearing her dark glasses and draped enchantingly in her long, blue silk scarf.

Laura ordered afternoon tea, tea that was faintly scented and came with a tray of small scones and strawberry jam and tiny, exquisite cakes which she explained were Shepheards's speciality. Seeing Mary's apparent diffidence she was quick to say, 'This is my treat, Mary. I wasn't looking forward to being alone in Cairo.'

'Oh, but I couldn't possibly . . . ' Mary protested.

Laura squeezed her hand gently. 'Please, you must. I can see that all this is giving you so much pleasure and you will have a lot to tell your sister when you get home.'

'Yes, indeed. This will interest her far more than all that treasure from the Pharaoh's tomb.'

There was a mystery about Laura, she just knew it, but she would never know what it was. Those eyes, like the pansies in the garden under the window of her cottage, held a tender sadness where there should have been laughter. She was young and beautiful and alone and Mary could only speculate on the cause of that wary desolation in their velvety depths.

Three English girls came to sit at the next table, their shrill girlish voices chattering happily. Beside her, Laura seemed to stiffen and she half turned away, and when Mary spoke to her she was aware that she was only half listening. She was concentrating on the conversation from the next table.

'What'll you bet she doesn't ask any of us to be

her bridesmaid?' the smallest of the girls was saying. 'I never invited her to any of my coming-out parties because she never really had a coming-out. One day she was with us at finishing school and the next she was engaged to Edward Burlington. It wasn't like Meg to be so secretive and I didn't even know she knew anybody like him.'

'My sister knows all about it. She'll be here with Mummy in a few minutes so we'll ask her,' said another girl, then the conversation regarding Meg was dropped in favour of talk about the boys they had danced with at Mena House the evening before.

A few minutes later two women came in through the door and crossed the room. Mary heard Laura's swift withdrawal of breath and the scarf was readjusted to cover what was left of her face.

'Do you know them?' she whispered.

Laura merely nodded, and almost immediately the younger girls started to bombard the older girl and her mother with questions.

'Dulcie, we've been talking about Meg Levison-Gore and her engagement to Lord Burlington. You know him, don't you? Weren't you at school with Meg's sister?'

'Yes, Laura. We weren't exactly bosom chums but we were at school together.'

'Didn't you like her?'

'Well, yes. We were all a little jealous of her because she was always so beautiful. Everybody heaved a sigh of relief when she didn't make the Season.'

'People are saying that Edward Burlington wanted to marry Laura, so why do you suppose he's marrying the other one?'

The older woman spoke for the first time. 'I've tried my level best to worm it out of Lavinia Levison-Gore, but I've got nowhere. One minute they were here in Egypt, then they were all haring back to England. Nobody talks about Laura and the last I heard from her mother was that she was living abroad. After that she closed up like a clam.'

'I was very friendly with Meg at school. Wouldn't you just think she'd invite me to be a bridesmaid?' one of the girls said plaintively.

'There's time yet. The wedding isn't until the spring.'

'Oh, I do hope she does! It'll be the wedding of the year – St Margaret's and members of the royal family there.'

'A fact which will add significantly to Lavinia's enthusiasm,' the older woman said drily.

Their conversation changed to other matters and, after a while, Laura said, 'Perhaps we should leave now. It's quite a little walk to our hotel.'

Conversation was minimal and Mary could see that Laura was deep in thought as they walked along the promenade beside the river. Reluctant to break the tenor of her thoughts, Mary entertained herself by looking at the great river and the ships of all sizes that moved, darted and anchored as they had done since the ancient land had been ruled by the Pharaohs.

After a while Laura turned to her with an apologetic smile, saying, 'I'm being a very poor companion, Mary, please forgive me.'

'That's quite all right, my dear, I'm enjoying myself just looking at the scenery. Did the conversation at the next table upset you?'

'It unsettled me. It made me remember things I've been trying to forget for the past three years.'

'Did you know them?'

'I knew one of them.'

'And are you the Laura they were speaking about?'

Laura smiled down at her before replying, 'If I said no, that it was merely a coincidence that they happened to be talking about someone with my name the matter would be closed, but you guessed rightly. I *am* Laura

Levison-Gore. My mother is never likely to tell anybody the true story and over the last three years the family will have swept any hint of scandal under the carpet.'

'But it changed your life?'

'Completely.' For a long moment she remained thoughtful, then, with a smile, she said, 'Oh, I wish I was sailing up the Nile with you! I'd love to see Karnak again and all those other wonderful places.'

'Places that you saw with someone who was very dear to you?'

'Some of them, yes.'

'Then seeing them with me would not be the same. Sometimes it's painful to look back.'

'I know. I promised myself four or five days in Cairo and I doubt if I shall ever come here again. I shall go home on Saturday.'

'Oh, I wish I wasn't leaving in the morning! It would have been nice to have looked around Cairo with you. We have a decent enough guide, but his English isn't very good and neither is his history, I'm afraid.'

'I think it's marvellous that you know anything at all about Egyptian history. I was terribly ignorant but Egypt cast a spell over me and I met someone who opened my eyes to her mystery, her history, and now it seems as if that pleasure-seeking girl was somebody else and not me at all . . .'

Her words left Mary wondering what she would remember most about Egypt; the glory of its past or the sadness in the beautiful eyes of her companion? There was some dark secret in the girl's life and she wished she knew what it was. Her sister Edna would have asked questions. Edna would have been frustrated with the little that Laura had said, but there was something about the girl's reserve that made Mary keep silent. She would not tell Edna about Laura when she got home. Edna would only say, 'Why didn't you ask her why she was living in Egypt and who she was living with?'

As they walked upstairs to their rooms, Laura said, 'After dinner, if you like, we could drive out to the pyramids. There's a full moon tonight and I can assure you that that is when all the ancient monuments should be seen. It makes them look whole again.'

'Oh yes, I would love that!' Mary enthused. 'We saw them the other morning and it was crowded everywhere. Is that when you first saw them, in the moonlight?'

'I've seen them several times but never with the person who mattered, so I can go out there unhampered by any feeling of nostalgia.'

She left Mary at her door and walked along to her own room. She had surprised herself at her sudden decision to return to the Fayoum on Saturday. For years she had been homesick for England. In the hot sun she had dreamed about soft summer rain and cool misted mornings, and now here she was thinking longingly of the Fayoum oasis, the gentle ripples on the Bahr Yussuf and the lushness of the vegetation. Bridget would be glad to see her home – and home now meant Rosetta and Ahmed's palace.

Things would be different when she got back. She would take an interest in the fields of cotton and sugarcane and bamboo. There would be grapes to pick and animals to care for. But more than that: she would take an interest in the fellahin and their wives and families. There was so much she could teach those uneducated women who were little more than chattels and saw nothing wrong in it.

20

Next day Laura stood in the foyer of the hotel watching Mary and her fellow tourists leave for their river-boat. They seemed a strangely ill-assorted group armed with cameras, fly-switches and guidebooks, their clothes unfashionable but eminently suitable for travelling in a hot country.

She had been touched by Mary's tearful farewell and the sincerity of her words. 'I've been looking forward to coming here for years and thanks to you I've seen so much more than I expected. I wish you could have sailed up the river with us.'

'Yes, it would have been nice,' Laura answered. 'One day I'll go back to Luxor but I have no idea when.'

'And you're going home tomorrow?'

'Yes.'

Mary did not ask for her address and Laura did not proffer it. Instead, she took her hand and held it for several minutes before releasing it.

After they had gone the hotel felt strangely empty and she was glad she had decided to go back to the Fayoum in the morning. She spent the day wandering around the museum and she bought three kaftans in fine Egyptian cotton. She took a long time choosing a heavily beaded silk one but there would never be an occasion to wear it . . .

There were crowds of people on the station platform the following morning but Laura guessed that most of them were waiting for the express train to Luxor. She was wearing a wide-brimmed straw hat with a veil that shaded her face, and all around her was the sound of English voices against which she steeled her heart.

The crowds seemed to evaporate with the departure of the Luxor train and, looking around, she saw that only a handful of people remained on the platform to await the desert train: two farmers with a couple of goats and a cage of doves; a slender young girl Laura had noticed earlier, with gold anklets round her slender ankles which tinkled delightfully whenever she moved. Laura was thinking it strange to find a young girl travelling alone but, after a few minutes, she saw an old man making his slow progress along the platform and the girl hurried forward to meet him. He seemed a very venerable old man with his snow-white beard and his long white robe and turban, a being who might have stepped out of the Bible, while the girl was a veritable Salome with her tinkling jewellery and the coy sparkle in her dark eyes.

Laura had removed her veil and the girl stared at her curiously, obviously intrigued that a European should be boarding the desert train. Three young men came striding down the platform, wearing well-cut European suits and bright red tarbushes on their dark heads. They stood in a group to chat and then, in the distance, the rumble of an approaching train could be heard. The young men shook hands and two of them walked back along the platform while the other moved forward to board the train.

He arrived at the carriage door at the same time as Laura and, with a charming smile, he indicated that she should mount the steps before him. She thanked him with a smile and placed one foot on the bottom step. At that moment there came a sharp report and suddenly Laura was flung to the ground and the young man was falling on top of her while his tarbush rolled along the ground.

Footsteps were running towards them and she looked up helplessly for assistance. A dark man with a black beard stood staring down at them, a man with a thin face and dark, tormented eyes. Suddenly he produced a gun which he fired twice at the young man lying above her. Laura felt his body grow heavy, and then his assassin was running away across the station yard and police whistles were being blown and other footsteps were bearing down on them.

The weight of the man's body was eased away from her and she was assisted to her feet. A dark red stain covered the skirt of her dress and she found herself staring down at the dead man's face, calm and emotionless in death. He was little more than a boy, and the thick, dark lashes that made fringed crescents against his cheeks reminded her suddenly of Ahmed. By now she was surrounded by police and railway officials, and then a stretcher was brought and the body of the young man was lifted on to it and carried across the yard.

'You will come with us, Madame. There are questions we must ask you.'

Laura stared at them aghast. 'But I am going home today! I don't want to miss my train. Believe me, I know nothing.'

'Nevertheless, Madame, you will come with us. Tomorrow you will get another train.'

'Really, you have no right to keep me here!' she protested, but all the while they were ushering her out of the station yard and there was nothing for it but to go with them.

They questioned her for what seemed like hours. Why was she visiting the Fayoum? It was not a favourite place with foreigners. When she told them that she lived there and gave them her address they gathered in a small group, speaking rapidly in Arabic. After a few minutes one of the men turned to stare at her, saying in a disbelieving voice, 'That is the house of Prince Ahmed Farag who was assassinated three years ago in train coming from Aswan.'

'I know, I was with him.'

'Why you with him?'

'We had been to Khartoum and were on our way to see his parents in Cairo. I was walking through the train when the bomb went off. I was hurt but Ahmed was killed.'

'Did you see his assassin?'

'No. I was taken to hospital. They told me there that Ahmed was dead.'

'But you saw the assassin today?'

'Yes.'

'You will describe him please.'

So Laura described the haunted-looking man, believing that she would remember his face for the rest of her life.

First one and then another man questioned her and by this time, with the heat in the room and a thirst that made her feel that her tongue was too large for her mouth, she felt she must surely faint.

But the questions went on: Why was she visiting Cairo? Why was she living in the Fayoum? What did she know of the man who had died?

'I never saw him before today!' she said wildly, 'I didn't know him at all. Who was he?'

'His name was Mohammed El Bakre and he was the son of Pasha Ali Bakre who is in the King's service. In the past year six people have been assassinated by the Nationals and we are not sure if the bullet was meant for him or for you, Madame.'

'But why me? I have nothing to do with Egyptian politics!'

'You were with Prince Ahmed and you live in his house.'

She stared at them fearfully but said nothing and, after a while, the man who appeared to be in charge said, 'You will stay here until tomorrow when we will release you to catch the train. It is obvious you can tell us nothing more.'

Laura was shown along several corridors until they came to a door which was unlocked and flung open. There was one small window which looked out on to a dusty courtyard. In one corner was a narrow bed and, in the other, a foul-smelling latrine. Laura believed that at any moment she would be sick with the stench.

They left her, locking the door behind them, and she could hear their footsteps walking away. She put her head down on the dingy pillow and sobbed. She had no faith in Egyptian justice. Suppose they didn't let her out? What would Bridget do about Rosetta? She struggled to her feet and went to stand where she could look through the narrow window. A tall, supercilious camel standing in the courtyard turned to look at her. She could see the incredibly long lashes over eyes that showed no curiosity, then, disdainfully, it turned away.

It was dark before a man came into her room carrying a small tray on which rested a pot of mint tea and a cracked cup. There was nothing to eat and she was hungry as well as thirsty by now. The tea was refreshing but there was very little of it, and when the man came back to retrieve the tray she asked if she could have some fruit. He stared at her uncomprehendingly so she tried to demonstrate the act of eating, biting into an apple or peeling a banana.

He shrugged his shoulders and left her alone. Although despair filled her heart, she made herself walk across the room to stand at the window. It was completely dark, but above her shone Egypt's jewelled sky and, faintly, she could smell the scent of jasmine.

She had no means of telling the time. It was too dark to see her watch, so she lay on the narrow, uncomfortable bed to await further developments. At first she merely lay there with her ears straining for any sounds from outside her room, and then with bitter amusement she started to think about her mother who would view her present plight with the utmost distaste.

Inevitably, her thoughts turned to her sister Margaret waiting happily for the day when she would become Edward's wife and she offered up a silent prayer that Edward would love her and be kind to her.

Edward was a nice man. He was kind and sincere, and one day, without the influence of his father, he would be his own man. She had behaved wretchedly towards Edward, encouraging him when she had thought she would never see Ahmed again, and then discarding him when the time was right. Surely Edward must see that her sister would make him a far better wife and Meg had always liked Edward, taking his part, being sweet to him. Laura hoped that girlish liking had turned into real love.

Her reverie was interrupted by the sound of footsteps in the passage and then the door was flung open and the same man came in carrying another tray which he placed on a shelf near the door. Laura looked at the tray with interest for it contained an orange and a small bowl of dates. She thanked him gratefully but he left her without saying a word.

She ate slowly, savouring the orange's sweetness. The dates were green and hard but she made herself eat them until the hunger pains diminished. She had only just finished when the man returned to collect the tray.

He threw a blanket over her feet without a word, then, dismally, she heard the closing of the door and the sound of his key in the lock. She had little faith that she would be released in the morning.

Sleep would not come to her. The mattress on which she lay was lumpy and the slightest sound made her think about rats and scorpions. She sat up and shrank into the corner. The stillness overwhelmed her, and then, from somewhere nearby, she heard the muezzin calling the faithful to prayer and looked up at the ceiling of her prison where shafts of bright moonlight illuminated the darkness.

In all that vast, teeming city there was nobody to care what became of her. A vision of the Cairo she had only glimpsed came to taunt her, a dark medieval city with its labyrinth of narrow streets and everlasting doors.

Bodily weary, sleep came at last, but it was a disturbed sleep, interspersed with cruel dreams. It was the sound of the key in the door that awoke her and she looked up, bleary-eyed, to see that her jailer had returned. She stared at him dully, and curtly he said, 'You come with me now.'

Her heart leapt with relief as she pulled on her shoes and followed him down the long passages. She was ushered into a room where a tall, thin man stood staring out of the window. He turned at her entrance and took his seat behind a vast desk littered with papers.

'I have questions for you,' he said curtly. 'You must answer truthfully. You knew the man who was killed?'

'No, I had never seen him before.'

'You were both going to the oasis of the Fayoum. Why?'

'I was going there because I live there with my daughter. I have no idea why he was going.'

'Yet you boarded the train together.'

'That is so, but it doesn't mean that I knew him.'

'Why are you in Cairo?'

'I came to look at the shops, to listen to music, to enjoy some of the things I have been missing these past three years. Is that so hard to understand?'

'Where you stay in Cairo?'

'At a small hotel on the east bank, the El Amahda.'

'Alone?'

'Certainly I was alone!'

'And how did you spend your time, Madame.'

'I went to the museum, to Shepheards, to the pyramids, to the mosques.'

'Always alone?'

'No. I met another Englishwoman visiting Egypt for the first time. She left yesterday to sail up the Nile as far as Luxor.'

'You not know this woman before you visit Cairo?'

'No.'

For what seemed an eternity he stared down at his notes, then, fixing her with a piercing glance, he said coldly, 'You will stay here, Madame, until we have corroboration of your statement. If we decide it is correct, you will be free to go.'

'But, please! I have a daughter who will be missing me terribly. I assure you I've told you the truth. I have nothing to gain from lying to you.'

'I must ask you to be patient, Madame. A young man has been killed. Prince Ahmed Farag, in whose house you live, was killed. We have to be sure. Now you will go back to your cell.'

The long, lonely night stretched in front of her, and how many lonely days? Was it possible to lose count of them? There had been no hint of compassion in the man's cold, impersonal face. How long would it take to check her story?

For three long days Laura saw nobody except her jailer who brought spasmodic meals of fruit, rice cakes and tepid tea. Twice he brought a shallow bowl of water so that she could wash and then, miraculously, on the fourth morning he returned with two other men. She stared at them dully, until one of them said, 'You must leave now, you are free to go.'

She continued to stare at them stupidly, then, collecting her scattered wits, she said, 'I am free to go home to the Fayoum?'

He nodded.

She looked down in horror at her bloodstained skirt and dirty jacket and, appreciating her dismay, he pointed to her luggage lying on the floor near her bunk and, for the first time, her tears were tears of relief.

After they had left her she washed in the bowl of water and then she discarded her clothing. It was a wonderful relief to step into the cool cotton kaftan she had bought but there was no mirror in the room to enable her to see if her hair was tidy.

Leaving the discarded clothing where it was she picked up her case and stepped out into the corridor. It was empty and she could not remember which way they had brought her into the prison. She walked on down the passage until she came to a door which she opened cautiously, only to find herself in the courtyard, stared at by the camel and two donkeys. Hastily closing it she moved on down the passage until she came to another door, then she discovered a small office where a solitary man sat at a desk near the window.

He stared at her in some surprise and she explained quickly, 'I'm looking for a way out.'

He rose to his feet and walked across the room to a door at the other side. This he opened with a flourish and indicated that she should walk through it. As she passed him with murmured thanks he smiled, the friendly smile of a man well pleased with himself.

She wanted to laugh. One minute they could be rude and arrogant, the next childishly gallant.

Once more she made her way to the railway station, only to discover that there would not be a train to the Fayoum until mid-afternoon. It would be dark when she arrived but there was no help for it. She had several hours to kill so she decided to look for a small hotel where she could get something to eat and perhaps find a ladies' room where she could attend to her hair and make herself presentable.

She was wishing fervently that she could get a message to Bridget but there was no telephone in the Fayoum house and she had little faith that a message would reach her if she telephoned the local police, even if she found anybody on duty. She would be home in the early evening so it was no use fretting about it now, she decided.

21

It was dark when Laura stepped down from the train at the Fayoum oasis but the glory of Egypt's sky aided her to walk confidently along the straggling street beside the river. Moonlight lent an enchantment to the waving palm fronds and the slender minaret across the river and she felt no fear that she would be accosted on her solitary walk.

Occasionally, laughter came to her from the houses hidden within their gardens, and she could hear the snuffling of animals and the cooing of doves.

She reached the gates of her house and was not surprised to find them closed. Obviously they would not be expecting her home at this hour. After pulling back the heavy bars and opening the gates, she closed them carefully behind her and then stared up at the house uncertainly. It was in total darkness. She had expected to find lights along the terrace and in some of the downstairs rooms but not a glimmer of light showed at the front of the house and, for the first time, a strange feeling of dread sent her running headlong up the path towards the house. She could see now why there were no lights. The shutters had been put across the windows and she could not understand why.

There was no need for Bridget to shutter the windows of those rooms that were used every day . . . Desperately Laura pulled on the bell to alert the servants inside the house and dimly she heard it pealing behind the closed door, but she was met only with silence, an oppressive sepulchral stillness. Again she pulled on the bell, then, before its sound had died away within the house, she started to walk through the gardens towards the rear.

Fear gave way to anger and anger turned to fear as she ran along the narrow paths that edged the pool. The scent of jasmine was powerfully sweet and the shadows of exotic shrubs only added to her fears as their branches tore at her kaftan like long, tenacious fingers. Then she was in the courtyard behind the house and pounding on the door with all her strength.

Again her hammering was met with an ominous silence and she was sobbing now with a frantic fear that she was alone and facing forces against which she had no armour. She sank on to her knees by the door, with her fists still pounding painfully against it. Then, when she had almost given up hope, from somewhere inside the house she thought she heard a sound. Heartened, she got to her feet and, adding her voice to her knocking, she cried, 'Please, somebody! Please come to the door.'

She waited, listening, then her heart lifted. She had not been wrong, there *was* somebody in the house! She heard, dimly, the opening of a door and shuffling footsteps crossing the tiles, then a voice saying in Arabic, 'I am coming, please wait.'

It seemed like an eternity before the door opened and then she was staring at Lutvi holding in his hands a lantern, his eyes wide with surprise. She staggered inside and sank down in the first chair she could find, with her hands against her face, shivering involuntarily.

Lutvi brought her a glass of cool water and stood silent while she drank it gratefully. She was glad of his silence. She had so many questions, but as yet words would not come to her. He continued to stare gravely down at her until suddenly she realised that he had made no effort to fetch Bridget. Breathlessly she asked, 'Lutvi, why are there shutters at the windows?'

When he did not immediately answer, she asked, 'Where is Bridget? Where is my daughter?'

'You not come home, my lady. All day and the next day Bridget wait. When you still not come, she very frightened.'

'But where is she?'

'At the home of Farag Pasha. Her Highness come for them and take them there two days ago.'

Laura stared at him in horror. Bridget should have known that she would come home. Surely she couldn't think that she would desert Rosetta willingly? Now Ahmed's family had charge of her daughter and Laura had to get her back!

'Lutvi, I have to go for her. I want you to come with me,' she said firmly.

'It better to wait until morning, my lady.'

'I am going now, Lutvi! I want my daughter here with me. If you do not come with me, then I shall go alone.'

For a long moment she looked into his grave, dark eyes, then with a small shrug of his shoulders he said, 'Very well, my lady, I come with you.'

She was glad of the lantern he carried as they made their way along the road to the white villa nestling in the midst of its gardens, a villa she had only seen and had never thought to enter. Lights from the terrace streamed out into the night as Lutvi opened the gate for her. Then, stepping in front of her, he led the way to the house.

In later years she was unable to describe either the gardens she walked through or the beauty of the house. All she was aware of was the confusion of warm, rich colours and soft lighting, the delicate coolness of alabaster floors and the subtle aroma of mimosa. Then she found herself staring into the proud, cold eyes of a man she had never seen before but whom she knew instinctively was Ahmed's father.

Ahmed might have looked thus in twenty years' time; haughty, with a hint of ancient arrogance. She could not imagine that this man's face would ever grow tender or that firm, chiselled mouth ever smile, but anger lent her strength to meet that cool, direct, uncompromising glance with her own. 'Where is my daughter?' she demanded. 'I've come to take her home.'

She was dimly aware that others had come to stand behind the prince's tall figure, his wife and people she didn't know, then Bridget was there, tearful, frightened. Laura asked, angrily, 'Why did you come here, Bridget? Surely you must have known that I would never leave my daughter?'

'Dade and I didn't believe you would, but you didn't come,' Bridget replied tearfully, 'and when the police asked your hotel they said you'd already left days before. Sure and I didn't know what to think, how could I?'

Suddenly Laura's anger left her. She could see Bridget's predicament. This wasn't England where communication was easy; this was the East, with all its pitiless uncertainty. Her incarceration in that Cairo prison had been without pity, a woman alone in a man's world, in a country where women were little more than chattels.

Farag Pasha was watching her face, recognising the thoughts that were passing through her mind, the mind of this English girl who had taken his son, his most beloved son, and made him her own. Now she had come to claim his granddaughter – and for two long days he had watched the child playing in the gardens and he had been enchanted by her.

When Bridget had brought the child to them his fierce pride had convinced him that the mother had returned to the West, hating her life in Egypt, yearning for its nightclubs and its decadence. Now something had happened to bring her back and before he relinquished the child he was determined to know what it was. In a cold voice he said, 'You will come into my study. I need to know where you have been that you did not return. I have to make sure that you are capable and worthy enough to keep your child.'

Furiously she answered him, 'How dare you question my right to look after my child! You have ignored our existence for three years and it didn't matter. We managed very well without your concern, and now you have the audacity to think I am not a good mother!'

'I am merely asking for an explanation of your absence,' he replied gravely, and his wife stepped forward quickly, saying, 'We have a right to ask this of you. Can you not understand how desperately worried Bridget was when you didn't return?'

For several moments they stared into each other's eyes, then Laura said, 'Very well, I suppose you have that right.'

Nobody spoke while she told them of the last few days in Cairo and, in the end, she said, 'If you do not believe me, I am sure you can check my story with the Cairo police. You are a very powerful man in Egypt, they will tell you all you need to know.'

Bridget was the one to break the silence. 'Aw ye poor wee thing,' she said. 'Dade and I should have gone to Cairo with ye like ye wanted mi to!'

Tears welled up in Laura's eyes and she brushed them away angrily. This family must not see her cry. She did not want their compassion – all she wanted was Rosetta, and to escape from their presence. She was scarcely aware of the kindness that was taking the place of haughtiness on the Pasha's face, or that his wife came forward to place a gentle arm round her shoulders. She only knew that weariness of mind and body overcame her and she would have fallen if strong arms had not come to her assistance and led her to a nearby divan.

They waited without speaking until she was able to composc herself, and then the Princess said, gently, 'You will stay here tonight, Laura. My servants will see that you are comfortable and will serve a meal to you. In the morning you are free to return to your home with Rosetta and Bridget.'

She allowed them to escort her to a room somewhere in the villa where a meal was served, a delicious meal of roast lamb and tender young vegetables, but she was so weary that she couldn't do it full justice or take note of her surroundings. At last the servants left her and she was allowed to bathe and step into the night attire provided for her. Then, almost before her head touched the pillow, she was asleep . . .

Laura stretched lazily, looking up at an ornate and unfamiliar ceiling, and then suddenly memory returned to her and she sat up, wide-awake, looking round at the most luxurious room she had ever slept in. Ahmed's house was charming, but it had been the home of a young man who had long been away and Laura had been content to leave it as a shrine to his memory. Now she was seeing Eastern opulence as Western eyes seldom saw it and, like a child in a fairy-tale, she wandered around the room, entranced with objects in jade and alabaster, allowing her hands to linger lovingly over rich brocades and silks while her toes curled luxuriously in rugs more beautiful than any she could have imagined.

She had been too tired to take in the details of the bathroom the previous evening; now she revelled in the green alabaster and marble and, in the huge mirrors that lined one wall, she stared in wonder at the image of herself wearing a turquoise silk nightgown which fell in exquisite folds around her feet.

The shutters were drawn against the windows but

she knew that it was morning by the gentle glow of sunlight that came through the chinks. She pulled them back and went out on to the balcony. She gasped with delight at the gardens all around her, where tall, stately palms vied with oleanders and where lotus blossoms floated tranquilly on the still pool. This was the East of her dreams, something from *The Thousand and One Nights*.

From somewhere in the gardens she heard laughter, then she saw a girl walking along a path accompanied by several children. The children darted ahead towards the pool and she recognised Rosetta among them, holding back a little from the exuberance of the others.

She called to her and the child's face lit up with a smile of pure joy. Then, with a wave of her hand, she was running after the others. The older girl paused underneath her balcony and, in a gentle voice, asked, 'You slept well?'

'Oh yes, thank you, very well. It must be very late.'

The girl smiled. 'It is almost noon.'

'Then I must dress quickly and come down.'

'There is no hurry. Rosetta is happy with her cousins.'

Her cousins! How strange the name sounded and for a moment Laura's smile faltered. The girl was about to follow the children to the pool and Laura called after her, 'Please, tell me who you are.'

The girl paused and smiled up at her. 'I am Fawzia,' she said simply, then she turned away and followed in the wake of the children.

Laura stared after her. Fawzia, the girl Ahmed would have married if Fate had not allowed their eyes to meet, so excluding everything and everybody from the passions that had consumed them.

There had been no sign of resentment on the girl's pretty face, no indication that she had not forgiven Laura for what they had done to her. But perhaps it didn't matter now, when she was married to Ahmed's brother and Ahmed was dead . . .

All the same, as Laura dressed in a freshly-laundered kaftan she was not relishing the thought that very soon she must meet Fawzia again.

She let herself out of her room and made her way along the corridor to where shallow marble steps descended to a hall decorated with panels of carved wood inlaid with ivory and mother-of-pearl.

For a moment she stood hesitantly in the centre of the hall, not knowing which way to go, listening for voices. But all she could hear was the tinkling sound of a waterfall and, dimly, the noise of children's laughter.

She made up her mind quickly and went in search of the laughter. Through a door that led into the garden, and came upon them near the pool, Fawzia sat in a chair watching the children play, a half-smile on her pretty face. When Laura joined her she indicated that she should take a chair and, after a few minutes' silence, Laura realised she would have to be the first to speak.

'Do you live here, Fawzia?'

'No, we are visiting. Our home is in Heliopolis.'

Again there was silence, and Laura was glad when Rosetta came running towards her, her arms outstretched. For a long moment she held her daughter close and Fawzia said, 'She is very beautiful – one seldom sees eyes of that colour in an Egyptian child.'

Laura smiled.

Again there was silence and Rosetta returned to her playmates. Laura said, tentatively, 'I do hope we can be friends, Fawzia, though I did you a great wrong.'

Fawzia said, softly, 'I did not know Ahmed well. We were affianced when I was only a child and he was in England more than he was in Egypt. My father told me what had happened and my pride was hurt more than my heart. There had been many times when I had doubted my capacity to make him happy. He had lived in the West, mixed with Western women, while I had been sheltered and cosseted in the way it is with us. I am happy with Ahmed's brother – he has not been conditioned to ask more of me than I am able to give.'

'I am glad, Fawzia! I would like to be your friend.'

'I am expecting my second child in the spring. I would like it to be another boy.'

'Yes, of course. You set such store by your sons. I think, perhaps, that Ahmed might have been disappointed to have been presented with a daughter.'

'Perhaps not. A daughter as beautiful as the morning with her mother's eyes . . . There would have been time for sons if he had lived.'

Fawzia had the beautiful turn of speech Laura had come to associate with the East, and she turned her head away so that the other girl could not see the tears in her eyes . . .

22

The rosy fingers of dawn crept serenely into the room through long net curtains that covered the tall windows. A shaft of pale sunlight fell across the rich counterpane that covered the bed, lighting on the pale tresses of the girl sleeping peacefully in the large bed. Gradually the contours of the room took shape. A large, beautiful room with its rose-coloured drapes and pale blue carpet, a room furnished in rich mahogany and smelling faintly of lavender.

The girl stirred and, from the street outside, came the steady clip-clop of a horses' hoofs and then the distinct clatter of milk bottles.

Sleepily she opened her eyes and scanned the room, then she caught sight of the wedding-gown hanging outside one of the vast wardrobes, its train spread deliciously across the carpet, and she smiled.

The house was still quiet and, wriggling up against her pillows, she could see by the clock on the bedside table that it was only a little after six-thirty. Her eyes returned to the gown, taking in the sheen of satin and the exquisite lace, the subtle gleam of pearls. With a little cry she slid out of bed and ran to where she could caress the gown, allowing her hands to pass lovingly along the folds of the skirt and the lengthy train. Inside the wardrobe were her white satin shoes and the froth of veiling. With no further desire for sleep she went to the window and looked out at the London street where she saw the milkman and his patient horse driving off slowly in the direction of the park.

A newspaper boy came down the street, whistling some popular tune, and the sunlight lingered on warm stone and trees bursting into new life. It held all the promise of a beautiful day and Margaret Levison-Gore could not be blamed if she rejoiced in the promise of a rich and rewarding life.

At twelve o'clock she would walk down the aisle of St Margaret's, on the arm of her uncle, Lord Mallonden, but before then would be the hairdresser, the dressmaker and the florist. Her mother would be fretting and fussing and there would be the bridesmaids and pages and their anxious mothers to cope with. The morning would be *hectic* and, as she lay relaxing in her perfumed bath, Meg endeavoured to stem her mounting excitement by reliving the events of the past few months.

She had been fortunate in her year as a debutante because the money put aside for Laura had not, in the end, been required and had been available for her own coming-out. Better than that, however, had been Poppy's marriage to a country squire from Gloucestershire. They had met at a country show, fallen in love almost on sight and had been married within three months of their meeting. Poppy had given birth to a son the year after and was again heavily pregnant. She was deliriously happy with her life in an ivy-covered manor house surrounded by rich farmland, happier than she had ever been as a debutante waiting for Edward Burlington.

Edward would never have fallen for Poppy or she for him, and there were times when Meg marvelled that he should have fallen in love with *her*. He had come back from the Far East and made a great effort to pacify his father by entering into the life of his social set. He had met Meg again at a dance and Mrs Levison-Gore did not allow herself to hope that Lord Burlington would spare her daughter Margaret a second glance after the trauma of his association with her other daughter.

To the surprise of them both, he did single Meg out for special attention. They chatted, they ate supper together, they danced – and then had followed all the rest of the London Season with Edward as her escort. Unable to believe their good fortune, her mother kept in the background. She did not push the match, as she had with Laura, and the Mallondens, too, kept a discreet distance.

Meg was taken for long weekends with Edward's parents, when his mother decided she liked the girl immensely. Even the Marquis had to admit that she was a vast improvement on the other one. True, she didn't have her sister's devastating beauty, but she was a pretty little thing and decidedly more malleable than that temptress.

Lord Mallonden had been generous with her dowry; they could afford to be, with Poppy off their hands. In any case, Margaret was his brother's child. It had been decided that she should be married from the Mallonden's house in Belgravia, and she had conformed readily in the choosing of her attendants.

Her uncle's grandson, Mark, and his younger brother, Allen, were to be groomsmen; their sister, Alison, was to be her chief bridesmaid and, because she was only twelve years old, Meg had little difficulty in choosing younger cousins to make up the number. Even Granny Mallonden, for once in her life, found no cause for criticism.

Meg snuggled into her bathrobe and went back to the bedroom. How slowly the hands of the clock moved! But from somewhere in the house she could now hear movement and, in a few minutes, there was a discreet tap on the door and a maid entered carrying a tray with her morning tea on it.

The girl smiled cheerfully. 'It's a beautiful mornin', miss, an' it looks as if it's 'ere to stay.'

'Oh, I do hope so! Is anybody else up?'

'You were the first I served, miss. I thought you'd be the one needin' it most!'

There was another knock on the door and Poppy's smiling face appeared round it.

'Oh, you're up,' she remarked. 'I'll have my tea in here, Mabel. I'm sure you'd like a bit of company right now, Meg.'

'Oh, yes please, Poppy. Is Timothy still asleep?'

'Yes, thank goodness. Did you sleep well?'

'Not bad. Wouldn't it have been nice if we could have had a quiet country wedding like you had?'

'Granny wouldn't have allowed it – nor Aunt Lavinia.'

'No, perhaps not.'

'Tomorrow you'll be Lady Edward Burlington and one day you'll be the Marchioness of Camborne. Are you ready for it, Meg?'

'I think so.'

Poppy sat on the edge of the bed, staring thoughtfully down at her hands, and there was something in her pose that prompted Meg to say sharply, 'You're thinking about Laura, aren't you, Poppy?'

Poppy smiled brightly. 'Well, I have to admit I do think about her from time to time. Surely you must think about her, too, Meg?'

'She had the chance to come back to England with us,' Meg said dully.

'On terms she couldn't accept,' Poppy replied.

'Well, I do think Mummy was right! How could she have coped with a baby? Who would have married her? She'd have had too much explaining to do.'

'Maybe she wouldn't have wanted anybody to marry her,' Poppy said. 'Anyway, it's no use thinking about it, I suppose. She made her own decisions and chose to abide by them. I don't suppose Edward ever mentions her?'

'No! Why should he? He had four years to get over her and now he's in love with me.'

'Of course! And you with him.'

'Well, yes, of course.'

Meg was not liking this conversation. It was wrong of Poppy to have brought Laura into the conversation this morning! *Particularly*, this morning. Poppy, too, was wishing she'd kept her thoughts to herself.

A few minutes later she said as much to her husband who seemed more concerned with amusing his son than listening to her.

Poppy looked at them both fondly. She'd been wishing for weeks that they could have got out of this occasion but they'd had no excuses to offer. Besides, Granny Mallonden had said that if Poppy didn't attend Meg's wedding people would only say it was sour grapes keeping her away. It was undoubtedly the wedding of the year, with the Duke and Duchess of York in attendance, as well as Princess Mary and several lesser members of the royal family. Her own marriage had been a quiet affair, with the church crowded with villagers and the village street lined with local well-wishers.

Poppy's husband was a handsome man of large proportions, with an honest, ruddy face and hands that were not afraid of hard work on the estate. They had horses and dogs and children in common – and she couldn't help wondering how much in common Cousin Meg had with Edward Burlington; Edward with his search after mysticism in far-flung places in the Orient, and Meg who had always been under her mother's thumb . . . Once again her thoughts returned to Laura – Laura who had been so very beautiful and whose conflicting passions had been her ultimate undoing . . .

Mrs Levison-Gore was in her seventh heaven. This was the occasion she had worked and schemed for since the day her daughter Laura was born; she would never forgive Laura for taking it away from her, but now here was Margaret – sweet, pliable Margaret, the bride of the year. After today things would be very different. She would be the mother of Lady Burlington and Meg would look after her wants and her needs. She would be able to afford to tell the Mallondens that, although she was only the second son's wife, she required nothing further from them.

Lavinia was pleased with the gown she'd chosen. Dark blue, elegant, falling to the floor in heavy folds, its bodice heavily encrusted with beads; and the large hat with its sweeping brim adorned with ostrich feathers balanced beautifully her tall, slender figure. At last she was satisfied with her appearance and at liberty to go to her daughter's room where Margaret was surrounded by the dressmaker, florist and hairdresser.

Her eyes filled with unexpected tears. How lovely her daughter looked in the white satin gown! The mass of white, frothy veiling covered her pale hair and streamed out over the length of the train as she stood surrounded by her admirers, the sheaf of Madonna lilies in her hands.

Lavina circled her daughter but could find no fault. With a gracious smile at those present she said, 'Thank you so much, you've all done *splendidly*. When the party have left for the church you will find a buffet lunch laid out for you in the dining room.'

They thanked her warmly. She then swept from the room and down the long, curving staircase to the hall where Lord Mallonden was waiting impatiently.

'She's quite ready,' she informed him, 'and looking very beautiful.'

'In that case there is no need for you to wait. The car is outside,' he said.

She was gratified to see people lining the street leading into the square and she took her place in the car with a serene smile.

Margaret walked cautiously down the staircase, her train handled efficiently by the dressmaker. The children came out of the drawing room with cries of admiration before they were hustled off to the waiting cars. Lord Mallonden went forward gallantly to greet his niece. He smiled and, tremulously, she smiled in return.

'Ready, my girl?' he asked briefly.

She nodded, then taking his arm they passed out through the open door. The sun was still shining . . .

23

It was the hour of sunset in Egypt – that magical hour when the most worldly mind is moved by the Infinite Being of God.

Laura Levison-Gore was coming out of the tiny schoolroom she had converted from an old summer-house in the garden of her house. Her long day's work was done.

Her pupils, who were all closely veiled women, were hurrying towards their homes. Some of them, though wives and mothers, were girls just emerging from child-hood. Most of them were Coptic, but there was also a sprinkling of Moslem women amongst them. The only distinguishing mark to segregate them was the tiny tattooed cross which decorated the wrists of the Coptic women, and Laura was careful not intrude upon the beliefs of any of her pupils.

Their attitude towards Laura resembled the devotion of English Sunday-school children to their teachers. Each day they brought her little bunches of jasmine and early sprays of tuberose because, during the year she had worked amongst them, she had endeared her-self to them.

At first they had only come in twos and threes and had shrunk from any form of intimacy, but gradually their number had increased until the summerhouse was now hardly big enough to accommodate them all.

During the past year her busy life had left Laura little time for reflection, but it gave her a satisfaction she had never experienced before – the satisfaction of feeling that she was at last of some practical use in the world, that her reason for existence was justified.

Bridget had remained unconvinced that she was accomplishing anything, but Laura could sense the joy of achievement when any one of her woman had mastered thc reading of a short sentence. The books she handed out were those her daughter had used several years before, children's stories of animals and fairy-tale adventures.

'Dade and I don't know why ye bother,' Bridget exclaimed. 'Don't they go home and jabber in Arabic? Why do they need to learn English?'

'It gives them something to do, Bridget,' Laura answered evenly. 'What would they be doing if they didn't come here? Gossiping round the well and sitting outside their houses watching their children playing in the dust. Isn't it better that they learn to clean their homes and care for their children in a proper manner?'

Fawzia, too, was unconvinced that Laura was not wasting her time. But there were mornings when she would sit at the back of the schoolroom, a half-smile on her pretty face.

Ahmed's mother was also interested in the work Laura had undertaken with the women from the villages. She was now occasionally invited to visit the Princess and her family at the large villa on the other side of the village. They drank scented tea from delicate cups, and tiny almond cakes were presented by the Princess's handsome servant Hassan who, Laura found herself thinking, would be more at home in charge of a harem of women, urbane and smiling.

'I feel that Hassan intrigues you, Laura,' the Princess said one afternoon. 'Why is that?'

Laura's face coloured. 'I find him very Eastern. I imagine him in charge of some harem.'

'I can assure you Hassan is not a eunuch,' Ayesha smiled. 'He has a young wife and several children. He has been with our family many years, as was his father before him. Coptic households do not go in for harems.'

Suitably chastened Laura said nothing, and the Princess said gently, 'You are still unable to look at us through Eastern eyes, Laura. I can understand, it is difficult for you. What do you intend to do about Rosetta's education?'

Laura's eyes opened wider and the Princess nodded. 'She is old enough to start her education in earnest. Is it your intention to acquire a private tutor or do you wish her to be educated in one of the schools in Cairo?'

'In Cairo?'

'Why yes. There are several good English schools in Cairo. I have not thought that you will want your daughter to grow up like a woman of our country whose formal education is minimal.'

'I must admit it has been worrying me considerably.'

'Things are changing in Egypt. The Nationalist Party is taking a greater grip on society and government. We are now no longer dependent upon the British and with the increasing power of the Nationalists it may be that one day there will no longer be a role for the King to play in Egypt.'

'You think that is possible?'

'It is something we must think about. In which case the old families will need to think seriously about their future. My dear child, you are out on a limb, neither fish nor fowl, neither British nor Egyptian.'

'Nor is my daughter.'

'Precisely . . .'

Laura was so thoughtful when she left the villa that afternoon she almost collided with a man leading his horse up to the gates. The horse was a purebred Arab, as beautiful as any she had ever seen. She apologised swiftly and he bowed, grave and gracious, and in that first moment he reminded her of Ahmed and their first meeting on the ship coming out to Egypt . . .

He was tall and attired in faultless riding clothes. On his head he wore a burnous edged with dark-brown fringing and she remembered that she had seen him riding through the village recently on several occasions. Always he had favoured her with that same straight, disconcerting gaze.

It was evident that he was visiting the Farag villa. When she reached home she mentioned him to Bridget who said, knowingly, 'I think oi know who that moight be, the Pasha's nephew, his sister's son. His mother's married to a Syrian and livin' in Damascus.'

'I see.'

'His mother was married when she was little more than a child, fourteen or fifteen I reckon. She only ever had the one son who'll be a year or two older than Prince Ahmed would 'ave been. I did hear a rumour that his father had taken another wife to give him more sons, but I don't know the truth of it.'

'You mean his parents are divorced?'

'Bless ye, no, love. It's likely he's allowed more than one wife.'

Laura thought no more about it until she met the man again a few days later. She was riding with Rosetta towards the ruins of the Roman city on the other side of the lake, a favourite place for both of them.

It was the horse which attracted her attention, galloping effortlessly along the edge of the lake, his mane and tail the colour of sun-kissed wheat flowing out in the breeze he created. Then she noticed the way the man sat his horse, as if they had been moulded out of a single sheet of bronze.

As they drew level he slackened his speed and once again their eyes met and he smiled. Her breath caught unevenly in her throat. He reminded her so much of Ahmed . . .

She looked down at Rosetta, trotting placidly beside her, unaware that her mother was vaguely troubled by the encounter. She would have to do something soon about Rosetta. The girl was bright and the time was rapidly approaching when she would deserve more than her mother could teach her.

As they rode up to the villa later, Bridget appeared on the terrace excitedly waving something in her hands.

'Dade and here ye are at last, love. Sure and it's a royal command that's come for ye. Better read it quick, Her Highness wants an answer as soon as possible.'

Curiously, Laura took the envelope, turning it over in her hands. For a minute she stared uncertainly at Bridget who was obviously anxiously waiting to hear what message it contained.

Laura stared at the single page of parchment and the neat, exquisite handwriting. Glancing at Bridget, she said, 'I'm invited to dinner this evening when formal dress is to be worn!'

'Formal dress, indeed! And what does Her Highness expect you to be wearin', and you buried here for the past few years? Pity ye didn't splash out on somethin' really expensive when you were in Cairo that time.'

'I'll have to wear the white evening dress I bought in London. Gracious, it's years old but it's the best I've got.'

Why had Ahmed's mother suddenly decided to invite her for dinner? Until now there had only been brief visits to the villa for coffee or afternoon tea. Now she was suddenly commanded to attend upon them for dinner wearing formal dress.

A servant was despatched with a message to say

that she would be there, and the dress was brought out of its mothballs and spread out across her bed.

'My, but it's a beautiful dress,' Bridget enthused. 'The Egyptian women'll have nothin' like this. It's like a girl you'll be lookin', all pure and virginal in that lovely thing.'

'Hardly virginal, Bridget! I think it's too young for me. We'll look for something else, perhaps we can do something with that old blue dress?'

'Oh no ye don't! You're to wear the white, love, and there'll be flowers for your hair and we'll 'ave to find some pretty shoes for your feet. They'll surely be sendin' somethin' for ye – they can't expect ye to walk to the villa.'

It was in a room tinted by the setting sun that Laura surveyed herself in the mirror. Suddenly the years dropped away and she was a girl again, dancing in Edward Burlington's arms at Shepheards Hotel. It was true that the porcelain pink-and-white English complexion had been replaced by sun-kissed gold, but she was still beautiful. Her figure was as slender and shapely as it had been on that night long ago, and as she twirled and danced in front of the mirror, the silk gown shimmered around her feet.

She sat while Bridget fastened a spray of gardenias into her hair. The diamond necklace Ahmed had given her sparkled against her throat and, for the first time, she wore the long, matching diamond earrings which gave her a sophistication more in keeping with her years.

Promptly at seven o'clock a horse-drawn carriage arrived for her and, giving Bridget a hug, she said, breathlessly, 'I feel like Cinderella leaving for the ball!'

'Dade and ye mustn't forget the handsome prince waitin' at the other end. Mark my words, love, there be somethin' afoot!'

Laura merely laughed. 'Oh Bridget, what a romantic you are! Of course there'll be no prince waiting for me. Her Highness will be gracious and the Pasha faintly disapproving as always.'

Laura had never set foot in the dining room of the villa before but, as she entered the room, she was aware of a long alabaster table set with flowers, of candlelight and the shimmer of glass and filigree gold.

The colours worn by the women were also rich and shimmering, their jewels blinking under the lamplight, and Laura stood in the centre of this jewel-clad family in the purity of her white silk gown adorned with the violets that Ahmed had said were the colour of her eyes.

Ahmed's father came forward to greet her, acknowledging her presence with a small, courteous bow. He was wearing evening dress, across which he wore a startlingly blue Order picked out in gold.

The Princess offered her cheek to be kissed and then Laura was being presented to the other guests: Fawzia and Ahmed's brother, men and women whose names she knew she would not remember, and an older woman who was introduced as Nakhela Kamel, a woman with a calm, beautiful face wearing a jewelled black kaftan and rubies which winked wickedly under the lights.

'You were surprised, no doubt, to get my invitation,' the Princess said frankly.

'Yes,' Laura answered. 'I was very surprised.'

'There is someone here who wishes to meet you. It will be to your advantage to make a good impression, Laura.'

Laura stared at her. Just at that moment the door opened and the man she had seen riding in the village entered the room. He was in faultless evening dress and the lamplight burnished his blue-black hair.

He smiled as he came forward to kiss the hand of the older woman before moving on to the Princess, then he turned and, for the second time that day, his eyes met Laura's. The Princess was saying, 'This is Omar Kamel, Laura, our Nephew, who made the request to meet you here this evening.'

Omar bowed gravely before Laura but did not take her hand and she stared back at him uncertainly while the Princess went on, 'You have spoken with his mother, my husband's sister. They have been visiting us for the last few weeks.'

She moved away and the charm of Omar's voice made Laura think how beautifully Arabic softened it.

'My aunt sent you a command,' he said softly. 'I would have sent you a plea.'

Again her eyes met his and he smiled. 'It seems I have heard about you for a very long time. When I heard them talking I found myself wondering what the real Laura would be like, the English girl who tempted my cousin Ahmed to forsake everything he'd known for the ecstasies of the present.'

She was taken aback by the words, which reached into the past and dragged it mercilessly into the light. Sudden anger made her eyes flash and hot words sprang immediately to her lips. 'You have no right, sir, to question me on our first meeting! My past is my own affair – it has nothing to do with you.'

His smile deepened. 'I mean no disrespect, please believe me. There must be honesty between us, Laura, neither of us should seek to hide behind the subterfuge of words. I have seen you during the time I have spent here and I admire you for the work you do in the village; I admire your beauty, and the courage you have brought to your life here which cannot have been easy. Before I invite you to become anything else, I would like to think that we can be friends.'

She stared at him in amazement. To presume to be friends on such short acquaintance seemed incredible, but to talk of 'something else' made her speechless. As they moved towards the dining-table he took her hand to escort her.

As the meal progressed she was aware of Omar sitting beside her, mostly silent and composed, and more and more he was reminding her of Ahmed. While other guests conversed quickly in cultured Arabic he turned towards her to say, 'You speak Arabic, Laura?'

The use of her Christian name on his lips startled her, but he was smiling graciously and she said, 'Yes, and I understand it very well now. I have to concentrate when it is spoken quickly, however.'

'My aunt tells me you are doing good work among the village women. Do you find that rewarding?'

'Yes. They are intelligent and most of them so badly want to learn.'

'Will that not make them discontented with their life in the village?'

'Oh surely not. I only try to teach them the things that will make them better wives and mothers.'

'Not to make them dream of a wider world and education which, alas, is at present only available to the rich?'

'If it does, then so much the better, I think.'

He smiled but offered no further comment. The meal over, she rose to leave the table with the other women. They would take no part in the men's talk around the table; it was not expected of them. They returned to the salon where Laura occupied herself by caressing the Princess's cat which sat, proud and distant, eyeing the company with unblinking amber eyes. She felt he should be adorned with a wide jewelled collar and earrings, exactly as the ancient Egyptians had adorned their cats, reminding her poignantly of the basalt cat which Ahmed had given her.

The cat responded with a deep throaty purr and Fawzia said, with a little laugh, 'You have made friends with Pasht – I've never been able to do that.'

'He is very selective,' the Princess said. 'There are many times when I would like to know what he is thinking.'

Madame Kamel said evenly, 'Have you ever been to the city of Damascus, Laura?'

'No. I'd never been to the East at all until I came to Egypt.'

'You would like Damascus. It is more cosmopolitan than Cairo, I think, and yet the old families retain many of their ancient customs.'

'My husband has said we will visit you one day,' Fawzia said. 'I shall look forward to it.'

This talk of travel made Laura feel, more and more, that she was a prisoner in Egypt, that for the rest of her life all chances of travel would be denied her because there was no man in her life.

While the rest of them talked, she wandered out on to the terrace. A full moon shone over the garden, throwing the palm fronds into sharp relief. Her future lay before her like a shadowed thing, but she knew that wherever it took her she would never smell jasmine without it taking her back to an Eastern garden and memories that would set her senses alight with a remembered pain . . .

The sound of footsteps made her turn quickly and she drew in her breath sharply at the sight of Omar Kamel walking towards her. At that moment he looked like Ahmed, and yet there was a subtle difference between them which she was as yet unable to recognise.

'All alone in the moonlight?' he said lightly. 'A moon goddess in a silver-white gown.'

'Are Syrians always so poetic, Mr Kamel?' she asked lightly.

'Please call me Omar since we are so nearly related,' he rejoined with a smile. 'The East is romantic, Laura. If you ever read our poetry you will come to realise it.'

For a moment there was silence between them, then, with a little smile, he said, 'The night is very beautiful. Shall we walk in the garden and absorb its beauty?'

'Wouldn't that be impolite?' she asked softly.

'Of course not! You are not interested in the women's talk and I have heard all I want to hear of the world's troubles.'

He took her elbow in his hand to guide her down the steps and then they were walking round the lagoon. The warm desert wind fanned her cheeks but she was not thinking of that moment, she was back near the temple of Abu Simbel with Ahmed, watching the Sudanese boatmen weaving the old patterned dances across the sand, her mind filled with their music, seeing Ahmed's eyes kindled with passion as he held her in his arms.

'Your mind is on other things,' Omar said gently. 'I watched you tonight at the dinner-table and you were far away from us. Will the time ever come, I wonder, when you can forget the past and look forward into the future?'

'You would be surprised how often I look forward into the future! It's true I can never forget the past, but the future is more of a problem than you can imagine.'

'There should be some man in your life so that you could think of it together.'

'There is no man in my life – my future concerns my daughter and only my daughter.'

'And one day your daughter will leave you to work out her own destiny. Do you not think of that?'

'Of course. But my daughter did not ask to be born. She is my responsibility.'

'Perhaps, but you also have a responsibility for yourself. Help yourself and you help your daughter.'

She stared at him uncertainly. He disturbed her strangely. There was the weird feeling that she was on the slope of a precipice and moving too quickly towards the edge . . .

24

A whole week went by before the Princess sent for Laura again. It was a request delivered by Hassan while she sat on the terrace eating her breakfast – and when she saw him walking through the garden towards the villa she had the strangest premonition that the day was somehow destined to change the course of her life.

She took the note he handed her with a smile and Bridget, who had come out to sit with her, eyed him curiously.

The note was brief but polite, asking her to wait upon the Princess a little later in the morning, as she had something most urgent to say to her.

She thanked Hassan and promised to comply with the request, then she handed the note to Bridget.

'Dade and what can she be wantin' now?' the Irishwoman said curiously. 'Have you any idea?'

'No; but it's obviously important.'

'Have their Syrian visitors gone back, then?' Bridget asked astutely.

'I'm not sure. I haven't seen either of them.'

'You'll not be able to have the women here this mornin', then?'

'No, I'm afraid not. Perhaps you wouldn't mind walking down to the village to tell them, Bridget? I'll see them tomorrow as usual.'

Bridget sat on at the breakfast table after Laura had left her and muttered darkly, 'There's somethin' afoot! Sure and why should Her Highness be after seeing Laura over something urgent? For six long years there's been nothin' *urgent.*'

The Princess received her in the summerhouse, a white, open pagoda where they could hear the tinkling of the waterfall and smell the blossoms.

The Princess received Laura with a gracious smile, her hand indicating that she should sit opposite while the niceties of almond cakes and fresh pomegrantate juice were served. As she sipped the refreshing liquid Laura couldn't rid herself of the memory of her grandmother's repeated words, that she wanted no taint of the pomegranate to illuminate future generations of the Mallonden family. The Princess, who was watching her, wondered what particular bitterness had brought that bleak look into the younger woman's face.

For several minutes they talked pleasantries – the prowess of Laura's pupils, the progress of her daughter – and then the Princess suddenly dropped all pretence by saying, 'It is the well-being of Rosetta of which I wish to speak, Laura.'

Laura looked at her enquiringly and the Princess went on: 'I cannot think that you are entirely content to live on here in the Fayoum. Have you given no thought to Rosetta's future life? The girl is six years old, time for her to be with other girls of a similar age, to be educated into the ways of the world.'

'Can it be so important, Your Highness, when most of the women in Egypt receive scant education? Though, with respect, I was not referring to you; you are possibly the most intelligent educated woman I know, but Fawzia received only an education I left behind me when I was ten years old.'

'That, my dear, is what I am trying to tell you. Fawzia is Egyptian; you are English and your daughter is half-Egyptian. What have you been able to give your daughter? Not a name, because you were never married to my son. If and when the Nationalist Party take control here we are not sure how much we shall be able to salvage and you, as an Englishwoman, will be totally disregarded.

'It is time for the child to be educated; it is time for you to put away the past and look to the future. You can expect no help from your own family. They have had six years to approach you but they have shown no interest in you or your child; now you have to think very carefully about where you go from here. Do you wish to continue in this dream world of living from day to day with only the past secure in your heart and no vision of the future, or do you want to ensure your daughter's future and your own?'

'How can I answer that question when I have no alternative to the life I am leading?'

'Perhaps I can give you that alternative. My nephew has a high regard for you. He sees in you the sort of wife who would grace his home when he goes to Paris as Ambassador at the end of the year.'

'But how can he? We hardly know each other! How can I possibly marry a man I scarcely know?'

'He has extended his stay with us so that you can get to know each other. Omar is well educated. He has spent many years in Europe, as Ahmed did. Next year he will be in Paris; marry him and you will be there with him and Rosetta can go to a school for girls in a similar station of life to her own. She will be Omar's daughter, a Syrian princess, courted and fêted in a city where there is not the same antagonism to those of a different race as there is in England.'

Stunned, Laura could only look at her in shock. The princess smiled. 'I can see that I have amazed you, Laura. Go back home and think about all I have said. Use the next few weeks to get to know Omar. Tomorrow you will ride with him – I will tell him you wish him to show you the oasis in the Libyan desert.'

Laura walked home as if in a dream. She could not believe that she had been more or less ordered to receive Omar Kamel, to receive him as a possible suitor. It was archaic. Yet was it any more archaic than listening to her mother extolling the virtues of Edward Burlington when she was only just out of the schoolroom?

The Princess had pressed her hand gently on her departure, saying 'Believe me, marriages planned in the head are quite often more successful than those dreamed of in the heart. Women of my class in Egypt never had any alternative and ask yourself quite honestly if it is such a bad idea. Think of all the advantages it can have for Rosetta.'

As Laura neared her villa she saw Rosetta waiting for her at the gate. Her face lit up with a smile and she came running eagerly along the path towards her. For almost the first time she began to see Rosetta in a new light, no longer as a child, and with a face as beautiful as it was intelligent.

The Princess was right. Rosetta was the one who mattered. Whatever she did in the future had to be for Rosetta, otherwise she might as well have obeyed her grandmother and left her baby in that Home for unfortunate women somewhere in the wilds of Scotland . . .

Laura did not immediately take Bridget into her confidence; this was something she had to think about quietly without Bridget adding her opinions, but the Irishwoman was not deceived. Laura's reticence told her more than actual words would have done. Her suspicions were confirmed when Omar Kamel arrived the following morning to invite Laura to ride with him.

She watched them setting out along the village road with acute misgivings. They made a very handsome couple, he with his dark romantic good looks, Laura delicately fair, but Bridget racked her brain trying to remember all she had heard about Omar Kamel and his life in Damascus . . .

Laura was finding him charming as he chatted amiably about the oasis he wished to show her, and riding with him was a joy as they stretched their horses across the miles of desert sand.

There was no room for conversation now, but after a period of intimate silence, little towns appeared on the far horizon of the desert – little towns with white minarets and green palm trees; and evidently there was water, for Laura could see the white wings of sailing boats, like birds, on the edge of the desert.

She reined in her horse sharply and Omar turned his horse so that they stood together staring into the distance.

'I had no idea,' she said suddenly, 'that there were so many towns in the real desert; I thought only bedouins and various sorts of tent-dwellers lived on its barren waste away from the Nile. But there must be water there. What are we coming to?'

He smiled. 'I'm afraid it would take you a very long time to reach that city,' he said. 'About as long as it took the boy to reach the end of the rainbow where he went to find the buried treasure. I doubt if any of the inhabitants of the Fayoum have ever been any nearer than we are now.'

'Why is that?' Laura said. 'Is there something sacred about it? Is it a forbidden city?'

'It is a city forbidden to all mortals and no mortal has ever trodden its streets; no prayer has ever been offered up by human lips from those white mosques; no call to prayer cried from those minarets. Laura, those beautiful eyes have seen their first mirage, a real desert mirage. That city over there doesn't exist at all . . .'

He smiled at the expression of wonder in her eyes

and, as they met his, the colour crept into her face although at that moment all she could think was that he looked like Ahmed, spoke like Ahmed, brought Ahmed back into her life with a disturbing reality.

All Omar was aware of was that he wanted this girl with her Western beauty as he had never before wanted anything in his life . . .

Bridget watched the friendship blossoming. Now Laura looked forward to his visits; she heard them laughing together, saw their restraint become anticipation. Laura was coming alive again and it was like watching a rose blossoming into full and glorious life after the chill winds of winter had gone.

Sagely, Bridget kept her comments to herself, but as she watched them ride out in the morning sunlight she said to herself, 'Dade and I'm not sure if it's any more right than the first one was, and her with her memories of the West pulling at her heartstrings!'

But Omar was blinding her with talk of life in Paris at the Syrian Embassy; the shops, the receptions, the fashion houses and an endless supply of money, all the things Laura had been missing during her years in the Fayoum. He brought her gifts, jewellery and perfume; gifts, too, for Rosetta, even perfume for Bridget who looked at it askance until Laura laughed at her doubtful face.

Omar told her that his mother was delighted with the way their friendship was developing and now she was welcomed into the Farag household as if she was one of them instead of the outcast she felt she had been for all too long.

When she told Bridget that Omar had finally asked her to marry him the Irishwoman said, 'And will ye be livin' in Damascus, then?'

'No, we shall be living in Paris where Omar is to be the new Ambassador. I want you to come with us, Bridget. I don't know what I should do without you.'

Bridget looked at her sadly. 'And what of Rosetta then?'

'She will be sent to a good school. It's time she had some real education, Bridget.'

'Then neither of ye will really be needin' me, love.'

'Bridget, you can't mean it! I'll need you more than ever, to talk common sense to me, stop me from spending money as if there's no tomorrow, remind me to be sensible. Oh Bridget, you can't think of leaving me now!'

Bridget kept her own counsel until Laura informed her that she and Omar were to be married at the Coptic Church in Cairo before leaving for Marseilles. She was to wear Eastern dress for the wedding, a kaftan which the Princess had given her, and she would shop for her trousseau in Paris.

'So you've finally made yer mind up, then?' Bridget said. 'If you're happy I'm glad for ye, but it seems to me that all I've heard is the sort o' life you're intendin' to lead in Paris; there's not bin a word about lovin' him.'

For a brief moment Laura's face clouded, then, more sharply than she intended, she said, 'I don't want to love anybody again in the way I loved Ahmed! I loved him with a sort of human bondage, Bridget. I'd have followed him to the ends of the earth. This time it's for *me*! But you are coming with me, aren't you, Bridget?'

'No, love, I'm not. I've made up mi mind that it's time I went home and made mi peace with mi kinfolk.'

'Home!' Laura echoed plaintively.

'Home to County Clare to see mi old father and mi sisters and two brothers. It seems like a hundred years since I walked out of mi father's house in a temper because I thought he favoured mi sisters more than me. I was young then, young and headstrong. I thought I knew it all. I took all mi savings out o' the bank and headed for London where I got a job with a well-off family as a kitchenmaid. I was good with children and when their nanny left I took care of 'em. That's when it all started. The husband came out here to work and I came with them. When they went home I stayed on with the Farag family and I haven't been unhappy. I'll always have good memories of them and of Egypt, but it's time I went home.'

'Are you sure you'll be welcome at home, Bridget?'

'Oh, yes, love, I'll be welcome. Which is more than you can say of that hard-hearted lot you called your family!'

'When will you go?' Laura asked dismally.

'As soon as you've gone, love. Now that I've made up mi mind I can't wait to see Ireland again. Have ye never bin there?'

'No, never.'

'Oh, but it's bonny. It's so green with the rain that falls on it, rain that lies on the wind like an angel's touch, and the sea's never so far away. Oh, sure and I'll miss the desert. I'll miss the sunsets and the warm sun; I'll miss the weight o' the years. Ireland'll seem so new after all this, and I'll spend the rest o' mi days lookin' out across the Shannon instead o' the Nile. I won't say there'll not be times when I'm missin' it somethin' awful!'

Laura's face was as bleak as Bridget's as they stared at each other, and there were tears in her eyes when she said, 'Oh Bridget, I'll miss it, too, all of it. And love that I thought would be for ever and which vanished so quickly, like a dream . . .'

25

Paris! Enchanting Paris with a beautiful house on one of the city's expensive boulevards and money, so much money she wouldn't have been human if she hadn't basked in the splendour of it.

Born into one of England's most aristocratic families, she could never remember a time when her mother hadn't bemoaned the fact that there was never enough money, for her education, her clothes, her holidays.

Now she had so much money she found it unbelievable. The fashion houses welcomed her into their perfumed salons where she could pick and choose as they vied for her custom. Jewellers tempted her with gems to enhance her gowns; and there were furs – the richness of sable, the glamour of mink, the delicacy of ermine. Expensive beauty parlours restored the honeyed gold into her hair while they pampered her body with massages and her hands with lotions and expensive varnishes.

Society came to know her as the beautiful Madame Kamel, the wife of the Syrian Ambassador, and the banquets the Kamels gave to their friends and foreign dignitaries became legend.

Laura did not love her husband as she had loved Ahmed. But she played the part of the gracious hostess, the model wife, the passionate lover. She felt she owed Omar a great deal, and she was still young and warm-hearted. She was also learning that passion need not necessarily be love. Her body could lie, her heart had never been able to.

Omar had insisted that Rosetta should be known as his daughter and she was enrolled as Rosetta Kamel in one of Paris's most expensive schools. Here she was in the company of the daughters of wealthy Parisians and Laura was happy to know that she was making friends.

Laura had a houseful of servants to do her bidding but she soon realised that she had no close friends. The European women who came to her dinners with their husbands were pleasant and charming; they discussed their gowns and their jewellery, the opera and the latest plays, but, as the days and months passed, she knew none of them any better than she had known them at their first meeting.

They never invited her to meet them for coffee or afternoon tea in any of the city's innumerable intimate café's where women gathered together to discuss their children and the hundred-and-one other things most women found to talk about. She began to wish Bridget was here. More so when Rosetta said to her one evening, 'Mother, why do I never get invited to birthday parties like the other girls? It was Claudia's birthday yesterday and I know she had a party. She's my friend, but she didn't invite me!'

'I don't know, darling. Perhaps she thought you wouldn't know many of the others.'

'But I do! I know quite a lot of them.'

'I'm sure you'll be invited when we've been in Paris a little longer.'

When she mentioned it to Omar he said, easily, 'Arabian women do not generally gossip with Europeans in the city shops and cafés.'

'But I am not Arabian, Omar!' she said sharply.

'You became so when you became my wife,' he said, sternly. 'Just as your daughter did.'

'You cannot take away my birthright, Omar! Do none of them realise that I am English?'

'No. I thought you wanted to leave the past behind. If that is true, it would be best to forget that you are English. When we go home, it is Damascus we shall be returning to, not England.'

She stared at him in silence. His face was courteous but grave. It was the face of a man who expected to be obeyed without question and, turning on his heel, he left her to think over what he had just said.

Over the months, Laura was made to realise increasingly that her role in her husband's life was purely ornamental. She was there to add lustre to the receptions and functions they attended; she was not expected to enter into discussions on world affairs or to have opinions outside the foibles and fripperies which he firmly believed made up a woman's life.

This was borne out forceably one evening when Omar heard her discussing the sad state of women in Egypt, where only the men in the towns and cities received an education and the women were expected to be little more than playthings or chattels. The Egyptian Ambassador listened to her with charming courtesy and, warming to her subject, Laura said firmly, 'Their men do not want them to read or write; it seems to me that their function in life is to bear as many children as possible before they are too old, and then quietly fade away.'

She was aware of Omar's eyes upon her from his place further up the table, and for the rest of the evening he pointedly ignored her presence. It was only when they arrived home that she became aware of the depth of his anger. He came into her bedroom, dismissing her maid curtly, and when she turned to stare at him she became aware for the first time of his face, so altered with rage that she scarcely knew him.

The change in him startled her. Hitherto all she had seen were his perfect manners, his charm, his generosity; now, for the first time, she was beholding a man she had never glimpsed behind the urbane civility he showed to the world.

No Arab wife would ever have behaved as she had done by expressing her own opinions, embarrassing her husband and the Egyptian Ambassador. 'Omar, I'm so sorry,' she cried sadly, 'What have I done?'

'Something you will never do again! You will not question any of our fellow guests on matters you do not understand. Is it because you are English that you feel you have a right to question and disagree with the traditions of other countries? I will not have my guests or any of our acquaintances embarrassed by my wife's preoccupation with their affairs.'

'But, Omar, the Ambassador listened to my views with a great deal of interest. I do not think they offended him.'

'He would not expect a woman of Syria to subject him to such criticism!'

'I am sorry, Omar, but I will probably never be a woman of Syria. You cannot alter the way I am. I was educated to think and feel, to see injustice and attempt to right it if it is in my power to do so.'

'It is not in your power! It will never be in your power. It is by my grace that you occupy your position in society – you will never forget it.'

She stared at him for a long moment before she asked, sadly, 'Why did you marry me Omar? Surely not because you loved me, or you would try to understand me.'

'I married you because I desired you. Now that I have possessed you the desire has changed somewhat. Now I *own* you. You are my wife and you will obey me. You will remember that it is your role in life to ornament my home with your clothes, your jewels and your beauty. I did not marry you for your intelligence or your nationality.'

After he had left her, Laura continued to sit at her dressing-table, staring at her reflection in the mirror. Sadness and fear engulfed her. How wrong she had been about her future with Omar! She had envisaged herself becoming like Ahmed's mother, gracious and looked up to. Now she realised that she was not like Ahmed's mother. Ayesha had known her place in her husband's household – she, Laura, had yet to learn it.

She had thought Omar would be like Ahmed, but whereas Ahmed had been educated to Western thinking, Omar had been brought up in the East and was steeped in Eastern prejudice. He had made it very clear that from now on he expected her to accept a role against which all her instincts rebelled.

She felt that she had sold herself for a pot of gold, and yet she hadn't wanted it to be like that. She had hoped to find love and protection for herself and her daughter. She had been prepared to give Omar children because she believed they would be important to him, but they had not come along and Omar had never reproached her, that much at least she had been grateful for.

Laura was careful never to make the mistake of airing her views again to any of their guests, but she was bored. Bored with nothing but women's talk; and conversation between her and Omar became increasingly difficult. There was a limit to what one could say about some play they had seen and passion was no substitute for love. As the months went by he came less and less to her bedroom and she was aware of the whisperings that went on around her and the sudden, continual appearance of another woman at their banquets.

The woman was a model for one of the fashion houses which Laura frequented. Half-French, half-Algerian, she possessed sultry dark eyes and an exotic beauty. Although she always arrived with an escort, he was eventually deserted in favour of Omar's attention. When her eyes met Laura's she was aware of the insolence in them and also of the gossip the woman's presence was creating amongst their acquaintances.

Within their society it was accepted that Omar should have his mistress, but one evening Laura remarked acidly, in the seclusion of their drawing room, that she deplored the talk going on around them and might at least expect that any indiscretions would not be conducted in her presence.

He came up behind her. She felt his fingers against the nape of her neck, as they unclasped the rope of pearls she was wearing. He faced her, the pearls draped through his fingers, his face wearing a half-smile, indifferent and cruel.

'You know how little it means,' he said softly.

'You would not like it if I behaved in a similar manner,' she replied, moving away from him.

'You are my wife – and, like Caesar's wife, I would expect you to be above suspicion. Women in my country have been stoned to death for less.'

She stared at him haughtily. 'I would expect to know more of your barbaric customs before we make our home there,' she said coldly.

Laura was trembling when she reached her bedroom. She had begun to realise that she had to accept what she couldn't change. She would play her part, be the sort of wife Omar wanted, but it was Rosetta who made her realise that for her daughter, at any rate, things had to change.

'Mother, why are all the girls talking about you and Father?' she asked innocently.

'Talking, Rosetta? What about?'

'Oh, some woman they call Chantal. They laugh and giggle about her all the time and I hate it.'

It was then that Laura decided Rosetta should go to school in England. When she informed Omar of her wishes he said, sarcastically, 'I would have thought England was the last place you would care to send her. She could find herself at the same school as the relatives who cast you aside years ago!'

'Rosetta knows nothing about my English relatives – and since she now bears your name it is unlikely that a connection with the Mallonden family will occur to anybody.'

She was surprised that he offered no objection except to say, 'I shall not be travelling to England with you; I have business in Nice.'

She could not keep the disbelief from her eyes and he laughed lightly before saying, 'What will you do in England? Try to recapture the life you threw away so lightly all those years ago?'

Laura didn't answer him, but she could not suppress a feeling of excitement at the thought of returning to England. She stared at her reflection in the mirror thinking: Will anybody recognise, in Laura Kamel, the girl I once was? That distant Laura had been young and innocent, trembling uncertainly on the edge of life, vain and foolish, desperately in love. Laura Kamel was a woman of a different mould, sophisticated and beautiful, a woman who had faced tragedy and learned to live with it.

She knew exactly the school she wanted for Rosetta. It had been too expensive for her mother to send her daughters to, but Poppy had gone there and all the Mallonden girls. The school she had in mind was run by a Miss MacNaughton, in Princes Avenue, South Kensington, a school that was modern in approach and luxurious in its appointments. The fees were high, its pupils gathered from the aristocracy and a fair smattering of wealthy Canadians and even wealthier Americans. Yet in spite of the luxury and freedom and the extreme modernity of the school, the girls were not spoilt.

If a girl was nice when she came to Miss MacNaughton, she was much nicer when she left her; if she was horrid when she arrived she was far less horrid when she went away.

Anne MacNaughton was American by birth, Scottish by ancestry and English by adoption, and there was a popular theory that, as she could pick and choose her pupils, she always chose in favour of good looks. This was not the case; but just as she had a genius for discovering the good points in even her worst pupils, she also had a flair for teaching them how to make the best of their looks. She could not bear stupidity and she declared that no woman who used her wits need ever look plain. No woman can make herself beautiful, but every woman can make herself attractive.

If she charged parents highly, she never grudged her pupils anything which appealed to her imaginative nature as likely to nurture their talents. She loved watching their mental development and increasing physical beauty, as a gardener loves watching the results of his lavish toil.

All this was in Laura's mind as she sat with her daughter in the taxi which was taking them to South Kensington. It was true that her cousin Poppy had never been strictly beautiful, but Poppy had always been nice, with a generous disposition that had made up for it.

Miss MacNaughton rose to greet her guests from an indulgently comfortable chair in her long drawing-room, a tall, well-proportioned woman with shingled silver hair, bright, intelligent blue eyes and a warm smile of greeting.

She was intrigued and enchanted with what she saw. A slender, beautiful woman, elegantly dressed in brown and beige, colours which complemented her honey-coloured hair and soft, pansy-hued eyes, a woman whose smile was strangely disturbing. And then she looked at the girl who accompanied her, the most strikingly beautiful girl she had ever seen.

Anne MacNaughton went forward to greet them, then she indicated two chairs set in front of the fire. Madame Kamel said, appreciatively, 'How lovely to see a coal fire shining on old mahogany!'

There was no trace of a foreign accent in Madame Kamel's voice, which surprised Miss MacNaughton considerably. She had been expecting a Syrian diplomat's wife and daughter and had thought to meet a woman with Arabian colouring, not this blonde beauty with perfect English. The child, though, was different. She had her mother's features and her mother's eyes, but that glorious blue-black hair proclaimed her Eastern origin and Miss MacNaughton's curiosity mounted.

'Who told you about my school, Madame Kamel?' she asked.

'It has a very good reputation, Miss MacNaughton – it seems I have been hearing about it for a very long time.'

'Your English is perfect, Madame. You, too, were educated in this country perhaps?'

Laura smiled. 'Yes, at Stourton in Essex.'

'A very good school.'

'Yes, but not as good as this one.'

'May I ask who recommended us? Was it one of my old pupils?'

'A great many of your old pupils, Miss MacNaughton.'

'Most of them keep in touch with me over the years and I like that. I feel none of my efforts were wasted. Your daughter has been at school in Paris?'

'Yes, for several years now. She speaks French fluently, of course, and Arabic.'

'Why have you taken her away from the school in Paris?'

'My husband is a diplomat. We entertain and are entertained a great deal and people gossip, sometimes unkindly. Girls can be cruel . . . Here, I feel sure, she will be safe from gossip about our everyday life.'

'You have my word for it, Madame. I have decided to put her with another girl who has been here since she was five years old. The girl she roomed with was involved in a riding accident in America during the school holidays, so she will not be returning here in the foreseeable future. I'm sure Rosetta and Angela will get along remarkably well.'

'Rosetta has always been good at making friends. I know she will be happy in London. Do you have many pupils from abroad?'

'From Canada and America, and I have had many girls from India. They all settle down well. It is a remarkably happy school, Madame Kamel, and I have a good staff, all of whom are popular with the girls.'

'Then I shall have nothing to worry about, Miss MacNaughton.'

Miss MacNaughton was intrigued by this beautiful woman who seemed totally unlike any other mother she had encountered on the day they brought their daughters to see her school. For many years she had considered herself to be a student of human nature, thinking that this was perhaps inevitable when she was responsible for the fashioning of so many young lives. Her pupils had come from all corners of the globe: the daughters of maharajahs, American senators and foreign diplomats, English peers and, lately, the daughters of men who had made money in trade and industry. But this woman had a certain something that set her apart. Her English was perfect and yet Miss MacNaughton could not believe that she was English. She sensed that in the past tragedy had played some part in her visitor's life, but why she should have this feeling she didn't know. Laura was gracious, and there was humour in her eyes and a certain, half-remembered gaiety. Most mothers talked about themselves almost as much as they talked about their daughters, but this mother was reticent, too reticent.

'Is it your intention to remain in London for some time, Madame Kamel?'

'No. I am here for a few days only but I would like to show Rosetta a little of London. We are staying in a rather nice hotel in Kensington and, if you are agreeable, I will bring Rosetta to the school on Monday morning. I hope to return to Paris the following day.'

'That will suit very well, Madame,' Miss MacNaughton said, somewhat surprised that her visitor had chosen to stay in a hotel in Kensington when she would have considered the Ritz or the Savoy more in keeping with the richness of the dark sable coat draped over Madame Kamel's knee and the array of glittering rings on her slender fingers.

After they had left her, Anne MacNaughton sat for a long while pondering about her latest pupil. She had felt strangely drawn towards the girl with her delicately exotic face and her mother's violet eyes. She would grow up with girls who would invite her to their homes, girls who would spoil and cosset her because she was beautiful and different. Anne MacNaughton had had long experience of girls from the East feeling English until their last day at school, after which they were somersaulted into an existence where women were shackled by conventions which an Englishwoman could have no conception of. Her mind went back to the tears that had been shed over the years, the questions asked to which she had had no answers, by girls from Arabian households whose mothers lived behind the veil in rooms filled entirely with women, and girls from India and the Far East facing marriages that had been arranged for them when they were small children.

Now here was this beautiful girl with all her life before her and Anne MacNaughton could not rid herself of the doubts and uncertainties that assailed her.

Her secretary seemed surprised to find her alone and Miss McNaughton said, 'Join me, Hester. Madame Kamel said they would have tea at her hotel. It seems we are to have another pupil, her daughter Rosetta, the first Syrian we have had. Her father is the Ambassador in Paris.'

'I saw them waiting in the hall,' Hester said. 'What a beautiful woman Madame Kamel is – and the girl too was lovely, such unusual colouring. I take it the mother is English?'

'I'm not too sure. Her English is perfect, but then she told me she was educated in this country. I sensed a reluctance to talk about herself. When the daughter matures, that raven-black hair and those incredible eyes are likely to cause mayhem among the menfolk of my other pupils.'

Hester laughed. 'I feel sure you're right,' she agreed.

They sat in companionable silence drinking their tea. Beech leaves tapped against the window and the late-afternoon sunlight fell on polished mahogany and bowls of flowers in the charming room. It was a very far cry from desert sunsets and the scenery of Rosetta's past . . .

Meanwhile, Laura and her daughter were walking in the direction of their hotel, unaware that a pair of inquisitive eyes watched them from the window of a taxi which was slowly passing by. Impatiently, the woman inside tapped on the glass between her and the driver.

'Please, stop a moment,' she ordered him, while the man sitting beside her followed her gaze as she turned to look behind her.

'Turn round,' she ordered the driver. 'I think we'll take tea here, it looks a very nice hotel.'

The taxi-driver obeyed. There was no accounting for the decisions or indecision of American tourists.

'Why are we stopping here, Lily?' the husband demanded. 'I thought you wanted to go to the Savoy?'

'We can go there later! Didn't you recognise her? I'm sure I'm right, but there's nothing to stop me finding out.' Lily Oppenheimer was every bit as inquisitive as she had been on the ship that was taking Laura to her destiny.

'Who? Who did you recognise?'

She had left the cab and, by the time her husband had paid the driver, she was waiting impatiently at the steps leading into the hotel.

'Who are we supposed to be looking for?' he grumbled.

'You'll see,' she said cagily.

The hotel lounge was quiet, with only a handful of people sitting at the tables drinking tea.

'We'll sit here,' Mrs Oppenheimer said quickly. 'We can see everybody who comes into the lounge.'

'You haven't said who we're looking for!'

'Hiram, I'm sure I'm right. I saw them leaving that house further up the road, and I recognised her. She's still very beautiful. I never forgot her, you know. She was the loveliest thing with those violet eyes and that honey-coloured hair. She'll be married now, of course, probably to some British nobleman. Her mother would have seen to that. She's probably in London for a few days, and the British stay in these smaller, discreet hotels. They leave the Savoy and the like to tourists like us.'

'Who are we talking about, for heaven's sake?' her exasperated husband finally managed to ask.

She stared at him, wide-eyed. 'You mean you didn't notice?'

'I didn't notice anything or anybody.'

'It was that girl, Laura. Surely you remember her on the boat going out to Egypt soon after the war? Her mother was that snooty woman with the two girls, and there was that Egyptian prince who was so terribly handsome. Laura was madly in love with him. Lady Hesketh sat at the captain's table with us – surely you haven't forgotten *her*?'

'Well, of course not. We met up with her in India and again in Singapore two years later. Aren't we supposed to be seeing them while we're in London?'

'Tomorrow. Didn't I tell you, Hiram? I'm sure I did.'

'You did not.'

'Oh well, I'm telling you now. I'll be able to tell her I've seen Laura. She'll be interested, I know. I remember she was very worried about her infatuation for that Egyptian prince.'

'Well, there's nobody in here who looks the slightest bit like that girl on the boat.'

'Have patience, Hiram, and order some tea.'

In their hotel bedroom, Laura had taken off her outdoor clothing and Rosetta was sitting at the small desk with a writing-pad in front of her.

'Aren't you coming down for tea, dear?' her mother asked.

'I don't feel like tea. I think I'll write to Celeste and Marie to tell them about the school I'm going to. They both said it would be *awful*.'

'You didn't think it was awful, did you?'

'No, I thought it was lovely! I'll be happy there, I'm sure. I'm glad it's for seven years, though. I might be ready to go to Syria by then!'

'Why are you so sure you are going to Syria? We could be anywhere in the world.'

'Father said when I left school in England you would be in Syria and I would go there, too.'

'And is that what you want, Rosetta?'

'Father said it is what happens to the girls in his family. They go home to be married to some man already chosen for them.'

Laura stared at her in dismay. 'When did he tell you that?'

'The night before we came to England.'

Laura stared at her daughter's dark head bent over her letter-writing. There had been no resentment in Rosetta's words, no questioning of Omar's plans for her future; only an Eastern acceptance that this was the way of things. Laura turned away with a feeling of utter helplessness.

Had she been wrong in bringing her daughter to school in England where she would learn independence, where she would listen to other girls talking about their futures and their right to fall in love with boys not chosen by their families? In the years ahead, how could Rosetta be expected to emerge from Western thinking unscathed?

'If you're sure you don't want tea, Rosetta, I'll see you in a little while. Give my love to your friends.'

Rosetta turned to smile and in her smile the years dropped away. It was Ahmed's smile, warm and embracing as it had been on that last day in the railway carriage, that reached out to her . . .

In the lounge, Laura went to her favourite table near the window where she could look out at the London street with its tall Georgian houses, unaware that from across the room Mrs Oppenheimer was saying, breathlessly, 'Now do you recognise her, Hiram? Why, she's hardly changed at all!'

Across the room her eyes met Laura's and she smiled and gave a little wave. Laura returned her smile but not the wave. She ordered tea and toast but all the time she was acutely aware of the man and woman staring across the room at her. To her dismay, the woman left her table and came across the room, smiling triumphantly. 'You are Laura, aren't you? I would have recognised you anywhere!'

Doubtfully, Laura returned her smile, but the woman had seated herself opposite and, not waiting for her reply, went on, 'I saw you in the street, and when you turned in here I just *had* to come after you. I told Hiram who you were – men never remember people – but he remembers you now.'

When Laura continued to look doubtful, Mrs Oppenheimer said, 'The boat out to Egypt, honey, just after the war. You left it at Alexandria and we sailed on to Bombay. We all sat at the captain's table, the Galbraiths and Lady Hesketh, you and your mother and sister and that *divine* Egyptian prince you couldn't take your eyes off!'

Laura recognised her now, the American woman who had revelled in her infatuation with Ahmed. There was no point in pretending that she was not that same Laura.

'I remember you now, Mrs Oppenheimer. I'm sorry, it is a very long time since I waved to you from the quayside in Alexandria.'

'Isn't it, just? And we've travelled about an awful lot. We go home to America in between our travels, telling ourselves that we'll stay there, that we've made our last trip abroad. Then we get itchy feet and off we go again. Now tell me about you. You're still the loveliest thing, and I can see you've married awfully well, I knew you would, of course. Who is he, some duke or some lord? He has to be!'

'Why do you say that?'

'Well, I remember your mother, honey. I spoke to her one afternoon and she said you were going to Egypt to meet some lord or other she hoped you'd marry. I thought it was a bit archaic myself, but I could see she was pretty determined. Now, tell me who the lucky man is, and was that your daughter I saw you with?'

'Yes, her name is Rosetta. I did not marry an Englishman, Mrs Oppenheimer. My husband is the Syrian Ambassador to France.'

Her companion's eyes opened wide in astonishment. 'Then you didn't marry your lord, then?'

'No. My sister married him instead.'

'And you married a foreigner? Well! Tell me, did you ever meet up with Prince Ahmed in Egypt?'

'We saw him at Abydos and he was kind enough to assist us with the buying of momentoes.'

'Is that all?'

Laura smiled and said nothing.

'We're going to see Lady Hesketh and her husband tomorrow evening at their London home – we've met up with them on several occasions over the last few years and she'll be so thrilled to know that I've met you again. How long are you here for?'

'My daughter starts at her new school next Monday and I shall return to Paris the day after.'

'So you'll be all on your own in London on Monday evening?'

'I shall be busy packing.'

'That won't take all evening, Laura. Now, Hiram and I are staying at the Dorchester so why don't you spend the evening with us? I'll invite the Hesketh and one or two other friends.'

'Well, I don't really think there'll be time . . .' Laura said, reluctantly.

'I'm not going to take no for an answer. We'll send a car round for you and, on reflection, there'll be just the Hesketh and us. We'll have dinner and chat about old times. Don't disappoint me, Laura!'

'It's very kind of you, Mrs Oppenheimer.'

'Until Monday evening, then. The car will be here at seven and Hiram will wait for you in the foyer.'

With a warm smile she rose and Laura watched her hurrying across the room to rejoin her husband. As they left the room both turned to smile and Laura sat back with a feeling of dismay. She had been so sure that if she and Rosetta stayed in this small, unassuming hotel she would not encounter anybody she knew. Now here was this woman with a memory as long as her tongue . . .

26

Mrs Oppenheimer produced Laura with a certain degree of triumph on Monday evening and Lady Hesketh took in at a glance the younger woman's reserve which was totally lost on her more ebullient hostess.

The jade beaded evening gown complemented her honey-coloured hair, now a little darker than Moira Hesketh remembered it, but Laura's eyes had lost none of their lustre and there was a haunting sadness in a face which had been so ready at all times to smile.

Lily Oppenheimer would have liked to talk about the past, to reminisce about that fateful voyage, but Moira Hesketh talked about life in India and the fact that they were now retired in England and enjoying every moment of it. The two men were gallant and, unable to restrain herself any longer, Mrs Oppenheimer said at last, 'And to think that this young lady is married to a Syrian. I'll bet he resembles that handsome Prince Ahmed. Now admit it, Laura.'

'He is quite handsome,' Laura said quietly.

'And you have a daughter?' Lady Hesketh said gently.

'Yes, Rosetta.'

'A name from Egypt, I think?'

'Yes, I thought it was pretty.'

'We only saw the back of her, but I'll bet she's a beauty,' Mrs Oppenheimer said. 'You're probably wise in sending her to school in England.'

'Perhaps. She's been educated in Paris until now and I would like her to know more of England.'

'Well, of course. And what does your mother think about it all.'

'I haven't seen my mother for some considerable time.'

'Your sister then?'

'Or my sister.'

'Oh well, I expect it's difficult with you living in a different culture, so to speak. There's a gentleman dining over there with a group of people who seems very interested in you. Do you know him? He looks kind of familiar to me?'

Across the room Laura looked at a tall, distinguished-looking man with silver-winged hair who smiled – and suddenly she was remembering John Halliday's smile and every moment of their last meeting.

Lady Hesketh said, 'Of course we should all remember him! He was also on the boat going out to the East. He's John Halliday, a diplomat. He's probably home on leave.' Moira Hesketh smiled in his direction and suddenly Laura was back on that liner again, watching him cross the ballroom with Ahmed on their way back from the bridge room and it seemed to her, at that moment, that all their lives were fatefully intermingled.

It was later in the evening before John Halliday was able to learn something of Laura's life since that day he had left her on the steps of the military hospital in Cairo. If her story amazed him, he did not show it. It was only when she told him she was in England to settle her daughter in to Miss MacNaughton's school that he said, quietly, 'So you had a daughter, Laura. I often wondered.'

'Yes. I called her Rosetta and she is very like her father.'

'And your husband – he knows everything?'

'Yes. He is Ahmed's cousin. We met at Ahmed's parents' home in the Fayoum with their approval. But Egypt is changing, though how it has affected them I'm not sure. I have never been back there.

And what about you? Are you returning to the Far East?'

'To Singapore, until my retirement. Can it really be eleven years since we all met on that fateful voyage to the East – fateful at least where you were concerned?'

'Those eleven years seem like a lifetime.'

'And what does the future hold for you, Laura?'

'Well, I'm not sure how long we shall remain at the Embassy in Paris, and then – have you ever been to Damascus?'

'No, though I've heard that it is an interesting city. It certainly has a long history. You will make your home there when you leave France?'

'I think so.'

At that moment Mrs Oppenheimer joined them, her bright, inquisitive eyes looking from one to the other expectantly, saying gaily, 'You two seem to have a lot to talk about! Why don't you join us, Mr Halliday?'

'Thank you, but I am with friends whom I've been neglecting.'

He bowed and went to rejoin his companions and Mrs Oppenheimer said, 'I really don't remember him on the boat. I'm surprised that you did, Laura.'

'Well, I met him in Egypt several times.'

'Is he married?'

'I really know very little about him, except that he is a diplomat and will soon be on his way back to Singapore.'

'Hiram and I liked Singapore – we had a lovely time there – but I doubt if we'll ever be going back. You know, we've never been to Syria . . . do you think we would like Damascus?'

'I really don't know – I have yet to discover it for myself.'

'Are you going to see your mother and sister before you go back?' she asked curiously.

'No, there won't be time.'

'Fancy your sister marrying that man your mother was anxious for you to marry. I except it pleased her, but was she as pleased about your marriage, honey?'

Laura smiled and, recognising the strain in it, Lady Hesketh who had come up to them, said gently, 'You look tired, Laura. I expect these last few days have been rather hectic.'

'Yes. I wanted to show my daughter as much of London as was possible and she has so much energy and curiosity! I do hope you don't mind if I return to my hotel now. I am leaving quite early in the morning.'

It had been an ordeal. First, Lily Oppenheimer's curiosity and then her meeting with John Halliday which had raised too many ghosts. All Laura wanted to do was get back to Paris and the continuing round of dinner-parties and the role she would be expected to play as an Ambassador's wife . . .

In Paris, life took up its familiar pattern. Omar was courteous and not in the least curious about her visit to England or Rosetta's new school, and it didn't take her long to realise that Chantal had been replaced, this time by a bold-eyed half-Negro woman who came to dinner in the company of a large man from the Russian Embassy.

Laura was neither unhappy nor happy. She seemed to be living in a kind of limbo to which she could see no end, waiting for Rosetta's letters which told her she was happy in England. The child spoke enthusiastically of her friends, the ballet and the theatres the girls were taken to, and she had developed a great affection for Miss MacNaughton who had been at great pains to make her feel at home.

More and more, as time passed, she asked permission to spend the school holidays in the homes of her friends and Laura readily agreed to this even when

Omar remarked, caustically, 'I suppose she had better make the most of it. She will find life in Damascus more limiting.'

Rosetta showed little inclination to return to Paris which gave Laura the excuse to visit England when ever Omar was away. These were the times she loved most, when Miss MacNaughton allowed her daughter long weekends so that they could explore London and the surrounding countryside together.

When Omar commented on her daughter's reluctance to visit them in Paris Laura said, 'Have you never thought, Omar, that Rosetta may wish to remain in England? That she may even want to take up a profession?'

'What sort of a profession is a woman fitted for?' he asked disdainfully. 'Clever women are unattractive, they are like men.'

'More and more the world is opening up for women. One day even Eastern women will see this.'

'Eastern women will not see it. Their menfolk dictate what they should see.'

'I want something more than that for Rosetta.'

'On the day you married me, you made Rosetta my daughter. She will obey me in all things, just as you will obey me. You will see how different life is when we live in Damascus.'

'Why do you never take me to Damascus? When you go there you go alone. We spend vacations all over Europe, yet you have never taken me to Syria.'

'When we go there together we shall be going there to stay. When I am no longer Ambassador in Paris.'

'I would like to go there before then, Omar. I would like to meet your mother again. I would also like to visit Egypt to see Ahmed's mother.'

'Egypt has changed. The Nationalist Party are in power now and they are making second-class citizens of the old families. You would not like Egypt now, Laura.'

On her visits to London Laura thought of visiting Lady Hesketh because she badly needed someone to talk to; but she always decided against it. Pride would not let her admit that she had been wrong about so many things. She had loved Ahmed with all her heart and soul but he had been right when he had said that their futures did not lie together. It was almost as though he had been able to look down the long road ahead and see its tragedies.

She wished she could take Miss MacNaughton into her confidence. She admired her logical approach to life, her humour and her courage, but something always held her back on the rare occasions when they met.

Miss MacNaughton had nothing but good to say about Rosetta. She was an excellent pupil, conscientious in her studies, amiable with her friends and popular with everybody. The girls enjoyed inviting her to spend time with their families because she was beautiful and intelligent and she had shown them she could ride well, dance gracefully and converse with people at all levels.

Rosetta stood out starkly amongst the bevy of European and American girls with their blonde hair and rosy faces, bounding enthusiastically across the tennis courts; nor was she at one with the girls from the Far East or Arabia. Rosetta was a hybrid with her slender grace, her shining dark hair and pale, porcelain skin, and Laura's unforgettable eyes.

Miss MacNaughton tried not to make favourities of her girls, but she loved beautiful things, whether they be girls, figures in expensive porcelain or exquisite flowers. She had grown to love Rosetta Kamel for her beauty and the clarity of her mind, for her natural yet sweet reserve.

She was unprepared for Lady Tarleton's questions on the afternoon when she came to collect her daughter for the Christmas holidays.

Angela Tarleton's mother was a tall, aristocratic woman of singular charm and quite unafraid to pose questions other women would have baulked at.

'I'm glad we're having this chance to talk, Miss MacNaughton,' she said evenly. 'We're spending Christmas at my brother's house and Angela has asked if she may bring her room-mate. Apparently her parents are abroad so she will not be able to be with them.'

'What is it you wish to know, Lady Tarleton?'

'Well, it's not so much me as the family. Granny Mallonden will be with us and she's always had this thing about foreigners. I admit it's quite illogical in this day and age, but Rosetta is Syrian, I believe?'

'Yes. Her father is the Syrian Ambassador in Paris. I have never met him but her mother is cultured and beautiful – and, to tell you the truth, I thought she was English.'

'And is she?'

'I don't know – only that she looks it.'

'We don't want any unpleasantness . . . My grandmother has always been like this. She never forgave Aunt Lavinia for being half American and, as she's got older, she's grown steadily worse. Something very unfortunate happened years ago and she hasn't managed to get it out of her system.'

'I am quite happy to have Rosetta spend Christmas with me,' Anne MacNaughton said. 'We can have a thoroughly enjoyable time here in London with the shops and the theatres.'

'And my daughter will be furious! No, my husband and I will be glad to have Rosetta. I must say Angela has shown more promise since she roomed with her and I, for one, think Granny is paranoid about what she calls the "shadow of the pomegranate". We've laughed about it for years. So we'll all make a great fuss of Rosetta, and make sure she has as little contact with Granny as possible!'

Lady Tarleton flashed her a bright smile and, collecting her gloves, bade Miss MacNaughton good afternoon. Then she went to the main hall and took her place among the rows of chairs rapidly filling up with mothers and fathers greeting each other warmly. She noticed that some of the mothers wore Eastern dress and she frowned. She did hope Rosetta wouldn't produce something as exotic as a sari. In fact, what *did* Syrian girls and women wear?

The girls sat up on the dais, all wearing the school uniform of pale grey skirts and pink blouses; fair girls and dark girls, plain and pretty. She smiled at Angela's pink-and-white face with her neatly brushed blonde hair. She hoped fervently that Granny Mallonden would appreciate Rosetta's rumoured beauty and ignore her nationality!

Rosetta had long since come to terms with the fact that in England she was foreign, though at Miss MacNaughton's she was not made to feel so. All in all, the girls were nice and she had made friends. She spent most of her time with Angela Tarleton because they shared a room and, in the first year or two, Angela was openly curious about her background, her time in Paris and what she expected from the future.

Rosetta had a natural reserve that had been fostered by her early life in Egypt. Her mother had always been reticent about her family and all Rosetta knew was that they were an aristocratic family who disapproved of her mother totally. That was the reason why they were living in the Fayoum, close to her father's family.

She knew that her father had been killed before he could marry her mother and that, presumably, made her some sort of outcast. But Rosetta was a survivor. She had welcomed her mother's marriage to Omar Kamel, though she was sorry to leave the Fayoum which had always been her home because she loved its beauty. She was sorry, too, to leave Bridget who was kind and fun to be with and she knew she would miss Grandmother Ayesha, who had swept through her young life like some exotic being from the *Arabian Nights* and brought her cousins to play with, and the grandfather who adored her.

Rosetta had enjoyed her time in Paris but people gossiped about her father's affairs, her mother's disregard of them. Here things were different. For one thing there was Miss MacNaughton who had taken great pains to make Rosetta's entry into English life run smoothly. For her fellows, Rosetta invented a stable and happy background. Her parents were lovers, her home was tranquil, Damascus was the city of *The Thousand and One Nights*, a romantic, enchanting city of domes and minarets. All she had ever heard or seen of Cairo she ornamented to make Damascus glorious and, when she heard the girls talking about ideas they might have of a professional life, she invented the Arabian prince who was simply waiting until she was seventeen to whisk her away on his magic carpet – with her father's permission.

This was the dreaming, vulnerable Rosetta, but there was another Rosetta, a girl with ideas of vengeance and atonement.

Now she sat on her bed watching Angela sitting on her suitcase in an attempt to fasten it. Angela had packed badly as always – she was a happy-go-lucky girl who did everything in a hurry and tended to forget things.

Rosetta got up to help with the case and Angela said, a little petulantly, 'I'd really much rather we were spending Christmas at home, but we do it in turn. Next year it'll be Aunt Poppy and the year after that, Aunt Louise.'

'So you only do one in four?' Rosetta said.

'Well yes, but this one's the grandest because it's at Grandfather's house.'

'And your grandfather is the Earl of Mallonden?'

'Yes. There'll be a lot of us there – aunts and uncles and their children – but I expect Great-Aunt Lavinia will be spending Christmas with her daughter Margaret who's married to the Marquis of Camborne's eldest son.'

'I suppose a marquis is very grand?'

'Very grand indeed. But Mummy says Great-Aunt Lavinia is very grand – she always has been.'

'Then it's just as well she won't be there at Christmas.'

'I suppose so. You'll like Aunt Poppy. I adore going to her place; they live in a lovely country manor with lots of dogs and horses, and Aunt Poppy's *nice.* I think it's awful not to be seeing your parents at Christmastime, Rosetta. Don't you really mind?'

'No. Mother's coming to London in January for a few days and we'll have our Christmas then.'

'But it's not the same, is it?'

'Not to you, perhaps. I'm different – I'm not English.'

'No, I suppose that *does* make a difference. I'm going to put this case in the storeroom downstairs – I suppose yours is already there?'

'Yes, since yesterday.'

Angela grinned. 'Thanks for not saying I'm awful! I know I am, without your telling me.'

After Angela had left her, Rosetta went to the bedside cabinet and took a letter out of the small drawer. It was from her mother, written in Laura's small wandering writing and covering several pages. She could imagine her mother sitting at her small lacquered desk in the white-and-gold Paris drawing room, her pen poised over the letter, a frown of concentration on her brow, her soft, honey-coloured hair framing her face, the face Rosetta loved more than any other. It was a letter of love and warmth, promising her a wonderful time during their next meeting in London in January.

Miss MacNaughton had written to tell her mother that Rosetta would be quite happy staying with her, over Christmas but she had followed this with a letter informing her that her daughter was to spend Christmas with Angela's family at her grandfather's house. Madame Kamel wouldn't mind, she knew. She would be glad that Rosetta and Angela were getting along so well.

Rosetta had never liked Christmas in Paris. At Christmas she'd been made to feel awkward. Her father had been disinterested, her mother sad. Here in England it was different. The top of her cabinet was filled with Christmas cards from the other girls, scenes of snow and choristers, pert little robins and stagecoaches in the snow. She was remembering what her mother had told her about English Christmasses when they were sitting out on the terrace of their house in the Fayoum; and she had hardly believed any of it since all she could see were waving palm fronds and the long fields of emerald green before the desert claimed them.

She could hear Angela's clear, high-pitched voice chatting to somebody outside in the corridor, and the next minute she entered the room with her mother.

Rosetta rose to her feet to take Lady Tarleton's outstretched hand.

'How beautiful you all looked this afternoon,' Lady Tarleton said sweetly. 'Angela tells me you're both packed and ready for the journey in the morning. We shall be calling for you about eleven. Now, Granny Mallonden will be with us for Christmas. She's eccentric and not always diplomatic. However, she's awfully old so we do make allowances. I hope you will, too, my dear.'

Rosetta looked puzzled and Angela gave her mother a stern look so that Lady Tarleton trilled gaily, 'Oh, she'll not be brusque with you, my dear, but she might well be with the rest of us. Don't let it bother you.'

'I don't know why she's coming,' Angela complained. 'She always grumbles about the journey; her room's always too cold and there are too many people. Why doesn't she spend Christmas at the London house with her friends?'

'My dear child, she's outlived most of her friends! No. She likes to keep her eye on the rest of us and she'd be quite miserable staying on in London, wondering what we were all up to. Have you grandparents, Rosetta?'

'I have my grandmother Ayesha and my grandfather.'

'Safely in Damascus, I'm sure.'

'In the Fayoum.'

'The Fayoum?'

'In Egypt.'

'Really? I had such a lovely time in Egypt – the dances at Shepheards and the Winter Palace, the garden-parties at the First Cataract. We must go back there one day, perhaps when Angela is old enough to come with us to enjoy those things. Of course, you will know all about them, my dear.'

Rosetta smiled.

It seemed that every day of her life she was learning more about the gulf which separated her from girls like Angela. If she had still been living in the Fayoum she would not even see girls like Angela, let alone talk to them . . .

27

Granny Mallonden arrived in the afternoon of Christmas Eve with a great deal of fuss and bother. The staff and the family took their places in the vast hall to greet her and Rosetta stood with Angela at the end of the queue, expecting to see a larger-than-life figure appear through the portals of the front door. Instead, she saw a small, bent old lady who leaned heavily on her companion but whose sharp, intelligent eyes scanned the waiting ranks, missing nothing.

Angela's grandfather and grandmother were the first to greet her, then she walked slowly along the row of children and grandchildren and great-grandchildren, knowing every face, occasionally asking questions. Angela's eldest brother, William, was at Eton and fixing him with a direct look she said, in her high, querulous voice, 'I hope you're working hard, Alistair, not like those boys I read about in the newspaper. I want to see you at Oxford next year, I'll accept nothing less.'

'Yes Great-Grandmother,' he said softly, his head bent, his face flushed.

'You only came to see me three times this summer,' she accused Angela's mother.

'I know, Granny, it was very difficult. Nigel was in America and I was with him some of the time, and there was the house to see to and visiting the children at their schools. Sometimes I wondered how I coped.'

'I coped when I was your age. Why do I get this feeling that the modern generation are less than we were, not the same sort of people at all? Why aren't you sending your girls to Miss MacNaughton's school in London, Poppy? Lavinia's grand daughter is going there and I don't like to think she's going to crow about that every time I see her.'

'It's very expensive, Granny, and Eric doesn't have that kind of money. Financially, it's not been a good year for us.'

'Are you doing well at school, Angela?' the dowager asked, ignoring Poppy's explanation.

'I think so, Great-Grandmother,' Angela said, looking down on her grandmother whose eyes slid towards Rosetta, missing nothing of her beauty which was too exotic for the garb of an English schoolgirl.

'Who are you?' she asked abruptly.

'Rosetta Kamel, Lady Mallonden,' Rosetta answered her, her eyes never wavering from the old lady's stern glance.

'You are not English?'

'No.'

'Is she with you, Angela?'

'Yes, Great-Grandmother. Rosetta's father is the Syrian Ambassador in Paris.'

'Syrian, eh? Well, you're the first Syrian I have met. I must say you speak remarkably good English. What other languages do you speak?'

'French and Arabic.'

As the dowager moved away to the servants' rank, the tension amongst her family lessened considerably.

'We always get this,' Angela whispered to Rosetta when she thought her grandmother was out of earshot. 'I was terribly embarrassed when she spoke to you.'

'There was no need for you to feel embarrassed,' Rosetta said with a smile.

'Oh, but there was. She thinks because she's old she can speak to everybody the way she likes.'

And not just because she's old, Rosetta thought.

On Christmas morning the family prepared to go to church and Lady Mallonden asked Rosetta if it was her wish to go with them, or did it conflict with her own religion?

'My family are Coptic Christians,' Rosetta answered her. 'I would like to go to church.'

'I know the Christians in Egypt are called Copts,' the Dowager Lady Mallonden said sharply. 'I did not think that applied to other Christians in the Middle East.'

Rosetta was saved from answering by Lord Mallonden, who came to hurry them up by saying that the cars were waiting.

'After lunch we drive round the villages distributing gifts to Grandfather's tenants,' Angela informed her. 'You might find that terribly boring.'

'I'd like to take a look round the house if you don't mind,' Rosetta answered her. 'I haven't really had a chance to look at the pictures in the Long Gallery and there is so much to see.'

'That's a marvellous idea. You'll love the family portraits and there's the Wedgwood Room that Grandfather is so proud of. I suppose in your home in Damascus you have lovely things like jade and ivory. Grandfather has some, but I don't suppose they can be compared to yours.'

Rosetta merely smiled, and immediately after lunch she stood at the front door watching the family pile into cars and set off down the drive. She was surprised to see the old lady going with them. She looked incredibly frail and yet she had eaten her Christmas lunch with every appearance of enjoyment and shown no signs of wishing to remain behind.

After they had gone, Rosetta began her inspection of the manor. Many of the rooms she found strange, like the gun-room and the vast library with its shelves filled with leather-bound volumes reaching to the ceiling. It was the Long Gallery which charmed her most, with the pictures of long-dead Mallondens in powdered wigs and silks and satins or splendid uniforms decorated with arrays of medals or colourful Orders. From one alcove a stern man looked down on her wearing the apparel of a judge and from another a silver-haired man with a benign expression gazed steadily down the corridor attired in the costume of a bishop.

It was the modern gallery, however, which gave Rosetta the most pleasure. Here she came across a huge painting of a family group and she had no difficulty in picking out old Lady Mallonden in the centre of the picture. She was considerably younger, sitting on a gilt chair with a small Pomeranian dog resting on her knee and behind her, with one hand on her shoulder, stood a tall man in officer's uniform, obviously her husband.

Around them were younger members of the family: sons and daughters, and one or two children. She thought one of the children could be Angela's mother sitting at her grandmother's feet while a boy, a little younger, hugged a black labrador while he laughed at a small girl playing with a puppy, a girl who looked remarkably like Aunt Poppy.

Rosetta moved on until she came to another painting, this time of a wedding group. A tall man in Lancer's uniform with a tall, slender woman on his arm, a woman with a proud haughty face, and behind them the towers and turrets of the house she was in.

Later she came across a tinted wedding photograph, this time of two younger people, the bride in a froth of white lace, surrounded by children in bridesmaids' dresses. There was something in this photograph that held her enthralled. What was it about the bride's face that seemed so familiar? This couple were not at the manor for Christmas so they could not have met, and yet that smiling face with its wealth of fair hair stared back at Rosetta like a friend. The tall man smiling down at the children meant nothing to her, and though the bridesmaids were pretty it was the bride who tantalised Rosetta so that she was reluctant to move away.

Angela found her there, staring up at the picture. 'That's Mummy's cousin Margaret. You know, the one I was telling you about, the one who's married the son of a marquis.'

'Don't they spend Christmas with you ever?'

'They'll probably drive over one afternoon while we're here because they don't live all that far away.'

They joined the rest of the party and immediately the dowager asked, 'What did you do with yourself, young lady, while we were busy on the estate?'

'I looked at the portraits in the Long Gallery. I found them very interesting.'

'Well, of course. Ours is one of the oldest titles in the country – there were Mallondens at Quebec and in the Indian Mutiny, wherever there was a threat to the British Empire. It would be interesting to know how far back you can trace your family.'

It was on the tip of Rosetta's tongue to retort that she could probably trace it as far back as the Pharaohs, but consideration for Angela's mother held her back. Instead she smiled sweetly, saying, 'The Assyrians are a very ancient race, Lady Mallonden.'

The old lady merely fixed her with a penetrating stare before leaving the table to find her seat.

'What are you two girls intending to do this afternoon?' Angela's mother asked as soon as lunch was over. 'It was awfully cold driving round the estate so I should stay indoors if I were you.'

'I know Rosetta would like to look at some of Grandfather's photographs and they're all in the library. Could we go in there?'

'Well, of course. We'll be spending a lazy afternoon, I expect, unless somebody suggests a rubber of bridge.'

A fire burned brightly in the huge grate in the library so the two girls made themselves comfortable on the rug in front of it. The tall windows were vast and yet the threatening sky outside made the room seem dark. Angela switched on several lamps before opening a row of cupboards under the bookshelves.

Rosetta jumped to her feet and went to help Angela carry the heavy volumes. 'How far back do you want to go?' Angela enquired. 'Grandfather dates them all, but we don't want to go back too far, do we?'

'Well, no. No further back than your parents, anyway.'

The girls were soon engrossed in an array of studio photographs of weddings and christenings, together with more light-hearted photographs of family groups taken in the gardens of various houses or at functions at home and abroad.

'This is Great-Aunt Lavinia years ago when she was presented at court. Her mother was an American and her husband was killed in India. Mummy says she's never really got along with Great-Grandmother.'

'Did she never marry again?'

'No. Whenever anybody starts to talk about her they always shut up when we younger ones are about. There must be some mystery somewhere, but I don't know what it is. Margaret's nice, though. She has two children, Elfreda and James.'

'I do love mysteries, don't you? Perhaps some of these photographs will tell us what it is.'

'Grandfather always catalogues everything. There'll be a volume on that branch of the family somewhere, I'm sure.'

They found nothing in the volumes on the rug, so Angela took several of them back to the cupboard and started to hunt inside. At last she gave a triumphant cry. 'It was right at the back but here it is! Colonel Robert Mallonden, MC,' she said, hurrying back to her place beside Rosetta.

Robert Mallonden was a handsome man in the uniform

of an Indian Army officer. His wedding to Miss Lavinia Proctor had been a fashionable affair, with the bride in traditional white satin surrounded by a bevy of bridesmaids. The next picture depicted them sitting side by side on a velvet couch. A little girl aged about two sat on the man's knee while his wife held a babe in arms, and Angela said, puzzled, 'I wonder who the little girl is I thought Aunt Lavinia only ever had Margaret.'

The little girls became schoolgirls with tennis rackets and thick pigtails under panama hats which were the order of the day, yet there was something allusively familiar in the smiles of both the girls.

'Doesn't it say their names?' Rosetta asked eagerly.

'No. It simply says the date, and where they were taken. That's not a bit like Grandfather.'

They turned the pages to find photographs of Colonel Mallonden and his wife attired for a ball in dress uniform and floating chiffon, and then they were sitting in the front seat of a car, smiling into the camara.

The pictures became more up-to-date: Lavinia in deepest mourning, surrounded by the family in some churchyard, her face hidden behind a dark veil, while underneath was written in large black print, 'Memorial Service for Robert'.

There were a great many blank pages, then came a picture of a group of girls who were obviously schoolgirls and Rosetta had no difficulty in picking out Margaret sitting on the floor in the front row.

'I wonder what happened to the other girl?' she asked curiously.

'She probably wasn't a relative at all, just a friend's daughter,' Angela replied.

'But she was very like Margaret,' Rosetta persisted.

'Yes, she was, wasn't she? And why are there so many blank pages in the middle of the others? It looks as though some of the photographs have been taken out deliberately. Do you suppose she died and they don't want to be reminded of her?'

'Or that there was some terrible scandal and the family disowned her!' Rosetta added and, as soon as the words left her lips, she knew that she had to find out more. It was imperative, too important to be passed over.

'Perhaps there's another album somewhere,' she suggested.

'No, there isn't. I looked.'

'But what happened to her?'

'We could look in the attics. There are a host of old pictures up there that Grandfather had removed from the walls to make room for others.'

'But not photographs?'

'There could be. We could at least look. We've nothing else to do.'

'Won't they mind us going up to the attic?'

'No, I'm sure they won't. Anyway, we can't go out, it'll be dark very soon *and* it's lashing down.'

Rosetta went to stare out across the parkland. The sky was a deep, haunting crimson and great hailstones had covered the grass as far as she could see. The fire inside the room was comforting and tempting and, although she had no wish to leave it, the mystery surrounding that other child was too tantalising to forget.

'Do you suppose the attic will be open?' she asked Angela, softly.

'I think so. We used to play hide-and-seek up there years ago – that's how I discovered the pictures.'

The attic door was open but it was so dark inside that they could see nothing. The light coming through the skylight hardly reached the corners of the room and Angela looked at Rosetta with some dismay. 'I don't think there's any electricity up here. At least, there didn't used to be. I was always terrified of the boys locking the door and leaving me here in the dark.'

'What can we do?'

'I can go downstairs and bring up one of the candelabras from the dining room.'

Rosetta stood in the doorway listening to Angela's receding footsteps, thinking it seemed an age before she heard her returning. She had lit three candles and the light from them flitted eerily along the darkened corridor.

Angela grinned cheerfully. 'They're all asleep – I thought they would be. We'll be back downstairs before any of them wake up.'

Angela placed the candelabra on top of a chest of drawers so that the light from it fell on the stacks of paintings, then the two girls began to move them around. They were all in heavy ornamental frames and the dust started to fly making Angela cough so that the tears rolled down her cheeks.

'I sneeze awfully in the dust,' she said in between coughs. 'I'll have to wait outside. You carry on and tell me if you find anything.'

Rosetta contemplated some of the pictures which were no doubt priceless: pictures depicting mournful Scottish lochs and lonely mountains; pictures of Edwardian beauties; hunting prints and pictures of noble gundogs. She had almost given up when she came across a painting which somebody had seen fit to wrap in thick brown paper. This is the last one, she told herself. Anyway, it's none of your business who the girl is.

Her fingers wrestled with the string and, removing the paper, she dragged the picture out into the centre of the room. Then her eyes opened wide in disbelief.

It was a painting of a girl in what was probably her first ballgown, a girl in a white chiffon gown with pink chiffon roses at the waist which trailed to the hem to match the roses in her hair. Her hair was a deep, honey-gold, falling enchantingly over one creamy shoulder, and dark violet eyes sparkled in a glowing, exquisite face.

Looking at that face Rosetta felt the world slipping slowly away. All her life she had wished for her mother's beauty – but what was her mother's portrait doing pushed behind a score of unwanted pictures in the attic of this great house? What had her mother ever done to this family to merit such treatment?

She sat down weakly on a dusty velvet chair with her mind in a turmoil. Suddenly, all the questions she had ever asked sprang into her mind, questions over which her mother had prevaricated until she asked them no more, and suddenly she was a little girl again, riding with her mother across the golden sand towards the house that was their sanctuary in a world where they were singularly alone.

That world was coming back to her vividly, a world peopled with obsequious servants within the house and, outside, villagers who stared at them curiously. How that little girl had longed to play with those laughing children who waited, with their conglomeration of animals, at the wrought-iron gates to catch a glimpse of Grandmother Ayesha as she passed in her carriage.

Was this where it had all started? What terrible thing had her mother ever done to turn her into an exile?

'Have you found anything?' Angela's voice asked from the corridor.

Quickly, Rosetta rewrapped the picture in the brown paper and thrust it behind the others. Gathering her scattered wits she whispered, 'No, nothing. We shouldn't look any more – there isn't anything to find.'

'I'll ask my mother,' Angela said. 'She's sure to know who the girl is and why there's been all that secrecy. I'll ask her when we are alone and I'll tell you what she says.'

'It doesn't matter,' Rosetta said shortly.

'I say, are you all right, Rosetta? The dust always does that to me – maybe the dust affects you too.'

'Perhaps. I think we should go back now. Are you going to replace the candles?'

'They're hardly used, so we'll take them into the library and say we lit them when it went dark. They're so much more romantic than electricity, anyway.'

'How long do you usually stay at your grandfather's?'

'The parents have a dinner date on New Year's Eve, so we shall be going home in the morning. We're allowed to have a party in the barn and all the village children come. It's great fun!'

'In the barn!'

'Yes, but it isn't really a barn any more. Daddy converted it into a room where we could entertain our friends.'

When Rosetta didn't comment, Angela said quickly, 'I didn't tell you before, I wanted to surprise you. You'll love it, honestly.'

'Oh, Angela, I'm sure I will.'

On Saturday afternoon, in a flurry of excitement and the barking of innumerable dogs, Great-Aunt Lavinia arrived in the company of her daughter Margaret, her daughter's husband, Edward, and their two children.

Mrs Levison-Gore was still a remarkably handsome woman, although her hair was now silver. Her tall, slender figure had lost none of its presence, and she entered the drawing room with a queenly air, offering her cheek gracefully to receive the family's kisses, treating even old Lady Mallonden with casual charm.

She afforded Rosetta a fleeting smile, unaware that something in Rosetta was reacting strangely – a mixture of curiosity, pain and a bizarre feeling of anger.

Margaret's daughter, Elfreda, showed off her new

dress while her brother stood with their father, a tall slim man who seemed content to remain in the background while his female relatives enjoyed the attention.

Mrs Levison-Gore took no further notice of Rosetta, but her daughter asked if she was Angela's friend and if she was happy at Miss MacNaughton's school.

Seen in the flesh, Margaret's resemblance to her mother was fleeting: in the turn of her head, perhaps, or the charm of her sudden, swift smiles. Lady Burlington was a little plumper than her mother and her colouring was not so unusual. On the other hand, as Margaret moved around the room Rosetta's eyes followed her, and now and again she was rewarded by the feeling that between this woman and her mother there was a family resemblance.

Afternoon tea was served, but Great-Aunt Lavinia intimated that they must be home before five as they were dining with Edward's parents in the evening.

'How is Camborne?' Lord Mallonden enquired. 'He wasn't in the House just before Christmas and I was told he was suffering from one of his attacks of gout.'

'He's quite well now,' Lavinia replied. 'Gout is a recurring condition, I'm afraid.'

After they had left, Rosetta overheard Angela's mother say to her husband, 'I'm relieved Grandmother went to sleep – there's usually an atmosphere when those two meet.'

She would have liked to have heard more, but Aunt Poppy was busily marshalling the children for one of her endless repertoire of games . . .

28

For four long days Laura had been aware that there was something odd about Rosetta. She had responded half-heartedly to her suggestions for their entertainment and, when they faced each other across the dining-table, she was only too aware of the searching stares her daughter conferred upon her. Disconcerted, she racked her brains as to why Rosetta should be behaving in this way.

Taking a leap in the dark she said gently, 'I was sorry not to have you with us at Christmas, darling, but Omar insisted that we went to St Moritz and there were no young people in the party. It would have bored you terribly.'

'I didn't want to go to St Moritz, Mother.'

Laura did not say that she had quite deliberately kept her daughter and her husband apart. Omar's discussions with Rosetta about marriage at an age when she would barely be out of the schoolroom had antagonised her more than she cared to admit.

'Tell me what you did at Christmas, darling. Did you enjoy it at Lady Tarleton's?'

'Well, we actually went to stay with Angela's grandparents for Christmas.'

'The Mallondens?' Laura's face had gone white.

'Yes. Do you know them, Mother?'

'I – I did. A long time ago.'

'You never said so when you knew I was rooming with Angela Tarleton.'

'I – I didn't think it was important.'

'They were very nice to me. Angela's great-grandmother was there – she stared at me a lot.'

'She probably thought how enchanting you looked.'

'Oh no, Mother. She stared at me for quite another reason. Apparently she doesn't like foreigners – and I am very foreign, aren't I?'

'You're half-English, Rosetta!'

'I know, but we've never talked about it, have we? We talked about my father and Egypt; we talked about my father's family but we never ever talked about yours.'

'Talking about my family made me very unhappy, darling. I preferred to remain silent about them.'

'And you don't want to talk about them now?'

She was aware of her mother's pallor and the anguish which darkened her eyes. Doubtfully Laura searched her daughter's face, seeing her set, almost hostile expression, and her heart lurched alarmingly in her breast.

Something had happened to bring that look into Rosetta's face and it concerned the time she had spent with the Mallondens. Laura had been dismayed when she realised who her daughter was sharing a room with at Anne MacNaughton's school. It seemed that Fate had been too cruel in placing her with Angela Tarleton who was her cousin Caroline's daughter. When Rosetta had asked if she could spend Christmas with her friend she had been reluctant to agree, but Omar was insisting that they spend Christmas in Switzerland and Rosetta would have demanded reasons for her refusal to allow the visit. Now it seemed that her innermost fears had been well-founded. Anxiously, she asked, 'What has happened, Rosetta? Why this sudden interest in my past when you have never been curious before?'

'I met Angela's great-aunt, Mrs Levison-Gore, and her daughter Margaret. I thought she was awfully like you, Mother.'

'Did you, darling? It's a long time since we met.'

'But you must have known her well, Mother. I saw a photograph of you with her mother and father on the lawns of some big house. Lady Burlington was only a baby, but you were a little girl.'

'So long ago, darling . . . but how did you know it was me?'

'I just knew. Then I found a painting of you pushed away behind some others in the attic. You were so very beautiful, Mother, in a white ballgown with roses in your hair. Why was your picture hidden away? And why have you never taken me to meet your family? Because they are your family, aren't they, Mother?'

Laura stared at her with tear-filled eyes and, in a voice choked with tears, she said, 'Oh, my dear! Of all the girls you had to meet at that school, why did it have to be Caroline's daughter?' She looked helplessly around the crowded tearoom and said, softly, 'We can't talk here, Rosetta, there are too many people. Suppose we walk in the park? I'll answer all your questions there.'

Frost hung on the air as they walked along the paths towards the lake where waterfowl sat dejectedly, waiting for people to feed them. For a long time they walked in silence before Laura said, 'Where do you want me to begin, darling?'

'At the beginning, Mother, when you were a little girl.'

Memories of the past were painful to Laura, but she made herself bring them to life; her vague memories of her life in India where her father was a serving officer; then, after his death, their arrival in England and the patronising behaviour of his family.

She talked about happier times at school in Essex and later at her finishing school set high up in the Bernese Oberland, perhaps the only time in her young life when she had been truly content. She talked about her closeness to Meg and her mother's preoccupation with finding suitable husbands for them both.

'The war hadn't been over very long,' Laura explained gently. 'England was rushing headlong into a sort of gaiety that people hadn't known for four long years. I was talked about as the debutante of the year, much to Mother's gratification. The only thing people could talk about in our circle was the Season, which girl was likely to capture which man – and Mother had already made it very clear that she wanted me to have Edward Burlington, the Marquis of Camborne's eldest son.'

'Margaret's husband!' Rosetta said sharply.

'Yes. We had only met once, at a children's party years before. But it was fun to go along with Mother; fun because I didn't know any different; fun because I had yet to fall in love.

'Mother heard that the Marquis and his wife were going out to Egypt to meet their son and intended wintering there, then she heard that the Mallondens were joining them with Poppy, that they wanted Edward for Poppy. A friend of the family had offered them a dahabiyah on the Nile. I'll never know how Mother managed it, but suddenly we, too, were going to Egypt and we were all sailing on the same river-boat.

'We arrived two weeks before the Mallondens and during that week I met Edward and he fell in love with me. Mother was delighted, the Mallondens less so, and Edward's family not at all. As for me, I must have been the world's most reluctant fiancée. I didn't want to marry Edward Burlington. I didn't love him, you see, because I was desperately in love with somebody else.'

'My father?'

'Yes. We met on the boat sailing out to Egypt. He was Egyptian and I was English. He was like nobody I had ever met before and he told me quite honestly that, although we might love each other, there could never be anything permanent between us.

'I pursued him relentlessly, Rosetta. And because he loved me he was very vulnerable. Together we forgot all the conventions we had sworn our lives to: family, friends, a way of life. Nothing outside our love was important. We went together to the Sudan and I forgot Edward and my family. I forgot everything except how much I loved Ahmed, how necessary it was for us to be together. And then things started to go wrong for us . . .

'Ahmed decided he needed to go back to Cairo. He felt that his father's life was at risk because of the political situation and that it was no time for dallying in the Sudan with me. I knew that he loved me, Rosetta, but the Eastern part of him made it clear that there were other things in his life – and I knew that I would have to accept it if we were to have a life together.

'We decided to return to Cairo by train and just outside Luxor there was a terrible explosion. I was in another part of the train, looking for our attendant, and I was slightly hurt. But your father – your father was killed . . .'

Silence fell again between them, then Rosetta said, 'Did you know when my father was alive that you were going to have me?'

'I thought so – but I decided to say nothing to Ahmed until I was sure.'

'But when you were sure, Mother, couldn't you have come back to England and the family?'

Her mother's face was etched with bitterness and gently Rosetta prompted, 'Please tell me, Mother. I'd rather know everything. Why did we stay in Egypt?'

Starkly Laura told her of the choice she had been presented with and tears flooded her eyes when Rosetta said softly, 'Just think, Mother – if you'd decided to go to Scotland I could be with some people you'd never know. That's if anybody had decided to adopt me at all!'

'Oh, darling, there was no way on earth I would ever have let you go!'

'We were happy in the Fayoum, weren't we?'

'Yes, of course. And eventually, as time went by, Ahmed's family came to accept us.'

'And you married Omar who is Father's cousin, and we have an awful lot of money,' Rosetta stated simply.

Laura smiled. 'It was fun to have so much money in those early days, darling. Now it doesn't matter. Money isn't happiness and you must never think so.'

'Do you love Omar as much as you loved my father?'

'I have never loved anybody as much as I loved Ahmed. I have never loved Omar – and you must not let him shape your future, Rosetta! I intend to talk to Miss MacNaughton while I am in London. I shall tell her some of the things I have told you today and I hope that she will influence you. Neither of us knows anything about Damascus and I don't want my daughter to be told that she will marry an unknown man my husband has chosen for her.'

'Does that mean that I am not to go to Damascus when I leave Miss MacNaughton's, Mother?'

'All sorts of things are happening in the world, Rosetta. There are those who believe the war clouds are gathering over Europe again, although in Paris and here in London life goes on as normal. Omar talks of returning to Damascus if the situation worsens.'

'I don't think I want to go to the Mallondens' ever again,' Rosetta said steadily.

'But of course you will go to them! Angela is your friend and you like her. It would be unkind to Angela to refuse – but what I have told you this morning must be our secret and ours alone.'

'But I couldn't be nice to Mrs Levison-Gore or that nasty old woman everybody runs around after!'

'It's the way they are, Rosetta. Grandmother Mallonden is very old. She was brought up in an age of rigid principles and unbending pride – she can't help the way she is. And my mother was made the butt of that pride so that it fostered a great bitterness in her. I'm well out of it, darling – and when the agony passed after Ahmed's death, when you were born, I learned to look back on the joy and only the joy . . .'

It was several days later when Miss MacNaughton sat in her drawing room listening to her guest's story. At no time did she interrupt her and, as she watched the light and shade cross Laura's face, she reflected anew on its beauty and the sadness she had perceived in her on their first meeting.

When the story was told they sat in silence for several minutes, and Miss MacNaughton was the first to speak.

'Thank you for taking me into your confidence, Madame Kamel,' she said gently. 'It was brave of you.'

'I must confess that it is a weight off my mind,' Laura answered.

'You know, I felt that you were English, but I couldn't be sure. You gave no hint of it – and I have foreign girls here in the school whose English is perfect.'

'I don't want Rosetta to feel that she must obey my husband with regard to her future. He is generous and is paying for her education – but if he has his way she will never need it – at least, not the academic part of it. I want Rosetta to decide her future for herself.'

'Is there no hope that your family would receive you? After all, this all happened a very long time ago. Memories fade, surely? Over the years your mother must have thought about you, longed to see you, as well as your sister with whom you were friends?'

'My sister is now the wife of the man I let down and although they will accept my daughter as Angela Tarleton's friend, they would be horrified if, at some later stage, a member of their family wished to marry her. My mother was half-American and my grandmother *despised* her. I have a letter she sent to me the day they returned home from Egypt and I have kept it all these years to remind me of her bitterness . . .'

Believing it was time to change the subject, Miss MacNaughton said, 'I have travelled in Egypt many times and one Easter I was employed on a dig in the region of Sakkara. I was an absolute novice, of course, but I thoroughly enjoyed it and one day I shall go back there. When I retire I have promised myself that when I feel the need for solitude and the benediction of the past, when the years in front of me are pitifully few and the years behind me powerfully overwhelming, then I will return to Egypt with its awe-inspiring sense of age. When I, too, am old I shall understand it better and appreciate it more.'

The two women smiled in sudden and complete understanding, then they shook hands and Laura said, 'Thank you for listening. I'm afraid I've taken up most of your afternoon, but I am glad to be leaving Rosetta in your care.'

'I promise you that she will continue to be happy here,' Anne MacNaughton said. 'Be assured that I will do everything in my power to make her so.'

They stood at the entrance to the school, looking down the darkened street where mist swirled eerily under the lamplight, and Laura said pensively, 'You know, in all those years when I felt myself an exile I never once remembered England in the springtime. Unlike Browning who says, "Oh, to be in England now that April's there", I remembered London with the mist lying low across the river, taxi-cabs appearing through the gloom and the eerie glow of gas-lamps.'

Miss MacNaughton smiled. 'I know. It's strange how we remember different things . . . and now you are going back to Paris. I'm always very happy in Paris.'

Laura smiled gently and, with a whispered goodbye, turned away.

Miss MacNaughton stood at the top of the steps watching until her figure was swallowed up in the mist. She could not say why, but she had the strangest notion that she would never see Laura Kamel in London again . . .

29

It could be the eve of Waterloo, Laura thought fancifully. The long table glittered with glass and silver; bowls of orchids and roses had been placed along its length and around it sat a great many distinguished guests from many countries. The women wore their jewels and their elegant gowns; the men wore evening dress resplendent with colourful Orders or dress uniforms, yet beneath it all was a tenseness, a desperate eagerness to preserve the normality of a way of life that was slipping away . . .

Laura sat between an official on her husband's staff and a Frenchman who, from the moment of their meeting, had not been afraid to show his admiration.

The Syrian spoke fluent French but no English and the Frenchman soon became aware of this. He made up his mind to address her only in English and appeared to achieve some perverse pleasure from the Syrian's angry glances and Laura's mischievous smile.

From further down the table she was aware of Omar's annoyance but decided to ignore it. No doubt he would make his displeasure known later in the evening, but for now she accepted the Frenchman's regard with friendly charm.

At first they talked about the theatre and the opera, the racing at Deauville and the art exhibition at the Louvre, then he said softly, 'I wonder if we shall be sitting here next year discussing the opera and the ballet? I rather doubt it.'

She stared at him without speaking and, feeling that she was waiting for him to explain his remark, he said, 'If there is war I cannot think that it will last very long, but war, however long it lasts, is disastrous. It may take a long time for things to become normal again.'

'You believe there will be war?'

'I don't see how we can avoid it. Hitler has to be stopped – he's got away with too much already.'

'But you say you do not think it will last very long. How can you feel so sure?'

'But Madame, we have the Maginot Line. No army could penetrate it. The British have the Channel and their fleet; the French have their Maginot Line. Together we shall be invincible.'

'I hope you are right, Monsieur . . .' Laura said pensively. 'May I ask your name? I don't believe we have met before.'

'My name is Armand le Grain.'

'Oh, I have heard of you – Count Armand le Grain who has just returned from Damascus?'

He smiled. 'And I have heard of you, Madame Kamel. I heard that you were very beautiful, but they did not do your beauty justice. It lights up this dismal gathering.'

'I did not hear that you were a flatterer, Count le Grain, only that you were a successful diplomat.'

'I could write sonnets about the beauty of your eyes – in spite of the fact that your husband is displeased at the attention I am showing you.'

'I am sure you are right.'

'Will you meet me one day? Oh, somewhere quite circumspect, I assure you. The Louvre, perhaps. Or the racecourse out at Longchamp. Somewhere where we could meet accidentally, pleasurably, and share a bottle of wine. Somewhere where I could look into your eyes and tell you how beautiful you are . . .'

Laura threw back her head and laughed. He was utterly audacious and totally charming. But then she said quietly, 'You should not flirt with me, Armand.

Arab men do not like their women to be subjected to flattery or the too prominent attentions of Westerners.'

'You can't tell me anything about Syrians. Four long years in Damascus afforded me many opportunities to study them and their womenfolk.'

'Armand, please tell me a little about Damascus. I have never been there, which makes me feel very ignorant. Is it anything like Cairo?'

'If you are thinking about mosques, minarets and decorated domes, then it is similar to Cairo. But Cairo is in Africa and it is also in Egypt. What do you conjure up when you think about Cairo? The Nile and the desert, the pyramids and the Sphinx, the life that flows and loiters along its wide pavements.

'Damascus, too, is old, but to my mind it lacks the variety of Cairo, the light and shade of its people and the deep, dark magic of Africa. But you will be going there soon.'

'Why do you say that?'

'If there is war the Syrians will not keep a large staff here – if the Embassy even remains here. They will return to Syria and hope that we lose the war.'

Her eyes opened wide with surprise, and he smiled. 'I can see I have shocked you, but I can assure you the Syrians have as little love for the French as the Egyptians and the Indians have for the British. Protectorates are not loved – they are tolerated. And if the French are embroiled in a war the Syrians will hope that their country becomes their own again.'

'My husband never discusses Syria with me, or the role of France there. It is regarded as men's talk – women should be content to talk about their clothes, their jewels, their children and their homes. Anything outside that is considered unfeminine and offensive.'

'Your husband wanted an ornament for his house and nothing more?'

'Omar is very generous with money, jewels, furs,

travel . . . most women would be only too happy to count their blessings,' Laura said wistfully.

'But not an Englishwoman with a tradition of freedom?'

'One would think I should have forgotten that tradition in all the years I have been away from England, but perhaps it is something that is bred in us.'

'Of course it is! Tell me, you have a daughter, do you not?'

When she stared at him, he smiled. 'I've asked people about you.'

'I have a daughter at school in London.'

'Kamel's daughter?'

'No,' she said shortly.

'Forgive me, it is none of my business, but if you leave for Syria, will you withdraw her from that school in England so that she can leave with you?'

'No, why should I? I want Rosetta to finish her education.'

'Even if England is at war?'

'Oh, Armand, I don't know! I would have to think about the consequences, but I am sure that I want Rosetta to live her own life, make her own decisions and mistakes. I don't want her to have a husband who has been chosen for her.'

'You would be surprised how well it works.'

'Oh, I know the French follow the same practice in a great many aristocratic families. A wife with the right connections – and a mistress who doesn't need them.'

He laughed, delighted at her frankness. 'Laura, I can assure you I have no mistress and no wife. Only a deep desire to be your friend and talk with you again.'

She rose from her seat with the other women and smiled down at him. 'Now is the time for men's talk,' she said softly. 'If I don't see you again this evening, thank you for your company.'

She turned to smile at the Syrian sitting on her other side but he was already chatting to the man next to him and, across the table, Omar favoured her with a long, cool glance.

Much later, on their way home, Omar said coldly, 'You appeared to have a great deal to talk about with Count le Grain.'

'He was telling me a little about Damascus.'

'French Damascus, do you mean?'

'I'm not sure what you mean.'

'He knows nothing about Damascus or Syria – just as the British really know nothing about India. France was our protectorate, although what they thought they were protecting us from, I never discovered. In actual fact we needed to be protected from them – from their arrogance, their ridiculous belief that we were a backward people who only existed in the modern world because they made it possible. Did they never ask themselves what the Assyrians were doing when the French were running around in loincloths and blue paint?'

'He talked about war, Omar. He thinks it is inevitable.'

'And I hope they lose it. They need to be taught a lesson; that other lands breed other men.'

'And if they lose it, do you think Syria would fare any better under Germany than it has under the French?'

'We would not be under Germany, we would be our own people again. Hitler has no desire to own Syria.'

'I thought he was another Napoleon with a desire to own the world? Perhaps I was wrong . . .'

'Well, of course you were wrong. Women are always wrong when they try to dabble in things they know nothing about.'

Laura was increasingly aware of the mounting activity in the weeks that followed, the comings and goings of diplomats and an influx of Syrians who departed days later carrying trunks that had not been with them when they arrived.

Omar did not need to tell her that their days in Paris were numbered but he offered no information about the date of their departure. When she suggested a visit to London to see Rosetta he said it was inopportune and ill-advised in view of the crisis that faced them.

When she replied that Neville Chamberlain had returned from Germany with Hitler's promise that there would be peace, he merely smiled cynically and she knew he didn't believe a word of it.

It was the beginning of summer. The streets of Paris were gay with summer dresses and flower-sellers. The trees along the boulevards were in pale-green leaf and the boulevard cafés were crowded with people who laughed and chattered as if there was no threat that the world they believed in was coming to an end.

Laura dressed unhurriedly, aware that her maid watched her carefully. The girl was new, replacing her French maid who had told her that she was leaving to take up other employment, but whose tears had told another story. The new maid was Syrian and uncommunicative. Laura had been given no say in her hiring.

Conversation between them was minimal but Laura was already aware that the girl showed an unnatural interest in when she left the house and when she returned to it; and she had constantly found her in whispered conversation with one of Omar's aides.

Laura had a good reason for leaving the house on this particular morning, but she dawdled over her dressing as though she was in no particular hurry. The day before, she had met Armand le Grain with a companion at one of the city's best-attended fashion shows. Across the room their eyes had met and he had smiled at her warmly, waiting only for a lull in the proceedings to approach her, bowing gallantly over her extended hand, his smile filled with charm and pleasure.

'I had begun to think I would never see you again,' he said softly. 'Are you still going to tell me that there is no opportunity for us to meet one afternoon and share a bottle of champagne?'

'I would like to meet you, Armand. I badly need a friend at this moment and the benefit of your advice.'

His face sobered. 'You are in trouble, Laura?'

'I need a friend, but I must be very discreet. I must not meet you where there are likely to be people who know me. Can you suggest somewhere where two people can be alone without being recognised?'

He smiled. 'I should be flattered, Laura, but I am not. You mean exactly what you say, don't you? You need a friend, nothing more.'

'Yes.'

'Tomorrow afternoon I am going to an art exhibition on the West Bank. The artist is unknown and not particularly good, but I bought a ticket because he is the son of an old friend of my mother's. None of the people we know are likely to be there – he is not that kind of artist. We could meet there by accident and, if we are unobserved, perhaps walk along the river-bank simply to chat. It is a place for artists, hardly the sort of place frequented by those around us.'

'Where do I find the exhibition?'

'Here is a ticket, Laura, on the edge of your chair. Around two o'clock. Who knows, you might like one of his pictures?'

For a brief moment he held her hand before kissing it and moving back to his companion who favoured Laura with a brief smile.

As she left the Embassy a man standing on the steps approached her with a smile, asking, 'Does Madame require a car this afternoon?'

'Thank you, no. It is such a beautiful day I would like to walk.'

She walked unhurriedly along the boulevard until she turned the corner, then she went quickly to a taxi-rank and instructed the driver to take her to the West Bank.

Armand had been right. The West Bank was crowded with people: young lovers sauntering with their arms around each other; shopkeepers with their wives and families enjoying an afternoon in the sunlight; and there was life and laughter in the antics of a small monkey sitting on top of a barrel organ whilst a little girl in a frilly pink dress danced joyously to the delight of her admiring grandparents.

The afternoon was full of sound: the music of the barrel organ and the children's carousel, the hooting of the river-steamers and the chattering and laughter of people determined to enjoy themselves.

As Laura handed in her ticket at the entrance to the exhibition tent, the girl at the desk seemed pleased to see her and she was surprised to find so many people at the exhibition, people probably well-known to the artist himself.

Armand had been right. The paintings were not brilliant but they had a certain robust earthy quality and she stood in front of one depicting a weatherbeaten old man gazing nostalgically across a field of waving corn.

'That's the one I like,' came Armand's voice behind her. 'André's grandfather surveying his farmland in Brittany. I think you'll agree that his country paintings are superior to those he has done here in the city.'

'I really think I ought to buy one of them.'

'I intend to buy one or two myself, so choose the

one you really like and then allow me to buy it for you.'

'No, please, Armand, I shall buy it for myself. This one, I think, unless it's one you've already decided on.'

Armand merely smiled. 'I'll ask them to put a ticket on it. If the crowd sees that the pictures are selling, perhaps one or two more of them might be tempted to buy.'

A little later they escaped from the exhibition tent and Armand pointed with his stick to the promenade.

'The lower promenade, I think,' he said softly. 'There are seats along the way and one or two small cafés – none of which serve champagne, I think.'

'Tea will do very nicely, Armand.'

'Ah yes, the English and their tea.'

For several minutes they walked in silence and it was Armand who was the first to break it. 'Why is it suddenly so urgent that you should have a friend, Laura?'

'I think we shall soon be leaving Paris. Documents are being removed from the Embassy in large quantities, strangers are appearing and disappearing and no one will answer my questions.'

'I, too, think that you will be leaving for Damascus very soon. Does that frighten you, Laura?'

'No. It is something I shall have to accept, to go where my husband goes, but I am concerned for my daughter. I do not want him to send for Rosetta, I want her to stay in England whether there is a war or not, but she must have sufficient money to pay for her education and to enable her to stay on there. Omar is paying for her schooling now, but if she does not come to us he could very well stop the payments. I need to sell my jewellery, and I do not know how to go about it. If I sold it to the women I know, he would get to hear of it and he would put a stop to it. It is jewellery that Omar has given to me over the years, but it is mine and I doubt if I shall be needing it in Damascus.'

'Would you trust me to sell it for you?'

'Yes, of course. You know someone?'

'I know a great many people who would be interested. Is it very valuable?'

'Of course. And I have furs I shall not need in Syria. I could, of course, have some of these placed in cold storage for Rosetta.'

They sat at a table outside a small riverside café and Armand ordered afternoon tea, before taking out his wallet and extracting a small card which he proceeded to scribble on the back of. Then he pushed it across the table towards her.

'This is the address of my broker. I will tell him that you will be letting him have the jewellery which you want him to sell. You must let him know where the money from this transaction is to be sent – and if there is anything you wish me to take to England, I shall be going there for a few days at the end of June.'

Her eyes filled with sudden tears. 'Oh, Armand, thank you for being so kind!' she said gently. 'I didn't know where to turn, who to approach . . . I'm so very glad I thought of you.'

'And here was I thinking you approached me for an entirely different reason!'

'This is better, Armand, it means more,' she said.

'You mean I make a better friend than lover?' he asked with a little smile.

'I mean that I am not looking for a lover – but I so very badly need a friend.'

In the days that followed, every time she took an item of jewellery from the safe she removed another piece and locked it in one of her suitcases which lay hidden at the back of her wardrobe behind a row of long evening gowns.

On the morning when she took her jewels to Armand's broker, she dismissed her maid who was busily engaged in sorting through her lingerie, making sure that the girl did not linger in the corridor outside her room. Then she took out of the wardrobe a small leather case and filled it with the jewellery she had removed from the safe. She stared down at it, sparkling dramatically in the sunlight, reflecting that once it had seemed so important; that she had taken pleasure in the sheen of emeralds against her throat, the sparkle of rubies in her ears. Now, all she could think of was how much money she would get for them.

She had kept nothing apart from the jewellery which Ahmed had given to her in the Sudan, including the three rows of pearls which she wore every day. She had yet to make a decision about her furs.

The broker was intrigued with her story and even more so with her jewellery and promised to let her know as quickly as possible what he had managed to accomplish. Then, later in the afternoon, when Laura returned to the Embassy, she found Omar pacing up and down in her bedroom, undisguised anger on his face.

'Where have you been?' he demanded as soon as she entered the room.

'Into the city,' she said more calmly than she felt.

'Come with me,' he said sternly, taking her hand in a firm grip and dragging her after him into the drawing room.

He pointed to the safe which stood open, saying, 'That is the safe where you kept your jewels. It is empty except for one or two leather cases containing jewels I never gave you.'

'I know.'

'You know! Where are the jewels?'

'I have asked a broker to sell them for me.'

'You want money? Why do you want money?' He

was bewildered. 'You are not short of money, Laura, and I always understood that your jewellery was important to you.'

'I loved my jewels, Omar, but did not think I would need them in Damascus.'

'How do you know we are returning to Damascus?'

'Oh, Omar! Do you really think I am so devoid of intelligence that I cannot read the signs? All the documents leaving the Embassy, the comings and goings, my Syrian maid whom I had no hand in choosing and didn't really want, and the threat of war which is on everybody's lips.'

'You think that was a reason to sell your jewellery?'

'I have sold my jewellery for Rosetta. It will pay for her education when you cease to do so.'

'Rosetta will return with us to Damascus.'

'No, Omar, Rosetta will remain in London. She is *my* daughter. She will not go to Damascus to marry some man you expect to choose for her while she is still a child.'

'When you married me *I* became her father! She will obey me.'

'I will go to Damascus with you. I will go anywhere in the world with you, Omar. You are my husband and *I* will obey you. But let Rosetta go. Allow her to grow up in England where she will know a freedom which your country will deny her. As long as I live I shall never ask you for anything else, Omar, but please, please do not fight me about Rosetta!'

'She is only half-English. Her father was my cousin and an Egyptian.'

'An Egyptian educated in England, loving our way of life, understanding our freedom. Ahmed would have understood!' Laura cried.

He stared down at her, his dark faced etched in anger, until something more cruel and vindictive took its place. Suddenly he grasped the neck of her dress and with a quick wrench tore it down its entire length, then he grabbed hold of her and forced her to the ground. She did not fight him even when his mouth was bruising her lips, when the cruelty of his hands on her delicate body brought tears to her eyes, when his unleashed passion made her want to cry out in terror. When at last it was over and he stood looking down at her, he said coldly, 'That is the last time I shall ever make love to you. There is no pleasure in making love to a dead thing.'

He strode away from her, slamming the door behind him.

For a long time she lay where he had left her, then she dragged herself slowly to her feet, collecting her scattered clothing which she draped around her body. There were red marks where his hands had gripped her arms and there was blood on her lips but none of that registered as she made her halting way across the room towards the door.

The corridor was quiet as she staggered towards her bedroom. Her maid looked at her curiously, her sly dark face, insolent, and suddenly anger consumed Laura, an anger that brought her defeated heart to life. Furiously she said, 'Leave me! Get out of my sight.' The girl fled.

Omar Kamel stood at his window staring out along the sweep of the boulevard. He was not proud of what he had done. He had treated his beautiful aristocratic wife with scorn and cruelty and the conflicting emotions beating in his breast were indicative of his self-loathing.

His mind went back to the first moment he had seen Laura riding her horse along the margin of the canal in the Fayoum. He had desired her then, but he had never truly known the difference between love and desire. Brought up in a Syrian household of women dominated by a despotic father, he had not had Ahmed Farag's years of Western training, but then Ahmed had been a fool to allow a woman to captivate him so that he forgot where his true loyalties lay.

His mouth twisted scornfully and a look of resolute pride extinguished the pain in his eyes.

Soon, now, they would be in Damascus. In Damascus his wilful, beautiful wife would come to know her place and accept it. He no longer desired her; desire faded and there were other women who would come readily when he needed them. As for Laura, she was his wife. He had bought her by giving her his name and the possessions he had lavished upon her.

30

It was the beginning of September and the start of a new term when Miss MacNaughton found herself sitting opposite a charming and gallant Frenchman in her morning room. He had kissed her hand, favoured her with his devastating smile and was now sitting back in his comfortable chair telling her that he was here on behalf of the mother of her pupil, Rosetta Kamel.

'Rosetta is on holiday with two friends in Scotland. One of the girl's parents has a cottage near Loch Lomond.'

'Very beautiful,' he said easily.

'Yes, very. I don't think she will be back until tomorrow or Friday.'

'It isn't necessary that I see her, Miss MacNaughton. My business is with you, on Madame Kamel's instructions.'

'I see. Or rather I don't see. Would you like coffee?'

'Coffee would be very civilised, I think.'

They chatted pleasantries until the coffee arrived, then Anne MacNaughton poured and set out a tray of shortbread.

Taking a piece he said with a smile, 'Also Scottish, I think.'

'Yes.'

'Madame Kamel and her husband are now in Damascus, Miss MacNaughton. The Syrian Embassy in Paris is left with a small staff and, until hostilities are over, that, I think, is how it will remain.'

'You are so sure there will be hostilities?'

'Yes, I am sure.'

For a long moment there was silence between them, then she said, 'I, too, think it is unavoidable.'

'London will be a target for bombing raids, Miss MacNaughton. Is it your intention to remain in the city?'

'I've tried not to think about it, but if war does come I shall have to consider taking my school to the country where the girls can get on with their education in peace. And you, Count le Grain, what will be your life when diplomacy has failed and France is at war?'

'We shall soon know, Madame. Within days perhaps.'

'How does Madame Kamel's life in Damascus affect Rosetta? Is she expected to go there?'

'Her mother has said quite adamantly that she does not want her daughter there. She wants her to remain in London and, to that end, she has sold all her jewellery and, on her behalf, I have placed the money in an English bank. Her jewellery has raised a great deal of money so the young lady will be well placed. Here is her bank book and certificates of shares – and two gifts which her mother asked should be given to Rosetta on the day she leaves you and not before.'

'And where is she to go when she does leave me, Count le Grain?'

'That, I think, will be up to you, Madame. You and Mademoiselle Rosetta.'

He stood up and went to pick up the parcel he had placed near the door and she watched while he unwrapped it. Inside was a large cardboard box which he opened, discarding several sheets of tissue paper as he did so, then he reached inside the box and took out a fur coat, a rich, glossy dark fur which he handed to her. Instinctively she allowed her hands to caress the silken sable.

'How beautiful it is . . .' she murmured.

'Yes. Perhaps one day when the war is over and

the world has returned to some sort of normality your pupil will caress its beauty as you are doing today. There is also this, Madame.'

He reached inside the box again and brought out a long leather box which he opened and placed on the table in front of her.

She found herself staring down at the diamond necklace and earrings which Ahmed had given to Laura many years before on the banks of the Nile: a long glittering rope of exquisitely matched stones that had once made every woman look at Laura in envious admiration. Now they nestled against the dark velvet in the drawing room of an English headmistress, and the two people staring down at them were both thinking how incongruous they seemed.

'I shall have to tell Rosetta that her mother has gone to live in Damascus. She will want to know when they are likely to meet again and if her mother is going to write to her.'

'I am sure Madame Kamel will write when she is at liberty to do so. But the war will alter many things. Life as we know it, Madame, is on the edge of a precipice. I have lived in Damascus for several years, Miss MacNaughton, and Madame Kamel will find her life there very different from the life she lived in Paris.

'Women in Syria do not take part in public life, they remain in the background, and Omar Kamel's father was a despot. His mother is Egyptian and both his father and his two brothers have never tried to hide the fact that they hate the French – nor do they have any love for the British. Kamel is returning to Damascus with an English wife and I rather think there are some unpleasant surprises in store for her.'

'Did you know the Kamels well in Paris?'

'I would like to have known Madame Kamel better.' The smile which accompanied his words was teasing.

With a shrug of his shoulders he went on, 'Madame Kamel was singularly alone. A very beautiful woman with enough money to spend on anything she desired, yet I pitied her.'

'Pitied!'

'Why, yes. I wanted to bring a smile to that enchanting face, to see her eyes light up with laughter. I love beautiful women, Miss MacNaughton. I am unmarried and it gives me pleasure to admire them and flirt with them. But I was unable to flirt with Madame Kamel – her cares were too many. The well-being of her daughter was all that mattered to her.'

'Have you ever met Rosetta, Count?'

'No, I have not had that pleasure.'

She moved over to the wall. 'This is a photograph of the entire school taken in the gardens this summer. That is Rosetta in the centre of the second row.'

He joined her and looked at the photograph. The pupils were dressed alike and among them were girls from all over the World – but Rosetta stood out like a jewel, alien and exotic. Raven-black hair framed a pale, porcelain face, making the girl next to her seem colourless.

'One day she will be as great a beauty as her mother,' he said seriously.

'That is what I thought on the first day I saw her.'

Armand smiled pensively and she knew he was thinking about Laura: Laura whose beauty had shone like a beacon yet had not been able to save her from desolation and loneliness . . .

Several days later Anne MacNaughton sat with her staff listening to the British Prime Minister telling the country that England was at war with Germany. It was a glorious September day. The sun shone brightly on a people enjoying the remainder of a summer that had been beautiful, yet only minutes after Churchill's declaration the air-raid sirens sounded a piercing warning and people on the streets looked at each other in disbelief before they ran to the shelters. It was a false alarm and, as they heard the all-clear, their faces brightened. Life would go on, nothing would change; it was comforting to believe in the sanity of governments and the invincibility of that narrow strip of water which separated England from the rest of Europe . . .

31

Laura had been in Damascus almost a year and none of it had been as she had expected it to be.

She had imagined that Damascus would be like Cairo with its mingling of East and West, but in the first few days she realised it was nothing like that city. The magnificence of the Nile, the ancient legacy of the past, the verdant green of the fields that bordered the Nile were missing, and in Omar's house, where she had expected to be the mistress, she found she was not.

Omar's mother was the mistress, ruling the women's quarters absolutely. With the memory of their meeting in Egypt to sustain her, Laura had greeted her warmly. At first Madame Kamel had been friendly, charming. Now she was distant, intent that Laura should understand that here things would be different.

Laura's bedroom and sitting room were luxurious in an entirely Eastern style but the whole effect was heavy and dark. The view from her sitting room overlooked the garden, however, and this afforded her her greatest pleasure.

She no longer ate her meals in the company of her husband. They were served to her in her room for the first few days, then Madame Kamel invited her to eat in a large room together with several other women.

Laura was immediately the object of their curiosity and her Western attire stood out in sharp contrast to their Eastern clothing. As she took her place in the richly appointed salon Madame Kamel said, evenly, 'This is Laura, the wife of my son, Omar. Laura, now you will meet my other daughters – Hebaka, the wife of my son Hassan; Shebeka, the wife of my son Sadek; and Fatima, who was Omar's wife until he divorced her.'

Laura's eyes opened in shocked surprise, and Madame Kamel smiled grimly. 'Fatima was a good wife and she gave him a fine son. When he was appointed to go to France as our Ambassador he did not think Fatima would be suitable because she has no English or French. She is a country girl, unversed in the ways of the world. She agreed that it was advantageous for Omar to have a wife who would do justice to his position and the first day my son saw you he believed you were the woman he should make his wife.'

'But why didn't he tell me?' Laura murmured unhappily.

The older woman shrugged her shoulders. 'He probably thought you would not understand. But there need be no animosity, Laura. Fatima lives here – indeed, she never went away – and her son has grown up under my supervision. It should not concern you. You have given my son no children and, although you remain his wife, he has great regard for the mother of his son.'

'Of course,' Laura said softly, looking down. She had little appetite for the over-spiced food set before her and she was relieved when fresh fruit was placed on the table. The meal was eaten in silence. Occasionally there were giggles from the two sisters-in-law sitting across the room, laughter that was swiftly silenced by a warning look from Madame Kamel.

When Laura looked up she was aware of Fatima's silent scrutiny. It was not hostile, but inquisitive, as though the girl could hardly believe in this golden-haired woman who had replaced her.

Laura thought that she had never been so lonely in her life. Madame Kamel kept her distance except when her son deigned to visit her. Then they talked endlessly together while he merely acknowledged Laura's presence with a brief nod and a distant bow.

None of the other women spoke English. They sat giggling together, with a plentiful supply of sweetmeats and, after their husbands' visits, were happy to show off the presents they had received. However, as the weeks wore on they showed some interest in Laura's clothing, both Hebaka and Shebeka venturing into her bedroom to pick up the toiletries on her dressing-table.

There were so many questions Laura wanted to ask. About Ayesha and life in the Fayoum; about how much Egypt had changed since she had left it, but her mother-in-law's attitude kept her silent. She seldom smiled, and whereas, in Egypt, her tone had been friendly, now her voice when she spoke to Laura was cold and indifferent.

Laura knew that Madame Kamel spoke English fluently, yet she insisted on speaking to her in Arabic; it was as though she had conspired with her son to obliterate every vestige of Western culture from Laura's mind.

Much was made of Omar's son when he arrived home from his school for the holidays. Ali was a handsome, well-built teenager with bold brown eyes but the insolence in them when he looked at Laura only succeeded in making her angry.

It was evident that his grandmother idolised him. She gave him presents every time he visited her, and one day, after his visit, she said to Laura, 'Isn't he a fine boy? And so like Omar was at his age. One day he will make us all proud of the fine things he does for Syria.'

When Laura remained silent she persisted, 'Do you not agree with me, then?'

'I hope he will justify the faith you obviously have in him.'

'But do you not agree that he is a fine boy?'

'I think he is very handsome. Handsome and bold – but there is no reason for him to look at me with insolence.'

'He is close to his mother so it is understandable if he resents you a little.'

'There is no reason why he should. I did not know of his mother's existence, or his for that matter, when I married his father.'

'One cannot expect the boy to reason so.'

'When I met you in Egypt I thought you would be my friend, Madame Kamel, but I am surprised to find that you are not. Why do you resent me?'

'My son wanted you and I saw the logic of his argument. I knew the thorn you had been in the flesh of my brother's family, how you had turned their world upside down. If you had stayed out of Ahmed's life he would not have gone to the Sudan and would not have been on that train.'

'How long must I go on paying for that terrible sin, Madame?' Laura asked passionately. 'If those assassins had been determined to kill him they would have chosen somewhere else and some other time. They killed a great many people.'

'I am aware of it.'

'Then why can't we bury the past? If we are to live in the close confines of this house, in a world of women, why can't we find some semblance of friendship? You are intelligent and have travelled. You have so little in common with the other women in this house – yet you treat the one woman you could converse with with ill-disguised hostility.'

For a long time they started at each other in silence, then Madame Kamel said evenly, 'You have not made my son happy. You have taken his gifts and sold them for money, you have said you do not wish your daughter to marry a man Omar would choose for her and you have left her in London to be brought up like an Englishwoman. You have turned your back on all the things I accepted when I came here, Laura. You have given me no reason to like you or make a friend of you.'

'You are right that I sold my jewels for money, Madame, but the money was for my daughter. One day, when this terrible war is over, Rosetta will be glad of that money. Omar no longer pays for her education – at least the money I was able to send her will pay for that.'

'If she had come to Syria with you she could have continued her education here.'

'What sort of education is there for women here?'

'And what sort of man will she marry? In England she will be neither fish nor fowl.'

'Her mother is English – that should count for something.'

'It counted for little with your family.'

Laura stared at her, unable to deny her words.

Madame Kamel turned away but impetuously Laura called after her, 'Madame, I would like to go into the city. I know nothing of Damascus. Is it forbidden that I visit the ancient sites in Damascus and around it?'

'You may go, of course, but not alone. I will instruct servants to follow you.'

So Laura went out into the city where she was conscious that always, a few paces behind, walked two servants. When she paused they paused; when she entered a building, they entered also, and after several weeks of this all desire to discover Damascus left her.

The other women were well supplied with glossy magazines but Laura could not enjoy them and books were unheard of. The others giggled together over the newest shades of kohl for their eyes, carmine for their lips and polish for their nails, and were totally uninterested in the world around them.

More and more Laura sought her own company. She enjoyed her garden but on one of Omar's rare visits she asked if she could speak to him alone.

He faced her in her sitting room, standing just within the door so that she had to address him from across the room. In some exasperation Laura said, 'I have offended you, Omar, and I am sorry, but there is really no need for you to treat me so discourteously.'

'What is it you wish to speak to me about?' he asked coldly.

'Omar, I need something to do. I am bored without books to read or people to converse with. Is there any work I can do – teach English to local women perhaps, or needlepoint? If I go on like this I shall go mad!'

'Omar Kamel's wife does not teach school, nor does she mingle with the wives of shopkeepers and field-workers. I will have books sent to you if that is what you want, but my mother speaks English – why do you not speak with her?'

'She has shown no desire to speak to me, unless it is to remind me of my many shortcomings.'

'My mother is astute and well aware of your shortcomings.'

'You, too, have been aware of them for a very long time, Omar. Why didn't you divorce me as you divorced Ali's mother?'

'Ali's mother was my affianced when I was still a schoolboy. She came to me with the blessings of my family and hers. When I set her aside she was desolate. You, Madame, would not be desolate. You would fly like a bird to the West where no doubt you would soon find yourself a lover. There will be no divorce for us. I bought you – with my jewels, my gifts – but instead of being grateful you set out to disobey every rule that I made, for you, for your daughter and for her future.'

'I have never disobeyed you, Omar! I am here in Damascus, living the life you planned for me. If I sold your jewels and furs, the money was for Rosetta. Why should you quarrel with that?'

'You did not sell the jewels that Ahmed gave to you! That told me his jewels were important, mine were expendable.'

The truth of his words hit Laura forceably. She had no argument for the man who faced her haughtily across the room.

She rose to her feet and went to stand in front of him, her eyes pleading. 'Omar, why don't you let me go? You don't love me and as long as I remain here I am a constant reminder of the West, the West that you hate. Why don't you remarry Ali's mother who loves you dearly? It would please your mother and your son.'

His dark eyes glittered in his proud, uncompromising face. 'Do not try to arrange my life for me. Understand this, I will *never* let you go. As long as you live you will be my wife and you will never see your daughter again. You will not go to England and she will not come here. And remember, Laura, it was your decision to make a Westerner of her, not mine.'

Turning on his heels he went out of the room, closing the door quietly behind him.

Laura's face was bleak as she stared at the closed door. There would be no mercy from that cold, implacable man. He meant what he said, and all she could do was accept it.

Months passed and the promised books did not arrive. She felt faintly lethargic. She had taken to wearing a kaftan while her Parisian gowns hung neglected in the wardrobes. She had lost weight which the loose kaftan helped to conceal but, as she stared in the mirror, there was no disguising the fact that the contours of her face were changing. She was so pale and her beautiful eyes, with blue shadows under them, now seemed too large for her face.

She spent long hours sitting in her garden with closed eyes, occasionally fanning herself to stir the warm air. One morning she felt somebody touch her gently on her arm and, opening her eyes, found Ali's mother, Fatima, staring down at her with a shy smile, proffering a glass containing what looked like tea.

Laura took the glass with a surprised smile. The liquid was tepid, not unpleasant to the taste and, after she had drunk it, she felt refreshed. She thanked Fatima with a smile, touched that this friendly action should have come from the woman whose husband she had taken and, as the days passed, Fatima visited her almost daily with the same potion.

If only she didn't feel so tired all the time! When she told Madame Kamel that she thought she should perhaps see a physician, the older woman shrugged her shoulders. 'You are not accustomed to our climate, which can be punishing for Western constitutions.'

'You forget, Madame, that I spent many years living in the East. I was perfectly well in Egypt, even in the heat of the summer.'

'In Egypt, even in the summer, there is the freshening breeze from the river. Here there is no Nile.'

'Perhaps if I were to see a doctor,' Laura insisted, but the older women shook her head.

'He will only prescribe drugs you do not need. Fatima's potion is excellent for the condition from which you are suffering and when the cooler weather comes it will pass.'

But it did not pass. The cooler weather came and Laura's lethargy increased. Her memory started to play tricks on her and her eyesight became blurred. She seemed to be living in a world of fleeting shadows so that her servants appeared like wraiths as they flitted in and out of her rooms, until only Fatima was real with her shy, sweet smile and her offering of refreshment.

Now after she had drunk the potion she experienced terrible nausea and the other woman's persistence in offering it seemed strangely sinister. The following day she laid the glass aside and refused to drink it, but Fatima's sad, tearful expression made her feel suddenly contrite and ungrateful. Of course it was not the potion that was making her ill; the woman was trying to be kind. Wasn't she the one caring individual in a world of people who were totally uncaring?

The potion no longer tasted pleasant; it had a bitter, acrid taste and Laura's symptoms were getting worse.

In her delirium she would call for Omar but he never came and then, after such a night, the morning would come and she would be better. The shadows retreated, faces became faces again and hands were gentler. The potion was no longer sour-tasting and when her eyes looked into Fatima's the other woman smiled encouragingly and murmured, 'No more camomile – camomile make bitter.'

For several days she felt more like herself so she started to write to Rosetta. It was a letter designed to assure her daughter that she was well and happy. She told her that Damascus was charming and historical; she enthused about the beauty of her garden and the magnificence of the house, but she did not tell her about Fatima or Ali. She ended the letter by telling her to be a good girl and always to obey Miss MacNaughton.

She was surprised when Ali offered to post the letter for her, but something prompted her to refuse. Instead, she smiled at him graciously, saying she felt so much better that it would do her good to take a short walk. She had the craziest notion that if she allowed Ali to take her letter, Rosetta would never receive it.

It was months since she had heard from her daughter

but she blamed this on the war. It seemed incredible to Laura that war raged in Europe and she should know so little about it. If her mother-in-law knew anything she never spoke of it and, when Laura mentioned the war, she merely said that since it did not concern Syria she was not interested.

Laura had almost reached the house again when she saw two men walking down the street, deep in conversation. Impulsively she stepped in front of them and, addressing the elder of the two, said, 'Please forgive me, but I am English and I desperately want to know if you can tell me anything about the war in Europe.'

Unthinkingly, she had addressed the man in English and her spirits rose when he answered her in her native tongue.

'What is it you wish to know, Madame?'

'Where the fighting is taking place and if England is still safe.'

'Madame, France and the Low Countries fell within days. The United Kingdom fights on.'

'But the Maginot Line! The French said the Germans could never cross the Maginot Line.'

'They ignored it. Now British ships are being sunk and British cities are being bombarded night after night. I regret I have no good news for you, Madame.'

'No, your news is very disquieting. Thank you for speaking to me in English.'

'Here in Damascus, Madame, I am a teacher of English.'

Both men smiled and, thanking them again, Laura returned to the house. The news the stranger had given her was frightening. Where was Rosetta in all this? London must surely be one of those cities attacked night after night and it had been months since she had heard from her . . .

That night the headaches came back and sleep was denied her.

Once again Fatima visited her in the garden, her soft eyes filled with gentle compassion, proffering her potion, standing beside her while she drank it.

The misty shadows returned, bringing with them agonising stomach cramps. Laura writhed in torment on her silken bed while her servants huddled together listening to her moans, until Madame Kamel sent them away.

Then the house was quiet. Moonlight flooded into her room and only the singing of the cicadas came from the garden. She stirred painfully before opening her eyes, blinking several times until she was able to focus. She was completely alone. Painfully she eased herself out of her bed and began a slow crawl towards the door.

Every torturing inch became more painful but her determination made her go on. It took both her hands to turn the knob on the door and open it, then she was in the dimly-lit hall with its tiled floor and the curving, shallow stairs leading to the rest of the house.

With the help of the balustrade she managed to pull herself to her feet and for a long moment she stood swaying at the top of the steps. Then with a little moan she sank to her knees and rolled helplessly down the stairs until she lay with her head resting on the rich carpet that covered the hall below. From somewhere near by a door opened and, through a mist of pain, Laura became aware of somebody bending over her. Lifting her head she breathed, 'Help me... Please, help me!'

Suddenly it seemed that the night was full of sound, doors opening, footsteps hurrying along tiled floors, voices raised in alarm and anger and the room they laid her in, her own, was filled with light so that she could not bear to open her eyes.

Omar Kamel stared down at the body of his wife, hardly daring to believe that this was the same woman who had enchanted him as no other. For long months he had banished her from his sight. Now he felt he was looking at a stranger. Her rich, silken hair appeared dry and lustreless as it spread across the pillow; her face was colourless, the flesh almost transparent, and her arms outside the coverlet were like sticks.

He stared at the physician who bent over her and the pain in his eyes was raw and punishing. The physician turned to him and shook his head dismally. In a corner of the room the women of his household stood huddled together: his mother and the wives of his brothers; and then, from the shadows, Fatima glided like a wraith to pick up the empty glass on the table near his wife's bed. She walked with her head down, but as she turned to walk away Omar reached out and took the glass from her hands.

She stared at him, startled, and as she shrank away, he demanded, 'What is in the glass?'

Her eyes looked round the room wildly but there was only silence and Omar demanded relentlessly, 'What have you given her?'

She crouched at his feet, her shoulders trembling. 'Only camomile, my lord, to help her sickness. Your mother will tell you it was only camomile.'

'Well?' he demanded of his mother.

'Fatima prepared the potion and I understood it to be camomile,' she answered quietly.

Without another word Omar handed the empty glass to the physician who sniffed at it and frowned, then he inserted his finger into the glass and tasted it. It seemed that time itself stood still, then he passed the glass back to Omar, saying quietly, 'Camomile there is, of course, but not enough to disguise the smell and taste of belladonna . . .'

Fatima moaned dismally at his feet and for a long moment Omar stood staring at the glass in his hand. Then suddenly he reached down and lifted her to her feet and with the back of his hand sent her reeling across the floor.

'Stay with my wife,' he said to the physician. 'Report to me later.' Then, turning to his mother, he said icily, 'You will come with me, Madame. You will tell me what has been your part in all this.'

The long night was almost over. In the east the sky was misted grey and pink, like the feathers of a pigeon, and the first faint, golden light of the rising sun fell gently on fairy-tale domes and minarets. In the still, shuttered room two servants sat beside Laura's bed, wafting their long ornamental fans over her still form while the physician nodded sleepily in his chair.

None of them were aware that the spirit of Laura Kamel had gone for ever into the land of silence . . .

An hour later Omar Kamel stood looking down at his wife's body. In the short space of a single night his whole life had changed. His wife was dead and his mother and son were banished from his sight. Fatima had been taken from the house, still shrieking her innocence, and was now in a prison cell, but it was his mother's perfidy which had hurt him the most. He did not believe that she had not known what was going on. The womens' quarter had been her domain and in it she was obeyed without question. Fatima and the wives of his brothers would never question her authority but Laura with her Western upbringing and independent spirit might have done so. In that case it would have been her undoing.

He had no pity for Fatima facing death in her prison cell, or for his mother raging impotently in exile. All his thoughts were for his son, his only son. One day he would bring him out of exile, when he was sufficiently chastened, when Fatima was dead and he was made to understand that what ever loyalty he possessed should be given to his father and none other.

Days after Laura's death Omar faced the Princess Ayesha in the solitude of her garden in the Fayoum. She had listened without speaking while he poured out his anger, the anguish he felt at the banishment of his mother and son, and the role Fatima had played in Laura's death. Now the Princess became aware of his resentment of Laura herself and the realisation dawned that, in many ways, Omar blamed her for introducing him to a woman who had been so disastrously wrong for him.

Accusingly he said, 'It was you who wanted me to marry her, you who pointed out the advantages a Western wife would have for me in Paris. If your son had lived, he too in time would have been aware of the impossibility of his marriage to Laura.'

'That we shall never know, Omar. Ahmed loved her, you only desired her. You should not allow this bitterness to go on now that she is dead. It is eating your soul.'

'It is because of her that my mother and son are banished from my home. You were only concerned with your granddaughter's future; that was why you wanted the marriage. How could you ever forgive Laura for what she did to you?'

'If bitterness is nursed too long it becomes a destructive thing. In time I came to see her courage as well as her beauty. I feel that you were so steeped in Eastern teaching that you never tried to understand her. You would not let yourself love her.'

'Why are women so obsessed with love? It is transient, other things are more important.'

'Laura was a woman who needed to be loved, Omar. All you offered her was second best – passion and the superficiality of possessions.'

'And what of her daughter? On our marriage she became my daughter, but Laura took her away so that she would never have to obey me. Surely you, as her grandmother, must see the wrong of it?'

'You would have brought her back to a house filled with women, to a life she would exchange for marriage to a man of your choice. I was brought up to accept that sort of life, Laura was not, and she could not accept it for her daughter. You have lived in the West, you must have absorbed some of their culture.'

'Oh yes, I have done that. Their affairs and divorces, their peculiarities.'

'You are speaking of a handful of people, Omar; you must know that it is not all like that. I take it that Rosetta has been informed of her mother's death?'

'Of course. I have no wish to see her, no desire to see her ever again. I am not as heartless as you think, Ayesha, I will make ample provision for her; indeed, she will be a very rich woman when she is sufficiently mature to handle riches.'

'She is little more than a child, Omar. What will happen to her in London?'

'I have asked her headmistress, Miss MacNaughton, to be her guardian. I cannot think that she will refuse to accept the responsibility until she becomes of age. Rosetta is your granddaughter, Ayesha. Do you intend to receive her here?'

'I loved her. I hope she will want to come here when this terrible war is over.'

'I take it you approve of what I have done?'

'You have been generous, Omar. Generosity motivated by pride, not love.'

'That is so. It seems to me that pride is all I have left when so much of my life has been destroyed.'

He turned and strode away from her through the garden and she stared after him with pain-filled eyes. He seemed like a man surrounded by a terrible loneliness and her thoughts turned to the beautiful woman who had been instrumental in bringing so much tragedy into their lives.

Ahmed had struggled with his love for the beautiful

English girl. He had tried to tell her that it could never be what he wanted it to be for them, but unheedingly she had worn down his resistance until she had possessed him body and soul. If Omar could have loved her as Ahmed had loved her, perhaps it would all have been very different.

32

It was impossible to believe that only a short distance away English cities were reeling from a night's bombardment. Fires were still burning, rescuers were searching for missing persons, people were staring helplessly at all that was left of their homes.

Miss MacNaughton stood at the window of her study looking out across the frosted fells to where Derwent Water lay, sublimely beautiful, under a blue winter sky. Sheep grazed peacefully on the fells and overhead, two curlews drifted dreamily before coming to rest on a sheer limestone crag. Smoke curled lazily from cottage chimneys.

She turned at hearing a tap on the door and Jenny's tousled head appeared round it to announce, 'The taxi's 'ere, Miss MacNaughton, an' Joe sez the roads are that icy.'

'I'm ready, Jenny. Is my secretary about?'

'I'm here,' called her secretary, Elinor, from the corridor outside. 'I don't like to think of you in London with all the bombing going on,' she said anxiously as they walked to the door.

'Don't worry, I'll be all right. I have the feeling that we are witnessing the death throes of the war, Elinor. Now, I'll be back during the middle of next week so don't try to contact me in London – I'll be far too busy seeing to things it's impossible to deal with up here.'

'I've got a list here of your appointments. This Mr Hadje El-Askar at the Dorchester – do you suppose he's the father of a prospective pupil?'

'I don't know,' Miss MacNaughton said thoughtfully.

'His letter came from Damascus, so something to do with Rosetta, I thought.'

'Will you be going to the art exhibition?'

'Most certainly! It's not every day one of our old pupils exhibits at the Tate!'

How strangely empty and silent the school in Princes Avenue felt without the sound of girls' voices echoing through the lofty rooms. Anne MacNaughton wandered from room to room, thinking nostalgically of how it used to be, then, with a philosophical shrug of her shoulders, she told herself not to look back. They had been lucky to find that beautiful stone house on the banks of Derwent Water for the duration of the war and the girls loved it. Long summer days when they walked over the fells with the young green grass springing under their feet, or sailed the lake with the vista of mountain peaks all around them. Faces glowing in the sharp winter frosts, burning logs and frozen waterfalls . . . Oh yes, surely it had been a time of enchantment never to be forgotten.

Perhaps it had been a mistake to arrange to meet her visitor from Syria at the old school in London, but time was short and they would just have to make the best of it.

The front door bell echoed hollowly through the deserted hall. Her visitor was punctual, at any rate. She hurried to open the door. A tall, slim man stood on the threshold, dark and distinguished-looking and wearing an elegant dark grey lounge suit.

She smiled and held out her hand. Gravely he bowed over it before staring curiously down the expanse of hall and up the shallow curving stairs.

'I must apologise for the emptiness, Mr El-Askar,' Miss MacNaughton said evenly. 'We have not been in residence since soon after the war started but I could not ask you to visit us in Cumberland and there were other reasons for me to visit London.'

He smiled but offered no comment and she invited him to follow her to her study where she indicated a chair opposite the large desk which she had decided not to move to the north and waited for him to state the reasons for his visit. As if making up his mind, he suddenly said, 'I am here on behalf of Mr Omar Kamel, Madame MacNaughton. Mr Kamel has asked that you break some very sad news to Rosetta. Her mother died a few weeks ago and has been buried in Damascus.'

Anne MacNaughton's eyes opened wide in shocked surprise. In that one swift moment she was remembering Laura sitting opposite her in this very room, beautiful and elegant, relating a tale filled with passion and bitterness, and sparing herself nothing in the telling. How could she believe that that beautiful, glowing woman was dead?

'Oh dear,' she said ineffectively. 'She was so lovely! What did she die from?'

'Some unusual malady. She was unhappy with our climate and Mr Kamel has been devastated by her death. She leaves a gap in his life that he can never fill. But now, Madame, comes the question of Rosetta.'

'Does he wish to see her? Are you here to take her back with you?'

'No, Madame, he does not wish to see her. He wishes to ask you if you will become her guardian until she is of age. I wish to leave with you details of a great many investments he has placed in her name and also amounts of money residing in London and Swiss banks. You will see from all this, Madame, that Miss Rosetta Kamel will be a very rich young woman. There are also these . . .'

He reached inside his briefcase and brought out a long leather case; then, standing up, he brought it over to her desk and opened it.

She was staring at a creamy three-stranded pearl necklace held together by a sparkling diamond clasp and her visitor was saying evenly, 'They were a gift to Madame Kamel from Rosetta's father. This was a gift from Mr Kamel . . .' He reached again into his briefcase and produced a small, square case which he opened to display a most beautiful square-cut emerald, sparkling and almost alien in that most English of rooms.

'Jewellery of that value should be placed in a safe, Mr El-Askar,' she said sharply.

'Of course, immediately after I leave here. Read the documents at your leisure, Miss MacNaughton. I am sure you will find everything in order, but if you have any questions please ask. I shall be staying in London for three or four weeks – here is my address.'

He reached into his pocket and placed his card in front of her, then, with a brief smile, he said, 'I hope Mr Kamel's instructions are quite clear to you, Madame.'

'I feel that Mr Kamel has presumed a great deal. But Madame Kamel was brave enough to tell me what she thought I should know of her past life – don't you think that perhaps now is the time to approach her family?'

'No, Madame, I do not. When Mr Kamel married the girl's mother he automatically assumed responsibility for her, a responsibility his wife chose to ignore. Now, after her death, he has decided to comply with her wishes. He does not wish Rosetta to visit him in Damascus – indeed, he does not wish to see her again – but he has made her financially independent.

'All her life Madame Kamel strove to preserve, in her daughter, that which relates to the West; perhaps if the girl's father had lived it would have been different, but we shall never know. What Omar Kamel does now is what his wife would have wished. All he is asking from you, Madame, is to make her the sort of woman her mother would have wanted her to become.'

He watched the fleeting emotions cross Anne MacNaughton's face, doubt and uncertainty, and then suddenly acceptance, and he smiled . . .

33

A taxi-cab drew up sharply at No. 123 Princes Avenue, South Kensington. Out of it jumped a slim girl in rich furs and a young man in American officer's uniform.

The girl held out her hand, perfectly gloved in pale yellow suede, to say goodbye. All the rest of her was lost in the rich darkness of her furs. It was only when she lifted her head that you could see the clear pallor of her skin and the youthful freshness of her scarlet lips.

'I really must go, Peter,' she said. 'Thank you for meeting me. I'll be writing to Gemma to tell her how very kind you've been.'

'I could be kinder – let me take you out to supper tonight,' the young man said, smiling down at her and thinking that his sister had done him an enormous favour by asking him to meet this most gorgeous girl.

'I'd like to have supper with you, honestly, but I haven't seen Naughty for such a long time and she simply won't expect me to leave her tonight. We shall have so much to talk about.'

'But you're going back to school!' he complained persistently.

'I know, but it's not really like that at all. She's my guardian.' With a swift smile she withdrew her hand from his and turned to run up the stairs to the front door.

Miss MacNaughton was sitting in her long drawing room awaiting the arrival of her ex-pupil, Rosetta Kamel. It was over twelve months since she had seen her off for North America with a Canadian and two

American girls and she felt faintly anxious. What would that brief time in the New World have done to the girl she had seen depart with many tears and misgivings?

When the drawing-room door opened and her secretary announced, 'Miss Kamel,' Miss MacNaughton rose from her deep-seated chair with the alacrity of a girl in her teens. She held out her arms and Rosetta flew into them. For a moment neither of them spoke, for the girl was in tears, tears of sheer joy at finding herself once more in the room she remembered her mother bringing her to years before and in the arms of the woman she loved and respected above all others.

'Oh Naughty,' the girl said between tears and laughter, 'I knew I'd do nothing but cry when I saw you! It's this room with the cool walls, the pictures and the roses! Oh, nothing's changed since the first time I saw it! I loved our time in the Lake District – but I love all this so much more.'

'But Rosetta, you've had a lovely time. You've seen all those wonderful places in America and Canada that I've only dreamed about. You've met the President of the United States and the Governor of Canada – it's all been so wonderful, you're going to find London terribly dull and ordinary!'

'London could never be dull, but now the war's over we can travel, can't we? I want to go to Egypt to see my grandmother and sail up the Nile; I want to go to Paris and Rome; oh, there's such an awful lot I want to see!'

'You're forgetting I have a school to run.'

'I'm not forgetting that this is your summer holiday! Gemma Proctor's brother met the plane and he asked me out to supper. He was very handsome and very nice, but I told him I couldn't possibly go out with anybody on my first night back in London.'

'Why not? I'm quite sure I can't offer you anything

as exciting as supper with a presentable young American. But would you find a musical evening in a private house very boring by comparison, Rosetta?'

'Nothing would be boring with you, Naughty. You can't imagine how much I've been looking forward to coming home!'

'Well, I received two tickets from an old pupil – you won't remember her, she was on the verge of leaving us when you arrived,' she explained. 'Her name is Leoni Sinclair and she's making quite a name for herself at Covent Garden. Tonight she's having a musical evening in aid of the Red Cross in the home of her aunt, Lady Moira Hesketh. I feel I ought to go, but if you'd rather do something else, I'm sure I could make some legitimate excuse.'

'I want to go, Naughty. I love music but I have no talent for it, I only wish I had. Did my luggage arrive? You must have thought there was so much of it and I have to admit I spent money wildly. You were very generous with my allowance, Naughty.'

'It was your money, my dear. And during the next few days I think you should be made aware of your stepfather's generosity. He has made you a very rich woman, Rosetta.'

'But he doesn't want to see me, or hear from me.'

'Perhaps he would find it too painful, perhaps you would remind him too much of your mother.'

'Perhaps . . . Naughty, what shall I wear tonight? Will it be very formal?'

'I think we ought to dress up, although nobody will be looking at me with you around.'

Her words were substantiated when, later that evening, she waited for Rosetta to divest herself of her furs. The girl who stood before her, waiting for her approval, was wearing a turquoise wild silk gown which hugged her slender waist before falling away in rich folds to her feet. Her creamy shoulders emerged from the draped neckline of her gown and Miss MacNaughton thought that she was almost too beautiful with her raven-black hair and golden skin. Pansy-blue eyes with that exotic colouring were an additional bonus, but the passionate curve of her red lips was strangely Eastern.

She was aware of the admiring glances of those around her and she walked like a queen with her head held high, tall and graceful as a swan.

Moira Hesketh stared after them as they mounted the stairs to the music room on the first floor. She had met Miss MacNaughton before but the headmistress's companion intrigued her. Somewhere she had heard her name before, but she couldn't remember where. And there was something in her appearance, some elusive resemblance to someone she had once met.

During a lull in the proceedings she said quietly to her husband, 'What do we know about the girl who was with Miss MacNaughton? Have we met her before?'

'I'm sure we haven't. I would have remembered the prettiest girl I've seen in years.'

'She reminded me of somebody, but I can't think who.'

'You're getting old, my dear. There was a time when you never forgot a face. I used to rely on that memory of yours in India.'

She said nothing more. She'd probably seen the girl's picture in a magazine or newspaper – hers was the kind of beauty journalists looked for to sell their magazines. She'd ask Mary Harborough. Mary knew all the London gossip, who was new in society, new in London as well as in the shires. A girl as beautiful as this wouldn't have evaded Mary's notice.

More people were walking towards her and then she was greeting Mrs Levison-Gore and her daughter, Lady Burlington. The younger woman said quietly,

'Edward wasn't able to come, Lady Hesketh. His father died this morning so he had to go to be with his mother.'

'I'm so sorry, my dear, I didn't realise the Marquis was ill.'

'He's not been well for some time,' she answered and, as they moved away, Lady Hesketh thought somewhat cynically, 'So her mother's finally got her wish, one of her daughters has become the Marchioness of Camborne,' and then she remembered where she had heard the name Rosetta Kamel – on that night in London when the Oppenheimers had invited Laura Kamel to dine with them. Rosetta was Laura's daughter . . . As she greeted a tall man with silver hair and a charming smile, she said, 'We have a very interesting situation, John. I'll tell you about it later.'

John Halliday mounted the stairs, aware that his hostess's eyes had been filled with wry amusement. At some stage in the evening she would tell him what had put it there.

Leoni Sinclair's voice was beautiful as it soared effortlessly through the lofty room singing Mozart and Bach, and ending her recital with the music of *Carmen*. The applause was rapturous and then their host was inviting his guests into the supper room. Across the room John's eyes sought Lady Hesketh's.

He waited while she made her way towards him, occasionally stopping to chat with her guests. Then she was at his side, saying, 'Let them all go in there, John. We can eat later.'

He smiled down at her. 'What is this interesting situation you want to talk about?' he asked gently.

'That Levison-Gore woman is here with her daughter, Margaret, the new Marchioness of Camborne. I can see the woman positively bristling with gratification from here. But that isn't all, John. *Laura's* daughter is here with Miss MacNaughton.'

He stared at her for a moment before saying, 'I don't think you need worry, Moira, they don't know each other.'

'Perhaps not, but one can't be sure. The situation has its poignancy, don't you think?'

'Yes . . . Is she like Laura at all?'

'Only her eyes. She is quite the most beautiful girl in the room, so you can't miss her. We'll go in there now and see what is happening.'

While Leoni Sinclair greeted her old headmistress joyfully and Miss MacNaughton congratulated her warmly on her performance, Rosetta took the opportunity to look around her.

She was accustomed to admiration but she was not vain. She had her mother's flair for clothes and her mother's charm and, although she didn't know it, she had inherited her father's seriousness, the gravity that had made him so attractive.

Her eyes flicked over the assembly of laughing, chattering people and came suddenly to rest on Lavinia Levison-Gore and her daughter . . . her grandmother and her aunt, two people who had never wanted to know her, who had banished her mother from their lives as though she had never existed . . .

Across the room her eyes met Mrs Levison-Gore's. After a few moments Lavinia nodded coolly while Rosetta merely stared, her eyes filled with a hostility the older woman couldn't understand. Really, these foreigners! The girl should think herself fortunate that she had even remembered her, let alone acknowledged her.

Miss MacNaughton took one look at Rosetta's bleak face as she stared stonily at a woman standing chatting to Lady Hesketh.

'Do you know her?' she asked softly.

'She is my grandmother,' Rosetta answered.

'Are you quite sure, Rosetta?'

'Quite sure. The younger woman is my mother's sister.'

'Do you wish to leave, my dear?'

'No. Why should we?'

At that moment Mrs Levison-Gore smiled brightly at Miss MacNaughton and, excusing herself from her group, came across the room holding out her hand. With a delighted smile on her face she said, 'Why, Miss MacNaughton! How nice to see you here! Of course, Leoni Sinclair was one of your pupils, wasn't she? I can't think that you've discovered any such talent in my granddaughter!'

Miss MacNaughton smiled.

Mrs Levison-Gore's gaze shifted to Rosetta. 'We have met, haven't we? But you must forgive me, I don't recall your name.'

'We met at the home of Lord Mallonden. I was at school with Angela Tarleton,' Rosetta explained baldly.

'Of course, I remember you now. Are you still in touch with my niece?' she asked Rosetta.

'I hope to be in the near future,' Rosetta answered, then, with a brief smile, she moved away and across the room.

Lady Hesketh murmured to John Halliday, 'I must talk to her, John. She knows who she's been talking to and the moment can't have been a pleasant one.'

She found Rosetta in the music room, staring through one of the windows at a London gleaming with lights after years of darkness. Lady Hesketh joined her at the window, saying softly, 'It seems very strange, still, to see London like that. I was accustomed to the gloom and the searchlights raking the sky. You spent most of the war years in the Lake District, didn't you?'

'Yes, it was very beautiful.'

'And since then?'

'I've been living in Canada and Boston. I went to a finishing school there with two other girls I knew at Miss MacNaughton's. Everybody was very kind and I loved it.'

'Yes, I'm sure you did. I have always found the Americans and the Canadians warm-hearted. That means a lot when one is away from one's own people.'

'Yes.'

'Are you expecting to stay in England some time?'

Rosetta turned to stare at her before saying, 'This is my home – I have no other.'

'Oh, my dear, do forgive me. I thought you would be returning to Damascus.'

'My mother died before I went to America so there is only my stepfather in Damascus and we don't really know one another very well. I have to think about my future.'

'Yes, of course. I'm so sorry to hear about your mother. She was very beautiful – I knew her many years ago.'

'You knew my mother?'

'Yes. I met her on the boat that was taking her to Egypt and me back to India.'

'Did you know my father too?'

For only a moment Lady Hesketh hesitated, then she said softly, 'Yes – a very charming and handsome Egyptian prince. His death was a great tragedy.'

While they had been speaking Lady Hesketh had been watching the play of emotions on the girl's exquisite face: memories that were happy, bringing a smile to her scarlet lips, and pain when she spoke of her mother's death. None of them on board that ship so long ago had known that beautiful, wilful Laura would follow her heart into a strange and alien world, and now her daughter, too, was poised on the edge of an uncertain future.

After a few moments' silence Lady Hesketh said, 'There is a gentleman here who also knew your mother.

He was a great help to her in Egypt, I know. Would you like to meet him?'

'Yes, I would like that very much. Who is he?'

'His name is Halliday, Sir John Halliday. He was also on the boat with your mother and her family. He worked at the British Embassy in Cairo and was a very good friend to your mother after your father was killed.'

'Then I would like to meet him.'

After Rosetta had been introduced, John asked her, 'What are you going to do with yourself in England?'

'I'm not sure,' Rosetta replied. 'Perhaps nothing for the first few months, until I find my feet. After that I want to do something useful with my money.'

She had mentioned money casually, as if it were of little account.

'Is it your intention to live in London?' he asked curiously.

'I haven't thought about it. I only arrived today, but Miss MacNaughton will give me the benefit of her advice, I know.'

'And in the meantime you will stay with her?'

She laughed. 'I honestly haven't thought about it. Isn't that silly? I've known I was coming back to England and I've never even thought about where I'm going to live and what I'm going to do. Will you tell me something, Mr Halliday. You met my grandmother on that voyage out to Egypt. What did you think of her?'

He stared at her, momentarily taken aback. 'I didn't know her very well, Rosetta. I remember that she was often indisposed and I can't think I exchanged many words with her.'

'I see. Her daughter, then?'

'Margaret? She was little more than a schoolgirl, a nice enough girl, I thought.'

'My father?'

'I played bridge with your father. I thought him charming, very handsome, rather grave.'

'I'm not going to ask you about my mother, she was the most beautiful, enchanting person in my life. Were you just a little in love with her?'

John laughed. 'It wouldn't have done me much good if I had been, I'm afraid. She was in love with your father and only your father.'

Rosetta nodded contentedly. 'Here comes Miss MacNaughton, intent on rescuing me from the most distinguished man in the room. I'm so glad to have met you, Sir John.'

34

Miss MacNaughton stood at her window looking down on the street below. From above she could hear the sound of girls' voices under the tutelage of the new music mistress, and she felt relieved that the beginning of term had got off the ground with few mishaps.

She was glad to be getting back into harness again. She'd spent six happy weeks walking in Scotland and now she was waiting for Rosetta to join her for afternoon tea.

They had explored the west of Scotland together before Rosetta had gone off to join her friends in one pursuit or another. She expected the girl to be full of news about her activities and she had a little advice to give her about slowing down and giving serious thought to her immediate future.

As she looked along the street a taxi-cab rounded the corner and two young men jumped out to assist Rosetta to alight with several large packages.

She sent them off, waving gaily before she ran up the steps and entered the front door. There were footsteps in the corridor outside and then the door was flung open and Rosetta rushed across the room to embrace her.

She was laughing. 'You're going to say I've been recklessly extravagant, I know, but wait till you see what I've bought you,' she said gaily.

'Rosetta,' Miss MacNaughton said sternly, 'I've told you I don't want presents from you. I have quite enough of everything.'

'But I get such pleasure from buying presents! And I have nobody else to buy them for.'

As she spoke she was busily tearing off sheets of glossy wrapping paper to bring to light a beige cashmere twinset, while another box revealed a crocodile handbag.

Anne MacNaughton looked at the girl helplessly. 'They're beautiful, Rosetta, but they embarrass me terribly. Presents like these put me under a terrible obligation.'

'Of course they don't! How could you possibly feel obligated to me when I owe you more than I can ever repay! Oh, Naughty, I've had such a wonderful time! The Pearsons took me to Ireland and we rode the most magnificent horses you ever saw – I've half promised to put some money into the stud farm they have there. It's doing awfully well but they do need some more bloodstock and the war hasn't helped. We must talk about it soon. And guess where I went last week?'

'My dear, how can I guess? You have so many things lined up.'

'I went to stay with the Tarletons and on Sunday we drove over to the Mallonden house and Granny Mallonden was there. I had to keep telling myself that she was my great-grandmother. She's awfully old – ninety – and she's quite deaf but everybody still kowtows.'

'Didn't it bother you to go to the Mallondens?'

'No. I sat back to listen to them talking about themselves and I was simply dying to drop my bombshell. What do you suppose would have happened if I'd suddenly said, "Look, I'm Laura Levison-Gore's daughter"?'

'There would have been great consternation, I'm sure.'

'Well, I didn't say anything. I listened. Margaret's daughter is in Switzerland and her grandmother is already lining up the right sort of men for when she comes back. Even Lord Mallonden was put out by it. He said, "Not again, surely, Lavinia! I haven't forgotten the last time." '

Anne MacNaughton studied Rosetta's face. The girl's expression was vaguely vindictive and there was something going on in that beautiful head that made her feel uneasy.

More light-hearted than she felt, she said evenly, 'And who has Mrs Levison-Gore decided to line up on this occasion?'

'Another marquis, would you believe! But this time the son of a duke. Lord Mallonden said it was unfortunate there were no royal princes of the right age she could have picked on. Do you know, it doesn't seem to worry her in the slightest when people are sarcastic. She treated me as if I wasn't there and even Angela's mother noticed and said it was a dreadful way to behave. I think her husband must have been a very nice man – Mother certainly never took after her.'

Miss MacNaughton laughed before deciding to drop the subject. 'The school got off to a fine start, Rosetta. Can't you feel it, we're really back to normal,' she said lightly.

Rosetta embraced her warmly again. 'I can feel it and I'm so glad for you, Naughty.' Raising her arms above her head she said, joyfully, 'Oh, Naughty, it's so heavenly to be rich! They were all talking about the Season, the balls they had lined up, Goodwood and Ascot – all the things Mother used to tell me about – and how much it was going to cost their parents and if they could afford it or would they have to share . . .

'I know I'm going to be invited to some of their balls and things, but I don't have to give the money side of it a single thought. I shall have the right clothes for every occasion and nobody will ride a better horse, or drive a faster car. I'll buy a boat for Cowes Week and hire a crew. I may not be the *English* Miss Kamel but I intend to be the *rich* Rosetta Kamel.'

'My dear, it isn't important. You are beautiful – and a very nice girl who knows how to be kind. Don't let the past shape your future. Don't open your heart to bitterness – your mother never did.'

'There, Naughty, you see the difference in us. My mother had forgiveness in her blood because she was English and the English know how to forgive. But I am Egyptian. One day I will make the Mallondens pay for what they did to my mother, what they were prepared to do to me.'

'My dear child, how are you going to make them pay? Are you going to tell them who you are? What do you want from them, an apology? Is that going to make up for everything, when all it will do is bring them closer together and possibly lose you your friend Angela?'

There was a strange smile on Rosetta's lips, then, with a truly foreign shrug of her elegant shoulders, she said, 'I haven't decided what I shall do. I am still thinking about it.'

'Oh Rosetta, have the Christian teachings you learned at my school counted for nothing?'

'Of course. But they have not obliterated an older and deeper hurt. You understand so much of me, but you cannot understand all of me. There is a part of me you may never know. It was born in me, Naughty, and I feel it in me, something old and deep and punishing. There was an old man in the Fayoum who helped to bring in the grapes. He picked me up one day in the road when I had fallen and I was crying. He dried my tears and put a huge black grape in my mouth, then he said, "One day, little one, you will be beautiful and you will suffer. The East knows well how to suffer." That is the part of me you will never understand because I do not understand it myself!'

Rosetta bought a very expensive flat in a new block overlooking Hyde park and Miss MacNaughton received an invitation card for the house-warming. Only a day or so later Rosetta was round at the school, throwing open the door of her drawing room and exclaiming, 'Naughty, you haven't answered my invitation!'

'I know, dear. Are you sure you want an old fuddy-duddy like me to be there with all your young friends?'

'I invited you, didn't I? If you don't come, then I certainly won't want the others. But honestly, Naughty, you don't have a thing to worry about. I invited Lady Hesketh and that nice man Sir John Halliday. *They've* both been gracious enough to accept my invitation.'

'I'm sorry, dear, of course I want to come. I didn't want to think you'd invited me because you thought you should.'

Rosetta smiled. 'I shall never do that with anybody. Oh, Naughty, I do want you to like the flat. It was terribly expensive, but the rooms are beautiful and I got such pleasure from chosing the furniture. But if you don't approve, then I'll just go ahead and change it.'

'Would you enjoy being so extravagant, Rosetta?'

She laughed. 'I love spending money on beautiful things I feel I can't live without – then I have the most terrible feeling that my stepfather is going to appear in a puff of smoke like an old Eastern genie and call a halt to everything!'

'I don't think there's any danger of that.'

'You'll know some of the younger people, Naughty. I've invited Angela Tarleton and her fiancé. She's getting married at the end of the summer to a Scottish peer who owns acres of land in the Highlands and the family are delighted. I'm invited to her wedding.'

'I'm so glad, dear. Angela was a nice sort of girl and you were good friends.'

'Still are. She's staying with me for a few days next week so no doubt I'll be hearing all about the family then.'

Miss MacNaughton remained silent, knowing full well that Rosetta had expected some sort of stricture but she had long ago decided to distance herself from any wild schemes in Rosetta's mind. Her role was to stay around to pick up the pieces – and she felt pretty confident that there would be a great many of them.

The flat was beautiful, as she had known it would be, and the younger element more than did justice to the champagne and the luxurious buffet which Rosetta had provided.

She was introduced to Angela Tarleton's fiancé, a tall Scot who was a good many years older than Angela but a very sound man who talked to her about his prize cattle, the welfare of his tenants and his disdain for fashionable nightclubs.

The flat was so spacious that the young people drifted away, leaving the older guests to their more staid entertainment of chatting together.

John Halliday would have preferred to be in the peaceful atmosphere of his club; instead, he had escorted Lady Hesketh who had seemed more than a little anxious to attend.

'Johnny wouldn't come,' she explained to him. 'He said she'd only asked us out of courtesy and there'd be too much noise. He's probably right but I wanted to come because Rosetta Kamel intrigues me. I'd like to know her better.'

'Why?' he asked laconically.

'Probably because she's here in London. I would have thought she would be required to go home to

Damascus once her education was over. Instead, she's bought this most expensive flat and rumour has it that she spends money as though there's no tomorrow. *I* think there's more to it than meets the eye.'

They watched Rosetta flitting among her guests, serene, beautiful, assured, and Lady Hesketh wished she wasn't feeling the same sort of disquiet which she had felt years before on that voyage out to Egypt.

She sensed a similar unease in Miss MacNaughton, who seemed strangely reluctant to answer questions as to why Rosetta was remaining in London when the stepfather who kept her so well supplied with money lived in Damascus . . .

Several days later Rosetta met her friend Angela off the train and later watched Angela prowling round her flat exclaiming ecstatically at the carpets and curtains, the furniture and the beauty of the ornaments she had surrounded herself with.

'What a lot of pleasure you must have had in furnishing this place! Why aren't you doing interior decorating, Rosetta? You'd be so wonderful at it!'

'I hadn't thought of it,' Rosetta admitted. 'When you're ready to furnish I'll help you with anything you want.'

'I'll not be able to change a thing. Ian's home is exactly the way it will stay, just like it's been for centuries!'

'Surely he'll allow you to change what you don't like?' Rosetta asked cautiously.

'I haven't dared to tell him – he thinks it's just perfect the way it is.'

'What does your mother think?'

'Oh Mother says I'll be able to do things in easy stages, and Great-Grandmother says I should be so pleased to have him I mustn't think of antagonising him.'

'He's Scottish, isn't he? Doesn't she object to your marrying a Scot? I take it *he* doesn't come under the category of foreign.'

Angela laughed. 'He just about passes muster, although I expect in her innermost heart she'd prefer him to be purebred English. She approves of everything else about him.'

'You mean his money and his estates, of course?'

'All of that. I'm really awfully lucky to have captured Ian without going through what Father calls the Silly Season. Even in the best families, money's awfully tight these days. Mummy says Cousin Margaret and her husband are having to pull their belts in. The death duties were absolutely appalling and, if the worst comes to the worst, they'll have to throw open the gardens to the public. You'd be amazed how many families are having to do that these days.'

'Including the Mallondens?'

'Great-Grandmother won't allow it, but when she's gone it might come to that. Granny pinches and scrapes – and you should see Aunt Poppy's clothes, they look as though she's bought them at the church jumble sale.'

'It rather looks as though all your cousins will be hoping to emulate you by marrying well. So the next few months should be very interesting,' Rosetta murmured drily.

'Heavens, yes. Daddy's already totting up how much my wedding's going to cost him. The society wedding of the year, Granny calls it.'

'Unless the daughter of the Marquis of Camborne exceeds all expectations.'

Angela laughed. 'You're beginning to get the measure of our family, Rosetta. Mummy and Aunt Poppy laugh about Aunt Lavinia but I'll bet Margaret's husband doesn't think she's at all funny. Actually I don't think he likes her very much.'

When Rosetta didn't comment she went on, 'I'd

have loved to have you for a bridesmaid, Rosetta, but I have to have my cousins, it's expected of me.'

'Well of course, and I am, after all, only half-English.'

Angela blushed and, looking at her friend unhappily, said, 'Oh Rosetta, you know that's never meant anything to me. You're my best friend, you always have been.'

'I know, and really, Angela, I'm not in the least concerned about your family's prejudices.'

'But you're coming to my wedding, Rosetta! Promise me you'll be there? And at the ball Father's giving to formally announce my engagement?'

'Of course. I shall look forward to it.'

Angela, wrapped up in her private plans, was unable to see Rosetta's expression as she looked out of her window across London. It was all starting to take shape and there would be no turning back from what she had planned. Kismet, she told herself silently.

She turned away from the window as Angela said, 'I'm going for fittings this afternoon. What are you doing with yourself.'

'I'm going to the museum.'

'The museum!' Angela said wide-eyed, and with as much consternation as if Rosetta had said she was going to the moon.

'I go to the Egyptian rooms. I've learned English history, it's about time I learned a little about Egyptian history and there's so much more of it. I also go to a class in the evenings. I'm becoming quite good at reading the hieroglyphics.'

'Heavens, what are they?'

'The ancient Egyptian writing. One day when I go back to Egypt I shall know what I'm looking at and what it all means.'

'You do intend to go back there then?'

'Yes, of course. To see my grandmother.'

'Is she really a princess living in a beautiful palace?

When I told my mother, she said it was probably something you'd made up, just like I used to make things up when I was young.'

Rosetta smiled. 'She really is a princess and all I told you about her was true.'

'That makes Granny Mallonden's high-handed attitude seem very silly, doesn't it?'

Rosetta merely smiled.

35

Edward, the Marquis of Camborne, was not a happy man as he surveyed his estate through the drawing-room window on a bleak February morning. The house and the estate needed a great deal of money spending on it and the death duties had been astronomical.

He felt angry with his father. He had kept so much hidden from his wife and his sons and now he had gone and it was left to Edward to pick up the pieces. Margaret was sympathetic but, like himself, she'd been domineered over all her life; his father and her mother had done a good job on both of them.

His mother-in-law was *astute*. His father had disliked her intensely, even while he had recognised her materialistic shrewdness.

'She'll run your life for you if you'll let her,' had been his constant harangue and, since the old man's death, she'd been a frequent visitor, making bullets for Margaret to shoot.

Every meal-time became a platform for her advice and interference and now she was turning her attention on Edward's daughter. Lavinia was a clever woman, even his father had admitted that much, but Elfreda? According to his mother-in-law, many of his problems would be solved if Elfreda made the right sort of marriage. Old families stuck together; it had always been so and it would continue to be so. Money married money; if girls had any sense they loved where money was and she was in a position to know. One of her daughters had been sensible, she claimed, the other had been stupid.

'I thought Laura had loved where there was a great

deal of money,' Edward had retorted, whereupon she'd snorted angrily, 'Money, in that case, didn't matter. Granny Mallonden would never have approved.'

Privately, Edward thought that it hadn't very much mattered to Laura whether her grandmother had agreed or not. Just occasionally over the years Laura had been mentioned, but only when Lavinia wished to emphasise something very strongly, like the obedience of children and the suitability of suitors.

She'd insisted on the finishing school in Switzerland for Elfreda and it was costing the earth. Edward considered it snobbish and unnecessary, particularly when he observed the conduct of a great many young people who were supposed to have benefited from that sort of education.

He frowned as his eyes fell on the figures of his wife and mother-in-law walking across the grass. They were both wrapped up warmly against the sharp wind but it appeared to be Mrs Levison-Gore who was doing most of the talking. He could see her hands gesticulating and he doubted if his wife would utter a word.

He would not argue with Lavinia over lunch. She talked as if the servants were not there and he felt pretty sure that the topics of their conversation were well and truly milled over in the servants' quarters. To his surprise, however, she was charming on this occasion and agreeable with the servants and yet he was aware that his wife's face was faintly troubled. He was doubly alarmed when Lavinia said, 'If you're having coffee in your study, Edward, I'll join you. There is something I want to say to you.'

He frowned. 'I have one of my agents coming this afternoon. If you have something to say, I suggest you say it over coffee in here.'

She frowned. 'This is very private, Edward. I would rather say it without having the servants overhear.'

'You say a great many things in the presence of

my servants,' he muttered, but in answer to his wife's appealing gaze he said, testily, 'Oh, very well, then. But I've only about half an hour to spare.'

Margaret made no attempt to follow them as they made their way to his study. Lavinia, who had made herself comfortable in front of the fire while he sat behind his desk, smiled appreciatively as she looked round the businesslike little room.

'I always liked this room, Edward,' she said. 'It's so cosy and warm. The rest of the place needs a fortune to heat it. You do realise, don't you, Edward, that this place needs a lot of money spending on it – and I know all about death duties.'

'I am aware of it.'

'You'll get no help from your mother, Edward. She's happy to be away from it all, living in that nice manor house in the Cotswolds. It's all very well going on about the family estate when there's enough money to look after it, but when there isn't one has to start thinking about other means.'

'You're suggesting I manufacture it out of thin air, are you?'

'No, Edward, I am not. When I was last at the Mallondens all the talk was of Angela. She's doing remarkably well for herself; got a presentable young man with vast estates in Scotland. She's only just met him, so you don't need to tell me they're ecstatically in love. They're not. It's all to do with expediency: two people who like one another and are agreeable to let it go on from there.'

'What has all this to do with what I need to spend on the estate?'

'It has a great deal to do with Elfreda. She's a nice girl, a very pretty girl, and she'll be back from that finishing school for Angela Tarleton's wedding.'

'So?'

'Most of the country's eligible bachelors will be at

that wedding, including the Duke of Sharne's son, the Marquis of Gleve. He is to be the best man and what could be more appropriate than that he should escort Angela's chief bridesmaid, Elfreda?'

'They could hate each other on sight.'

'That is defeatism, Edward! I think you and Margaret should put yourselves out to be quite charming to the Duke and Duchess of Sharne and I will help in any way I can.'

'I suggest you keep out of it, Lavinia! My father never liked your slippery meanderings over Laura and me and I don't want anybody saying you had a hand in my daughter's marriage.'

Not at all put out by his words, but rather reassured, Lavinia said, 'Very well, Edward. Just as long as you realise I have all your interests at heart. And before you spend too much on your property, see that Elfreda has the most lavish gown you can afford for Angela's ball!'

She left him staring pensively into the fire.

Edward hated her interference. His father had always said he'd been a fool to marry Margaret. He could hear the old man saying, 'Mark my words, you'll have that woman breathing down your neck all your married life. The girl hasn't a thought in her head that her mother hasn't put there – it should have been anybody but her.'

There had been a lot of wisdom in his words. Margaret was sweet and malleable but he always knew when her mother had been at her. Why had he married her? In his innermost heart he knew that it was that elusive similarity, that mischievous resemblance to her sister. It wasn't always present, it was something he had to look for; then, miraculously, it was there in the turn of her head, the sweet, swift smile. Suddenly there was Laura and an old, remembered pain . . .

Margaret never spoke about Laura – none of them did – it was as if she had never existed. And yet, somewhere, there was Laura and her child.

There were times when he'd been tempted to make enquiries about her, but something had always stopped him. She had never pleaded with her family for forgiveness, never crawled to them to be taken back and he knew, in his heart, that when he married Margaret he had settled for second best.

He wasn't going to push Elfreda on to anybody; it would be different, of course, if she fell for the chap. Edward began to think of what he had heard about Paul, the Marquis of Gleve . . .

Angela decided she would be married in November. It wasn't the best month but there were several points in its favour.

Her brother Ernest was in the Far East and was not likely to be home until early October; her cousin Elfreda would not be leaving her school in Switzerland until the summer and the gaggle of cousins who were to make up her bridal retinue were either taking exams or looking forward to holidays.

Winter weddings could be charming, her mother said brightly. The bridesmaids could wear velvet, Tudor-style with ermine muffs, and she could have her ball at the beginning of October. Summer balls were a nuisance because they interfered with Ascot and Goodwood; people were out of town and, when they returned, their guests would all be looking forward to something nice to prepare them for the winter months.

Angela's prospective bridegroom offered no objections so the wedding was arranged for the beginning of November, from the Mallondens' London home, a fact which pleased Great-Aunt Lavinia enormously, since it gave her a little longer to plan her strategy.

Elfreda emerged from her sojourn in Switzerland

like a delicate English rose, a faithful copy of what her mother had been with pale, flaxen hair and china-blue eyes, fine-boned and soft-spoken, jolly and gentle, so that even Great-Grandmother Mallonden received her graciously and seemed well pleased with all that breeding and money had managed to accomplish.

Her father thought it was a blessing that all that debutante nonsense had been shelved since the war. His daughter would be launched into society without any obvious hint that her grandmother might be manipulating events. By the end of the summer Elfreda found herself being escorted to race meetings, Cowes Week and a great many parties and summer dances by blue-blooded young men who did things in the City, or served in one of the Guards' regiments. They all liked horses and dogs and invariably drove fast cars.

None of these escorts quite measured up to what Lavinia wanted for Elfreda; her sights were set firmly on Paul whom Edward steadfastly refused to invite to the house because he knew all their friends would interpret his action as one coming from Lavinia.

Lavinia was furious and Margaret was made the target of her anger but Elfreda was quite oblivious to the undercurrents going on around her. She was enjoying herself. All this gaiety was a far cry from Switzerland and the stern chaperoning of Madame and her staff!

Receiving no help from her son-in-law, Lavinia decided she must encourage the match alone, or rather, with the aid of friends. An old chum was giving a dance at the end of August for her granddaughter whom Elfreda knew quite well and Lavinia had heard that the young Marquis had been invited to it . . .

Elfreda wore a gown chosen by her grandmother, a confection of pure silk pink chiffon with a trail of white silk roses from the shoulder to the hem. She looked extremely pretty and ethereal. Delight shone in the eyes of her handsome escort who arrived looking as smart as paint in his subaltern's uniform. The family stood on the steps to watch their departure and it was doubtful if they were even through the gates when Edward said pointedly, 'I take it this is not just any dance, Lavinia. You've gone to an awful lot of trouble to choose the gown and the escort.'

'Don't be silly, Edward!' Lavinia snapped. 'I'm always interested in where she's going and what she's wearing.'

Edward retired to his study, unconvinced, and Margaret whispered to her mother, 'Don't go on pushing it, Mother, or Edward will be furious. They might not even like one another.'

'I'm not a defeatist like you are, Margaret! I have great hopes of this evening.'

Long before the supper dance Elfreda had fallen in love with a young man she had danced with only briefly; a tall dark young man with a charming smile and grave dark eyes that looked down at her with friendly awareness.

'Who is he?' she hissed to a friend standing near by.

'The Marquis of Gleve, the Duke of Sharne's son. Dishy, isn't he?'

'Oh yes, I think he's georgous.'

'Have you been introduced?'

'No.'

'I'll introduce you if you like – he's a friend of my brother's.'

The introduction came shortly afterwards. The young Marquis bowed gravely over her hand and asked if she would dance with him later in the evening, then he took her dance card, filled in a vacant dance and handed it back with a smile.

She was disinterested in every dance throughout the evening until he walked across the floor and bowed before her. Slipping her hand in his she gave herself up to the intoxication of gliding round the floor with him. Before he returned her to her escort he said, coolly, 'I'm sure we shall meet again, Elfreda. Perhaps at Goodwood? Do you enjoy racing?'

'Oh yes, but I haven't really done very much.'

'You will,' he said, bowing over her hand, then she was watching him crossing the hall to claim his next partner.

Elfreda remembered very little about the rest of the evening . . .

Miss MacNaughton listened with a great deal of interest as Rosetta spoke delightedly of her plans for the summer.

'I'm having such a lovely time, Naughty,' she said gaily. 'I'm being taken to all the nicest places and it's so wonderful to be able to buy the right clothes.'

'And who is taking you to these nice places?' she asked lightly.

'Oh, we generally go in a party and sometimes it's one escort, sometimes another. Don't look so doubtful, Naughty! They are all extremely circumspect, eligible and charming.'

'Eligible?'

'Why, yes. They're not married and I don't want to marry a single one of them. It's all very light-hearted and charming.'

'Is one of these nice young men going to escort you to Angela Tarleton's ball in October?'

'Darling Naughty, it's only the beginning of August! How do I know who will be escorting me in October?'

Miss MacNaughton had to be content with that, but inwardly she hoped Rosetta had given up all thoughts of punishing the Mallondens for the past.

Angela had spent much of the summer in Scotland and, when she did take the opportunity to spend time with her friends in Rosetta's flat, all her talk was of her wedding, the engagement ball and what people would be wearing.

'I've chosen my wedding dress,' she said, then in the next breath, 'I'm not telling a soul what it's like so you'll all have to wait to find out, but the bridesmaids are wearing velvet. Mother suggested it. They'll all look like people out of Romeo and Juliet with pearl head-dresses and beaded collars.'

'I suppose the family will be there in force,' Rosetta said evenly. 'Including Great-Grandmother.'

'Most definitely Great-Grandmother! And it's getting to seem like launching a battleship. There's that long walk down the aisle, and getting up and kneeling down in church. Aunt Poppy manages her very well, so I hope they can sit together.'

A small titter went round the rest of the girls and one of them said archly, 'What about Elfreda? She's cutting all sorts of a dash with her marquis. Will it come to anything, do you think?'

'Oh gosh, I do hope so. She's absolutely head-over-heels about him,' Angela replied.

'And the family are head-over-heels, too, I suppose, particularly her grandmother.'

'Well, of course. If she captures Paul, one day she'll be a duchess. We've never had one of those in the family before.'

Rosetta sat back to listen, her face inscrutable, her insides churning with a strange, unaccountable anger. Why should it matter so much that Elfreda had fallen in love? She'd hardly known the girl at Miss MacNaughton's school and they'd only exchanged brief smiles when they'd met at Angela's parents' house.

She was glad when, one by one, her friends made their excuses to leave. Angela was the last to go and, as they parted at the door, she said, 'Why not come for the weekend, Rosetta? We're all going to the races on Saturday afternoon. One of Daddy's horses is running and he seems to think he has a good chance. Ian won't be down this weekend because he's judging cattle up in Scotland. Dad's horse was a good reason for me to cry off.'

Long weekends at the Tarletons were always the same, casual and easy-going. Walks with the dogs, rides along the country lanes, mornings spent poring over the newspapers, evenings at the bridge table. In between there were the races at Chepstow and it was on the second day, when Angela waved gaily to a couple entering the catering tent, that Rosetta immediately recognised Cousin Elfreda in the company of a tall, extremely handsome man.

'We must go over there,' Angela said. 'I do want to meet him because if all goes according to plan hers will be the society wedding of the year, next year!'

Rosetta would not have recognised Elfreda from the ordinary little girl she remembered from school with her delicate, pretty face and pale blonde hair.

Now that pretty, childish face was all smiles. She seemed, to Rosetta, like some pink confection in icing sugar with her pink-and-white complexion, her pale blue eyes and rose-lipped mouth. The dimples came and went with her smiles, and then Rosetta found her hand taken in the firm grip of the young man accompanying Elfreda, who looked down at her curiously while his lips murmured a conventional greeting.

Whether it was Angela's words of introduction or her appearance that made Paul seem curious she didn't know. Angela said lightly, 'This is my friend, Rosetta Kamel. Rosetta was the most beautiful girl in the school, the one who carried off most of the prizes and always looked as though she'd stepped out of the pages of the *Arabian Nights*.'

'Oh yes!' Elfreda enthused. 'I thought you were so very lovely, Rosetta. I wished I was like you but there was never any hope. I'm like my mother, a typical Mallonden.'

'Don't scoff at the Mallondens,' Angela retorted.

'I'm one myself! Take a look in the Long Gallery next time you go to Grandfathers' – we've had our share of beauties.'

'But none like Rosetta,' Elfreda said firmly.

'Well, of course not. Rosetta's Syrian. Dad's horse came in second, so it wasn't a bad performance, he'll be pleased. Are you having a good day?'

'Mixed,' Paul answered her. 'Actually, we're thinking of leaving. We just came in here to look for some friends we're with. Elfreda's mother is giving a dinner-party this evening so we promised to be back in good time.'

'We won't keep you, then. You've some way to drive.'

The two cousins kissed and, over their heads, Paul looked into Rosetta's eyes, a straight look from blue-grey eyes like polished steel. Rosetta's eyes were sombre but, as he escorted his companion out of the tent, they were all he could think of . . .

It was several mornings later when Rosetta called at Miss MacNaughton's school to introduce herself to Naughty's new puppy, a bundle of white mischief called Hamish, a West Highland terrier.

Rosetta picked him up and cuddled him. 'Oh, Naughty, he's beautiful! Why did you never have one before?'

'I vowed I wouldn't when Patch died years ago. It hurt so much, I said then that I'd never ever give my heart to another dog, but Hamish was so adorable I couldn't resist him. Besides, it will do me good to get out across the park with him. I'm becoming far too sedentary.'

'Will you enjoy walking in the wind and rain with him?'

Anne MacNaughton laughed. 'Hmm! Can I rely on you to be one of his walkers?'

'Well, of course. Now, if you like.'

Miss MacNaughton looked at her in comical surprise. 'You mean you actually have a day when you're not out and about with one young man or other?'

Rosetta merely laughed and Miss MacNaughton said, with a little sigh, 'I was thinking how nice it would be in the park this afternoon but I have a staff meeting. Here's his lead. He's remarkably good, so I don't expect him to give you any trouble.'

It was a mellow September day, a day of white scudding clouds and silver ripples on the lake with a breeze that brought a sparkle into her eyes and a glow into her cheeks. She was halfway across the grass leading towards the Serpentine when a man who had been walking towards her suddenly stopped and said, hesitantly, 'Hello, it is Rosetta, isn't it?'

She turned and looked up at him, then, smiling, she said, 'Yes, we met at the races in Chepstow. You were with Elfreda Burlington.'

'Yes. Is this your dog?'

'No, he belongs to my old headmistress. His name is Hamish.'

He bent down to pat the dog who promptly rolled over on his back so that they laughed delightedly at his antics.

'Would you mind if I walked with you?' Paul asked.

So they walked together and fell in love. They took sudden shelter under the trees in a light burst of rain, and they sat over tea and scones in the company of office workers and shop assistants enjoying the park during their lunch break.

Looking around her, Rosetta said swiftly, 'Oh, this is what I've always liked about London! Ordinary people enjoying something as ordinary as lunch in the park under the trees. It's so sweet and sane – indestructible, too, if that doesn't sound too silly.'

'This is something you were not accustomed to before you came here?' Paul asked curiously.

'There was much of the same thing in Paris, ordinary people enjoying themselves on an ordinary day, but before then my life was very different.'

'In Syria?'

'No. In Egypt.'

'But I understood Angela to say you were Syrian.'

'I know, but I have never been there. My father was Egyptian and my mother was English. All my early childhood was spent in the Fayoum, in Egypt. Then when my mother married Omar Kamel I became Syrian.'

'I see.'

For a long time there was silence. Rosetta stared out across the lake which gave Paul plenty of time to study the contours of her face with its mane of raven-black hair, and the incredible violet eyes that made him catch his breath sharply. Since their first meeting he had been unable to erase her image from his mind; her beauty was a magnet that drew him towards her with tentacles of steel for she made all the other women he had ever met seem insipid and uninteresting.

He knew what his family and Elfreda's family expected; and he liked Elfreda. She was a decent, friendly and thoroughly *nice* girl. But the sight of her had no power to make his heart beat one bit faster; and the most poignant thing of all was the knowledge that Elfreda was in love with him . . .

Miss MacNaughton stood at her window watching them walk down the street with the puppy trailing along behind and there was deep disquiet in her heart. She knew immediately who Rosetta's escort was; she'd seen him constantly in the society pictures. And she knew that the young Marquis of Gleve had been Elfreda Burlington's constant companion over the past few weeks. Now here was Rosetta with her tantalising Eastern beauty and, as they paused to say goodbye, there was no disguising his feeling for her.

He was holding her hand, looking down into her eyes, and she in turn was looking up at him with wide-eyed fascination.

'Will you have dinner with me one evening, Rosetta?' he asked her urgently.

'I would like to have dinner with you, Paul, but aren't you engaged to Elfreda Burlington?'

'No.'

'But you hope to be?'

'No! I don't hope to be *anything* without you. I don't want to think about a future without you.'

She hadn't thought to hear this sort of undying protestation of love so soon, and while one half of her wanted to be circumspect, to refuse to see him, she was doubtful about the other half. Paul Gleve attracted her more than any man she had ever met – but she wasn't sure whether it was because she had thought he belonged to Elfreda or if it was real.

If she could take him away from Elfreda simply to prove that it could be done she might have been satisfied with that, but she already knew that while she could hurt Elfreda, she couldn't bear to hurt Paul. On the other hand, she thought savagely, there can never be anything permanent between Paul and me. Had she but known it, these had been the sentiments expressed by her father to her mother many years before . . .

Miss MacNaughton saw little of Rosetta in the days after her meeting with Paul and she believed she knew why. The girl did not answer her telephone when she tried to speak to her; she did not come to the school; and twice one of her teachers said she'd seen Rosetta arm in arm with a tall young man in the park.

Then, at the beginning of October, came Angela Tarleton's ball. Rosetta appeared in the early evening to show off her ballgown. She threw of her dark sable wrap and flung it over a chair, then she waltzed around the room in her gold kid slippers with the sheen of coral-coloured wild silk swirling about her feet, her only adornment the diamond necklace and earrings her mother had bequeathed to her. She was as beautiful and exotic as a poppy.

Rosetta would stand out like a brilliant jewel amongst a bevy of girls in frothy white lace and chiffon and Miss MacNaughton asked, 'What made you choose coral, darling? You look quite lovely in white.'

Rosetta grinned at her wickedly. 'You know they'll *all* be in white, Naughty. White or sugar-pink-icing dresses. I am different and I want to *look* different. Don't tell me you don't like my gown?'

'Oh but I do like it. It's beautiful. But when you first came here, Rosetta, you desperately wanted to look exactly like every other English girl in my school. Now, suddenly, you want to be different, the orchid not the rose.'

'The pomegranate . . . isn't that how Great-Grandmother Mallonden described me?'

'Rosetta, what are you trying to prove?'

'Why, nothing at all, dear Naughty! Except that I am the way I am. None of them ever wanted to know the English part of me, they only admired the Egyptian in me because it was different, because I was different. Well, tonight I'm going to *be* different. I'm going to shine like a star and they'll *have* to take me for what I am!'

She picked up her sable wrap and draped it round her shoulders, then, with a small, defiant smile, she left her to go running lightly down the stairs.

36

Angela stood with her fiancé, her parents and his parents at the top of the stairs, waiting to greet their guests. She looked pretty and predictable in white lace and, as she kissed Rosetta's cheek, she murmured, 'You look gorgeous, darling! I wish I'd had your courage instead of this ordinary white.'

'You look beautiful, Angela,' Rosetta whispered, then moved on to greet the others. She appeared in the ballroom under the scrutiny of eyes filled with admiration, doubt, curiosity but, as her gaze swept the room, she was only aware that the Mallondens were there in force. Great-Grandmother Mallonden sat at the far end of the room on a huge velvet chair, looking a little like Queen Victoria, and surrounded by her large family.

In the group was the Marquis of Camborne and his lady, his mother-in-law Mrs Levison-Gore and the Duke and Duchess of Sharne with the Lady Elfreda. Rosetta's eyes searched for Paul but could not find him among the Mallonden clan and, as she was immediately asked to dance, she had a better view of the family when they reached the top of the room.

All eyes turned to watch her being spun along the floor, and she was aware that, to most of those present, she was the complete alien, a creature as far removed from them as is the sun from the stars.

She saw Paul enter the room and stand for a few moments looking around, then unhurriedly he crossed the room to join Elfreda and the rest of them.

There were many exchanges of looks within the family when he invited Elfreda to dance, and, over the head of his partner, his eyes met Rosetta's and she smiled.

It was the dance before the supper dance when Paul came to claim Rosetta. Nobody seemed to think it strange; after all, Rosetta had been a family guest at the Mallondens' for a good number of years. What they did think was strange was the way he looked down at her, as if she was something precious, so that in a roomful of dancers they seemed singularly alone.

Elfreda and her grandmother were not pleased, nor was Great-Grandmother who prodded her son with her evening bag, asking, 'Who is that girl Paul is dancing with? She's not in our party, is she?'

Rosetta did not enjoy Angela's ball. Although she danced the night away with a host of admiring partners and was the recipient of fond appraisal from a great many eyes, both male and female, young and old, the occasion was spoilt by the fact that Paul was there and everybody at the ball knew that he was intended for Elfreda.

They might as well have been engaged already, she thought savagely. Mrs Levison-Gore was making herself charming to the Duchess; Elfreda's father was viewing the scene with cynical detachment and the Mallondens were making more fuss of Elfreda than they had done for years. Paul was the one who seemed strangely aloof; he was courteous and attentive, but Rosetta had seen nothing of the lover in his attitude towards Elfreda.

He asked her to dance a second time after supper and, for the main part, they danced in silence. It was only when he left her that he said, 'Rosetta, when can I see you again? It must be soon!'

'Do you really see any point in our meeting again?'

'Yes, I do. Can it be tomorrow?'

'I thought you were returning to the country tomorrow?'

'I've changed my mind. I shall be staying on in London for the rest of the week. Will you meet me in the park, at the usual place?'

'Very well.'

'Please, Rosetta, trust me. Things are moving far too quickly for me. I feel as though I'm on the edge of a precipice, that one touch will send me plummeting into unknown depths. Take a look at them all, annoyed that I'm still here talking to you when I should be over there playing the anxious lover when I never felt less like one.'

'It would be such a good marriage for you, Paul.'

'For the rest of them, you mean!'

'Isn't that how it's always been?'

'I expect it is – but it's not going to be like that for me.'

'I told you . . .'

'I know what you told me, Rosetta – that there could never be anything between us. The British have been conditioned to look no further than the Anglo-Saxon race for true nobility but that's outdated and silly and one day it's going to change dramatically. It only takes one person change things and the rest will follow. Why shouldn't we be the first ones?'

'Would you be brave enough for that?'

'Would you?'

Rosetta watched him cross the room and she knew in her heart that she would be brave enough. She would glory in taking him away from Elfreda; glory in flaunting her conquest before the entire bunch of them before she told them who she was. But could Paul forgive her? Could she reassure him that her love for him was greater than her thirst for revenge?

It was several days later when she faced Miss MacNaughton in the quiet of her room. She paced the room as she talked and Miss MacNaughton couldn't help being aware of her anxiety.

'I love him, Naughty!' she said passionately. 'Oh, I know you will think I only love him to hurt Elfreda and my grandmother, but it isn't like that. When I was very young you told me that a woman loved a man and wished to give herself to him because he responded to all the intellectual interest in her nature as well as the other feelings; because he awakened new qualities in her; because she admired him . . . Will you believe me when I tell you that is how I feel about Paul?

'I think he was meant for me, Naughty, for we loved each other right away. I feel quite unworthy of him and he feels unworthy of me. I ought to be grateful to you for having made me what I am, the kind of me, at any rate, that he approves of, the kind of me that he thinks so wonderful.'

'My dear, I had splendid ground to cultivate. Anything I planted grew in it. I can take very little credit for myself. I just don't want you to be hurt as your mother was hurt.'

'That's what I'm so afraid of! I think I would die if they refused to accept me.'

'Oh my dear, what can I say? You don't need me to tell you about their stiff-necked prejudices. What is going to happen at Angela Tarleton's wedding? Who is he going to single out for his attention, you or Elfreda?'

'He has said he loves me, Naughty.'

'I know. And surrounding him will be all the force of his parents, Elfreda's parents and the Mallondens. He will be a brave man indeed if he can ignore them – and what sort of burden does it place upon you?'

Rosetta was not left long in doubt.

Only two days later she was alone in her flat when she received a visit from Angela. She knew as soon as she opened the door that something was wrong. Normally Angela greeted her with affection; today her face was sombre and when Rosetta invited her to sit down before the fire she said stonily, 'I can't stay, Rosetta, I have to go for fittings and I'm late as it is.'

Rosetta looked at her doubtfully and did not press the point.

Angela seemed uncomfortable, but she had always been a forthright girl and, suddenly deciding to take the bull by the horns, she said quickly, 'Rosetta, what are you doing? Everybody's talking about you and Paul Gleve. You've been seen all over London with him and neither of you have eyes for anybody else. Why are you being so mean? You know very well he's Elfreda's fiancé. Now the society columns have picked it up.'

'They're not engaged, Angela.'

'They're as good as! They both have the family's approval and we were expecting them to announce their engagement after my wedding.'

'Even if they're not in love with each other?'

'Elfreda is besotted with him, you know that.'

'But is he besotted with her?'

'He won't be if you continue to set yourself out to steal him! Obviously he's attracted to you – probably because you're so different from Elfreda – but that's all it can ever be. He'll never be able to marry you, Rosetta. You're not even English and his parents would never agree to it.'

'He does happen to be of age, Angela.'

'That's not important. He won't fly in the face of their disapproval. One day he's going to take on his father's title and he has to have the right sort of wife beside him.'

Rosetta didn't speak and, after a few moments, Angela said quickly, 'Oh, Rosetta, I didn't mean it like that! You're very beautiful and talented, you're probably streets ahead of Elfreda intellectually, but I've been listening to them talking and they're all looking askance at Paul's behaviour – and yours.'

'I see.'

'It's not that they don't like you, Rosetta – Mummy was very quick to tell them how much we'd always loved you – but that didn't carry any weight. Great-Grandmother was horrified and Aunt Lavinia was too. You know what she's like.'

'Oh yes, I know what she's like.'

'Rosetta, I really don't think you ought to come to my wedding. They'd make you feel very uncomfortable – Paul too. I want you there, but not if it means there's going to be trouble. It's my day after all, and I don't want it spoilt.'

'Of course you don't. Very well, Angela, I'll make some excuse not to be there.'

'I'm sorry, Rosetta, I really am. I thought I should warn you as your friend that it's all going to be terrible if you keep on seeing Paul. It's better to end it before it gets any worse.'

'Even if I love him?'

'But you can't love him, Rosetta! You haven't anything in common – your whole life has been different to his.'

'You think that makes a difference, do you?'

'Well yes, it has to!'

'Oh, Angela, it must be very comforting to feel that today, next year, fifty years on nothing will be changed. The war changed so many things for a great many people yet it seems to me that it would take a direct manifestation from God to change things for you! I think perhaps you should go; you did say you had fittings this afternoon.'

'I'm sorry, Rosetta,' Angela faltered. 'I do want us to be friends. Surely when this is all over we can still be friends?'

Rosetta didn't answer and, after a few moments,

Angela turned helplessly away and let herself out through the door.

After she had gone Rosetta stood for a long time looking out of her window at a dismal wet afternoon, an afternoon which was very much in tune with her feelings of sorrow and impotent rage.

All those long years of her mother's exile came back to torment her – years when she had often seen the desolation in her mother's eyes without knowing the true reason for it – and she found herself remembering snatches of conversation between her mother and Bridget.

' "Dade and she's beautiful! How could they ever have talked about the shadow of the pomegranate and this beautiful child?" '

Those words had seemed nonsense to her then. Now she understood them perfectly.

She was shaken out of her reverie by the telephone ringing shrilly in her ears and she went quickly to answer it. It was Paul, telling her that he was on his way to London and would be with her within an hour.

'Is everything all right, Rosetta?' he asked gently. 'You sound a little strange.'

'It's nothing, Paul. I'll tell you when I see you.'

He received her news with restrained fury. 'Who do they think they are?' he stormed. 'If they don't want you at Angela's wedding, then I'm not going either.'

'Please, Paul, I don't want to spoil things for Angela. She's been my friend a great number of years.'

'Fine friend she's turned out to be.'

'Perhaps, but the pressures put upon her must have been tremendous. I told you at the beginning that anything between us was impossible. Now you must see just how impossible it is.'

'I'll go to her wretched wedding! I'll keep the peace

and I'll play my part, but after it's all over I intend to tell my parents what I want. There'll be no announcement of any engagement between Elfreda and me; as soon as possible I shall tell my parents about us. With or without their approval I intend to have you, Rosetta.'

37

Rosetta sat at the back of the church on the day of Angela's wedding. Outside, the London skies were grey and a thin drizzle of rain was falling when the bride walked into the church on the arm of her father. Her retinue of bridesmaids clad in crimson velvet with pearl-encrusted collars and muffs glowed on the chill late autumn day but Angela looked beautiful and ethereal in white.

Rosetta hid herself behind a dark raincoat, wearing a large black trilby on her head and dark glasses. She felt confident that nobody in that vast crowd of guests and well-wishers would recognise her.

Miss MacNaughton sat in the congregation. She had not seen Rosetta for several weeks and though she looked for her in the conglomeration of guests she failed to find her. The men, resplendent in their morning suits, handled their duties with the right degree of efficiency and charm and she was able to appreciate why the young and handsome Marquis of Gleve should have captured the heart of her favourite pupil. At the same time she noticed the way Elfreda's eyes followed his every movement, and her anxiety for Rosetta's future mounted.

Rosetta hurried away before the wedding party emerged from the church and, walking quickly, did not stay to see who walked or stood with whom. She made her way towards St James's Park, feeling the need to walk, to distance herself from the wedding pageantry and the man she loved, who was welcomed in their midst even when she was not.

It was there, standing near the water's edge, that

Miss MacNaughton found her later. She stared in surprise at the darkly-clad figure gazing miserably across the water and without saying a word, she went towards her and took her in her arms.

The girl's body felt cold and she was appalled at the tear-stained cheeks and her look of misery, from which all the beauty seemed to have fled.

Holding her arm, she walked her quickly along the edge of the lake and, in a light voice, she said sharply, 'We're going home to tea and hot muffins, Rosetta. You'll catch your death of cold if you stay here much longer.'

Rosetta made no objection. She seemed incapable of any action or thought of her own, and although Miss MacNaughton talked brightly on their journey to the park's entrance she offered no conversation in return.

Miss MacNaughton hailed a passing taxi and soon they were letting themselves into the school where they were met with the distant chatter of girls' voices from the rooms above and the sound of laughter.

The drawing room was lit by firelight and, after Rosetta had stood staring down into the flames for a few minutes, she shrugged her arms out of her coat and took off her hat.

In a passion of weeping she knelt down on the rug before the fire, and Miss MacNaughton left her alone. There would be time later for comfort; tears were meant to heal – it would have been harder if she'd been unable to cry.

It was much later, when Rosetta sat on the rug at her feet, that she learned of all that had happened during the last few weeks, from Angela's visit to her flat on the same night Paul had told her that he intended to face his parents.

'They hate me, Naughty, and they don't really know me,' she said plaintively. 'They will hate me even more when Paul tells his parents about me. I loved Angela, she was my best friend after you, but that morning when she came to my flat she looked at me as she might have looked at a stranger. No, not even a stranger, an *enemy*.'

'I don't expect she really meant it,' Miss MacNaughton said with more confidence than she felt.

'She meant it, Naughty. Remember how they hated what my mother had done? If they could do it to her, they can do it to me.'

'When does Paul intend to tell his parents?' she asked.

'Tomorrow. He said he would drive up to Yorkshire in the early afternoon and tell them before dinner.'

'I see . . .'

'They won't approve, you know. They've been conditioned to accepting Elfreda. She was the ideal wife for Paul until I came along.'

Silently, Miss MacNaughton had to agree with her. She knew the state of mind Rosetta would be in during the next few days and wished she could do something to help. On the other hand, she knew that this was something Rosetta and Paul had to face on their own.

The day after Angela's wedding dawned with leaden skies and heavy rain. By lunchtime thunder echoed dismally over the city, interspersed by raking fingers of forked lightning.

All Rosetta's thoughts were on the man she loved, driving north, and her imagination filled in what she was unable to see. Swollen rivers and crashing trees with the dark, dismal Pennines shrouded in mist . . .

During the day the radio announced a string of accidents throughout the country and, with the dark, the storm seemed to increase, tearing wildly at the last shreds of leaves which still lingered on the trees. As the wind and rain lashed at his speeding car, Paul felt a swift surge of relief as he recognised the towering crags above the swirling river.

Another half-hour and he would be driving through the gates of his father's estate . . . he did not see the sudden flash of lightning that struck the giant elm, sending it crashing down in front of his car . . .

Rosetta heard on the radio that the Marquis of Gleve had been seriously injured and was fighting for his life in a North Country hospital; then, in the morning paper, there was a photograph of Paul and Elfreda at Angela's wedding. Elfreda and her family were staying with Paul's parents in North Yorkshire and Rosetta thought she would die from the pain in her heart . . .

She spent long hours in her flat overlooking the park, pacing, always pacing, and the hours turned into days and the days into weeks.

It was late one evening when the shrill sound of the telephone echoed while she sat curled up on the window-seat, staring out into the night. At first she did not answer it, believing it was Miss MacNaughton asking if she was remembering to eat properly. Such calls were a regular occurrence but this time the insistence of the ringing made her finally get down from her seat and walk lethargically to answer the telephone.

A voice she did not recognise asked, 'Is that Miss Rosetta Kamel?'

'Yes, speaking.'

'This is Margaret, the Duchess of Sharne, speaking.'

Rosetta's heart missed several beats, and she sank down weakly on to the nearest chair.

'Hello,' the voice continued. 'Can you hear me?'

'Hello. Is it about Paul?'

'My son is very ill, Miss Kamel. He is still in hospital in Leeds and he is unconscious. In those rare moments when he is lucid he has asked for you; the doctors seem to think it would aid his recovery if you were to visit him. Would that be convenient?'

'Yes, yes of course! As soon as possible.'

'Within the next day or so then?'

'Tomorrow. I will drive north tomorrow.'

'Thank you. We shall all be very grateful. I expect to be at the hospital when you arrive; if not I, then Elfreda will be here or some other member of the family.'

She replaced the receiver without another word.

When Rosetta told Miss MacNaughton of the telephone call she said immediately, 'I shall travel with you, Rosetta. I'll remain in the car while you go into the hospital – they won't allow you to stay too long – and I feel you might need to be with someone when you leave. Besides, it's a long journey to make on your own.'

Rosetta had given little thought to the hazards of undertaking such a journey in early December and it was Naughty who insisted that they both wrapped up warmly. She also had the presence of mind to pack flasks of hot soup.

It proved to be an uneventful journey. There was frost on the trees but very little wind and the roads were reasonably quiet. It was one of those clear, sunny days England enjoys in early December before the real onslaught of the winter bites hard and, at any other time, Miss MacNaughton felt she might have enjoyed the trip. As it was, Rosetta drove like an automaton, declining to stop for a meal and resenting those times when Miss MacNaughton insisted they pull into a lay-by to drink the soup.

Fortunately, Miss MacNaughton knew Leeds reasonably well and they had little difficulty in finding the hospital.

Rosetta was trembling as she stopped the car and Miss MacNaughton said anxiously, 'You have nothing to be afraid of, Rosetta. Paul has asked for you and that should surely tell you something. You are not here to stand any nonsense from any of them.'

Rosetta's sad, swift smile tore at her heart and she watched her making her way across the car park to the vast hospital behind.

At the desk she enquired after the Marquis of Gleve's room and was told that Her Grace, the Marquis's mother, was at the hospital and had made a request for her to be taken directly to her. Rosetta's heart sank, but with her head held high she followed a nurse along one long corridor after another until they came to a closed door marked Private. The nurse knocked and opened the door and Rosetta found herself facing an array of people, most of whom she recognised although she had prayed they would not be there.

A tall, white-haired woman came forward to meet her. She did not extend her hand and, although she smiled, it was a remote, impersonal smile. 'I am Paul's mother. Do you know Mrs Levison-Gore, and the Marchioness of Camborne and her daughter Elfreda?'

They bowed their heads without greeting and, in turn, Rosetta acknowledged their presence with the briefest inclination of her head. She was glad they were there; it meant that anger replaced the fear she had been experiencing before entering the room.

'I am glad that you are so early,' the Duchess was saying. 'You have made good time. But we must wait until we have the doctor's permission to go into Paul's room. Perhaps you would like to sit here with me.'

She led the way to a seat near the window and Rosetta followed, watched by the others. The Duchess had heard a great deal about the beautiful Rosetta Kamel, the Syrian girl with whom her son was in love. She had seen her dancing with him but had thought nothing more of it until their names had been linked in the society columns. Then Paul had been ordered home so that the appropriate chastisement could be given.

She had spoken to Paul on the telephone on the evening before he travelled north, and his words had done little to quell their sudden doubts about his future.

She had told him that his father wished to have a long talk with him and he had said, in return, that he wished to have a long talk with his parents.

'What is all this talk about this girl the papers are linking you with?' she had demanded.

'I want you to meet her mother. She's beautiful, cultured and I'm in love with her,' he'd answered firmly.

'And what of Elfreda Burlington?' she'd enquired haughtily.

'Mother, I'll explain when I see you tomorrow. We can't talk on the telephone.'

She had had to be content with that, and then had come the horrific accident and Paul's desperate fight for life. Now here was this girl who was undeniably beautiful in an alien way, with her raven-black hair and the Eastern immobility of her face. Her eyes fascinated the Duchess; pansy-blue eyes in a face that might have been fashioned to adorn the wall of some Egyptian temple.

Mrs Levison-Gore had told her the girl was Syrian. With that in mind she said evenly, 'I believe you are Syrian, Miss Kamel?'

'No. My stepfather is Syrian. When he married my mother I became Syrian.'

'I see. What is your nationality, then?'

'My father was Egyptian, my mother was English.'

'So you have relatives in this country?'

'I do not need them. Please, tell me about Paul. He will be well eventually, won't he?'

'We hope and pray so. Occasionally he responds to our presence. Indeed, the nurses assure us he is aware of it. But when he speaks all he says is Rosetta, Rosetta. We hoped by sending for you that it might help to bring him back to us.'

Rosetta gave the Duchess the full benefit of her exquisite profile as she stared out of the window across the windswept hills. The Duchess had not known what to expect when she asked Rosetta to travel north. Some girl on the make perhaps, some Eastern beauty who had captured her son and who wished to make her mark in English society. Indeed, Lavinia Levison-Gore had hinted as much, but now here was this girl with her aloof patrician beauty, the richness of her sable coat thrown carelessly round her shoulders, and her calm remoteness.

Rosetta consulted her watch and the Duchess said quickly, 'I do hope they will come for you soon. Are you wishing to get back?'

'I have a friend sitting in my car – not exactly the best place to wait on a chill December afternoon.'

'No, of course not. Perhaps I should see what is happening.'

She rose to her feet but before she could reach the door it opened to admit a young doctor who said quickly, 'Is the young lady here?'

Rosetta rose to her feet and, with all eyes upon her, she followed the doctor out of the room and along the corridor.

Elfreda sat beside her mother, staring dismally down at the floor, but across the room Mrs Levison-Gore's eyes met the eyes of Paul's mother.

'She's very beautiful,' was all the Duchess was prepared to say.

Mrs Levison-Gore decided that silence was the best way to deal with such a remark. Men had been losing their heads about girls like that for as long as she could remember. Ruining their careers over such women, putting family life at risk. It was a great pity the girl had come. Obviously the Duchess wished to do everything possible for her son's full recovery but the bones were healing; eventually he would come out of his coma with only half-forgotten memories of the past. And with Elfreda near at hand to comfort him all would be well.

She'd said as much to Edward, who had been difficult as usual.

'If he's so much in love with that girl then I don't want him marrying my daughter,' he'd said acidly.

'Your daughter happens to be very much in love with him,' she'd retorted, to which he'd replied, 'Exactly. That is one of the reasons why I don't want her marrying a man who is not in love with her. That spells disaster to me and I don't want any part of it for Elfreda.'

'You know as well as I that love passes,' she'd argued. 'What has he got in common with this girl who has probably been raised in a harem and knows precious little about Western thinking?'

'You don't know that, Lavinia, and I'd prefer you to keep out of it. As I intend to. That is, unless I see Elfreda's future threatened in *any* way.'

She had had to make the best of it. Edward was adamant and Margaret wouldn't cross him. All she could hope for was that she had the Duke and Duchess as allies.

Meanwhile, Rosetta was sitting at Paul's bedside holding his hand as she stared at his bandaged head and still, white-sheeted form.

'Talk to him,' the doctor said, smiling at her. 'Say anything you like; remind him of the places you went to together, talk about the people you both know. Tell him that you're here.' Then he had left them alone.

It was hard to talk to a face that showed no expression and when there was no answering voice, but

Rosetta continued to hold Paul's hand and spoke to him about ordinary things which he might have loved: the park in a shower of summer rain; red leaves scurrying across the grass in the autumn and the winter snows. She spoke of things they had done together which might evoke memories; but when she spoke of love it remained a pale, fluttering shadow that had blossomed briefly before Fate had conspired to sweep it away.

She did not hear the opening of the door until suddenly there was the Duchess standing beside the bed, saying in her cool, clipped voice, 'How sad that nothing seems to have changed. We were hoping for so much from your visit.'

She reached out and covered her son's hand with her own.

'Rosetta has to go now, darling, but you know that there will always be someone here.' Then, turning to Rosetta, she said evenly, 'Your friend will be tired of waiting in the car. Thank you so much for coming. Elfreda hasn't been home for days – I doubt if the poor child has slept.'

Rosetta got to her feet and looked at the Duchess steadily for several minutes. The older woman was the first to look away. Then, picking up her sable coat, Rosetta draped it round her shoulders and left without another word.

Deep, dark anger filled her heart and, as she reached the room where she knew the rest of them waited, she paused. Now she could have her revenge, now she could fling open the door with words that would wipe the condescension off their faces for ever and the thought of that revenge was incalculably sweet.

Her hand was on the doorknob; she started to turn it, then something sane and rational seemed to take hold of her and, without a backward glance, she walked along the endless corridors and out of the building.

Miss MacNaughton watched her walk across the car park. It was like watching a robot, a creature that moved and spoke and did things, but not a creature of flesh and blood that could suffer and fail.

It was not the time for conversation; that would come later, as would the tears. For now she had to be content to sit back in her seat simply watching Rosetta . . .

38

As they neared London, Miss MacNaughton said, 'It's very late, Rosetta, or rather it's very early. You must come home with me – I can't have you going back to your flat at this hour.'

'I don't really mind,' Rosetta replied.

'But I mind, dear. We are going to eat some breakfast and then you are going to bed. I shall ask the girls to be quiet because I have a guest who is very weary and tonight, over dinner, we shall talk.'

'You think there is something to talk about?'

'Yes, indeed I do. The rest of your life, Rosetta. I think you have spent most of this journey in the realisation that a chapter of your life is closing and whatever you decide for the future I shall be here and ready to listen.'

Rosetta turned her head and smiled, the saddest smile Miss MacNaughton had ever seen . . .

She did not do full justice to the excellent breakfast Miss MacNaughton cooked herself in her own private kitchen. There were shadows of weariness etched on Rosetta's face and immediately they had eaten Miss MacNaughton insisted that she went to the guest room.

'Sleep as long as you like, dear,' she said, 'I doubt if the sounds of London will wake you.'

Rosetta believed she would not be able to sleep at all, in spite of the weariness of her body. There was still too much anger, too many hurts and the memory of a lost love to prevent it. But she was wrong. Mercifully, weariness overcame her and she slept dreamlessly until late afternoon. When she went to pull back the drapes at the windows she was amazed to see that already it was dark and the street lamps were lit . . .

A maid came to tell her that dinner would be at seven, so she bathed and dressed unhurriedly before making her way to Miss MacNaughton's private dining room on the ground floor. Her eyes lit up at the sight of the dining-table lit by candlelight. The table had a festive air with its bowl of dark red roses in keeping with the tall crimson candles and immediately on her entry Miss MacNaughton handed her a glass of sherry, saying, 'We'll drink our sherry in front of the fire and I've asked Cook to prepare all your favourite foods. We'll have a bottle of Chablis and we can talk after we've eaten. Did you sleep well, Rosetta?'

'Like a log. I thought I'd not sleep at all – there seemed so much to think about – but I have been thinking while I dressed, though not very comprehensively, I'm afraid.'

'Two heads are better than one, my dear.'

'And your head is such a logical one, Naughty!'

'Well, I don't know about that, but I might hopefully be able to help.'

They dined without any mention of the matters which troubled them both but later, when they sat before the fire drinking their coffee, Miss MacNaughton said gently, 'It's not enough, is it, Rosetta, to live as you have been living? God gave you intelligence and a great deal of your mother's courage; you want more from life than race meetings and shopping, theatres and country weekends. Times are changing. At one time if a girl had money she was expected to marry well, do a little charity work, entertain her guests and leave the running of her home to her servants. Very soon now girls are going to look further than this.'

'I think you have forgotten that I am not like ordinary girls, Naughty. I am *not* English. In this country it would be difficult to marry well, at least into the British aristocracy, so it would have to be some man who was rich, and perhaps even a little dubious.'

'The Marquis of Gleve is not the man to end all men, Rosetta.'

'I was in love with *him*, Naughty, not his title, not his money. With Paul himself. I am not looking for matrimony to forget him.'

'So now what are you going to do, my dear? Get on the merry-go-round that never stops, or are you going to find yourself?'

'I'm going to find myself, Naughty, and to do that I have to go back to my roots. I've never been able to forget it, that long, straggling road beside the stream and the houses covered with palm fronds. I used to dream that I was a little girl again, peering through the railings, waiting for somebody to call, so terribly disappointed when nobody came. I shall go back to the Fayoum and perhaps I will find my grandmother there!'

'And if there is nobody there any more?'

'Then I shall try to discover Egypt, the Egypt my mother discovered with my father.'

'You'll write to me, Rosetta? I shall be very anxious until I know you are all right.'

'Of course, Naughty! I'll write as soon as I have something to tell you.'

'When will you go?'

'As soon as possible. The weather will be perfect now; if I leave it too much later it will be too hot.'

So Miss MacNaughton had to be content with that. She watched her pupil fly out on a cold grey morning just before Christmas, a morning when Christmas trees adorned shop windows and frost lay heavy on the ground. On that morning she prayed that Rosetta would find the sunshine she was looking for, the sunshine that would illuminate the rest of her life . . .

Rosetta was the only woman dressed in European clothes to step down from the desert train at the oasis of the Fayoum. With her were villagers carrying crates of chickens, others accompanied by goats, the bells around their necks vying with the lowing of buffalo cows. A strange excitement took hold of her because, in spite of the long, intervening years, all her memories were coming to life.

The enchantment of little rivers, and grapevines, trees and luxurious vegetation, not growing in patches but everywhere. She was remembering the waving palm fronds and weeping willows, the wonderful fields of cotton and corn and sugarcane, and her heart lifted as she left the tiny station and set out along the road towards what had once been her home.

The white villa was still there, hiding amidst its lush garden, but the tall, wrought-iron gate was locked and barred and, peering through it, all she could see was the wandering path up to the house, overgrown and green with moss. Oleanders and jasmine were growing rampant below the feathery palms and the windows of the villa were shuttered and unwelcoming.

Her heart sank dismally, but she made herself skirt the gardens in case there was a wicket gate at the side of the house which had been left open. Everywhere was barred and, dejectedly, she sauntered back on to the road and stood uncertainly looking along it.

An old man appeared with his goats, looking at her curiously and with old-world courtesy touching his breast, his lips and his head in the graceful Arab greeting he smiled. As a child she had spoken Arabic as easily as English but she had forgotten most of it and she doubted if the old man would know any English. Somewhat disconsolately she made her way back along the road. It was possible that her grandmother's house would also be shut and barred, but she had to try.

She could see the large white villa standing high

above the road with windows that gazed down on a scene of indescribable beauty and she approached the gates with misgivings. Then her heart suddenly lifted when she saw that they were not barred. Tentatively, she opened them and passed into the garden with the meandering path up to the house before her. There were gardeners working there but they paid her scant attention as she walked up to the entrance hall. She could distinctly hear the tinkling sound of the waterfall and the scents of an Eastern garden were heavy on the still air. For a long moment she stood hesitantly on the threshold, then, taking her courage in both hands, she stepped into the cool, tiled hall – and back in time.

In that first moment it seemed to Rosetta that she was a little girl again and that at any moment Laura would come towards her, gentle and beautiful, out of a past burdened by memories. Instead, however, came a tall, stately Egyptian who gazed down at her enquiringly but with grave courtesy.

She asked, in English, 'Is this still the home of Princess Ayesha Farag?'

The servant inclined his head and admitted that it was.

'Is the Princess at home?'

'She is resting.'

'Please may I see her? I am prepared to wait.'

At that moment another servant entered the hall. He looked at her curiously, and then his face lit up with recognition and he smiled as he came forward to greet her with hands outstretched.

'Miss Rosetta!' he said eagerly. 'You know me, Miss Rosetta?'

She stared at him, and then she took hold of both his hands and relief flooded her being. 'Oh Lutvi, I am so glad that you are here! I was so terribly afraid that everything would be changed.'

He was talking excitedly in Arabic to the other servant who was smiling now and, with a bow in her direction, disappeared towards the back of the house.

'Ali will inform Her Highness that you are here, Miss Rosetta. Come, come, you wait in here where it is cool.'

He ushered her into a smaller room overlooking the garden and she remembered it instantly, the sound of tinkling water and birdsong, the perfume of jasmine.

She stood looking out into the garden intrigued by the strutting of a hoopoe bird and the sudden flashes of blue when a kingfisher swept from the branches of a jacaranda tree towards the river below.

Her heart raced suddenly when she heard the closing of a door and swift, light footsteps crossing the tiled hall outside. Then the door opened and she stared across the room at the tall, erect figure of the grandmother she hadn't seen for over fifteen years.

Her grandmother's hair was grey where once it had been black, but she was still a beautiful woman, graceful and elegant in a dark blue kaftan, her fine dark eyes viewing Rosetta at first with dismay and then with tenderness until the girl flew into her embrace.

There were so many things to talk about, and as the sun-filled room grew dark the servants came in to light the lamps. Outside in the garden the palms were silvered with moonlight and the night sky became a jewelled dome.

They talked of the past as if it was yesterday, of Laura whose beauty still haunted that other villa shuttered against the night, and of Omar who had loved her and hated her. They spoke of Ahmed who had laid his life at Laura's feet and it was only much later, when Rosetta lay in bed listening to the light desert breeze rustling through the palm fronds outside her window, that she realised they had not spoken of why she had suddenly decided to seek the shelter of her grandmother's house . . .

39

The young Marquis of Gleve sat beside the lake in St James's Park, idly watching the waterfowl squabbling and courting under the summer sun. Lovers walked arm in arm under the trees or sat on the grass, absorbed only in each other, and his thoughts were bitter.

He tired easily. He could not do without his stick, although his doctors and surgeons assured him that, given time, he would be perfectly fit and well again. Family and friends had been supportive since his accident and his mother, bless her, had been worried out of her mind that her oldest son would never be fully restored.

Convalescence had been slow, and with it had come the decision that had shocked his parents, causing them untold pain and the breaking of Elfreda's heart. He only knew that the man who had emerged to full consciousness had somehow left his boyhood behind him. He was faced with the reality that in life there was no such thing as happiness without pain, victory without defeat, nor would he ever fully escape from the feeling of guilt for the hurt he had caused those he loved.

He knew in his heart that he could never love Elfreda as he loved Rosetta. In the end, his mother had told him that they had brought her from London but he had not emerged from his unconsciousness to recognise her. She had gone away and they had all hoped that would be the end of it because Elfreda was young, lovely and suitable.

He was well aware of the distress he had caused them all when he insisted on travelling to London in search of Rosetta. But she was no longer at her flat; a strange voice had told him on the telephone that Miss Kamel no longer lived there and Angela Tarleton had not been any more forthcoming, saying she had absolutely no idea where he could find her former friend.

For days he had frequented the shops where he might have expected to find her, expensive shops where charming girls and sumptuously-dressed women were selecting gloves and feminine fripperies of all sorts.

He was hailed joyfully by a great many young women who had known him in the past and, always on the pretext that he was looking for a lady with whom he had an appointment, he strode through the various rooms, satisfying himself that Rosetta was not one of the seated customers who were critically surveying the garments worn by the mincing mannequins.

Disappointed but not defeated he passed from one shop to the next and then, suddenly, his limbs started to protest and he had to resort to the peace of the park and face up to the fact that he did not know what to do next.

Where had Rosetta gone? Back to Syria, for all he knew. Or she could be with some man who had come into her life. He racked his brains in an endeavour to remember what she had talked about. The latest plays, music, the ballet, race meetings and art exhibitions, all the usual tantalising things London had to offer. And then, as he made his way slowly back towards the taxi-rank, a name sprang into his mind. He had seen it somewhere on a poster advertising a concert, but where?

All the way to his London house he kept his eyes open for hoardings displaying concerts – and then he saw it: Leoni Sinclair. Rosetta had told him she had been to one of her concerts in London and he made a note of the date and venue of the concert now being advertised.

He had no difficulty in obtaining a ticket for the concert which was to be held in a small and exclusive hall in Belgravia and he knew, as soon as he entered the room, that here in the audience were genuine music-lovers as opposed to dilettantes. His disappointment, however, was almost too much to bear when the concert began and there was no sign of Rosetta. But from across the room a lady with soft grey hair and fine dark eyes surveyed him with a great deal of interest and, returning her glance, she smiled. He decided she was probably a friend of his mother's and, later in the evening, over refreshments, he found himself standing beside her.

'Did you enjoy the concert?' she asked.

'Oh yes, she has a lovely voice. I've heard a lot about her.'

'Yes. It is wonderful to have such a talent. I never quite realised it when she was a pupil at my school.'

'So every time she gives a concert you come to hear her?' he asked with a little smile.

'This is only the second time. She is going into opera but this is for charity and she agreed to take part.'

'You came to her last concert, then?'

'Yes, at her godmother's house near by.'

'A friend of mine must have come to that one: perhaps you know her, Miss Rosetta Kamel?'

The smile on his companion's face deepened and, had he but known it, there was now a decided twinkle in her dark, intelligent eyes.

'Yes, I know Rosetta very well. She too was one of my pupils.'

'Then you must be Miss MacNaughton?'

'Yes. She spoke to you of me?'

'Many times. I am Paul Gleve.'

'I know who you are. Rosetta spoke of you to me, also. I travelled with her to see you when you were ill in hospital after your accident. I hope you are now fully recovered.'

'I'm doing very well. Miss MacNaughton, I've spent days looking for Rosetta all over London. I've been to her flat but she no longer lives there; I've haunted the shops where I thought she might be. Can you tell me where I can find her? You must know.'

She stared at him thoughtfully, undecided. Then she said quickly, 'The second half of the concert is about to start. Perhaps we should go back to our seats now. We can talk another time.'

'Is Miss Sinclair singing in the second half?'

'No. We are to be entertained by a young and exciting Russian pianist.'

'Are you desperate to hear him or could we slip away without hurting anybody's feelings? Are you with anyone else?'

'No, I am quite alone.'

'Then will you come? My house is nearby and I could entertain you to sherry and coffee.'

His face was so eager, so disarming, that Anne MacNaughton had no qualms about accompanying him, and it was not until he had seen her settled with a glass of sherry in a charming room overlooking one of Belgravia's most renowned squares that he began to talk about the months since he had regained consciousness: his pain over the hurt he had caused his parents, his regret over Elfreda and the anger of her grandmother towards him. But through it all she recognised that nothing counted with him except his feeling for Rosetta, his desperate longing to see her again.

It was not for her to tell him Rosetta's story; that could only come from the girl herself. But in telling him where he might find her she had to be sure that he loved her enough, that there would be no more pain for Rosetta in loving him.

Her hesitation prompted him to say urgently, 'You're

wondering why it is so necessary that I find her. I will tell you. I have told my parents that if Rosetta won't marry me then I won't marry anybody. They hoped it would be Elfreda Burlington, but although I am very fond of Elfreda I was never in love with her. I hope she soon finds somebody who is more worthy of her than I am. If I find Rosetta and she still loves me then I shall ask her to marry me. I don't care about anything or anybody else. Nothing else is important.'

'Then I will tell you where she is. She has gone back to Egypt, to the Fayoum, where she is living with her grandmother, Princess Ayesha Farag. She made this decision entirely on her own and she writes to me with whatever news she has. She has reopened the schoolroom her mother had many years ago and she is working with young Coptic and Moslem women, teaching them how to care for their homes and their babies, showing them how to sew and how to read.'

'Does she say if she is happy?'

'Only that she is busy. She did not go back to Egypt in search of happiness. I can only tell you that her days are full and rewarding. More and more a class of woman is rising in Egypt who looks for something more than being a pretty toy or a child-bearing machine. The women in Ancient Egypt were highly respected and they were a power to be reckoned with – a fact that did a great deal for their civilisation, I think.'

'I'm afraid I am abysmally ignorant of the sort of things Rosetta will be interested in.'

'May I ask what you intend to do now?'

'I shall go to the Fayoum and hope that she will receive me. Do you suppose her grandmother will agree to her marrying an Englishman?'

'She did once tell me that her grandfather had little love for the English, but apparently he died several years ago.'

'Will you wish me well?'

'I do not know how much of the past Rosetta will wish to tell you, perhaps very little to begin with. She was with me many years and I love her. I watched the Eastern side of her nature warring with the Western part of her and I saw her prettiness blossom into the sort of beauty that I knew men would find desirable – and I knew there could be hurt in it. It made me very sad when she fell in love with you, but all I could do was watch her suffer. I was glad when she made the decision to return to Egypt – at least it was one way of helping her to forget you. Now I just hope that something good will emerge from so much pain.'

He took her hand and held it firmly in his. 'I swear to you, Miss MacNaughton, that I will spend the rest of my life trying to make her happy. Do you believe me?'

She looked long and earnestly into his eyes; then, with a smile, she replied, 'Yes, Paul, I do. I think I can safely leave my child – for she is my child – in your hands.'

40

Rosetta Kamel was coming out of the schoolroom where she had been teaching, her long day's work done.

Groups of black-clad, veiled women walked along the street in front of her, chattering excitedly like children, although some of them were young married women with small children of their own.

They had accepted her at once because they remembered her, the little girl from the white villa at the other end of the village staring at them soulfully through the latticework of the white stucco wall, sitting with the other children at the back of the schoolroom listening to her mother's attempts to teach their mothers basic English.

Now it was only when she locked the schoolroom door that their lives separated: theirs to go to their tiny houses covered with palm fronds to keep out the heat of the sun, hers to the large villa and the company of Princess Ayesha.

Rosetta felt she was existing in a sort of limbo and yet she was not unhappy teaching the wives and daughters of the fellahin. They had quickly overcome their initial shyness and, although their English was minimal and her Arabic still rusty, together they had reached a state of rare understanding.

She had come to look forward to the evenings when she dined alone with her grandmother, waited on by quiet-footed servants, listening to Ayesha's stories of her youth in an Egypt of unending luxury in exquisite Mameluke palaces where, at only six years old, she had known the name of the boy she would one day marry.

She talked freely of her husband and her children, and Rosetta came to know her father as seen through her grandmother's eyes. Once she had asked, 'Did you blame my mother for everything?'

Ayesha had not replied immediately. Instead, she stared out across the garden in brooding silence before she took hold of Rosetta's hand, saying gently, 'At first I hated her. She had taken my son and made him someone we could not know. Then, when he was killed like that, I blamed her and my husband was very bitter. But she was very brave. She came to me and asked for my help and when I met her I knew why my son had loved her. She was lovely and with a rare courage. She had a childish faith in a world she expected to play fair; when it didn't, she turned to something else with a faith hardly diminished. I wanted to know her better, but in those early days my husband would not allow it. Then, when my nephew Omar Kamel took her away, it was too late.'

'I thought you wanted her to marry your nephew?'

'For your sake I wanted it, Rosetta. He gave you a name, he made you rich.'

'My mother died in Damascus. I know so little about it.'

'Omar came to see me so that he could tell me himself. It was hard to believe that that beautiful, vital woman was dead,' Ayesha said gently.

She would tell Rosetta nothing more about her mother's death, believing in her heart that all the pain and anger should be allowed to die with her.

It was almost dark when Rosetta turned the bend in the road, with the villa before her. She was surprised to see Lutvi walking towards her carrying a lantern, while beside him walked a man in Western dress. She saw Lutvi raise his arm and point in her direction, then the other man quickened his stride and she noticed that he carried a stick and limped slightly.

He was almost at her side before she recognised him. Quickly he reached out and took her in his arms and at that moment it seemed that the earth started to spin. Words would come later, but at that moment there was nothing beyond the joy of his lips on hers. They were surrounded by the afterglow of the setting sun, that supreme hour of Egypt's beauty, when Rosetta unreservedly surrendered herself to the joy of her new happiness . . .

Later, under the lamplight, they sat with Rosetta's grandmother and they allowed her to talk about the past. It was only when the long tale was told that Paul asked, curiously, 'Why did Laura come to you, Your Highness? Why not to her own people?'

He saw the look that passed between Rosetta and her grandmother, then Ayesha said softly, 'That is something Rosetta must tell you herself, whenever she is ready. Now, if you will excuse me, I am rather tired.'

He rose to his feet and took her hand. 'I hoped Rosetta would marry me. I intend to tell my parents that I have found her and that we are coming home. I promise that I will put no chains around her, that whenever she wishes she can return here to be with you.'

'That is kind,' she said gently. 'And of course I shall always be delighted to receive her. Your pupils are going to miss you, Rosetta.'

'And I shall miss them. What shall I tell them?'

'Tell them that you are going to England to marry the man you love. They will understand the truth.'

Rosetta smiled wistfully. 'Do you know, I have lived in Egypt for several years but all I know is the Fayoum – I have so much wanted to see the rest of it.'

'Then we shall, my darling,' Paul said stoutly. 'We shall come back and cruise the Nile as your parents did, perhaps next year. But there is a ship docking at Alexandria in two days' time, on its way from Singapore. I was hoping you would agree to marry me and that we could sail on her.'

Ayesha left them to their plans. She had never expected to keep Rosetta with her indefinitely. Her granddaughter had come back to lick her wounds and now the wounds were healed. And she had no doubt that they would return.

Two days later Paul and Rosetta waited in Alexandria to board the *Empress of India.* There were few other people waiting with them – times were changing and now people were flying back to England.

From his position on the deck John Halliday looked down on the teeming quayside, but his thoughts were tinged with a strange melancholy.

It was the last voyage he would make from the Far East. He had looked forward to his retirement, to the years ahead in that small manor he had purchased in Devonshire on his last leave, a house surrounded with long, sweeping lawns, ivy-clad and unpretentious, a house on the outskirts of a village which he had known as a boy where the winds from the sea flirted endlessly with those from the moor.

Moments like this had been his joy, but already they were numbered. The ship was only half-full, carrying people like himself, refusing to let go, clinging to a past that had once seemed important, and he looked up, shading his eyes against the sun as a large aeroplane flew overhead.

Some of the passengers had gone ashore for a last glimpse of Alexandria but he had decided to remain on board. He was aware of a rare lethargy, a reluctance to recapture old sights and sounds, and his conversation with the captain over lunch had only added to his regret.

He now merited a place at the captain's table together with a retiring brigadier and his wife, a tea-planter from the hill country with his daughter, and two empty places which would be filled by people boarding in Egypt. The captain had been disposed towards sentimentality. 'You'll see,' he'd said unhappily. 'In another year or two the only ships sailing to the Far East will be cruise ships. The ordinary passenger ships will have been replaced by planes. I shall be glad to be handing in my ticket after this voyage.'

Nobody had attempted to disagree with him. To those people sitting round the table the old ship seemed as ready for the scrapyard as they considered themselves to be.

John had few regrets. He'd had a good life; experienced more than his share of excitement. He turned away. For the first time that he could remember, he didn't want to be on deck when the ship sailed.

As he dressed for dinner that evening he reflected, somewhat cynically, that the cruise ships would carry a different sort of passenger. Instead of the old diehards with their talk of polo and tiffin, mess bills and regimental balls, there would be holiday-makers, vainly looking for old times and old places.

There was a hush of expectancy around the captain's table as they waited for the two newcomers to join them, then suddenly they were there, and introductions were being performed. John found himself smiling into a pair of eyes that seemed to have haunted him for a great many years and, as the girl's face lit up with a smile of recognition, he took her hand.

The Marquis was charming, but he explained that they had had a very long day and he tired quickly after his accident. Indeed, his face was pale and, as soon as the meal was over, he excused himself by saying he had decided to retire early; that tomorrow he would be better company.

Rosetta accompanied him out of the dining room and immediately the brigadier said, 'What goes on there, do you suppose? She's a beautiful girl and I noticed she was wearing an engagement ring – one couldn't miss it.'

'She obviously isn't English,' his wife said sharply.

'Half-English,' John said evenly. 'I knew her mother.'

Their interest quickened, but, rising to his feet, John said, 'I think I'll take a turn about the deck, get a bit of fresh air.'

'Are you for bridge later?' the brigadier asked.

'I'm not sure. I'll look in and if you're all made up then I won't bother.'

The sea was calm, silvered by moonlight, and for a while John contented himself with standing at the rail, engrossed by a pair of dolphins that raced beside the ship. He was about to turn away when he saw Rosetta walking towards him along the deck, her pale gown billowing in the gentle breeze, her dark hair a silken halo about her face.

She smiled and joined him by the rail.

'How strange that it should be you sitting opposite me at dinner,' she said softly.

He smiled.

'Do you always travel by boat, Mr Halliday?' she enquired.

'Yes, but this is the last time. This time I'm going home for good, retiring.'

'I see. Will you like that?'

'It comes to us all, Rosetta. I've spent the last twelve months visiting friends in the Far East whom I may never see again. Now I'm going home to take root in Devonshire. May I ask if you enjoyed your stay in Egypt?'

'I've been staying with my grandmother in the Fayoum, the only corner of Egypt I know. We have promised ourselves that we will come back one day.'

She looked directly into his eyes, saying calmly, 'I am going back to England to get married. I don't know what to expect – hostility, perhaps sadness – but we love each other. That should count for something, I think.'

'Perhaps that should count for everything, Rosetta, I wouldn't know; matrimony is something I don't know a great deal about.'

She smiled. 'I find it very strange that I should meet you on a boat returning from Egypt when I remember that you met my mother on a voyage coming out to Egypt years before. I'd call that Kismet, wouldn't you, Mr Halliday?'

'It certainly seems that way.'

'May I ask you something?'

'Of course.'

'Paul and I are hoping to get married quietly in a small church on his father's estate. It will be better that way. Could I ask if you will be kind enough to give me away?'

He stared at her, momentarily disconcerted. Her beautiful eyes were wide and awash with tears so that he wondered how difficult it had been for this proud girl to ask her question. He reached out and took both her hands in his before saying, gently, 'Rosetta, I shall be very proud and honoured to give you away. And you must never be afraid of the future again.'

'For years bitterness ate into my soul and I wanted to punish the Mallondens for what they did to my mother. For a long time I agonised over how I would do it – and then, when the opportunity came, I couldn't do it. It is ironic that I have punished them by loving Paul, by having him love me. I thought I had friends in England but when they had to make a choice between me and the girl they thought Paul would marry they chose her, not me.'

'I think you might find that the very same people who did not approve of Miss Rosetta Kamel will vigorously cultivate an acquaintance with the Marchioness of Gleve.'

'I would rather have no friends at all than false ones!'

'And you are right. You know, Rosetta, your mother was never afraid of the future. Time and time again she was hurt by events and people but she had a childlike faith in the ultimate fairness of life. For your mother, time ran out. But for you, fortune seems to be smiling.'

'Even when Paul is taking me back to a country where I have few friends and where his family may not be able to hide their disappointment at his choice of a wife?'

'Even then. You have youth and beauty and the love of a good man. Given time, I think you will realise that you have been well blessed.'

Suddenly she smiled, a radiant smile that took him back over the years and he was seeing Laura again, happy and smiling as he had seen her on the train taking her back to Cairo with Ahmed before cruel Fate had ended her happiness for ever. And, as he watched Laura's daughter walking away from him along the deck, it seemed to John Halliday that life had come full circle . . .